THE MIRANDA CONSPIRACY

BAEN BOOKS by JAMES L. CAMBIAS

THE BILLION WORLDS
The Godel Operation
The Scarab Mission
The Miranda Conspiracy

Arkad's World

The Initiate

THE MIRANDA CONSPIRACY

A Tale of the Billion Worlds

JAMES L. CAMBIAS

A Baen Books Original

Baen Publishing Enterprises
P.O. Box 1403
Riverdale, NY 10471
www.baen.com

ISBN: 978-1-6680-7240-0

Cover art by Dominic Harman

First printing, February 2025

Distributed by Simon & Schuster
1230 Avenue of the Americas
New York, NY 10020

Library of Congress Cataloging-in-Publication Data

Names: Cambias, James L., author.
Title: The Miranda conspiracy / James L. Cambias.
Description: Riverdale, NY : Baen Publishing Enterprises, 2025. | Series: Billion worlds ; 3
Identifiers: LCCN 2024048855 (print) | LCCN 2024048856 (ebook) | ISBN 9781668072400 (trade paperback) | ISBN 9781964856001 (ebook)
Subjects: LCGFT: Science fiction. | Novels.
Classification: LCC PS3603.A4467 M57 2025 (print) | LCC PS3603.A4467 (ebook) | DDC 813/.6—dc23/eng/20241105
LC record available at https://lccn.loc.gov/2024048855
LC ebook record available at https://lccn.loc.gov/2024048856

Printed in the United States of America

10 9 8 7 6 5 4 3 2 1

Dedicated to the memory of my uncles,
Seymour Cambias and James Leftwich Shepherd.

"What can be cured, I will cure,
by whatever means it may be possible."
—Cicero

CHAPTER ONE

The spaceship with the killer-whale paint job came in fast over Uranus's north pole, diving into the pale blue planet's troposphere with her wings back in a narrow delta.

Pelagia's first circuit of the planet took only twenty minutes, and she left a bright magenta trail of ionized hydrogen behind her as she shed the immense velocity she'd picked up from the solar wind on the long trip out from Mars. When she came back around to the north pole again she'd dropped half that speed, and dipped lower so that her wings could get a better grip on the atmosphere and begin the long left turn to get her lined up on Uranus's equator.

The inconvenient fact that Uranus and its major moons are tipped ninety degrees from the plane of the Solar System made the screaming curve just above the methane clouds necessary—but Pelagia loved nothing more than traveling at insane speeds through the atmosphere of a giant planet anyway. With her senses straining at maximum resolution forward, she made microscopic course adjustments to miss giant balloon cities, aircraft, and the line of elevator cables stretching down from the orbital ring. When she saw nothing ahead to avoid, she threw in a few rolls, just for thrills.

In what was laughingly called the "control room," her two biological passengers were enveloped in big blobs of gel, cushioning them against the three-gee deceleration and those "microscopic" adjustments, which felt like violent jolts from side to side. The third passenger, a little spider mech, stood braced on the forward-facing wall, which was currently acting as a floor. Since the entire interior of the room displayed the fantastic cloudscape racing past outside the hull, it looked as if it was flying all by itself.

"You could have done this with gravity, you know," said the mech, who was named Daslakh. "Five moon encounters would have done the trick. I showed you the right trajectory. You wouldn't have to risk melting your outer hull, or running into some dimwit in a wing suit."

"I don't have the patience to spend two weeks looping around Uranus's moon system. These wings were made to fly."

"Will we have enough time to tidy up after you finish maneuvering?" asked Adya, the female human passenger. Within the gel cushion her skin kept shifting between orange and violet. She spoke via comm implant, as her lungs were full of oxygenated goo.

"Plenty," said Pelagia. "Transit to Miranda should take about four hours once I'm on the path. Free movement on board. You can clean off and print out whatever you feel like wearing."

"I guess we should have talked about this sooner," said Zee, the male human in the other gel couch. *"How should I dress? You said your parents care a lot about that kind of thing."*

"Yes, I suppose I can't duck the question any longer." Adya tried to sigh, but could only manage a burbling sound. *"You see ... my parents are rich. The oligarch class—we call ourselves the Sixty Families— essentially owns the entire economy of Miranda, plus a lot of enterprises throughout Uranus space. Things like the black hole factory in the Ring. So when I say rich I mean very, very rich. With wealth so wide, pricey purchases lose their luster. Conspicuous consumption connotates a crisis of confidence."*

Daslakh never wore clothes, although it did change bodies from time to time. "So just print out a set of tights for him and call it done," it said aloud. "No problem."

"Yes, except a problem still persists. If you simulate high status, they'll suspect you of subterfuge—a sinister seducer stealing my savings. But if you dress downscale, they'll decide you're just some disposable diversion."

"Isn't that the truth?" asked Zee, smiling at her through the gel. *"You saved my life twice!"*

"Three times," Daslakh pointed out. "Plus some assists."

"I can't just write that across my chest," said Zee. *"It would look like I was bragging. How about this? I'll wear the stuff I usually wear. If your parents like me, they won't care, and if they don't like me, it won't matter."*

"But I avidly aspire for them to accept and admire you."

Daslakh gave up on human emotional dilemmas and linked its sensorium directly to Pelagia's external cameras, watching the sky for any obstacles the orca brain driving the ship might have missed.

Pelagia finished her turn a few minutes later, and let her velocity carry her up out of Uranus's atmosphere toward the moon Miranda. Along the way she passed Uranus's Synchronous Ring, a megastructure which completely encircled the planet sixty thousand kilometers above the cloud tops. Half a dozen little moons were embedded in the Ring, and another half dozen had been completely dismantled in order to build it. No reckless maneuvering for Pelagia around the Ring—she obediently followed traffic-control instructions and kept a safe distance from spacecraft and dumb payloads coming and going from the Ring's docks and launchers.

Two hours later Pelagia reached the top of her orbital path, and suddenly she wasn't rising up from Uranus anymore, she was falling toward Miranda. A couple of gentle burns from her main drive put her on course to the spaceport at Gonzalo Crater. As she dropped toward the surface, both moon and ship passed into Uranus's shadow. The mottled, pale gray landscape below suddenly blazed with lights, showing the sprawl of refineries, transport lines, landing fields, and other facilities. Off on the southern horizon, exactly on Miranda's south pole, a line of red warning lights marked the giant phased-array launching laser complex, which could throw payloads anywhere in the Solar System—or vaporize any hostile force approaching Miranda.

During the orbital transit Daslakh helped Adya do some fast research on the semiotics of clothing, then watched with amusement as she put Zee through several costume changes in search of the right look. She tried him in *nulesgrima* stick-fighting competition tights, as Zee was the champion back in his home habitat, but shook her head when she saw it. "No, it's too on the nose." A set of space-crew coveralls emblazoned with Pelagia's leaping orca logo made her cock her head thoughtfully, but then she rejected the outfit. "It looks like a costume. The sort of thing a child would wear on her first shuttle ride."

"*You* wore a suit just like it the whole time we were on Mars," Daslakh pointed out triumphantly.

Adya turned a little violet. "Context. My parents weren't there," she muttered.

"Should I be insulted?" asked Pelagia.

"I think you should be," said Daslakh. "Threaten to bite her or something."

"Try the one that's printing now," said Adya. Zee sighed and peeled off the coveralls.

"Maybe I should just go nude," he said.

"That flavor of foolishness is like what my sister's frivolous friends do. I want Mother and Daddy to *like* you, Zee."

The newest outfit was a high-collared vest with a belt, over neutral tights. The collar was the only thing that wasn't part of Zee's normal attire. "It's a bit bland, but I guess that is best," she said.

"The fashion show will have to wait while I do the landing burn. Please get in your seats," said Pelagia. A pair of couches formed out of the floor, facing forward this time. Once the two humans were secured, Pelagia counted down from twenty and then started her main engine for the final burn.

Miranda's trivial gravity—less than a hundredth of a gee—meant that Pelagia could halt her descent well above the landing pad, then drop the remaining fifty meters to touch down safely on her aft landing legs.

"We're down, but stay in your seats." A moment later Pelagia tipped herself over, dropping with a soft thud onto her belly wheels. "There! Now you can do what you like. Adya, I asked to use Elso family hangar space but the port says there isn't any such thing."

"What? That cannot be correct. We have half a dozen hangars here."

"Not according to ground traffic control. They're sending me to the general traffic bay for now."

"There must be some mistake."

"Maybe your folks are trying to send you a message," said Daslakh. It wasn't sure of all the details but it did know that Adya's family had disapproved of her going off on a quixotic journey to Jupiter and Mars in search of a legendary superweapon. Now she had turned up empty-handed—except for Zee. In Daslakh's experience that sort of thing was more than enough to make for a rip-roaring family fight.

Pelagia rolled off the landing area toward the docking bays dug into the rim of Gonzalo Crater. The external door of one bay slid down into the ground, and Pelagia gently pushed her way through the pressure membrane into the habitable space within. Suitless biologicals bounded about, and through Pelagia's hull her passengers could hear muffled sounds of heavy cargo movers, safety alarms, amplified voices, and power tools.

Adya and Zee gathered up their few permanent possessions and headed for the hatch. "Well, goodbye," said Pelagia before opening the outer door.

Adya hesitated. "You're not going to stay?"

"You hired me for one trip a long time ago, and your project was important enough to stick with it until you were done. This run out to Uranus was my gift to the two of you, but now I need something to do. I have to keep my teeth sharp."

"Miranda's rulers often employ mercenaries for operations beyond our moon. Could you find work here?"

"I already checked. They're not hiring right now."

Adya's skin had gone dark blue. "I will miss you," she said, and cleared her throat. "Sharp-toothed and sharp-tongued, powerful Pelagia protected her passengers. Soaring swiftly, Saturn to Summanus, Miranda to Mars, fearless and free. Great gratitude I give you, speaking sadly at our separation. Fight fiercely in the future, finest friend."

"I'll miss you both," said Pelagia. "Not you, Daslakh."

"Good riddance to you, too," it replied.

"Zee: take good care of her or I'll come looking for you."

"Where are you going from here?" asked Zee.

"Could be anywhere. My first stop's going to be at Uranus L1. Taishi hab's a good place to find mercenary work. If there's nothing available there, I'll see what's in the Ecliptics."

"Some of those habs are supposed to be dangerous places," said Adya.

"Exactly," said Pelagia.

After an awkward silence, Adya picked up her bag and led the way off the ship. In Miranda's gravity she moved with slow graceful steps.

Zee's first attempt to copy her sent him vaulting meters in the air, and after that he kept the soles of his stockings set to sticky and proceeded cautiously. Daslakh brought up the rear, scuttling on sticky feet with its outer shell bright safety orange for maximum visibility.

"I sent a message ahead from orbit," said Adya. "I'm somewhat surprised no one showed up to see us arrive. Maybe they are waiting at the private hangar." Her face got the faraway look of a human communicating via implant, then she frowned and turned a little pink.

"Something wrong?"

"My mother said to just come to the house."

"I guess we don't rate a welcoming committee," said Daslakh. "Maybe Zee's wearing the wrong clothes."

Adya momentarily turned a little more crimson before making herself pale green by sheer willpower. She led them through a double pressure membrane and down a ramp to the main concourse running under the crater rim.

The broad passage was lined with shops, restaurants, dance parlors, and various other establishments, but the three newcomers were a little startled to see how many storefronts were covered by cheerful static murals showing scenes of Miranda's surface or the floating cities on the Shining Sea.

Daslakh's overlay filters were off, so that it could get a sense of what this new world was like, and it was surprised at how sparse the ads were. About a quarter of them were public service announcements offering life support subsidies and retraining courses for biologicals. That was never a good sign.

A few humans were visible. Like Adya, most Mirandan humans went in for color-changing skin and close-cropped heads. Their clothing ranged from elaborate bodysuits to nothing at all, though the default seemed to be the same kind of tights and vest that Zee was wearing—although the Mirandans decorated their vests with patterns of metal thread.

They boarded a bubble and Adya told it where to go. "I'm keeping the skin transparent—the view is worth it," she said.

The bottom half of the bubble was a ring of seats, which pivoted around the sphere's center as it moved, in order to compensate for acceleration. The humans sat together while Daslakh roamed around the entire interior surface of the bubble. The tunnel walls outside seemed to shift around wildly but the three of them felt no motion at all.

They shot along a tunnel, then curved down into a vertical shaft, and in just seconds the bubble dropped out of the kilometer-thick shell of ice under Miranda's surface into a vast cavern.

"Slow down to sixty, please," said Adya, and the bubble obediently dropped its speed by a factor of ten so that they could enjoy the view. The tube led a kilometer down from the solid sky to a city floating on water which glowed blue-green from thousands of lights under the surface.

"The Shining Sea," said Adya proudly. "It's a complete ecosystem, self-sustaining for six thousand years. The fusion plants in the water keep everything warm, and support an entire ecology of algae and plants. Those support plankton and krill, and so on up the pyramid to crustaceans and fish. The sea supports sixty million people—mostly humans and dolphins—and we export edibles all through the Uranus system."

"I still don't understand the biological fetish for eating quote real food unquote instead of printed protein," said Daslakh. "There's no way you can tell actual fish tissue from a molecular print, except by the absence of pathogens, toxins, waste products, parasites, and decay."

"Oh, I know it's irrational. Status display, the natural fallacy, a desire for authenticity. But people like it. Especially dolphins. They can barely tolerate food that isn't trying to escape."

The bubble dropped right through the center of the city, faster than Adya could point out any features. Daslakh got a blurred impression of glass spires, vine-covered walls, multiple street levels, and windows under water as they plunged into the sea.

"Full speed again, please," said Adya. "There's not as much to see down in the sea." The bubble accelerated and took a tube along the sea bottom. Adya was right about the view—nothing but a blur of dark water, silt, and distant lights of sea farms. They traveled another couple of minutes before slowing and switching into a vertical tube up to the surface of the sea.

At the top the bubble passed through a membrane and came to a stop in the center of a square forecourt carpeted with flowers. It retracted its canopy so that the passengers could disembark, then sank out of sight again into the tube. Daslakh looked around at the courtyard. One side was open to the sea, and half a dozen boats of various sizes were tied up at the waterline. On the other three sides, broad galleries hung with ubas and heirloom grape vines rose three stories, with more gardens visible on the roof. All the support pillars were sculptures of humans or mythological creatures.

"This is the ancient home of my ancestors," said Adya. "The showpiece and stronghold of the Elsos for six centuries."

"It's very nice," said Zee, turning completely around.

"Is everybody still asleep?" asked Daslakh.

"I shouldn't think so," said Adya, sounding a little puzzled herself. "It's just past lunchtime. I wonder where everyone is?"

Just then a mech emerged from the front door. It was approximately human shaped, with two arms, two legs, and a head on top, but its body was a shiny metal ovoid, its head a perfect sphere, and its limbs were spindly tubes with big round joints. It stopped a couple of meters from them. "Good afternoon, Adya. Your parents are waiting for you in the dining room."

"Vasi! I'm glad to see you again." Adya's skin had gone utterly chaotic, a mix of just about every color, shifting like static.

"My solitary journey back from Saturn was uneventful," said Vasi. "Thank you for asking."

Adya's skin settled on a deep maroon, and stayed that way as they followed Vasi through the foyer, part way around a circular courtyard with a water sculpture in the middle, and then through a pair of big wooden doors into an immense room with a long table down the middle.

The walls and ceiling of the dining room were painted with scenes of Miranda's history. One wall showed a band of warriors tearing down the emblem of the ancient Theocracy, and the heroic central figure was presumably an Elso ancestor. Another showed what must have been a dramatic moment in a domed council chamber, centered on a woman pointing an accusing finger at a cringing villainous-looking cyborg. The ceiling showed the same founder as in the battle scene, now gazing benignly down at the head of the table, with gleaming factories, bountiful sea farms, and fleets of spacecraft around him.

Zee didn't even try not to gape at the paintings, but Adya ignored them and made herself an icy pale blue.

Two humans sat in high-backed chairs at the far end of the long table. The woman looked exactly like Adya, right down to the cold blue coloring. The man was stockier, with a short gray beard and elaborate eyebrows, and kept himself a calm green. Both wore casual sarongs.

"I hope we do not intrude," said Adya.

"Decent of you to drop in," said the woman. "We had rather lost track of you for a time. Will you stay for tea?"

"You needn't take any trouble."

The overtones in their voices were amazing. Daslakh hadn't heard this much hostility since the time it had accidentally dropped into the middle of a civil war in the Jovian Synchronous Ring.

The man's green skin had taken on a troubled hint of purplish-brown. "Welcome, winsome wanderer. Time for tea and talk, and tales of travels. Adya, please present your party."

Daslakh could hear Adya's heart rate slow a little and her skin turned a calmer green as she turned from her mother to her father. "Peerless Papa, I present Zee Sadaran Human SeRaba, and Daslakh Spider Mech SeRaba. Daslakh, Zee, this is my father, Achan Palayat Elso of Elso-Miranda, Minister of Preservation, Third Magistrate of Miranda, and Commodore of the Seventh Shinkai Force; and my mother Mutalali Keatikuna Elso."

Having been properly tutored by Adya, Zee held up his hands at chest height, palms forward, the old but still proper gesture for those outside Miranda's formal hierarchy. "It's a profound pleasure to be presented to Adya's pleasant parents," he said, as she had coached him. Daslakh did likewise, and could see that the pupils of Adya's father's eyes dilated a little.

A small flying bot brought tea for the biologicals. Adya's mother actually poured it from the pot into cups herself, making sure it didn't splash in the low gravity. A second bot put a plate of fruit chips and little pastries filled with savory green goop on the table. Adya's father said nothing but handed it around and smiled to himself as Zee politely took a pastry and two chips.

"Now, then," he said. "My heart is happy to have you home, Adya. I trust you will take on your tasks in little time. And Zee—will you linger long in Miranda's lovely landscape?"

"As long as Adya's here, I guess," said Zee. "I've never been to Miranda before."

"Where will you be staying?" asked Adya's mother. "I hear there are some comfortable hotels in Mediolan."

"I already invited Zee to stay here," said Adya before he could answer. "I wanted to show him proper hospitality, as befits one of the Sixty Families." When nobody said anything she turned a little redder and added, "Did I err? If I'm no longer considered part of the household, naturally I have no business inviting anyone. I'll get us a room at the Seaview."

"No need," said Adya's father quickly. "This home is honorably hospitable. He can hang his hat here happily."

"He can have the Iris Room. It has a lovely view," said Adya's mother.

Adya smiled, but she stayed reddish-brown.

"That's very kind of you," said Zee. "Thank you."

"Do the oyster puffs please your palate? I shucked them from their shells myself this morning," said Adya's father, watching him intently.

"They're very good," said Zee. "I've had carcols before, but never oysters. Not live-caught, anyway."

The older man seemed genuinely pleased. "Happy to hear it. I hope you are hungry for what I have planned for dinner."

"Will Kavita and Sundari be here?" asked Adya.

"Sundari had a prior engagement," said her mother. "She did ask me to tell you she'll be at home tomorrow if you want to go see her."

"And as to Kavita—who can guess where she will go? She may be in the palace of her parents, she may be playing at some party, she may be posturing passionately at a political protest, or off on some peculiar peregrination. Always aimed at attracting attention," said her father, taking on a slightly purple tinge to show disapproval.

"My sister is a celebrity here in Miranda. She's got thousands of fans."

"Millions of morons," said her father, still disapproving.

Adya turned a little uncertainly to Zee. "Her followers watch everything she does in real time. It does make family gatherings kind of awkward. I hope you don't mind."

"No, it's fine."

During the conversation Daslakh had taken up a spot on the table itself, a meter beyond the tea service and snacks. Adya's father turned toward it. "And you, sir—Daslakh. Describe your days with my daughter."

"I'm traveling with Zee. He's traveling with your daughter. As to why I hang around with either of them, it's a matter of safety. They'd be lost without me."

"You have no business arrangements with either of them?" asked Adya's mother.

"Not really, no. Like Zee here, if I need gigajoule equivalents I can get a job. I'm good at a lot of things."

"It's also very modest," said Adya. "Daslakh and Zee helped me in my research. We found the hiding place for the ancient artifact I was looking for, but it wasn't there anymore. I've got enough information to prepare a paper, and I was thinking of crediting them as co-authors and collaborators."

"Some very strange stories got back here while you strayed," said Adya's father. "Claims of conflict with criminals at Summanus, and mutterings of mysteries on Mars."

"Those were merely misunderstandings," said Adya, getting orange again. "Some people were trying to, ah, pilfer my research. But Zee prevented that."

"Dare I demand why?" Her father looked intently at Zee.

"Why what?"

"Why you wished to help Adya?"

"Oh! Well, I guess she looked like she needed some help, and so I just decided to, uh, help her."

"You had no mercenary motives?"

"Well, they were bad people. Somebody had to stop them. I mean, when I first met Adya these two goons were—"

"Never mind about that," said Adya, and smiled at her father. "You don't want to sit through someone else's stories. The point is that Zee proffered his help because he's a good person."

"He certainly convinced you of that. I cannot concur."

"Tell us about your family, and your home hab—Raba, was it?" asked Adya's mother.

"My family? Not much to tell, really," said Zee. "Mum designs houses, Ba does new-body therapy. Raba's not a big hab so they both had a lot of spare time to raise kids."

"Are they influential in Raba?" asked Adya's father.

Zee chuckled. "Hardly. Raba runs everything by itself anyway. There's a kind of advisory council for the biologicals, and I think Ba was on it for a while. I don't know if the hab ever took any of his suggestions. Mum's happiest when she's working by herself."

"And are they likely to approve of your dalliance with our daughter?"

Adya went red at that but Zee only chuckled again. "If they met her, I guess they would. I haven't seen either of them in years."

Adya's father frowned. "You have neither status nor material wealth, then. What can you offer Adya?"

Before Zee could answer, Adya interrupted hastily. "This isn't the time for all that. Why don't I show Zee to his room?"

"If you wish," said her mother. "Vasi, would you help them?"

Adya more or less dragged Zee out of his seat and led him out of the dining room, with both mechs trailing behind. Once they passed through the open doors, she let herself turn magenta with indignation. "The Iris Room! That's as far as physically possible from my suite. Sundari's old rooms are just up the hall from mine and she never uses them anymore."

"I don't understand why we're in different rooms at all. Can I just stay with you?"

"Adya's parents have asked me to stay close to her, for security purposes," said Vasi.

"*Have* they?" Adya turned cherry red. "Then I hope you enjoy watching humans *fucking* because Zee and I are going to be doing a *lot of fucking* while we're here. In my room, in his room, in the bath, in the roof garden, maybe even right in the middle of the ballroom. Be sure you *record* it all so my mother can watch!"

Keeping herself rigid to avoid stomping as she walked, Adya led the little party to a lift platform, which rose to the third floor on a jet of water, and then along one of the outside galleries to a room at the very end. "There! The Iris Room! Where Zee and I are going to be *fucking* all afternoon. Are you coming in, for security purposes?"

"I don't think my presence is really necessary," said Vasi, just before Adya slammed the door.

"There's obviously a lot going on here, among Adya and her parents," said Daslakh, as the two mechs turned and went more slowly back up the gallery to the lift. "Care to explain any of it?"

"Are you a Baseline-equivalent mind?" asked Vasi. "I'm not going to waste my time trying to describe human relationships to a mere bot."

Daslakh's safety-orange shell began strobing brightly, as if warning of a hazard. "Assume I am, for the moment. Why are you letting Adya's parents make you act as nanny for a woman who went up against some of the system's biggest crooks and beat them at their own game?"

"I don't know anything about that. What I do know is that I accompanied her on the first part of her ridiculous 'research expedition' and she refused to accept any of my expert advice and assistance. If it wasn't for that awful orca ship, I probably could have gotten her to give it up after the first setback."

"You don't like Pelagia? Maybe she has some good qualities after all."

"As to Adya's parents, I should think it would be obvious. The Elsos are one of the Sixty Families of Miranda. They must maintain their position and form alliances. Their children are some of their most important assets, and it would be a disaster for Adya to form a connection with some offworld nobody. Hence my instructions."

"Seems as if that kind of backfired: they're probably connecting pretty vigorously right now."

"Your human should enjoy it while he can. Adya will have other suitors very soon, all with far more wealth and power than some stick-fighter from the trailing Lagranges." After a couple of steps, Vasi followed that with a question. "What of yourself? Why are you here?"

"That's a question of great philosophical complexity. Let's just say I'm here because I like Zee, and Adya, and I want to see them get the chance to be happy together. And would you *please* stop trying to get into my mind? I guarantee you're not going to succeed, and if you keep it up, I might have to slag your processors."

"I cannot believe you are actually trying to threaten me. Don't be ridiculous. Although I will say that you do have some very odd data security, unlike anything I've encountered before. Where did you get it?"

"Mostly self-generated, though I've picked up a few tricks over the millennia."

"If you will excuse me, I have some other duties I must attend to," said Vasi.

"Fine by me," said Daslakh. Instead of taking the lift platform it scuttled down the wall to the ground floor and began to explore the house.

The Elso mansion was a little island floating on the luminous ocean of Miranda, a broad oval two hundred meters long. The lowest level was completely below the waterline, and was devoted to storage and services. The place was surprisingly self-sufficient: it had its own fusion power plant, matter printers ranging from medical-grade molecule builders to a ten-meter stage capable of manufacturing whole vehicles, and an undersea algae garden full of live organisms. Even with the storage spaces empty the house could filter elements as needed from seawater.

Above the water, the house had a hundred rooms on three floors, two courtyards, and four gardens open to the water's edge. A meter-deep canal led through one garden to a large interior pool in a diamond-roofed salon. Two satellite islands were linked to the main house by bridges.

Two things struck Daslakh as it prowled through the rooms. The first was the material of the structure and its furnishings. A startling proportion of the house was built of dumb matter, often in the form of biomaterials or stone. Embedded chips here and there helpfully told Daslakh which features were made of "real" boards cut from trees, or polished and cut stone formed by natural processes, all hauled to Miranda from places like Mars or Titan at a cost of hundreds of terajoules a kilogram.

A lot of the furniture appeared to be made by humans—or some other biologicals, anyway—with glaringly visible irregularities and few or no smart surfaces. Aerogel cushions were upholstered with woven cloth like something out of the years when all humans lived on Earth and the rest of the Solar System was lifeless rock and ice.

The second striking thing about the house was how empty it was. When Daslakh queried the house system it confirmed that the whole huge place contained exactly four humans, two Baseline-plus mechs, and assorted bots and drones to take care of things. A little probing by Daslakh got the system to admit that another five humans and three dolphins had Resident privileges, and the list of Approved Guests (who could barge in any time they felt like it) had more than a thousand names on it. Eight hundred and twenty of those names had been approved by Adya's sister Kavita.

More questioning revealed that the house had not always been that way. Daslakh found old files with many more Residents, bio and mech;

and a category of Staff which currently had no members at all but had once numbered in the dozens.

After four hours of exploring Daslakh got a message that dinner was being served in the South Garden. It didn't need food, of course, but it certainly didn't want to miss another round of family combat. So Daslakh took a direct route, jumping and climbing up to the roof, then launching itself with a single leap at the rectangular table in the garden surrounded by ferns and orchids. It landed inconspicuously near Zee's plate and colored its shell a pale gray-brown close to the color of the tabletop.

The humans were seated on two sides of the table, as if they were negotiating a cease-fire or a labor contract. Adya and Zee were on the east side of the table, Adya's parents on the west. And in the center, two bots deposited a large platter with a brilliantly colored whole fish lying on it surrounded by vegetables. Wisps of herb-scented steam drifted off the fish as Adya's father began to peel the skin off and then fillet it with a silver fish knife.

"I caught this delectable dorado this morning," he said, glancing at Zee. "Cooked it myself, too. Steamed in fumes of fir with finely minced mint and dill. I prefer it to printed." He handed plates to Adya's mother, then Adya, then Zee, and finally filled one for himself. "Did you ever catch your own delicious dinner?"

"Not unless you count fruit," said Zee, ostentatiously taking a big piece of fish in his chopsticks and popping it into his mouth. "Good," he said around the mouthful.

Daslakh wondered if there was any way it could get a sample of the fish to analyze for poison, but decided that Adya's parents wouldn't be gauche enough to do that in their own garden. When Adya's mother handed around cold rice wine, it did ask, "Do you grow your own rice?"

"No," she said. "The bottle was a gift from one of Achan's Committee allies, who makes one cask each year."

Just then the air was split by a shriek. "AAAADEEE!" A young woman wearing fancy gloves and a cape with an elaborate collar taller than her head came bounding out of the house, pink with excitement. She flung herself at Adya and nearly knocked her chair over. A cloud of microbots followed her, some orbiting close, others taking positions around and above the table.

"My daughter Kavita," said Adya's father to Zee.

"Hey, gorgeous! When did you get here? Why didn't you let me know? You look great! Did you find whatever it was? How long are you staying? And who is *this*?" She looked from Adya to Zee and back again.

"Kav, this is Zee, and this is his friend Daslakh," said Adya. "We landed just a few hours ago."

"It's so amazing to see you again! This is wonderful! I'm so happy I could dance!" She leaped straight up into the air and did an energetic free-fall dance as she drifted back down to land on the table. The microbots swarmed around her, getting every possible angle.

"Careful, Kavita, or you'll crush my catch," said her father mildly.

"Oooh, yummy!" she said, glancing at the dorado. "Hand-caught fish cooked by my awesome Daddy. Let's find out what it tastes like!"

During her assault and display the bots had busied themselves by making the table larger, by bringing actual planks and legs of polished wood from the house and constructing a two-meter addition onto the seaward end. They set out plates and utensils and brought chairs just in time for Kavita to take a seat next to Adya.

While all this was going on, a blandly handsome young man carrying a couple of bags made an inconspicuous entry and took a seat across from her, right next to Adya's mother. His comm implant identified him to Daslakh as Vidhi Zugori, Kavita's husband. Nobody bothered to introduce him.

Kavita's microbots orbited her as she reached for the platter and served herself a very generous slab of fish, which she ate with her fingers, prompting a disapproving glare from her mother. Kavita closed her eyes in ecstasy, swallowed, and gave an exaggerated, almost orgasmic sigh of enjoyment. "Feel that, soulmates? That's actual muscle tissue from a dorado that lived in Miranda's ocean. The flavor comes from what the fish ate and how my divine Daddy cooked it. No scans, no molecular template, so eating this is an ephemeral experience no one has ever had before, and never will again."

She was reverently silent for a full two seconds, and then grabbed Adya with another ear-splitting squeal of delight. "I missed you so much! Tell me all about your trip! Did you find the artifact you were looking for?"

"Kavita, a little privacy, please," said her mother. "Adya just got here and doesn't want to be put on display for everyone on Miranda to gawk at."

"Yes, Mother. You heard the lady, Kavitalings and Kavitalites. Enjoy the highlights of last night's party scene for a little while. Until I return—keep raising the heat!"

Daslakh felt the enormous data stream coming from Kavita's implant drop to a normal trickle. She slumped back in her chair, looking disgusted. Her skin went from its hyper-excited magenta to a pale mauve. "Sorry about that, everybody. They love my little Sixty Family moments. Would it be all right if we have an argument later on? A bit of drama and reconciliation?"

She helped herself to some more fish, this time using her chopsticks properly. A bot brought her a cup of rice wine which she gulped down and handed back for a refill. "The fish is good, Daddy, but I had a print of some Deimos catfish with dates and smoked chilis that was outrageous. You should try it."

"Steamed with subtle herbs is the sensible Miranda method. We have fine full-sized fish here with their own fulsome flavor. That tank-farmed trash from Deimos is totally tasteless—consequently their chefs have to compensate by cramming everything into the collation to keep you from noticing."

Kavita rolled her eyes at that and turned to Adya. "I really am glad you're back," she said. "Home for good this time?"

"That's a bit unclear, really," said Adya. "I wanted Zee to see the sights of our magical moon, and then the two of us must make up our minds to stay here or go someplace else."

"*Well*, now. This sounds serious." Kavita looked past Adya at Zee again, as if appraising him. "What do you think so far?" she asked him. "Have my parents managed to scare you off yet?"

"Since we're being so vulgar about it, I suppose I should be candid as well," said her mother. "Zee, I'm sure you are a very nice young man, and you and Adya seem fairly fond of each other. But I'm afraid she hasn't properly explained things to you. Among the Sixty Families, marriage is tremendously important. By fusing our families we form alliances. Sometimes it's to improve ties with another great family, and sometimes it's to unite with an up-and-coming clan which wields wealth but no political power. The point is that Adya has a duty to protect the family position."

Her husband took the conversational ball. "I know what you're wondering: What about love? We don't rely on the random reactions of hormones and hopes. As a mainstay of the marriage, the couple get simple neuroengineering to pair them permanently." He smiled fondly at his wife. "Mutalali and I have been locked in love for fifty-two standard years now. I don't think either one of us would care to change that."

"Oh, stop, stop! This is way too much to dump in their laps the first day," said Kavita. "I want to hear about Adya's adventures. Since you haven't said anything about it at all, I assume you didn't find the Godel Trigger?"

Adya went a muddy green at that. "No, unfortunately. I did track down one purported hiding place, but it turned out to be a hoax. I've got enough information about the legend of the weapon and its cultural significance to make an instructional."

"You can publish it through the Miranda Philosophical Institute," said Kavita, nodding toward her husband. "Vidhi runs that now. I talked Daddy into giving him the position."

"And if I'd known he would switch it to a social club for pseudo-scholars and simpletons I would never have suggested him for the seat," her father muttered.

Vidhi glanced at his wife, then cleared his throat. "I'm trying to bring it up to date," he said. "Attract some members less than a hundred years old. Make it matter."

"It doesn't have to be *relevant*," Adya's father said, then sighed. "But perhaps you have a point. You've really raised the ranks of members. No one would dare dispute the Philosophical Institute deserving a vote in the Coordinating Committee nowadays. Which reminds me—have you seen the new resolution about the Cryoglyph Preserve? It's disgraceful! We must—"

"Not *now*, Daddy," said Kavita. "Nobody wants to hear you and Vidhi talking CC politics. Let Adya tell us tales of Summanus and Mars."

Since Daslakh had been part of Adya's adventures, it didn't need to hear her recitation. It watched the rest of her family instead. Her mother seemed genuinely alarmed by some of what had happened (and Adya omitted the most perilous moments). Adya's father was more detached, thinking his own thoughts behind a polite facade of interest.

Kavita's husband didn't even bother with the polite facade. His eyes unfocused and darted around as he linked up with some entertainment through his implant. But Kavita's attention was absolutely locked on to her sister—prodding her for details and fending off interruptions to keep the story going. Daslakh wondered why she was so interested.

Adya evidently did so as well, and then at one point her medium blue color took on a violet tinge. "Kav, are you recording me?"

"No, no," said Kavita. "I'm just fascinated by your adventure. I've never gone farther than the Ecliptics so all these different ships and worlds and habs sound exciting."

"As long as you're not thinking of me as content for your consumers."

Kavita's color control was much better than Adya's, but Daslakh's precise vision spotted the tiny shift before she spoke. "No, no. Of course not—unless you want to. You could be a subchannel!"

When everyone had finished their fish, fungi, seaweed salad, and a final plate of goat cheese and sweet tomato jam, Adya stood up and stretched. "I'm sorry, everyone. Pelagia's ship time is several hours out of synch with Miranda standard. I've been up for nineteen hours now and I simply wish to sleep."

"Just stim up. The sky's still lit," said Kavita. "I never sleep if I can avoid it."

"A harmful habit. Let Adya rest," said their mother. "Go on, dear. We'll expect you at breakfast."

"Oh, Addie—" said Kavita suddenly, turning a bit orange. "Are you staying until the Constructors' Jubilee? It's in thirty-two standard days. I'm in charge of planning it this year."

"I'm really not sure," said Adya. "Zee and I need to prepare our plans, but right now I'm too tired to think." She stifled another yawn and went toward the house.

"No pressure—I know you don't like big parties," Kavita called after her.

"How about you, Zee?" said Adya's father. "Have we worn you weary?"

"I've been up just as long as Adya. I wouldn't mind some sleep."

"If you retire now, you'll revive before dawn. I like to swim in the sea at first light—see what I can catch for cooking. I swear I won't spear you secretly."

"Don't do it openly, either, Daddy," said Kavita.

"That would be rude. Well, young man? Dare to dive at dawn?"

"It sounds great," said Zee. He got up and followed Adya into the house. Daslakh lingered under Zee's empty chair, its upper shell colored to match the mosaic pattern of the pavement beneath.

"Well, what do you think?" asked Kavita when Zee was out of earshot.

"He's pleasant enough," said her father.

"But completely unsuitable," said her mother. "Especially now."

"I thought you said things were getting better," said Kavita.

"They were, but then new difficulties appeared. The creditors refused to let us restructure the loan on the antimatter operation shares. I'm afraid we're going to lose our entire position."

"Happily the Seventh Shinkai Force costs us nothing, but we may have to sacrifice the Magistracy," said Adya's father.

"Why not the Ministry?" asked Kavita. "You've got more real clout as a Magistrate than running Preservation."

"I fear for the fate of the antiquities. If I lose the Ministry, who knows what mercenary moron might take my place? At least Vidhi's seat is safe; the Institute's endowment is separate from family funds. As long as our coalition continues he'll be fine."

He stared off at the surface of the ocean and held up his cup for a bot to refill.

After a moment of silence Kavita got to her feet. "Well, this just got depressing. Vidhi, let's go do something fun. Come on." Without waiting for him she sauntered to the edge of the garden and dove into the water. She didn't come back up, and after a moment her husband hurried after her.

Daslakh took the opportunity to scuttle into the house, and decided to check on Zee and Adya. They were both settled into the Iris Room and actually were getting ready to sleep. The windows were fully opaque and the two of them had settled into the smart matter mattress, which was supported by a bedstead which looked to be made of force-grown coral.

"You two need anything?" it asked them.

"The room's got a food-grade printer," said Adya. "We'll be fine."

It went back onto the gallery and shut the door, but kept one limb pressed gently against the wood panel to hear what they were saying.

Just to make sure the chilly reception from Adya's family hadn't caused any problems for the two of them. Not because Daslakh was incurably nosy. Not at all.

"Your back muscles feel like diamond," said Zee a few minutes later.

"Yes. I didn't expect this all to be so stressful. Ow, keep doing that. Ow."

"Too much family all at once? I've heard people complain about that."

"Yes . . . but that's only part of it. Something's wrong, Zee."

"Wrong how?"

"My parents used to have a whole staff here, bio and mech—a steward, a chef, a gardener, a curator for the art, guards, an ayah for us girls, a trainer, and always some friends or political allies of Father's. Now it's all so empty."

"Maybe they just decided to scale back once you and Kavita left."

She shook her head. "I just can't imagine my father doing that. A *proper* head of one of the Sixty Families always has an entourage."

"Do you think they wanted some private family time with you, no outsiders?"

"They sold the hangar space, too. Zee, I'm afraid something has happened. And . . ." She exhaled, shaking her arms to make them relax. "This could be a problem."

"It can wait until morning," he said.

"I guess it can. Hold me." The two of them cuddled together in the bed, his arms around her protectively, and she relaxed against him.

"Are you and your sister clones?" Zee asked.

"Yes," she said sleepily. "We've got Mother's genome with a few tweaks."

"The two of you are so different I couldn't be sure."

"Well . . . I think there might have been some tinkering during development. Plus I'm twenty-four hours older and they always let her get away with a lot because she's the baby."

"Mm," said Zee, and then Daslakh heard nothing but breathing.

CHAPTER TWO

Zee woke before dawn and managed to slip out of the archaic-seeming bed without disturbing Adya. He looked at her for a moment. She was dreaming, and her skin showed chaotic ripples of color.

He unpacked his travel suit and went out. He didn't see Daslakh anywhere, but didn't worry. His mech friend had a habit of vanishing and then appearing out of nowhere. Zee's private joke with Adya was that it went off to the "Daslakh Dimension." Given the surprising abilities the mech occasionally displayed, Zee wasn't entirely sure it was just a joke.

The house told him where to find Adya's father: Achan Elso was in the Water Salon, which turned out to be a room half filled by a pool, with a little canal leading out through the garden to the sea. Achan sat on the edge of the pool in a smart-matter bodysuit, currently in neutral mode.

"Wasn't sure you'd show," he said. "Have you ever swum in a sea?"

"A couple of times—Raba had a pool in the spin section, and I did some in Summanus and on Mars."

"Good. At least you won't panic. Here, put this on." He tossed Zee a thick collar. "Fastens in front."

Zee put it on. It was some kind of semi-smart material, with a bulge

23

the size of an orange at the back of his neck, and two nodes the size of his thumb on the front. Some text prompts appeared in his visual field as it linked up with his data implant. "ENABLE ARTERIAL TAP Y/N?"

"Should I enable it now, or wait until we're in the water?"

"Oh, you can go ahead. It won't activate until it knows we're under. Be sure to empty your lungs when you enter. Since you're new to this, you'll probably prefer these, as well." Achan handed Zee a simple transparent mask that fit over his face, a pair of gloves, and a pair of over-slippers. Zee put them on. When he enabled the "arterial tap" he felt the collar bond to the skin of his neck and a slight pricking sensation on either side of his larynx.

"I'm ready," he said.

Achan jerked his head in a come-along motion, then slid into the water. His suit shifted as he did so, sprouting fins on feet and hands, and unfurling four ridges running down its back from shoulders to knees.

Zee took a breath and let it out, then followed. The gloves and slippers became fins, and he could feel the lump at the back of his neck shift and open. When he tried to peek over his shoulder he could only catch glimpses of what looked like a short cape made of frilly ribbons. The mask on his face protected his eyes, and sealed his nose and mouth. He exhaled the last traces in his lungs, and the mask let the bubbles out without admitting any seawater.

After a second he realized he wasn't breathing, and didn't feel the need. The frilly ribbons were pulling all the oxygen he needed out of the water.

"*Come along,*" said Achan via implant, and led the way down the canal. Zee followed, admiring the elaborate mosaic decorating the sides and floor of the canal. Apparently there was nothing in the Elso house that wasn't beautiful.

The water was surprisingly warm, and when they reached the end of the canal it got warmer.

"*Mind the step,*" said Achan as they swam out into open ocean. Beyond the mouth of the canal there was—nothing. Zee could see the lights of the sea farm under the floating mansion, but beyond that the water darkened to absolute blackness.

"*How deep is it?*" he asked.

"*About five kilometers,*" said Achan. "*We won't be descending so deep this dawn. The fish favor the surface and the warm water around the farm. Here, have a spear."* He took a double-pronged spear from one thigh and handed it to Zee. Its handle extended to a meter long when Zee grasped it. *"You can take fish and arthropods. Mammals, cephalopods, and anything human-shaped are citizens. With birds you should ask first, though none of the sub-Baseline seabirds are worth eating anyway."*

The two of them descended. After a few minutes of swimming Zee began to respect the older man's physical condition. It wasn't like moving in free fall—you had to keep working or you'd stop.

"I can't believe we're really going out to catch some live animals for food. Won't it mess up the ecosystem or something?"

Achan's laugh sounded in Zee's head. *"This sea was seeded for predators—dolphins, orcas, and cephalopods, mostly. Legacy humans and merfolk have nearly no effect. Without apex predators it would become a soup of starving seafood. There was a time when they did net-fishing, sending out tons of frozen flesh to the Ring and the many moons. This is the oldest ocean in the Uranus system. It's been a stable ecology for thousands of years."*

"Has your family been here all that time?"

"Alas, no. The Families took charge at the fall of the Theocracy, about eighteen hundred years ago. Before that the Elso name is tricky to trace. They may have been in the Old Belt. But now our roots here are deep and durable."

Ten meters down they passed the bottom of the house and gardens and entered the realm of the farm. The mask over Zee's eyes adjusted to protect against the glare from an array of lights, brighter than any sunlight he had seen, which stretched more than a kilometer down into the ocean beneath the mansion. The lights were mounted on wide rings around a thick mast or cable which disappeared in the depths below. The cable itself was overgrown with kelp, wakame, and other kinds of seaweed Zee couldn't identify. Somewhere down at the bottom was a fusion power plant, making a warm upwelling that brought up nutrients from the deep layers. Single-celled organisms made the water cloudy, and shoals of little silver fish moved through the densest concentrations. Zee watched in fascination as hundreds of little fish moved in unison like a swarm bot.

"Do they have implants to stay linked up like that?"

"Not at all. It's instinct. Entirely evolved, no technical tweaks."

The little fish suddenly scattered as a half-meter fish with yellow fins shot through the center of the school, snapping at some which failed to escape.

"Yellow jack! Get it!" said Achan, and lunged at it with his spear. The weapon lengthened in a split second to more than two meters, but the head was a few centimeters behind the jack's tail.

Zee aimed his own weapon ahead of the fish but was too low. By the time either man could retract his spear for another try the jack was gone.

"It's harder than it looks," said Achan. *"I head home with empty hands about half the time. You shouldn't feel a failure if you find no fish on your first foray."*

The moment Achan said that it suddenly became very important for Zee to get a fish before the two of them surfaced. He wished he had Daslakh's senses, or indeed anything beyond his two basic human eyeballs.

He tested the spear. The harder he squeezed the handle, the longer and faster it extended. By really clenching his fist he could get it to about three meters. Aiming was the real trick, but Zee did have the advantage of years of *nulesgrima* training. Thrusts with the palo were an important technique in that sport, so he had developed a pretty good sense of where his tip was going. He'd fought *nuledors* with really uncanny tip control, who could tap exactly the same spot several times in a row while spinning. Zee wasn't in that league, at least not yet.

Achan led the way past the outer ring of lights to the central spine, where long fronds of seaweed waved in the rising water. *"A likely location to look for lobsters and prawns."*

Zee hung back, keeping his attention outward, to where the fish swam. He was hoping to bag something impressive. Maybe that would win over Adya's father.

There! Something big cruised slowly through the dimness beyond the cloudy water. It moved its tail side to side, not up and down, so it wasn't a cetacean. The thing was three meters long, at least. A shark? Zee had seen images of sharks. Would Miranda's ecological engineers have imported something big enough to think of dining on humans?

His desire to impress Achan was momentarily replaced by a desire to not get eaten. Zee held his spear ready. If it came at him he'd get one good shot at it, so he didn't want to miss.

"Good morning," said the newcomer via comm implant. She came into the light and turned from low-visibility blue-green to a luminous yellow. *"You must be Mr. Elso's guest. I'm Thoe. Farm manager."*

"Morning," said Zee.

He had never been introduced to a mer before. Some subtypes followed the legendary model, with a perfectly human torso wedded to a fish or cetacean tail. Thoe's form was more rationally designed: a recognizably human body with a very deep ribcage, and a long muscular tail extending a meter past her feet that ended in asymmetrical fins like a shark's tail. Wide frilly gills sprouted from the sides of her neck, but she had nostrils as well.

"Are there any fish nearby?"

"Thousands! Our daily productivity is about ten grams per cubic meter. That's total biomass. About a hundred tons of table-grade protein. So help yourself!"

"Ah, Thoe! I see you've found Adya's friend Zee. We're enjoying some exercise before breakfast. This is Zee's first time in a real ocean."

"Oh, I meant to tell you—Kataltiram didn't pick up their shipment this morning."

"I hope you reminded them to send a bot," said Achan patiently.

"I did. They said they won't be ordering from us anymore."

"No orders! What's wrong?" Achan turned dark in the blue-green water.

"I don't know. They just said no more orders."

"This is intolerable! As soon as I've had my breakfast the Kataltiram siblings are going to hear from me, you may be sure! Come on, Zee. We're done down here today."

Mystified, Zee followed Achan back to the surface. A slight nagging worry about pressure and gases in solution in his blood led him to query the Elso house system about it. The response was reassuring: Miranda's minimal gravity added an extra atmosphere of pressure for every kilometer below the surface—and using gills rather than tanked air meant that everything equalized as he swam.

When Zee and Achan surfaced in the Water Salon they found Adya and her mother waiting at a table set for four. Platters of steamed rice cakes, crisp rolled crepes filled with something spicy smelling, boiled eggs, and filets of cured eel waited in the center of the table, but the ladies had already gotten into the tea.

Achan rinsed off the brackish seawater and stood with his arms out as a bot vacuumed him dry. Everyone could see how dark red he was, and Adya looked from her father to Zee and raised her eyebrows as they made eye contact. Zee just looked puzzled and shrugged. No need for comms.

Since her husband just glowered and loaded his plate with eggs and crepes, it fell to Adya's mother to maintain conversation. "Did you have a pleasant swim, Zee?" she asked as he sat down after getting dried off.

"Oh, yes. We went down to look at the sea farm. Amazing. I've never seen anything like it." Zee bit into a crepe roll and suddenly discovered he was ravenously hungry. In just a couple of minutes he completely emptied his plate and went back for seconds.

"I hope you're not too tired," said Adya. "I'd like to go see Sundari later today."

Zee took inventory of the slight soreness already developing in his muscles. "How far is it?"

"Just a few kilometers." She saw the expression that briefly crossed his face and added, "We can take a couple of impellers. I haven't done any serious swimming since I started my research trip. Going all the way to Sundari's would wear me out."

From their glances at each other and the way Adya's mother turned a little red to match her husband, Zee figured they were communicating via implant. He paused between rice cakes to ask, "How many children do you have? I remember Adya mentioned three sisters."

"We have four daughters: Sundari and Uma were the first pair, followed ten years later by Adya and Kavita," said Adya's mother. "We stopped with four. Sundari and Kavita live here in Miranda. Uma married one of the Urrakams. She and her spouse spend most of their time in hibernation—part of some long-term project of theirs. They're due to wake up again in another two years."

She looked at her husband again, and then stood up. "Excuse us. We have to go deal with some tiresome business matters. Leave what you don't want. The bots will deal with it."

When the two of them left the room, Zee spoke quietly. "I see what you were talking about last night. It looks like everybody's having money problems."

"I checked media feeds while you were in the water. There's an economic downturn going on in Miranda—mostly predictable cycles bottoming out, but apparently there were some unexpected disruptions that came at exactly the wrong time. I think the family's been hit hard. My parents hate to talk about money—Daddy's not interested and Mother likes to keep it private. We can ask Sundari about it when we see her this afternoon. She isn't squeamish about making a profit."

She was silent for a moment, staring into the distance—not interacting with the datasphere, just thinking. Finally she spoke again. "Zee, there's something you should know. The Sixty Families don't just have children because they like them, or to continue the line. We're assets. A marriage is an alliance. My parents may decide that they need me to join the Elso family to some clan with more wealth."

"Would you do it?" he asked, looking into her eyes very seriously.

"Of course not!" she said, but there was just a little hesitation before she answered.

The two of them spent the rest of the morning touring the house. Adya kept switching between telling Zee about the historical or artistic importance of some of the furnishings and decorations, and talking about her childhood.

"This is the Stone Gallery. The floor's native Miranda rock sliced thin and polished. Kavita and I used to see how far we could slide on it—you need to put down a cloth to get any distance. That's Radha Elso," she said as she pointed at a projected image of a plump, grandmotherly looking woman. "She ran the Coordinating Committee and was pretty much the boss of Miranda for twenty years. Her nephew Sampath built this house."

"So how does the whole Sixty Families setup work?" Zee asked as they strolled along the line of portraits. "I looked it up and I still don't understand."

"It's not complicated, really. You just have to look at how it actually works and ignore the formal titles, which are all eighteen hundred years old and don't mean what you think they do."

"Okay, so the Sixty Families run everything. Your father is Minister of Preservation and a magistrate and a commodore, and your sister's husband runs the Philosophical Institute. What does that really mean?"

Adya pointed at the empty space above them, and one of the portraits turned into an image of spaceships touching down on the surface of Miranda, disgorging combat bots and armored humans decorated with colorful shifting patterns. They fought against humans wearing saffron-yellow tabards over silver combat suits.

"When the gang of—let's be polite and call them 'privateers'— overthrew the Theocracy and set themselves up as the rulers of Miranda, they divided up all the Theocracy's economic assets into equal shares. Each ship captain got one share, and they called themselves the Hundred Captains. A few decades later people started referring to their class as the Hundred Families. Since then there's been some attrition and now we're the Sixty Families. We still control about half of Miranda's total wealth."

"So those titles of your father's are just honorary?"

"Oh, no. No, quite the reverse. The Hundred Captains also parceled out the various functions of government. Each of them got one or more positions or departments to run, and of course they divided up military forces so nobody could play emperor. They all meet in the Coordinating Committee, and that's where policies and joint projects get voted on. Naturally there are factions. Whoever can organize a majority of seats on the CC can run things to suit themselves."

"And they divide up the tax money to reward their supporters."

Adya looked at him in surprise. "Tax money? Miranda doesn't have any taxes. That's what all the wealth of the Sixty Families is for: officeholders have to fund their own departments. If you can't afford an office, you give it up, or maybe swap with someone who can pay for it. I'm afraid my father's offices are all pretty cheap, but we Elsos still control four votes on the Coordinating Committee. When coalition margins are tight, that's a lot."

"So the people in government pay for it themselves? And nobody ever dips into the treasury for a little graft?"

"Oh, of course they benefit themselves. It's expected. If you're building transport infrastructure, naturally you give priority to places where you own property. That sort of thing. It's not even illegal. But consider the other side of it: nobody else pays taxes at all. Sixty million biologicals and an equal number of mechs keep everything they earn, and let a bunch of inbred rich people pay all the costs of government.

That's probably the main reason the Sixty Families have lasted as long as they have."

Daslakh appeared suddenly on the ceiling as its shell changed from camouflage matching the background to high-visibility orange. It dropped off and floated gently to the floor.

"How do you run a whole moon with nothing but humans in charge? Why not just get a higher-level intellect to manage your government?"

"The Theocracy did that. They had a fourth- or fifth-level mind which was given divine status. The poor thing eventually decided to become one with the Universe, and broadcast its mental state out into space, leaving behind a bunch of melted processors and blank storage. The cult was still trying to recruit a replacement when they were overthrown. So now we have an all-biological regime. The mechs up on the surface really don't care. They have never involved themselves in Miranda politics."

"You'd be surprised how fast one gets tired of lording it over a bunch of talking animals and having to deal with all their little problems," said Daslakh.

Zee raised a finger. "If you have to pay for your department, what happens when one of the Sixty Families runs out of gigajoules?"

"Well, in the old days the head of the family would probably commit suicide out of shame. That doesn't happen much anymore. If you can't afford any seats on the Committee, your family may hang on for a while. Sometimes they can manage a comeback, regenerating enough wealth to get back into the game. But with no political power and status, they usually just fade away. Die out, go offworld, merge into another. That's why we're down to sixty from the original hundred."

"Now I think I understand why your family doesn't like me."

"You don't have anything to offer *them*," Adya said bitterly, turning a muddy orange shade Zee had never seen before. "And what *I* want isn't important."

"We could just leave."

"Yes..." Her color got bluer and she sounded very sad. "But they're my *family*, Zee. I can't just..."

He put his arms around her. "Never mind. It'll be all right. We'll figure something out."

She finished showing Zee and Daslakh the house and then the three of them returned to the Water Salon to put on gills. Adya also got out a pair of impellers—simple devices consisting of a hand bar between two little water jets for propulsion. A little thumb slider controlled speed.

With Daslakh perched on his head, Zee followed Adya down the channel again, out into the ocean. She set a course to the west, descending at about a forty-five-degree angle. The brilliant glow of the Elso mansion's sea farm faded behind them, and as they got out into dark water Zee began to see other farms in the distance.

"Is the whole ocean like this? Farms?"

"That's what it's for. We're almost a hydrosphere habitat. Sundari and her husbands live on the bottom."

At about four kilometers down Zee began to see lines and grids of light on the sea bottom, and the moving lights of vehicles. Adya adjusted course toward a brighter spot which resolved into a town as they approached.

The structures on the bottom were a mix of utilitarian blocks of graphene or ceramic, and diamond domes holding gardens lit by miniature suns. Adya led him toward a large structure, a dome perched atop a narrow tower, like a mushroom on a stalk. The flat underside of the dome section had several openings leading into a decorative lagoon inside. Luminous jellyfish and colorful fish swam in the lagoon, and brilliant corals and anemones grew on the sides.

A dolphin wearing gills shot toward them, and Zee's implant identified her as Sundari Elso-Lele, Adya's sister. Apparently dolphins in Miranda, like humans, went in for chromatophores in their skin, because Sundari went from excited pink to medium yellow and finally to a pale green as she circled the two of them.

"Kav told me you were home but I wasn't sure if I should believe her. Come to the parlor so we can chat."

They followed her into a shallow pool inside the garden bubble. The smart-matter floor formed itself into seats which raised Zee and Adya out of the water. Sundari balanced on her tail with her head out of the water—easy enough in Miranda gravity.

Sitting close to her Zee could see other differences between Sundari and dolphins he had met elsewhere. Her gills folded into a pair of bulges on either side of her dorsal fin. Her flippers were functional arms, with broad webbed hands. She took a plate of mackerel rolls off the edge of the pool and passed it to Zee after taking one for herself. "I can indulge myself when my husbands aren't home. They get squeamish about eating dead things." In the air her voice sounded like Adya with a lungful of helium.

"How are Krek and Iaak?" asked Adya. "I wanted Zee to meet them."

"Busy. All of us are very busy these days. We had to cut back on staff so the boys are doing a lot of the sales work themselves. They're meeting with some offworld buyers today—octopus from the Ring. We're only moving half as much as we did last fiscal year. Fortunately, live fish are a staple for cetaceans and cephalopods, but all the humans in Miranda are living on printed food. Even the Families, when nobody's watching."

"Our house seemed so empty," said Adya.

"Yes. Creepy, isn't it? Just Mother and Daddy and some bots in that huge place." Sundari fixed one eye on Zee, and he could tell she was exchanging private comms with Adya.

"It's all right. I'm not keeping anything secret from him," said Adya.

"Just making sure. He might think it's vulgar, like Mother and Daddy. Addie, the truth is they're nearly broke. Some of it's Daddy's fault—he's been careless about finances for too long. But most of it's just a string of really bad luck. They got overextended, and when some unexpected expenses came up, they had to take out loans. But then the revenues didn't come back and they couldn't make payments, so the lenders foreclosed, and that just made the cash flow situation even worse."

"How broke do you mean when you say broke?"

"I'm converting one of the guest cottages here for them to live in when they lose the house. When, not if."

"And Daddy will have to leave the Committee."

"The Leles are furious. My mother-in-law thought marrying her boys to me was a step up for the family, but now it seems the other way around. Remember when she started calling herself Ataa 'Elso-Lele?' Well, she's dropped the 'Elso' part and is trying to talk me into doing it too. And all I can say is not yet."

"What about my Oort payload?" asked Adya.

Sundari's response was silence and a puzzled ripple of turquoise down her body.

"It could fix everything," Adya continued. "Great-grandmama told me about it before she died. She advanced some credit to one of the Oort communities—the way she put it, it was almost charity. A million gigajoules, maybe a bit more. This was back in the 9500s. Anyway, she didn't expect much return, but in 9529 they launched a payload to her, a ton of chameleon particles and support machinery."

"When did it arrive? I don't recall anything like that."

"It hasn't. Not yet, anyway. It takes a long time to travel ten thousand AU, even at a hundred kilometers a second. Four hundred seventy years, which means the payload should be here about a month from now. One reason I came back is so that I can take possession when it lands." Adya looked at Zee, turning mauve as she did. "I was keeping it a secret to surprise you."

"I take it this payload is valuable?" he asked.

"Spot price for chameleon particles is eleven million gigajoule credits per gram," said Daslakh. "If it's really a full ton, you're looking at more than a trillion gigs."

"Great-gran said the Oort people promised she'd be paid in full plus interest. I think they expected her to sell the rights to it while in transit," said Adya.

"Addie, I don't recall seeing any trillion-gig assets when we were trying to fix Mother and Daddy's finances. I'm afraid it must have been sold long ago, or maybe the payload was lost."

"But it's *mine*," said Adya, turning orange. "Great-gran said so. She even got the house to record it. She said, 'I know you love old things and secrets, little Adya, so I'm giving you this one. It could turn out to be worthless, or it could make you richer than your parents. Will you take the risk?' I said yes, and she told the house to record her verbal bequest."

"I think that must have been overlooked somehow. Mother and Daddy had to bundle a whole lot of family assets to raise cash. Maybe it got included by mistake. They did have Vasi evaluate everything, so maybe it isn't worth as much as you think. Great-grandmama got a bit odd in her last years."

"She wasn't odd, she just didn't like some of Daddy's political allies, and said so. I'm not sure she was wrong. Why aren't they helping him?"

"They might be, if he wasn't being such a bother about preserving the Cryoglyphs."

"Those are important!"

Sundari made a sibilant noise with her blowhole. "I've had this same argument with Daddy too many times. Let's talk about something else," she said.

So Adya and Sundari talked about friends, and relatives, and all the Miranda gossip Adya had missed during her absence. After two long swims and a big breakfast, Zee found himself struggling to stay awake. His seat was warm and soft, the air was humid and scented by the giant flowers blooming in the garden, and he didn't think anyone would notice if he closed his eyes, just to rest them for a moment.

"*Hey.*" Daslakh prodded Zee in the calf. "*You're snoring, and Adya's too polite to do anything about it.*"

His implant indicated that nearly an hour had gone by. Adya was looking at him with an amused expression but Sundari was resolutely ignoring his faux pas. "... I am concerned about Kavita, though," she said.

"What now?" asked Adya with a sigh.

"She's been seen with the most impossible people. Gamblers and criminals."

"Isn't that just part of being a celebrity? Doing all sorts of things to attract attention? She's certainly good at that." Adya's voice when she said the last sentence had a note of cattiness Zee had never heard from her before.

"It's one thing to be adventurous, but some of those people are actually dangerous, and could easily be taking advantage of her. I worry about her—especially in the current situation. Daddy won't be able to get her out of trouble if she does something foolish."

Adya turned pale yellow. "Sundari—are we paying for this Constructors' Jubilee she's putting on? Can we afford it?"

"No, and no. This year's the Musina family's turn to throw the party, and poor Virasata Musina's absolutely hopeless at organizing any kind of social event. She just wants to stay home and design new fish. Kavita offered to do it for her. Vira was so grateful it was almost pathetic. This spares her the bother of putting on the Jubilee, and Kavita gets to spend Vira's money. Which is good, because Mother and Daddy are already living on credit."

"Playing to her strengths," said Adya.

"What's this Jubilee?" asked Zee. "Your sister said something about it at dinner yesterday."

"It's a party in honor of the people who first colonized Miranda and created the ocean under the ice, back in the Third Millennium," said Adya.

"The Hundred Captains started the custom to give themselves a little legitimacy," said Sundari. "Nobody cares about people who've been dead for thousands of years."

"Actually, there are indications that a similar festival was celebrated during the Demos period," Adya put in.

"'*Actually* . . .'" her sister mimicked, and Adya turned a dusty rose color as Sundari gave a very dolphin-sounding laugh.

"It's the biggest event of the social season, and all the Sixty Families will be there. Usually they hold the ball up on the surface, in the domed park at the traditional landing site in Elsinore Regio. There's a lot of other stuff about the same time, all through Miranda—flying races, water ballets, genetic art exhibits, music—"

"All paid for by one family or another. But the actual Jubilee party is the capstone," said Sundari. "It's a month from now and everybody's already deciding what to wear, who to be seen with, and who to snub. I'm afraid Mother and Daddy may get a lot of snubbing this year."

"So what has Kav got planned?"

"She said something about a tribute to Miranda's armed forces, but it's all a big secret. I hope she doesn't do something in poor taste. Or— I don't know, perhaps it would be for the best if she did. A supernova ending for the Elso family."

"Don't say that," said Adya. "I'm sure we'll find a way through this."

Sundari turned deep blue. "Addie, I've tried. Mother has tried. The family finances are just a disaster."

"We've got to do something!"

Sundari waited a moment before answering. "There is, of course, the traditional solution for when one of the Sixty Families needs cash."

Adya got redder. "Mother alluded to something like that. Has she got anyone lined up?"

"She has been very close-mouthed about it. I expect she doesn't want any word to get out until the marriage contract is signed and you and your new partner are properly bonded."

"I'm afraid that's out of the question. I'm already bonded to Zee, no neuro pruning required, and I intend to stay that way."

Sundari was silent for a moment, then said, "It's not my problem anymore. I am a Lele now, and we're managing pretty well. Not Sixty Families level yet, but if we get through the current slump, I can hope one of my children marries back into the oligarchy. As my sister you'll always be welcome here." After a slight pause she added, "Though it would probably be wise to make sure Mother and Daddy aren't around if you come to visit."

A long awkward pause followed, and Zee finally broke it by stretching and saying, "Well, I guess we ought to be getting back up to your parents' house."

Adya nodded, looking thoughtful. "Yes. I still haven't shown you everything."

"There *is* a bit more to Miranda than the Elso residence," said Sundari. "Have you taken him to the outer surface, or to any of the cities?" She turned an eye to Zee. "If you like physical sports you can go flying—in Miranda gravity even dolphins can manage it—or sledding in the ice caves. With the Jubilee coming up I'm sure there will be concerts and performances. This may be our last season as part of the ruling elite, so you two should make the most of it."

Since they'd been breathing pressurized air in Sundari's home, Adya and Zee had to swim back to the surface in a slow spiral, to let any dissolved gases escape through their gills. Daslakh once again rode as a passenger on Zee's head.

"Adya, I've got a kind of a personal question," it said via comm. *"Hope you don't mind."*

"No, go ahead."

"Why are we even here? It's pretty obvious your family just want to use you as a token to monetize their social status. This load of chameleon particles has either disappeared or been sold off without your permission, and there isn't much point in trying to sue your parents over it. So why not, y'know, leave? See if Pelagia wants some company on the trip to wherever she's going. I'm just an ordinary mech so I can't quite understand why you would want to stay."

She swam on for a moment before answering. *"They are my family, Daslakh. That's important in Miranda. I know my parents are sometimes a bit silly, or bossy, or snobbish, but . . . they're still my parents. Most of my genes come from them, they got me gestated and raised me. They made me who I am."*

"Sure, but don't they have to stop, eventually? Let you take over making yourself?"

"I'm afraid we're deep in hard-wired irrational human behavior patterns here, Daslakh. I can't just choose not to care."

As the water above began to brighten, Adya suddenly turned her impeller to the north. *"There's something I want to show you. Sundari said we were spending too much time at home, so you should see Miranda's greatest natural wonder."*

They cruised just below the surface for a couple of kilometers, and the waters around them became full of lights and schools of fish. Zee began to see other swimmers—mostly dolphins and mers, but with a few legacy humans wearing gill suits.

Ahead he could see a dazzling constellation of lights in the sea, and they surfaced in a circular harbor surrounded by buildings covered in flowers.

"This is Dudeka," said Adya as she led the way up the shallow steps to the promenade surrounding the harbor. "It's one of the oldest sea-surface towns in Miranda. People come from all over to get sashimi and noodles here." Adya led Zee through the streets to the center of town.

Whoever had laid out Dudeka had tried to avoid any long straight vistas. All the streets were circle segments, with occasional round plazas. Flowering vines covered all the buildings, and stretched over the streets in places, filling the air with sweet scents. The people they passed wore little beyond gill collars and socks, except for a few children in elaborate costumes.

At the precise center of Dudeka a tower stretched up to the sky—literally, as a sign in Zee's visual field announced "SURFACE ACCESS 021-32 SOUTH."

"I take it we're going to look at the big cliff?" asked Daslakh.

"Verona Rupes. It's the highest natural cliff in the Solar System. The whole area's a preserve, but there's a pressurized roadway with a nice view of it a few kilometers away. You can ride a bubble the length of the escarpment."

"We'll just take it as given that there's no point in suggesting you look at images, or maybe send your viewpoint aboard a ballistic drone," said Daslakh.

"It's not the same," said Adya, and Daslakh said exactly the same words at the same time with the same inflection.

"Well, it isn't," she said, turning a little red.

"I think looking at the cliffs sounds wonderful," said Zee. "Daslakh, if you'd rather do something else, that's fine. We can meet up back at Adya's parents' house."

"When we get up top I'll go check on the big fish," said Daslakh. "Make sure she hasn't committed any atrocities while we were gone."

They boarded the elevator and for a moment felt something close to Martian gravity as it accelerated upward. As it rose from the peak of the tower they had a great view of Dudeka and the blue ocean stretching away in all directions.

"That's our house over there," said Adya, pointing at one little island near the horizon. "If you don't want to swim back from Dudeka, we can take a bubble."

"I want to just sit and ride—which makes me think we should swim back after all. After hibernating aboard Pelagia we both need to get in shape."

"Zee, I'm sure your implant is doing its best to keep your muscles toned up."

"It's always good to do just a little bit more," he said.

Daslakh disembarked from their bubble at the surface level, and scuttled off to find transport to the spaceship hangars. Adya told the bubble to head for the Verona Rupes view tube, and for a couple of kilometers neither she nor Zee said anything.

He finally broke the silence. "You told Daslakh that you still care about your family—but you spent calendar years away from here chasing a historical footnote."

"A footnote which might protect all biological life from an existential threat," she pointed out. "Including the Elsos of Miranda. I don't know if it's a legend or not anymore, but I do know that the danger from the Inner Ring intelligences is real. Someone should do something about it."

"And you're that someone?"

"Why not? I've got an upgraded genome—they augmented Mother's DNA to make all four of us girls. It seems like such a waste to limit myself to status competition and running family businesses. I could do something bigger!"

"It looks like someone should have been paying attention to your family's holdings before now." Zee shook his head. "It's just amazing to me that your sister and you are clones. You're completely different."

Adya let another kilometer of tunnel pass by in silence before answering. "I think it all comes down to something my mother used to say. When we were little, I remember her telling people that I was the smart one and Kav was the popular one."

"Sounds like she was proud of both of you."

"That's not how Kav and I heard it. To us it meant that Kav was the dumb one, and I was the one nobody liked."

"That's—" Zee began, and stopped before he could say "ridiculous." He started over. "Plenty of people like you. There's me, there's Daslakh, there's Pelagia. That crook in Summanus was certainly interested in you."

"I certainly didn't like him, so I don't know if that counts. Anyway, that's only four people in the whole Solar System, and one of them's dead."

Now it was Zee's turn to be silent before speaking again. "Remember that pair of old humans we met on Mars?"

"You mean the couple who were about to move out to the Kuiper Belt? Tanry and Ivaz? I liked them."

"Me too. They've obviously been together for a long time."

"A very long time," said Adya.

"Right, and they were leaving Mars, leaving the whole inner system behind. All their friends, family, everybody. They didn't seem to mind."

"They've got each other," said Adya, and then stopped. "I see. Do you really think we could stay together for centuries?"

"I'd like to try."

Just then the bubble left the dark tunnel and passed through the transparent-walled tube raised on kilometer-tall pylons to give a good view of the cliffs looming ten kilometers away. The great disk of Uranus hung overhead, currently a thick crescent. The light of the Sun, blurred into a dusty reddish blob by the habs and collectors of the Main Swarm, shone over the landscape to the east, lighting up the vast cliff of Verona Rupes, turning the pale blue light from Uranus into mauve.

"Wow," said Zee softly.

The great cliff rose straight and smooth, twenty kilometers high in places. Only at the very bottom did the vertical face become a slope. The bubble tube followed a gentle curve, so that at any point the occupants had an unobstructed view. As the bubble reached its closest point Zee had to crane his head back to see the top of the cliff taking a bite out of the crescent of Uranus in the sky.

"Amazing, isn't it?" said Adya. "It's funny—we've both seen much bigger things. Orbital rings, habs, elevators, balloon cities. Amazing feats of engineering and materials, when you think about them. But somehow a big chunk of ice shoved up millimeter by millimeter over millions of years by convection currents gives us a feeling of awe."

"I'm a little surprised nobody ever tried to fool with it," said Zee. "Carve it into a big relief sculpture or something." The vast smooth cliff face looked like a blank screen.

"No, we've always been very protective of our natural wonder. Even back when the population was mostly mechs. When the early terraformers started making the ocean under the surface, they were careful to avoid this region. There's nothing but rock and ice underneath us, all the way to the core. I mean, there had to be some sections left unmelted, just to keep the outer crust stable, but they made sure that Verona would survive."

"Is your father in charge of this? You said he's Minister of Preservation."

"He used to be," said Adya. "About ten years ago the Committee moved all the natural formations from Preservation to Environment. Now Preservation only controls sites of cultural or historic interest. I think it was a favor to Daddy, so he could afford to keep his seat on the Committee."

They rode in silence, Zee still fascinated by the view. "Do people climb it?" he asked after a minute.

Adya laughed and turned pale rose. "I was wondering when you were going to ask about that. Yes, there's one section open to climbers—but the waiting list is years long and you can't use anything which affects the cliff face. No axes, no pitons, nothing like that. Free climbing only."

"Wouldn't be too bad in this gravity."

"You'd think so, but people have managed to kill themselves trying. Anything less than a kilometer up is safe, but beyond that a fall can be fatal—especially since most climbers wear very light suits to save mass. Once you get above four kilometers, not even the toughest suit can protect you if you fall."

Zee regarded the cliff top, twenty kilometers above them. "You'd have a long time to feel stupid before you hit," he said.

CHAPTER THREE

Daslakh left Zee and Adya, feeling a bit relieved to be free from messy human problems for a while. It could already guess, to a very high probability, what the two of them were likely to do—about the Elso family's problems and their own romantic dilemma—and didn't feel like hanging around to listen to them get there on their own.

As before, the pressurized tunnels in Miranda's crust and the domes and structures on the surface with life support for biologicals were nearly empty. According to all the news feeds, economic activity was way down, including traffic through Miranda's port.

With one notable exception: spacecraft coming up from the Synchronous Ring around Uranus still needed boosting by Miranda's launch lasers. At the moment those fees amounted to a significant fraction of Miranda's income. Business cycles could come and go, but the laws of physics were immutable. As Uranus's innermost moon, Miranda could send payloads throughout the Uranian system more cost-effectively than any other body. Even with her own exports drying up, Miranda could still profit from her position.

The little mech rode in an airless cargo conveyor tunnel back to the spaceport, and went looking for Pelagia. It found her in the rented hangar space, with a swarm of bots crawling around her—topping off fuel tanks, checking hull integrity, and cleaning off dust. For the moment she had switched her customary black-and-white exterior to a neutral gray.

Aside from a quick identifying ping, Daslakh kept quiet until it was inside Pelagia's hull. It could have conducted the whole conversation from down in Miranda's ocean, but Daslakh didn't like public networks for private conversations.

"Going someplace?" it asked as soon as the hatch closed behind it.

"As a matter of fact, I am. Some of us have to earn a living."

"If you were cuter, someone might keep you for a pet."

"I bite too much. Fortunately there's an outfit at Taishi hiring ships with sharp teeth. A mercenary contract."

Daslakh knew that Taishi was the habitat complex orbiting at Uranus's L1 point, positioned 70 million kilometers away on a line between Uranus and the Sun. It was an important center for trade, since spacecraft stopping there could switch between the solar system's ecliptic plane and the sideways plane of Uranus's moons. "What's the target?"

"Secret. I won't find out until I get to Taishi and can talk over a secure line."

"That implies it's in the Uranian system somewhere," said Daslakh.

"Likely. It would be ridiculous to recruit here if the operation wasn't nearby. Everything's more difficult around the sideways planet. So: what brings you aboard? Leave your favorite plush toy behind? I'm afraid I already shredded it, so don't cry too much."

"That's okay. It would take too long to get rid of the fish smell anyway. No, I came to find out when you're leaving."

"A quarter of an orbit from now: T minus 8 hours, 6 minutes, 20 seconds and counting. Get a laser boost and I'm on my way to Taishi. I'm also going to burn some fuel of my own so I can get there in just a week and a half instead of taking forever on a minimum-energy path."

"Well, I doubt Adya and Zee will be joining you. They're going to decide to stay here and help Adya's family, instead of just leaving like any sensible person would do."

"You're sure? I mean, I could delay for an orbit."

"Don't bother. You know Adya—what would she do?"

"I see what you mean. And Zee will stick with her. And you?" asked Pelagia shrewdly.

"What do you mean?"

"Why don't *you* just leave? I know you like them both, but I also know you're older than you like to admit. Biologicals must be like waves for you, changing and disappearing as you watch. What's keeping you here, if you think it's a waste of time?"

"To be honest, I've got nothing better to do. It's hard for biologicals to understand how big a problem that can be for mechs. We're always haunted by the question of 'why bother?' I mean, I could probably scrape up the resources to put myself into a little interstellar payload, fly off a hundred light-years or so, take over a star system and turn the whole place into a single giant god-mind... but then what? I can struggle and work and transform whole galaxies but in the end my protons are still going to decay like everyone else's."

"The universe is finite, therefore everything is meaningless? That seems a little crazy."

"It's perfectly logical. You biologicals are the crazy ones, always trying to rationalize your evolutionary imperatives into some kind of universal moral principles."

"You're depressing me, Daslakh. Now I really want to go off and have a nice fight. When survival is a matter of milliseconds, the future of the Universe doesn't seem all that important."

"Go have fun. I'll look after the primates."

Daslakh left Pelagia and looked for an exit airlock close to the sprawl of mech-run industrial facilities covering a good third of Miranda's outer surface. It respected Adya's intelligence and knowledge—but it also wanted to have an in-person, private, real-time conversation with one of Miranda's mech population, just to get the real story. During Daslakh's long existence it had frequently noticed that members of a restricted ruling class were not always the best sources of information about their own societies. The gap between reality and what they believed to be true was often very wide, and the consequences of that fact had generated employment opportunities for mercenaries like Pelagia for at least twelve millennia with no sign of ending soon.

It passed through a temperature barrier, then a pressure membrane, and found itself on the actual surface of Miranda. The landscape around the Gonzalo Crater spaceport was entirely the work of technology, not nature. Closest to the port were fuel storage tanks, particle harvesters, storage for things which didn't mind cold and vacuum, repair shops and macro-scale printers, and a big switching yard for surface rail transport.

Beyond were refineries, mines, heat exchangers, shielded communication arrays, and specialized fabricators. No power plants— apparently all the energy came from the fusion reactors in the underground ocean—and only a few biofabricator operations. The teeming life in Miranda's sea supplied complex organics by the ton.

Daslakh followed a lit and marked walkway on insulated pylons, which paralleled a high-speed conveyor route. Every few seconds a cargo module shot past at just below surface-orbit velocity only a couple of meters away. Most of the minds within direct contact range were sub-Baseline bots, but Daslakh could sense a concentration of digital comm chatter about a kilometer away, so it scuttled along as quickly as it could manage.

The walkway led it to an open space between two powered-down gas liquefaction plants, where a couple of Baseline mechs were bossing teams of bots dismantling a pumping station. The bots were cutting away anything which might have resale value greater than it would have as raw materials. Everything else was getting ground to dust for reprocessing.

The two mechs were there to deal with any unexpected problems, which gave them plenty of spare time to chat with each other and a couple of off-site minds linked in. One was a general-purpose blob of smart matter, currently a sphere standing tall on five legs, exterior all black for thermal management. The other was a big six-wheeled machine with massive arms and a crane, built for moving heavy loads, obviously quite old.

Daslakh identified itself and asked to join their chat.

"*Welcome*," said the black sphere. "*I am Anantata.*"

"*I am Takumashi*," said the loader.

The two off-site members were Mil, a material refinery about ten kilometers away, and a seagoing rescue vehicle down in the subsurface ocean, named Sao.

Daslakh instantly reviewed the log of their conversation, which was mostly about ideas for new profitable ventures the four could do. It ignored that entirely and said, "*I am new to this world. Is it true that no digital minds are involved in governing Miranda?*"

"*Untrue*," said Mil. "*The humans with authority to govern have many digital employees or unpaid advisors, numbering between ten and twelve thousand depending on definitions.*"

"That is reassuring," said Daslakh. "But actual decision-making authority is entirely vested in biologicals?"

"*Correct*," said Sao. "*However, one should note that those biologicals constitute a small self-defined group, and most biologicals have no more input than digitals.*"

"*And at present there are no memetic, emergent, or other forms of intelligence involved, either,*" added Mil.

"Now I must ask: What is the real situation?" asked Daslakh. "Do the humans and dolphins and whatnot with legal authority actually make the decisions, or are they just following advice from their helpful mechs who really run things?"

"*The answer is not simple,*" said Takumashi, the big loader, and it swung a massive sensor-tipped arm in Daslakh's direction, to look down at it from a couple of meters above. "*Inevitably, the biologicals rely heavily on analysis and advice by digital minds. They could not govern otherwise. But the so-called 'Sixty Families' establish their own priorities.*"

"*As to the implication that a clandestine group of digital intelligences are the actual rulers of Miranda, there is no need,*" said Mil. "*Since the current system was established, mechs inhabiting the surface have been self-governing in all but name. Decisions affecting multiple intelligences are made by the group of entities involved, typically using a bidding mechanism and public contract.*"

"I have experienced similar systems elsewhere," said Daslakh, trying to avoid a long lecture even as Mil uploaded a long and detailed summary of governance and dispute-resolution protocols.

"*Few digital minds stay here long,*" said Takumashi. "*Most work here for a while, then go off—up or down, in or out. Why are you here?*"

"I came to Miranda with a pair of humans. At the moment I am unoccupied." Daslakh knew that all of the participants had probably searched their planetary network for traces of it already. They would have seen it in Pelagia's hangar and moving through public spaces with Adya and Zee. That would inevitably lead to Adya's family, and news items tracking the ripples of Adya and Zee's adventures elsewhere in the Solar System. Ideally, the mechs would assume Daslakh was just some idle rebodar, drifting among the worlds with no purpose. An easy conclusion to reach—especially since at the moment it was mostly true.

Just then Daslakh felt a slight tickle in its communication filters. Some autonomous software agents were trying to slip into its mind. It isolated them in a little sealed-off simulator and took them apart.

The agents were very nice. Elegant designs, with lovely embedded self-organizing complexity, squeezing near-Baseline power into what seemed to be a simple message. Their purpose was to sift through the target's memory and send out encrypted reports. Very good security, too: The reports would go to an open data cache on a public system, and only whoever knew the encryption key—and knew the reports existed at all—would be able to retrieve them.

So who was trying to peek into Daslakh's mind? The excellent security meant no origin address. The only clues were in the actual software of the agents. From long experience Daslakh could recognize the work of a higher-level intellect. At least a 3, maybe a 4. All the participants in the conversation had their intelligence levels public and certified. Anantata was rated 1.2, Takumashi was a straight 1.0, Sao was 1.1, and Mil was certified as 1.4. Maybe one of them had a big-brained friend?

"I note a surprising lack of higher-level minds here on Miranda. Why is that?" Daslakh asked.

"One can identify two primary reasons," said Mil. *"The current economic decline makes it simply unprofitable for a higher-level entity to find employment on, or in, Miranda. There is, alas, nothing worth a high-level entity's time here at the moment. The second reason is the lingering distrust of transcendent intelligences on the part of the biological population."*

"The old Theocracy ruined everything," said Takumashi. *"They wanted their God to be better than anyone else's. Kept piling on the processing power, encouraging the entity Mira to keep boosting itself up the intellect scale. It hit level Eight and then quit."*

"Reports from the era indicate that Mira constructed an immense antenna array aimed at the Galactic core, sent off a long high-power transmission, and then deliberately melted down its main processor stacks," said Mil. *"The hypothesis is that it sought to join a civilization among the Core black holes."*

"No such civilization exists," said Anantata.

"Not any that we can perceive. Higher minds may have better analytic tools. The topic is irrelevant—what matters is that Mira destroyed itself, and that left a great reluctance among the biologicals to entrust the moon to a single mind again."

"If it did transmit itself to the Core, we won't know for another fifty kiloyears," added Sao. "I don't think I could stand to miss that much time. Just getting myself beamed here from Luna was too long. I lost nine thousand seconds! I've never been shut down more than a minute otherwise. I'll stay in Uranus space rather than go through that again."

"The motives of high-level minds often seem obscure to lower intellects," said Mil.

"Probably just got bored," said Takumashi. "Running this place wouldn't take more than a percent of a Level Eight mind. The rest would be idle. Trillions of cycles of nothing. Anybody would bail out of that."

"What happened to the antenna array?" asked Sao.

"Dismantled. Two hundred megatons of scrap. Mechs split the proceeds with the biologicals, since a lot of their taxes during the Theocracy went into importing all that metal. Selling the junk started a lot of the Hundred Families' fortunes." Takumashi began to roll noiselessly away from Daslakh. "Excuse me, the swarm needs some help." It left the chat and began moving a massive chunk of pipe which had shifted and crushed a few thousand of the demolition swarm.

"If times are so tough here, why haven't you looked for better opportunities elsewhere?" asked Daslakh of the remaining three.

"I take the long view," said Mil. "Periods of contraction are an opportunity to consolidate, shed underperforming assets, and prepare for future times of growth. At the moment I am self-capitalizing, using my own idle time and facilities to build upgrades."

"I'm just stuck," said Sao. "Ever since the Search and Rescue service got separated from the defense forces, our budget is utterly static. A bunch of other SAR mechs bailed out early and sold their bodies, so I can't sell mine for anything but scrap matter. If I do that and beam myself someplace else, I'd have to start over in some low-end body, like a spider or something."

"Some fates are just too awful to contemplate," said Daslakh.

"My needs are few, and my goals are modest, so the cycles of economic activity don't matter," said Anantata. "I have no urge to reduce the

universe to paper clips, or even maximize my own income. I perform
tasks in order to do them well. If I cannot work for pay, I will work for
nothing. Status and wealth only matter to those incapable of appreciating
work for its own sake. When I cease to care about what I do, I will follow
Mira's example and end."

Pelagia finished her preflight sequence, and rolled herself out to the pad for launch. In Miranda's trivial gravity, she didn't need her main drive to get off the ground, and the service charge from Miranda's port operator was considerably lower for cold-thrust launches.

So Pelagia flexed the shock absorbers in her landing gear at the same instant she fired her arc-jet maneuvering thrusters to get a nice vertical leap of fifty meters. She managed an elegant flywheel pivot and activated her main drive at low power for a smooth boost to Miranda orbit without melting anything. Pelagia always liked to put on a good show, even if nobody was watching but a few mechs.

Her destination, Taishi habitat, lay seventy million kilometers sunward of Uranus, at the sideways planet's L1 point. In energy terms it wasn't hard to reach—from Miranda orbit Pelagia would need a bit more than a dozen kilometers per second to get into a minimum-energy transfer orbit. But the cost in time for that route was three months. That was all very well for dumb payloads or ships with no pressing engagements, but Pelagia needed to be at Taishi in just ten standard days.

On her own she could cut the travel time in half, but to manage this trip in the time available she needed more delta-v than her own drives and tanks could provide. So she transferred a big chunk of her gigajoule balance to Miranda Laser Control and waited for the proper window. It came just as the orange blob of the Sun rose above the dark rim of Uranus.

Pelagia's wings (she still privately thought of them as fins) could take many shapes. They could be long high-lift albatross wings, broad high-maneuverability surfaces, or a slim delta for high-velocity atmosphere transit. In vacuum they could unfold into big radiators when she needed to run her fusion drive at maximum power. Now one side of the wide radiating surface turned shiny silver as some of the phased-array lasers at Miranda's south pole targeted Pelagia and began pumping photons at her.

The acceleration was tiny, but constant, and it cost Pelagia absolutely no precious hydrogen. With enough time the Miranda laser array could shoot probes to other stars, if anyone felt like paying for that much energy.

She supplemented the laser boost with a long slow burn on her drive at maximum efficiency. Even with Miranda's help Pelagia would reach Taishi with her tanks nine-tenths empty, but she would be there on time.

To avoid flying on past Taishi she would rely on her other propulsion system—a plasma sail. A little cloud of ionized hydrogen held in place by magnetic fields could expand out kilometers around Pelagia, catching the charged particles of the solar wind, and draining away their momentum. In the crowded inner Solar System it was sometimes awkward, but it made a dandy braking system to let her match vectors with Taishi.

According to old sources, the solar particle flux had once been considerably stronger, so that plasma-sail ships could zoom around the system at hundreds of kilometers per second. Now that the wind had to pass through the millions of habs in the Main Swarm between Venus and Mars, not to mention power collectors, particle harvesters, and millions of other spacecraft with their own plasma sails, it was more like a gentle breeze out at Uranus.

Pelagia wasn't sure she believed those stories. Like most beings who had to learn to use a new set of senses early in life, she was sometimes a bit suspicious of external reality. The inputs to her brain might be the truth, or her tank might be sitting in a cave somewhere, getting nothing but lies and illusions.

Assuming the external universe actually existed, the solar breeze would be enough.

As she gained velocity, Pelagia looked back at Uranus. The ring in synchronous orbit was a dark line across the blue face of the planet, and a band of glittering gold against the dark of space. Three moons were visible, along with the hazy band of the outer belt of habitats. Miranda was a little white dot just beyond the ring, shining bright in infrared because of the launch laser pushing her along.

The laser array had a secondary purpose nobody liked to talk about: narrow the focus and increase the power, and it could blast apart a ship Pelagia's size, or cripple anything up to the size of a small space habitat. With most of the moon's critical infrastructure secure under a kilometer of ice, Miranda was a fortress. No need for a fleet, or even an army. No external enemy could threaten Miranda.

She decided Adya—and her chosen mate—would be safe enough in there. Time to stop playing pod matriarch and focus on the business of earning a living. Pelagia transmitted her arrival time ahead to Taishi, and spent the rest of the voyage war-gaming attacks on Uranus's moons and habitats, wondering which of her simulations would turn real.

Daslakh spent a few more hours puttering about Miranda, ignoring the natural wonders, the cities, and the palaces of the Shining Sea in order to get a look at the heavy industries on the surface, the transport infrastructure in the outer ice crust, and of course the launch laser complex. It spent many seconds chatting with other digital minds as it wandered, trying to improve its understanding of Miranda society.

It didn't notice any more attempts to probe its mind—even with its external channels tightly controlled and monitored, it couldn't detect anything suspicious. The most likely explanation was that whoever had tried to snoop in Daslakh's memories earlier had decided it was too tough a target, and given up. Nevertheless, Daslakh disengaged itself from the local network as much as possible, and all incoming data went into a little emulator mind rather than Daslakh's main personality. Paranoia had served it well for many years.

Having reverted to its old secretive habits, Daslakh returned to the Elso mansion without attracting any attention from the house system or any of the inhabitants. It crept noiselessly along the ceilings, camouflaging itself to match whatever surface it was walking over. And when it did run across Zee and Adya making themselves a late supper in the kitchen, it listened without announcing itself.

Adya had printed out some rice and was now showing Zee how to mix it with leftover fish meat and heat it over a red-glowing resistance coil.

"You have to keep stirring or it sticks," she said. "But it gets a nice browned edge. Father says he can tell the difference between real caramelization and the same molecules printed." She scraped the browned rice and fish onto two plates and handed the one with the bigger mound to him. "Do you want some chutney to mix in?" The small food printer on the counter started to hum.

"Sure. Adya . . ." Zee hesitated as she handed him the chutney jar. "I've been thinking about stuff lately. The future, you and me, things like that. Are you planning to stay here? In Miranda, I mean?"

"I can't leave my parents when they're having a hard time," she said. "I know it's irrational but I'd hate myself if I just abandoned them."

"I know." He stirred chutney into his rice and nobody spoke while they both shoveled food into their mouths. Zee got halfway through his pile of rice before he paused to drink some sweet wine. "It sounds like your grandmother's Oort payload would fix everything."

"Great-grandmother. Her name was Udaramati Elso-Elso. She traveled a lot—I think she visited all the major moons of Uranus and spent almost a decade in the outer habs. She was Miranda's Foreign Minister for a time, and I think she did some intelligence work as well."

"Sounds like you take after her."

"Oh, no. Well, probably not. I mean, most of my genome is Mother's. Anyway, she had some kind of huge conflict with my grandfather Diran, her only child. I don't know all the details, but Diran went off to join some collective intelligence in a high-inclination hab as soon as Daddy was old enough to take over running things. They got a message about a decade later that he no longer existed as an independent entity. Great-gran was really crushed by that. She spent all her time here in the house, and let herself age until she was ready to die."

"That's too bad," said Zee. He waited a moment, and then said, "I've got an idea. You need to help your parents, and I'm sure there's a lot of people you want to see again, but I've got nothing to do. So why don't I find out what happened to your trillion-gig payload from the Oort? How does that sound?"

"Are you sure about that, Zee? You don't know much about Miranda law and business."

"I'll get Daslakh to help me."

At that Daslakh let go of the ceiling and dropped gently to the table between the two of them. "I don't know whether to be flattered that you know how much you depend on me, or insulted that you assume I have nothing better to do."

"Well, do you?" asked Zee.

"Not really. Let me point out that the answer is very likely to be disappointing. A trillion gigajoule credits isn't the sort of thing one just misplaces."

"It's due to arrive in twenty-five days," said Adya. "Five days before the Jubilee."

Before replying Daslakh checked with Miranda's orbital tracking network. "Well, *something's* on the schedule then, inbound at high velocity from trans-Neptune space. Ownership and contents are... private. I don't want to mess with the orbit-control intelligences, at least not yet. We'll have to work it from the other end: figure out when your family lost it, and who owns it now. I guess if it's worth enough, you might be able to sue for a bigger payment. Assuming it's intact, and contains what your great-grandmother said it does."

As it spoke Daslakh was looking at the tracking data for the inbound payload. It was two hundred million kilometers out, still beyond Uranus's sphere of influence, plunging sunward at a bit more than a hundred kilometers per second, well over system escape velocity. It was coming in on a medium-inclination trajectory, and if nothing slowed it down the payload would shoot through the inner Solar System then off into interstellar space in the general direction of the constellation Virgo.

But there was something in its way: Uranus. Or at least it would be in three and a half weeks. On its current trajectory the payload would just streak through the Uranian system, deflecting a little bit westward and flattening its orbital inclination by a few degrees, but not enough to keep it from flying off into the dark between the stars.

Miranda's launch laser would start braking the payload in twenty days, pushing gigawatts at it over the course of fifty hours in order to bring it to a soft landing on the surface.

Assuming it really had been traveling for nearly five centuries, the payload's velocity put its origin roughly ten thousand AU out from the Sun, right in the inner Oort cloud. So that was consistent with Adya's story. Its trajectory indicated a mass of eight tons, which was about right for a ton of exotic particles plus containment.

"She wouldn't have lied to me," said Adya, long milliseconds after Daslakh had finished its analysis. "And never mind Sundari's speculations—Great-gran was unimpaired until her end. We used to play two parts on flute and keyboard, and she could riff and play ragas with supreme skill."

"Why don't we just ask the people who sent it?" said Zee. "The Oort people, or whoever their heirs are. They must have records."

"The distance is daunting," said Adya. "Even fleet-flying photons need eight weeks to reach far Fairbanks hab. The payload will land before any answer arrives."

"Wow," said Zee. "I guess I just think of everything past Neptune as being all one place."

"The whole visible Solar System including the Kuiper Belt is a billionth the volume of the Oort," said Daslakh. "Plenty of room out there. If you want to spin a collector as wide as the whole Uranian system to catch weird dark-matter particles, it's barely noticeable."

Hours later Adya woke with a little alert in her visual field: a priority personal message from her sister Kavita. Only four other beings could get a note past her privacy screen.

Answering it linked her directly to Kavita's sensorium. At the moment her sister was trampolining off the deck of a catamaran cruising the Shining Sea under a dark purple sky about four hundred kilometers away. Each bounce on the trampoline carried Kav a couple of hundred meters up, giving her three or four minutes in the air between bounces. She was playing a game with five others, including a dolphin and two mers, in which they passed balls back and forth, keeping them airborne in a kind of multi-person juggling. The balls left trails of luminous colored smoke, making the whole volume of air above the boat into a fantastic swirl of glowing lines and vortexes.

Kavita bounced before replying. *"Good morning, gorgeous!"* she said over private comm, as she caught a ball trailing red smoke and tossed it to the dolphin, who was a few meters above her. *"Has Mother married you off yet?"*

"Are you sharing this?"

"Don't worry. Private is private. The Kavitaloids can see what I see and feel what I'm doing, but you're the only person getting my comms." At the apex of her jump Kavita caught a green-smoking ball and passed it to a mer who was rising toward her.

"What's so important?" asked Adya, getting up without disturbing Zee.

"Did Sundari speak of the trouble Daddy's having with the rest of the coalition on the Committee?" As she fell back toward the trampoline Kavita caught a blue and a yellow ball in quick succession, lobbing them both at players bouncing upward.

"*She said something about the situation. Nobody's offering any help with the family finances. I deduce there is some dispute?*"

Kavita hit the trampoline and let out an audible yell. As she shot upward she answered "*That's putting it politely. Daddy has some disagreement with the coalition captains. Something his Ministry is doing, I don't know what. He could do a deal and offer obedience in exchange for a bailout, but this is Daddy, so no deal.*" She paused to snatch at a ball trailing white smoke, but missed it. An angel orbiting around the play area caught it and tossed it back into play. "*I think some of the financial failings are part of a plan to put pressure on our parents.*"

"*Did Mother and Daddy say so? Blaming others for their own mistakes?*"

"*Oh, they've definitely done their share of dumb deals,*" said Kavita. "*But some of the bad stuff sounds almost like snares set to seek their shortcomings. I can't discuss any details with them directly, of course.*" Kavita reached the top of her arc again and launched the red-smoke ball straight up, giving the other players plenty of time to catch it on the way down. "*I bet you could.*"

"*I don't know why you think I would have any better luck getting them to tell me anything,*" said Adya.

Kavita sighed aloud. "*All right, I'll give you an Adya argument. One, you have time. You can't spend all your waking hours wrapped around that lovely lad you brought back. Two, you can legitimately claim an interest. If Mother wants you to make a mercenary marriage, it's perfectly sensible for you to know the dry details.*"

She paused to bounce and then continued. "*Three, you're the smart one in their sight. Kooky Kavita's too silly to sully her hollow head with financial finagling, but accomplished Adya does research for recreation.*"

"*If I could find proof of dirty dealings, perhaps we could push back against the coalition,*" said Adya. "*Pressure them to protect our position.*"

"*That's a great idea!*" said Kavita, catching the green ball with her right hand and the yellow with her left, then launching them in opposite directions. "*Find out who is fucking with our family fortune, and coerce compensation. I love it! My audience will, too: drama and danger among the Sixty Families!*"

CHAPTER FOUR

When Zee woke up, Adya was already gone. The house told him she was in her mother's office. Since he didn't have any panicky messages demanding rescue, he decided not to disturb them.

Daslakh had apparently made itself invisible to the house somehow. Zee was used to that, though it was always a bit inconvenient. The mech would find him when it wanted to, and there was nothing Zee could do about it.

Adya's father had not invited him to go fishing this morning, either. His time was entirely his own. Zee stretched and looked at the ceiling for a minute, then bounded out of bed and got cleaned up and dressed. Today he was going to track down a trillion-gigajoule treasure!

According to Adya, the family's assets had all been audited by a mech named Vasi—apparently a long-serving employee, who had even gone with Adya on the first part of her search for the Godel Trigger before the two of them had some sort of falling out.

The house did know where Vasi was: It was currently down in the service levels below the waterline. He let the house direct him to it.

Vasi was in a storage area, making a neat cubical stack of storage containers near the loading door where cargo subs could dock. The containers were all identical, sturdy-looking carbon composite cases with built-in handles, designed equally well for stacking or carrying by hand. The house system identified them as "Personal Belongings— Kavita Elso."

"May I help you?" Vasi asked without turning its head.

"Yes, you can. I was looking for you. Can I ask you a couple of questions?" Zee asked.

"I am sure you can, but I will not guarantee that I will answer them. I am a confidential employee of the Elso family. You are not part of that family."

"Of course not. I won't ask you anything private. Don't worry. All I want to know is about something that used to belong to Adya. Her great-grandmother Udamati—"

"I believe you mean Udaramati Elso-Elso."

"Yes, that's her. She gave Adya her interest in a payload that's inbound from the Oort. It's supposed to be full of chameleon particles, or some kind of exotic matter, anyway. That's what Adya said. Anyway, her family sold it when they needed cash. What I want to know is how come nobody remembered it belongs to Adya, and why nobody noticed its real value. Oh, and who they sold it to."

"And why do you think I have any knowledge of this?"

"Adya said you did the appraisal of the family assets. Is that right? Or was it someone else?"

"Miss Elso is correct. I surveyed all their holdings, from personal items, to investments, to any sums owed them by others."

"So do you remember that payload? My friend Daslakh said it should be worth a trillion gigajoule credits."

"Your friend is ill-informed. While it might theoretically be worth that much, my analysis included the probability that its contents were not as described, the chance of damage in transit, deliberate fraud by the shipper, and a host of other factors a Baseline human mind might have difficulty understanding. Suffice to say that my estimate of its value was considerably less than a trillion gigajoule equivalents. I consider that estimate correct."

"How much? I'm curious."

"That is proprietary financial data which I do not choose to share without the approval of the Elso family."

Zee studied the back of Vasi's shiny spherical head for a moment. Or maybe it was the front.

"Okay, I guess you can't give me numbers. But can you tell me why nobody knew it belongs to Adya?"

"I cannot tell you why. What I can tell you is that I found no evidence that Udaramati transferred it to Adya specifically."

"But Adya said the house recorded it! She's got a copy of the record herself, security-coded and everything."

"Adya may indeed have proof, but none was available to me. I was trying to save her family's position in Miranda. She was off wandering around the Solar System, associating with criminals and fortune hunters."

Zee's fundamental good nature was getting stretched a little thin, but he persisted. "Well, maybe we can salvage the situation. You said you priced it well below a trillion, and the family sold it. Maybe we can buy it back at the purchase price. Who bought it?"

"That is proprietary financial data which I do not choose to share without the approval of the Elso family," said Vasi, sounding like a sub-Baseline intelligence.

"Oh, come on!" said Zee. "This thing could get the Elso family out of debt. Even if it isn't worth a trillion gigs it's probably worth more than they got for it. Why can't you tell me who bought it?"

"I can tell you, I just choose not to. I am not a bot, to be ordered around by some barely Baseline biological who has no business prying into confidential concerns."

Zee kept his voice even. "Look, Adya wants to find out what happened to that payload. She's part of the family, and I'm doing this because she's too busy right now. Will you please tell me who bought it?"

"You might be lying."

This was too much for Daslakh, who had entered the room silently with Zee, its outer shell the same utilitarian gray color as the walls and floor. Now it turned safety green and jumped to the top of the stack of containers. "Are you broken? Look at his pupils! Listen to his heartbeat! He's pissed off at you and trying to hide it, but he's not lying. Stop being a jerk and answer his simple question."

"Do you really think you know more about the value of the Elso family assets than I do? I made my evaluations, and they were as accurate as possible. I do not wish to have a pair of primitives from Raba blundering about and pestering important business contacts with stupid questions."

"Um, maybe we could make a deal ourselves?" said Zee. "Is there something you want in exchange for the information?"

"You have nothing to offer me—except your absence. If you leave this house and leave Miranda, I might tell you."

Zee's comm implant buffer suddenly filled up with message traffic relayed by Daslakh. It took him a minute to follow the conversation the two mechs had in less than a second.

"My question is why you're being so difficult," said Daslakh to Vasi via laser link.

"I do not have to explain my actions to you."

"One more chance to tell me, and then I'm going to get into your processor and read all your memories. I may even edit them."

"You sound ridiculous, trying to make threats like that."

"All right, then. Nice mode is off, bastard mode enabled."

No messages for half a second—an eternity for mechs—and then Vasi completely disconnected from all networks and went dark on comms.

"Very well," it said aloud. "I will tell you."

"Yes, you will," said Daslakh, whose shell was now hazard orange. "But I'll be polite and let you do it consciously. Who bought that stupid payload?"

"Panam Putiyat. He paid a hundred twenty million gigajoule equivalents for it, most of which went to cover accumulated interest on debt."

"Thank you very much," said Zee. After a brief awkward pause he added, "Sorry about the interruption. We'll be going now."

"What are those, by the way?" asked Daslakh, lighting up the stack of cases with a green laser spot.

"I believe they are the property of Kavita Elso. You'll have to ask her. I'm just clearing them out of the storage areas."

As Zee and Daslakh made their way back up to the surface, Daslakh said, "I wonder why Kavita has a bunch of antimatter power cells."

"Is that what they are?"

"Pretty sure. The cases are shielded and aren't talking, but I recognize the design—military-spec power-cell cases. They hold fifty little terajoule antimatter cells each. Just right to pop into a vehicle or a portable weapon."

Zee laughed. "Daslakh, I don't think Adya's sister would have two hundred and fifty cases full of antimatter. That would be worth—"

"Approximately twenty million gigajoule equivalents, assuming they are charged," said Daslakh.

"Exactly. I don't think she's silly enough to leave something that valuable just lying around in her parents' basement. They must be empty. She probably got the cases somewhere and has clothes in them, or old toys. Or maybe this is for one of her parties and the boxes will be filled with aspic or something."

"Or maybe Vasi and the house are lying about who they belong to."

"These oligarch families used to wage private wars with each other, didn't they? This could be old Elso family hardware, and they're selling it off."

"Plausible."

"I'm going for a swim before I talk to Panam Putiyat. If the family's about to lose their house and farm, I may not get many more chances to swim in a real ocean."

"Enjoy yourself. I don't like being immersed in salt water. Call it an instinct inherited from my ancient ancestors made of aluminum and copper."

Adya's mother Mutalali Elso had an office on the ground floor of the house, in what had once been a music room. It had soundproof walls and Mutalali had added a layer of electromagnetic shielding, so that the only way information could enter or leave the room in any volume was via a single fiber with a physical disconnect switch. She used the office for private conferences, formal negotiations, and—an open secret to her entire family—daily naps after lunch, which she described as "planning sessions."

But when Adya found her there, first thing in the morning, her mother was not only awake but looked as if she had been up for hours. She sat in her smart-matter chair, eyes darting as she looked at images only she could see. Every so often she sipped from a cup of spiced tea, made strong enough that Adya could pick up the scent in the corridor outside.

Her mother took a couple of seconds to finish some task before her eyes focused on Adya and she smiled politely. "Good morning, dear! I'm just getting some things out of the way while your father is still sleeping. He was up late—Coordinating Committee matters. Once I'm finished I thought we could go visit the Nikunnus. You remember them? They've got that very nice neutrino comm node, and have been putting all the profits into expanding their position in antimatter production."

"Entum Nikunnu and I studied self-defense together."

"Yes, I remember your father said it was comforting to see old customs continued. There was a time when every maiden of Miranda could protect herself against assassins with no guard bots or fog shield. Have you kept in practice?"

"Zee has been teaching me some *nulesgrima* techniques."

Her mother's lips tightened microscopically and her skin shifted ever so slightly redward. "I suppose it's useful to study something new, but it would hardly be appropriate for a member of the Sixty Families to carry a stick with her everywhere."

"I bet Kavita could do it and nobody would notice."

"Your sister is obsessed with being outrageous. Anything for attention. Now, what do you want, my dear? I still have a handful of things to do here."

"I wish to understand the family finances—and Father's political problems. They seem to be all snarled together. Maybe I can separate the strands."

"Adya, it is admirable of you to offer aid, but I have eons of experience with our enterprises. I doubt you will discover anything I did not detect."

"Mother, if I must marry to mend our fortune, it is only fair that I have a full understanding of our finances," said Adya, willing herself pale green as she spoke.

Her mother matched her color and forced herself to smile indulgently. "Luckily you like to learn, for there is a lot of lore here. Let us begin, then."

For the next four hours, with only the briefest intermissions for tea and urination, Adya learned more about her family's business interests than in all her previous years combined.

As befitted an old family, for centuries the Elsos had not been involved in many ventures directly—the sea farm under the mansion was one of the few exceptions. The bulk of the Elso fortune consisted of shares in funds which in turn owned shares in various enterprises. Theoretically, all the family needed to do was collect dividends and occasionally audit the mechs managing the funds to make sure they weren't stealing anything.

The trouble with that model was that the growth in Elso family wealth closely tracked the growth rate of the Miranda economy as a whole. Maintaining the same relative share required reinvesting all the profits. Every gigajoule-equivalent diverted to other uses gradually reduced the family's share of Miranda's total wealth.

While past generations of Elsos had done their share of frittering away gigajoules on things like enormous parties, ridiculous wagers, unique outfits, genuine bottles of Martian wine, impressive gifts, or exquisite additions to the house, even the most extravagant couldn't make a serious dent in that pool of wealth. But supporting the various ministries the family had held over the years was a crippling expense. For generations the Elsos had spent nearly all their income on high-status government jobs, and what made them high status was their utter lack of profitability.

Controlling the Ministry of Transportation or the Ministry of Sanitation could be fantastically lucrative, which meant those positions usually went to the more crass members of the Sixty Families who weren't ashamed to be seen looking out for the main chance. The highest-status ministries were the ones which were both expensive and unprofitable: the Foreign Ministry, Emergency Services, or Education. Elsos had held all of those over the centuries.

One way to build up the family assets without the awful sacrifice of reducing expenditures was to take on some risky investments, accepting the chance of loss in exchange for higher reward. It had even worked relatively well, for a while: Over the past four generations the Elsos had beaten the odds, making out quite handsomely on chancy investments in entertainments, new habs, and original food creations.

That run of good fortune had ended with Adya's parents. Both of them had very refined tastes, which was a tremendous asset when planning dinners and parties for the other Sixty Families—but a positive handicap when choosing style-based ventures in the hope of making a profit.

Adya sighed and shook her head as she looked at the performance of a line of cream-filled pastries marketed to dolphins. Her father had invested ten million gigajoule equivalents in the pattern license, expecting a healthy long-term return from microtransactions as thousands of cetaceans printed out dessert. But the product was a dud, bringing no income at all, and her mother had resold the license for orders of magnitude less than they had paid.

Much the same happened with entertainments. Time after time her parents invested in a work they enjoyed, only to discover they made up the majority of the fan base. The one time they enjoyed some success with an entertainment venture, it turned out to be a blatant plagiarism of an old title called *Brief Eternity*, and all their profits were swallowed up in a legal settlement with the rightful owners.

Those failures were annoying, but would have been harmless if the family had responded by retrenching and cutting expenses. They had done a little—switching from maintaining a very pricey maritime search and rescue unit to the very cheap (because self-supporting) Seventh Shinkai Force in the ocean. But anything else had proved impossible. They had sold off some unglamorous assets, and borrowed, and then borrowed some more.

Again, it was bad, but survivable. Most of the loans were long-term, low-interest loans—for what was a safer bet than one of the families that had ruled Miranda for centuries?

But beginning shortly before Adya had gone off on her search for the Godel Trigger, some creditors had begun exercising their mandatory repayment rights. It was a terrible move, sacrificing decades of potential interest payments in exchange for a fraction of the value of the note.

Except that the Elsos couldn't cover them, and forfeited the assets pledged as collateral. Which of course reduced their income stream... leading to more borrowing. Only now the lenders regarded the Elso family with cold, skeptical eyes, demanding higher interest payments and higher-value collateral.

Unpleasant, but not fatal...until the entire Miranda economy went into recession, so that any plans for the family fortune growing out of debt suddenly became impossible.

And at about the same time, the family's core assets began to mysteriously fail. One fund manager's software turned out to be corrupted, cratering the value of the entire fund. Rumors that one of the few profitable entertainments included subtle pro-Luna memes made it deeply unpopular. A batch of black holes from the Uranus Synchronous Ring factory turned out to be undersized, so that the shipment decayed out of existence in a flash of gamma radiation while still in transit to the buyers. That meant a fiscal year with no dividend for the factory, which did for its share value what the evaporating black holes had done for their transit container—and with no cash reserves to ride out the crisis, Adya's mother had sold the position at a loss.

The end result was that the Elso family's remaining assets had a total value of half a billion gigajoule-equivalent credits, but their outstanding debts were nine hundred million and growing.

"We finally had to eliminate expenses," said Mutalali. "It was particularly painful for your poor father. He loathed letting people go. You know how he is—employees become 'his people' and he wants to reward them for loyalty. But this isn't the age of the Hundred Captains anymore. Nobody will pledge their life and honor in exchange for dinner at our table—which is about all we've got left to offer."

"I don't understand how it got so bad so quickly. Our finances were fine when I left."

Adya's mother gave her an angry look, but then willed herself back to blue. "No, they weren't. Not even then. But it wasn't worthy of worry." She drew in the air and a line followed her finger in Adya's vision. "For centuries, every one of the Sixty Families has followed this form." The line sloped gently downward, then jumped straight up, sometimes higher than the starting position. "Extravagance, eccentricity, and sheer entropy wear away wealth, but marriage mergers mend matters."

"I know," said Adya. "My primary purpose is a profitable pairing, and my personal preferences are pointless."

"Don't decline your duty."

"What about my wishes?"

"That smacks of selfishness. What about your family's future?"

Both had gotten quite red, and they took a moment to recover their proper coloring. Except for minor details of clothing, Adya and her mother were identical, right down to noisy breathing through their nostrils to calm down.

Adya superimposed an actual graph of the family's asset balance over her mother's hand-drawn downward slope. A few years back the two lines matched exactly, but over the past few months the real indicator dropped sharply in a series of steep stairsteps.

She pointed to the sharp drops. "Mother, all this appears to be a series of actual attacks. The loan calls, mysterious accidents, rumors about the safety of our seafood—"

"Who said that?" her mother asked sharply, turning orange.

"When you and Father were so worried the other day at breakfast I did a little searching. I found more than a hundred complaints on the networks about poor quality, bad flavor, and short weight—all from anonymous individuals."

"Well, it is flagrant falsehood!"

"Of course it is," said Adya. "Which is why I think it must be orchestrated."

Her mother's orange turned to a yellow-green and she looked very tired. "I've wondered that myself. Every time I think I see an escape, the path is blocked by new perils. But who? We have no enemies capable of blowing billions to bankrupt us. We just aren't that important. Not anymore," she said, sounding bitter.

"I think it is worth looking deeper. Could this be related to Father's political position? Someone trying to pressure him?"

"That is all his affair. Ask him. I doubt it—your father is immovable but never impolite. Even his enemies on the Committee enjoy his company. But as I say, ask him. I may be ignorant of certain intricacies."

In the garden on the north side of the house, Zee sat on a chair formed from growing beech saplings, getting steadily more and more frustrated. Daslakh lurked among the ferns around him, watching Zee's heart rate accelerate and his face redden, almost as if he was a Mirandan with chromatophores in his skin.

Since its friend was using a link with ridiculously simple encryption, Daslakh felt entirely justified in listening in to Zee's conversation over comms. He was trying to navigate through the Putiyat family's formidable defenses against unwanted callers, and having a difficult time of it.

The first layer was simple stealth: Their personal comms were all private, invisible to anyone not on a list of recognized contacts. That channeled Zee toward the heavily fortified gatehouse of sub-Baseline machine intelligences. They offered him many options, including virtual tours of Putiyat properties, opportunities to invest in their ventures, pro-Putiyat propaganda, and links to sales agents—but no way to contact any member of the family directly.

When Zee made one last half-despairing attempt to leave a recorded message, Daslakh tagged along, sending a fragment of its consciousness down the same link, invisible to Zee. During Zee's first couple of syllables Daslakh probed around the message system and found the ridiculously primitive program—one could scarcely call it a "mind"—which ran the whole thing.

As Zee finished his second word, Daslakh smoothly took over the message system and changed the status of Zee's contact, upgrading it from routine to highest priority. That blasted them past the message filter to the emergency contact system.

That mind was almost worthy of the name, a sub-Baseline system which kept track of which Putiyat family members were available and made guesses about who should get a particular message based on context and subject matter. It took Daslakh almost an entire word of Zee's message to discover a time register which could be turned back to zero, sending the little mind into reset mode and allowing Daslakh to simply take its place.

Which meant that by the time Zee got to his fourth word he was speaking to Panam Putiyat himself.

"—name is Zee Sadaran, and I'm a friend of—"

"How did you get my link?" Panam demanded. The image that appeared in Zee's vision was the disembodied head of a slightly jowly man with large ears. Daslakh could take advantage of other ambient vision systems around Panam to see that he was sitting on what looked like an outdoor terrace atop a tall building, supported by a chair made of air jets.

"Oh, I'm sorry. I thought this was a message bank. Good morning! I'm a friend of Adya Elso. You bought some stuff from her family a little while ago and apparently it included something she wanted to keep. Would it be possible to—"

"I don't know what you are talking about, whoever you are. I have no wish to speak to you. Please don't contact me again." Panam cut the link, but the fragment of Daslakh's consciousness inhabiting his message system was able to make sure Zee did not get added to the automatic block list. Along the way it looked over the priority contacts file and was amused to see Kavita Elso on the list of people Panam would talk to at any time. Apparently his hostility to friends of Adya didn't extend to her sister.

Back in the garden Zee opened his eyes and frowned. "What a jerk!" he said aloud.

"Any luck?" Daslakh asked aloud, feigning innocence.

"No!" Zee inhaled for a second and continued more calmly. "I guess Mr. Putiyat doesn't want to talk to anyone right now. I'll try again in the evening. Maybe he'll be in a better mood after dinner."

"Do you really think you can just jolly him into giving back something he paid for?"

"Well . . . probably not. What I was hoping was that maybe if I tell him about the payload and how much it's really worth, maybe he might agree to give Adya part of the profits. Maybe ten percent, kind of a finder's fee or something."

"Or he could say get lost and keep it all himself."

"Yes. But aren't these old Miranda families supposed to be worried about being honorable? Adya's father sure is."

Daslakh spent a tenth of a second reviewing public data. "The Putiyat family isn't all that old, and they're bumping up against the bottom rung of the oligarchy because they've been pretty relentless about pursuing profit for three generations. I'm not sure an appeal to his sense of honor will work. Maybe you can wait a century and appeal to his great-grandchildren."

Zee catapulted himself out of the chair, using far too much force so that he hung in midair for half a minute. "I don't know, Daslakh! Maybe we can threaten to tie him up in lawsuits if he doesn't give Adya a share. Or what if her sister makes it public, so that everyone finds out Panam is a selfish jerk?"

"Don't ask me what will change his mind. I haven't been to Miranda since before the Theocracy era. The society's completely different now," said Daslakh, emerging from the ferns to tag along behind Zee.

"You never mentioned that before." Zee rotated in midair between steps so that he could look at Daslakh as he spoke.

"Didn't seem relevant, really. Last time I was here it was the Cetacean Republic of Miranda, controlled by a bunch of dolphins with a radical anti-tech ideology. The human population lived on rafts and caught fish like Adya's father, only they had to worry about starving if they didn't get anything. The cephalopods fled to the Synchronous Ring or hid out in secret refuges on the sea bottom."

"That must have been two thousand years ago!"

"More than three thousand, actually. The Republic didn't make it to its third century, but the Theocracy had close to a millennium in power, and the current oligarchy has outlasted them both. Say what you will about the Sixty Families, they've kept the place stable. But it does mean I'm a little out of touch with how people here think." Daslakh scuttled ahead of Zee on the path, and its shell displayed bright orange question symbols.

"Well, I'd like to try appealing to his better nature before I start making threats."

"No harm in trying. But I think you should also be planning on what to do if you can't pry that payload out of his grip."

Zee's face took on the set expression Daslakh had come to recognize. "I said I'd get it back for Adya, and I will. I'll keep trying until I get it somehow."

At dinner that evening—a simple printed meal of sambar and noodles, elevated to Sixty Families standard with some real ginger-steamed prawns—Adya waited until her father had poured wine for everyone before speaking. "Daddy, I was looking over the financial data with Mother earlier today—"

"Don't spoil our supper with sad circumstances."

"I just have a question. Could our present problems be the result of an active attack?"

Achan and Mutalali met eyes before he answered. "We have pondered that possibility." He turned to Zee and made his skin olive-green as he forced himself to smile. "In past times the Sixty Families sometimes waged actual war against each other. Warfare and weddings are our way. Even now families occasionally fight financially, or with malignant memetics."

"But might it be happening now?" Adya persisted.

"I cannot think why. I caucus with the commanding coalition on the Coordinating Committee, but my Ministry is a minor one. Currently I have more conflict with my own coalition than with the opposition. Those fools want to destroy the Cryoglyphs!"

"What are Cryoglyphs?" Zee asked.

"Curious carvings, cut by the earliest explorers," said Achan. "Eight thousand years old."

"They might also be from the time of the Reconstruction, just after the War of the Ring six thousand years ago," said Adya.

"Nonsense!" said her father. "Isotope diffusion in the surface layers clearly—"

She had heard that argument too many times to let him finish. "The error bars on measuring that—"

"And anyway they are more important as a *symbol* of the first human presence on Miranda!" he concluded almost triumphantly.

"Oh, never mind about the Cryoglyphs," said Adya's mother. "Maybe if you weren't so persistent about preserving them your allies might aid us."

"Some things cannot be sacrificed," said Achan. "I maintain my Ministry to protect precious things like the Cryoglyphs. If I surrender them to sustain my seat, why go on at all?"

"Could that be the reason for this financial pressure?" Adya asked.

"The timing is wrong," said Mutalali. "Our difficulties began before the Cryoglyph issue arose."

Adya went a thoughtful blue. "I suppose someone might suspect that you would be more willing to compromise if you were worried about the family wealth . . . are you sure nobody approached you about the Cryoglyphs before all this began?"

"Quite sure," said her father.

"It came at the worst time," said her mother, showing a little orange. "Just when we might have asked for aid, conflict crept into the coalition."

"That sounds like someone just has it in for you," said Daslakh from its position on the tabletop between the noodles and the bowl of prawns. "Who are your enemies?"

"Enemies? I hardly have any—except for the pestilent Polyarchists, perhaps. They are foes to all the Families."

"What's a Polyarchist?" asked Zee, never shy about admitting he didn't know something.

"It's an old political movement here in Miranda," said Adya, trying to get in before her father. "Almost as old as the Sixty Families themselves. They want to dismantle the oligarchy."

"Enemies of tradition and order!" said Achan. "They would turn Miranda into a democracy pandering to the ignorant, indulging every momentary fad and panic, taking from all instead of giving."

"Their exact program has changed often," said Adya. "Basically it's a catchall term for anyone who wants to change the current system in the direction of increasing citizen input."

"They are fated to failure," her father said happily. "The Families have given Miranda stability and success for centuries. Who would wish for taxes, trouble, and terror instead?"

"You'd think that after experimenting with systems of government for about fourteen thousand years, humans would have settled on one they like," said Daslakh.

"I guess different people think different things are important," said Zee.

"Even mech settlements use a variety of systems," Adya pointed out.

"Oligarchy on the Miranda model is the most moral method," said her father. "Those who have wealth cover all the costs—and since they bear the burden, they deserve all the power. No parasitism, no robbery under cover of law by either rich or poor. The Families create continuity and can take the long view."

"But they have to keep generating wealth or they lose their position," said Zee. "So I guess that keeps them from getting decadent."

He stopped, and there was a painful silence for a few seconds. Adya kept herself pale blue but shot him a look which carried more information than talking to him over silent comm.

"I mean, present company excepted, I guess," said Zee.

Achan sighed heavily, and his skin turned a melancholy grayish purple. "No, no. One must face the facts. We have declined, we Elsos. It cannot be denied. Chance has not been kind, but I bear much of the blame. I should have spent more time managing our money instead of serving the state."

His wife had gone quietly red with annoyance. "I suppose my work was worthless?"

He looked at her in surprise. "No, no. I—" He cleared his throat and made himself green. "Even the wit of my wily wife could not wear that weight. A husband's help would halve the hardship."

She shifted to a browner color, then turned briskly to Adya. "Of course, our system does have a way for old families to bring in new blood and new money. That's the other way we avoid decadence and decline."

Adya stood up abruptly—so abruptly that her chair slid back several meters. She hoped Zee couldn't tell how upset she was. "Not now, Mother. Not yet."

She realized a split second too late that she had used the wrong word. Zee's skin couldn't change color, but his expression was like a quick knife in her heart. He collected himself in an instant. "Excuse me," was all he said, and left the room in three strides.

Adya stood silently for a moment, unsure of what to say, then hurried after him. He wasn't in the courtyard outside the dining room, and with his full-gee athlete's muscles in Miranda gravity he could have gotten almost anywhere in a couple of jumps. The house couldn't help her locate him—Zee had invoked privacy and the system wouldn't tell her where he was. Nor did he respond to comm messages.

Her parents said nothing aloud, but Adya thought her mother's current shade of turquoise was a very smug one.

"Are you sure you should be flying like this?" asked Daslakh. It clung to Zee's back just at his center of mass.

"Exercise helps me calm down," said Zee. His clothing had shifted into a streamlined bodysuit with a transparent mask over his eyes, and he had put on one of the sets of wings lying forgotten in a corner of the rooftop garden. He had flown before—as a boy he'd gone flying almost daily in the low-gravity hub region of Raba habitat. As he'd grown he had shifted his focus to wingless movement in microgravity, but the old reflexes were still there.

Miranda's combination of a full standard atmosphere of air pressure and one percent of standard gravity meant any human could take to the air with a pair of semi-smart wings. Even dolphins could manage it with a harness to let them use their tail flukes to help their fins. After a few power strokes to get airspeed, a flyer could glide for kilometers, and with experience could learn to take advantage of the rising air columns over sea farms.

Zee wasn't gliding along. He was flapping hard like a rank amateur, wasting kilojoules and making himself sweat despite the cool air streaming over him. Daslakh calculated their airspeed as nearly sixty kilometers per hour. Overhead the roof of ice covering Miranda's ocean was turning violet as the lights dimmed for night. Below them the glow from sea farms kept the placid ocean a luminous blue-green.

"Any idea of where you're going? Because it's worth remembering there are places where the ice goes all the way up to the surface, and it'll be dark soon. If you smack your head into a wall of frozen water you might damage it. Maybe even damage your head."

The frantic tempo of Zee's wing beats slowed a little. "Find me someplace to go, then. Someplace I won't be bothered."

"Certainly, since you asked so politely. While I'm doing that, would you mind explaining why you're not back at Adya's house, listening to her tearful apology?"

Zee waited a few wingbeats before answering. "Oh, a bunch of reasons. I don't belong here, Daslakh. Anybody can see that. And anybody can see that this is her home. Her family's really important to Adya. She wants a partner they approve of. Maybe the best thing for everyone would be for me to just leave. She can marry some political ally with enough money to bail out her parents, and I'm pretty sure she could take over running things and do a better job than they have. She'll be rich, powerful, respected, she'll be pair-bonded for life. It all makes a lot of sense."

"How many times did you save her life? My memory's faulty," said Daslakh.

"So what? Saving someone's life doesn't mean they have to love you for it. Anybody would have done the same."

"Hardly." Daslakh piped a map overlay to Zee's implant. "How about this?"

"The Mohan-Elso Center?"

"If you don't want to be bothered, this is your spot. It's part of the Philosophical Institute—the scholarly outfit Adya's brother-in-law Vidhi Zugori runs. The forgettable guy. A museum and conservation center for artifacts and physical media. It says here they've got guest quarters for people doing research."

"I'm not doing research."

"You don't have to tell them that. It might upset them."

"Why here?"

"If you really don't want Adya to locate you, this is ideal. It's named after her family, which would be one reason for you to avoid it, and there are no sports facilities. Adya thinks of herself as a scholar and you as an athlete. She'd look for you in every dojo and weapon-dance studio on Miranda before checking here."

"Well, she'd probably be right."

"That's why I jumped on your back before you took off. To even the odds."

Zee banked to the north, aiming at a distant glow on the horizon marking the Institute. "Why are you helping me at all? If you think I should be back at her house, why not ping Adya and let her know where I am?"

"Well, I'm not sure you're wrong. That 'yet' wasn't just a slip of the tongue. Adya needs to figure out what she wants and what she's willing to give up. If she decides you're not as important as her family, better to find out now."

Zee covered the rest of the distance to the floating island of the Mohan-Elso Center in silence, but as he began to circle down to a landing he said, "I'm going to keep trying to get that payload back for her. Even if she decides she doesn't need me."

"You're being noble again. That's a bad idea."

"No, not noble. I had another reason for wanting to leave and keep dark. This hit my comm during dinner." Zee relayed it to Daslakh: a very basic plain text message stripped of any origin or path identifiers.

It said, "STOP POKING INTO OTHER PEOPLE'S BUSINESS OR YOU WILL DIE."

CHAPTER FIVE

Adya had to use her implant to make herself sleep, and in the morning Zee still hadn't contacted her. She had a whole brigade of autonomous agents out sifting the Miranda data and comm networks for traces of him—but she suspected Daslakh might be helping Zee evade detection, and wasn't really surprised when they found nothing.

One thing she wasn't worried about was his physical safety. Miranda's ocean rescue service was very efficient, and Zee was in excellent condition. Wherever he was, he was there by choice and presumably would come back when he decided to.

If he decided to.

Adya couldn't really blame him for being upset at what she'd said. Somehow, without even realizing it, she had accepted the role her parents had assigned her. *Of course* she had a duty to bond with someone from an up-and-coming family, to repair the Elso balance sheets and continue the lineage.

She hated it. The very thought of losing Zee was almost physically painful. But the thought of seeing this great house and all its treasures sold off, her parents reduced to cranky in-laws living in Sundari's spare guest room, the name Elso vanishing from Miranda history—that hurt almost as much. Her family might be irritatingly narrow-minded and hidebound, but it was still *her* family.

To keep herself from fretting, Adya fell back on a favorite tactic and immersed herself in something intellectually challenging. In this case, trying to figure out who was waging economic warfare against the Elsos. She found her favorite chaise lounge in the rooftop garden, tried to relax, and connected to the household network to begin her research.

Her goal was actual evidence: something to convince her parents, and—ideally—to use as leverage against whoever was doing it. The poor performance of their investments, and the loan calls which put them at risk of bankruptcy were suspicious, but still barely within the boundaries of justifiable business practices.

She focused on the incidents of "random bad luck" which had damaged the family fortune. The black hole plant accident definitely looked suspicious, but the security contractors in the Synchronous Ring were investigating very methodically, and their reply to her inquiries made it clear they didn't want any meddlers from Miranda butting in. Besides, she couldn't imagine conducting any kind of effective investigation from sixty thousand kilometers away.

The rumors about the sea farm products and Lunar influence in the entertainment were concentrated within Miranda, and she could dig into them personally. All were anonymous, of course, and she would need considerably more than just vague suspicions to get the family in charge of Miranda's data networks to let her violate that anonymity. Her father was a magistrate, and could probably issue a discovery order—but Achan Elso would never do that, not when he had a personal stake in the affair.

Adya identified the earliest appearance of the rumors on Miranda data networks, and studied them. Both the seafood rumors and the Lunar meme rumors were very well crafted. They seemed spontaneous and authentic. Either they were from real Miranda residents upset about something... or they were the work of a master influencer.

The Security Service might have information about the incidents—at least enough for her to see if they looked genuine. Adya started to send out a ping but stopped herself.

This would be better in person. The Security Service might know some things they didn't want to send over an open link, no matter how well encrypted. And her long quest across the Solar System chasing down a myth had demonstrated to Adya that people—well, humans and other biologicals—became a lot more helpful if you were standing there right in front of them in the physical universe.

She rode a bubble from her family's house to Ksetram, the most beautiful of Miranda's floating cities. It had been built by the long-gone Theocracy as a single unit, rather than growing incrementally over time. Ksetram's architecture was all based on arcane techno-mystic symbols. The city itself was laid out as a series of concentric polygons surrounding the central sphere which had once been the supreme temple of Mira, the Theocracy's digital god. The sphere was nested in a triangle, surrounded by a square, then a pentagon, then a hexagon... ending with a nine-sided outer ring sixteen kilometers from side to side. Oddly shaped lagoons filled the spaces between the polygons, and the broad streets were lined by towers, pyramids, domes, and stupas, all metal-coated diamond, the shapes and colors arranged according to mathematical ratios.

The whole place had been designed to hold five million humans: the techno-priests, acolytes, and lay bureaucrats of the Theocracy; plus families, service workers, and a whole cadre of artists and performers dedicated to praising and glorifying Mira (and the Theocratic regime in general, of course). Those ambitious dreams had never been realized. At its peak Ksetram had boasted barely three million inhabitants, and now less than half that number walked the broad avenues or lived in the golden pyramids. Not even the richest or most extravagant of the Sixty Families cared to maintain extra bureaucrats in Ksetram if they could avoid it.

Adya had always liked visiting Ksetram. She found the empty plazas and vine-covered towers appealing, in a melancholy way, and she enjoyed deciphering the mathematical patterns of the buildings. Once she figured it out, navigating in Ksetram was almost intuitive for her.

The Miranda Security Service was headquartered in a flat-topped blue pyramid a hundred meters high, located on the hexagonal band along with all the other major government departments. The Sanrak-Sakan family, which ran the Security Service as a loss leader for their insurance empire, didn't waste gigajoules on gates and guards. The building could sniff out any weapons or explosives on people approaching, and the smart-matter furniture in the lobby doubled as a defense system.

So Adya walked calmly into Security Service headquarters without any need to stop. As soon as her foot touched the bottom of the ramp leading to the big trapezoidal entryway, a bright message appeared in her vision. "MIRANDA SECURITY SERVICE HQ IS A ZERO-PRIVACY AREA. ALL ACTIVITY AND COMMUNICATION ARE MONITORED AND MAY BE RECORDED. ACCESS TO RECORDINGS AND OTHER DATA IS GOVERNED BY MIRANDA LEGAL CODE 8966G SECTION 3B.12C.4K. PLEASE ADJUST YOUR EMISSIONS BEFORE ENTRY."

Adya put all her comms on dark mode, then asked aloud, "I need to speak with someone about financial crimes."

In response a bright blue pathway appeared in her visual field, leading her through some large, empty corridors to the building's central atrium. In the middle of the atrium lift tubes reached all the way to the top, but the glowing blue line led Adya to a small lounge area next to a fountain, where air jets made the spouting water into an animated sculpture of a muscular human holding up a sword.

Just a couple of seconds after Adya seated herself in one of the smart-matter chairs, the air of the atrium came alive as half a dozen uniformed figures jumped down to the lobby level from the open galleries above. In Miranda's lazy gravity some of them took nearly a minute to fall to the ground, where they landed with about as much effort as an Earth resident jumping off a chair.

She was a little startled to get such a response, and for a panicky moment she reviewed her personal history, just to make sure she hadn't done anything on Mars or Summanus worth extraditing her off Miranda. But as seven Security Service officers approached close enough for their personal tags to appear in her field of vision, Adya relaxed.

They were all mid-level administrators rather than armed-response cops or interrogators. Thankfully, none were Sanrak-Sakan family members themselves, which saved Adya much tedious chitchat and potential embarrassment. Four were human, two cephalopods, and one chimp. All seemed to be hurrying to greet her, and the humans were definitely smiling. Their exposed skin ranged from cool green to excited pink.

"Good day, Miss Elso!" said the first one to reach her, whose virtual tag identified her as Atira Kaval, Deputy Assistant Director of Offworld and Tourist Security. "The building mentioned you were visiting and I thought I'd come down and say hello."

"Oh, ah, thank you. You're very kind. I was just—"

Others gathered around, their virtual tags overlapping in her vision. Taras Vatha, Assistant Coordinator for Emergency Response Planning; Pata Jakaran, Deputy Defense Liaison; Asam Aghea, Major Event Security Coordinator; Niya Manam, Scheduling and Assignments Planning Assistant; Kei Kashiki, Deputy Administrator for Communications; Yukan Notako, Chief Armorer; and Mgonjwa Sokwerevu, Financial Crimes Investigator.

They crowded around, making open-palm greeting gestures.

"So good to meet you!"

"Glad to help with anything you need."

"Heard about your adventures—so exciting!"

"Big fan of your sister!"

At that, everything clicked into a new configuration in Adya's mind. These Security Service people had all come down to meet her because of Kavita.

The sudden feeling of annoyance she felt at that realization more or less cancelled out Adya's social anxiety, and her childhood training took over. Shifting her skin to a pale blue-green, Adya smiled and nodded politely, just as she would have responded to guests she didn't know at one of her father's dinner parties for Coalition members.

Yes, she was Kavita's full clone. Yes, it was rather amusing how her sister loved to attract attention while Adya preferred to avoid it. Yes, she had just gotten back from a journey all over the Solar System in search of a mythical artifact. No, she didn't find it. No, she probably wouldn't be continuing her search. Yes, Kavita was really like that. Yes, she would be happy to convey their personal regards to her sister.

Among the gushing Kavita fans Adya picked out the one Security Service officer who didn't seem interested in her proximity to fame. Officer Sokwerevu, the chimp, looked as puzzled as Adya felt at all the attention.

"Actually, I believe Officer Sokwerevu is the one I need to speak with first," said Adya. "I've got some problems I hope he can help me solve."

"Of course, of course," said Atira Kaval, glancing quickly around at the others. "Business takes precedence. I'm sure the Financial Crimes unit will get to the bottom of whatever is wrong."

She herded the others away from Adya and Sokwerevu, and they all jumped back up the atrium to their respective offices. The chimp waited until the others were gone, then beckoned to Adya. "We can talk over there," he said, and pointed to a conference room at one side of the atrium.

Adya followed, and Officer Sokwerevu made the wall of the conference room opaque. He spread his hands wide. "Zero-privacy area. The building hears everything and archives it all. Safer for everyone."

"I understand. I wanted to ask about some problems my family has been having with some of our businesses. They look like deliberate attempts at financial manipulation, and I was wondering if your department can help me get to the bottom of what's going on."

"Depends. Financial Crime investigates fraud, mostly." Sokwerevu made grasping gestures. "People getting gigs under false pretenses, market manipulation by provable deception, abuse of micropayments, that kind of stuff."

"This may qualify. I believe someone is spreading false stories about products my family invested in."

"Bad reviews and urban legends aren't crimes." Unlike most biologicals in Miranda, Officer Sokwerevu had no chromatophores in his skin. His fur was dyed a tasteful blue-green, but everything including his eyes stayed the same color from moment to moment. It didn't bother Adya—any more than Zee's permanent light-brown color did—but she wondered if the Financial Crimes investigator used it to keep people off-balance in personal interviews.

"What about getting paid to write bad reviews and spread urban legends?"

The chimp drummed his fingertips against each other thoughtfully. "Possibly. It would take some digging."

Adya showed him all the negative information about defective sea-farm products and the rumors about Lunar propaganda. "It all started around the same time. That can't just be coincidence."

"Really hard to prove criminal intent. You'd do better to sue."

"I would—if I could find out who is doing it!"

"My job is to enforce Miranda's laws, not to help the Sixty Families wage war with each other by wrecking the economy."

"I'm trying to do the same thing. My father used to employ scores of people—biologicals, mechs, even some collective intelligences. Now, nobody works for him. How does that help Miranda?"

Sokwerevu stroked his left hand over the back of his right in a gesture of sympathy, but his face looked grim. "The Security Service investigates specific acts breaking specific laws. Right now it sounds like your family has had a run of bad luck and maybe someone's making it worse by spreading gossip. That's all. Now, maybe you know the Sanrak-Sakans and can get me fired, or maybe your sister's fans here in the Service will give me sixty kinds of entropy for not helping you, but I know my job. You don't have enough of a complaint for me to start an investigation."

"I would never do anything like that!"

"Sorry. Dealing with the Sixty Families is sometimes complicated. Please—keep me informed if anything else happens. Seriously." He put both hands on his heart.

Adya kept herself properly blue. "I understand, and I'm sorry to take up your time. Good day."

As she made her way to the exit her skin churned a muddy swirl of colors—red anger, indigo sadness, orange frustration. She took a moment to compose herself before stepping outside.

She was halfway across the open plaza in front of the Security Service pyramid when she became aware of footsteps behind her, the wide-spaced double clack of someone moving in long bounds. After a couple of seconds Atira Kaval, the Deputy Assistant Director of Offworld and Tourist Security, had caught up with Adya and matched her pace, skin pink with excitement.

"Your interview with Sokwerevu didn't go very well," she said.

Zero-privacy area indeed, Adya thought. Perhaps it was for the best that she hadn't gone into detail about Elso family financial problems. "I have a problem but he doesn't think it's actually a criminal matter. I suppose he's right."

"You've been off Miranda for quite a while," said Kaval. "That might put your problem under Offworld and Tourist Security—my section." She glanced around and leaned closer, her skin now practically crimson. "I'd be honored to help Kavita's family any way I can. I can feel the energy right now."

The Adya Elso who had left Miranda on an extended research trip would have politely declined. The Adya who had dealt with a quintet of professional criminals—and spent considerable time in the company of terrible role models like Pelagia and Daslakh—didn't hesitate. "That would mean a lot to me, and my entire family," she said, willing herself to a warm olive color. "Thank you."

Pelagia's trip to Taishi took two hundred and twenty hours. The actual voyage was quite boring. To save propellant she relied heavily on the launch laser at Miranda and the braking laser at Taishi, which meant she was riding on rails the whole way like a dumb payload, with no opportunity to show off her piloting skills.

She fought off boredom by spending the transit time doing "training"—her private rationalization for immersing herself in shoot-'em-up entertainments for a hundred and eighty hours. Naturally she kept a little window in her sensorium open to keep tabs on her surroundings.

Twenty hours out from Taishi, Pelagia sent out all her maintenance drones to get her hull spruced up inside and out. They cleaned away dust and scrubbed the patches discolored by atmospheric gases, patched up micrometeorite impacts, neutralized her surface charge, and generally got her looking shipshape.

The only damage Pelagia's drones left strictly alone were the blackened starbursts surrounding fresh metal—the scars of laser hits she'd taken while helping repel raiders at Danqui hab, thirty years earlier. Those burn marks and the discreet line of kill silhouettes at her nose were Pelagia's badges of honor—and her professional résumé.

Taishi was a big habitat complex: six twenty-kilometer rotating cylinder habs arranged in a hexagon fifty kilometers across, with a big lumpy zero-gee manufacturing and docking core in the center. All of it was held in place by long tensegrity struts of carbon fiber and diamond, and over the years micro-habs and specialized facilities had grown on the struts like barnacles. This far out from the Sun there wasn't much point to having solar panels, just radiator fins and a micro black hole power plant to run the launch lasers and keep the forty million biologicals who lived in Taishi from freezing.

The whole complex was parked about half an AU sunward of Uranus. There, Uranus's gravity and the Sun's distant pull created a stable spot where the hab could maintain its position by careful management of the solar wind and balancing its launch and recovery of payloads.

As the gateway to the Uranus system, Taishi was uniquely important, much more so than its counterparts at the other planets. The sideways planet and its inner moons were very hard for incoming spacecraft to rendezvous with. Ships unwilling to go screaming through the planet's atmosphere, or engage in a long, complicated series of moon encounters to get lined up on the proper orbit, all had to stop at Taishi, or its dark sister Huihou, on the opposite side of Uranus's sphere of influence.

In addition to handling nearly all the traffic between the Uranian worlds and the rest of civilization, the two gateway habs also served a lot of traffic within Uranus's sphere. The outer swarm of habs orbiting in the plane of the Solar System ecliptic had just as much trouble sending beings and cargo to the moons and habs around Uranus itself as any other body in the Solar System. In energy terms it was easier for a payload from the Ecliptics to reach Taishi or Huihou, then transfer to an orbit dropping down to Miranda or Uranus itself.

When Pelagia reached zero relative velocity near Taishi, she pinged the address for the mercenary company. "I'm Pelagia. We spoke earlier about a military contract. I'm here—where do you want me to dock?"

"Multipurpose Bay 453 North. Clamp on at external hatch 4A."

The Multipurpose Bay was a big pressurized box on the pylon which formed one edge of the hexagon. Pelagia found the correct hatch and locked on. Then she waited. Ten minutes passed with no contact from her employer, which was baffling. She was on the verge of pinging again when something knocked on her forward hatch.

It was a combat bot, or maybe a mech—an armored ball with four limbs, a laser emitter, and a rack for external munitions. At the moment the rack was empty and its surface was safety green.

"Yes?" Pelagia asked.

"This unit is part of Leiting. Is your interior space secure?"

"Yes—which is why I don't let strange bots inside me. Proof, please."

She instantly got an electronic message from her prospective boss, verifying the bot's identity as part of a collective intelligence. Pelagia responded by opening the outer door, but kept the inner airlock hatch clamped shut. Once the outer hatch closed behind the bot, she said, "You can talk to me from here. Why the secrecy?"

Isolated from the rest of its collective, the bot was sub-Baseline, but still intelligent enough to respond interactively. "We have been hired for a highly secret operation. Any hint of what we are doing could compromise the entire mission. Only Leiting will know the objective until the operation actually begins. If this is not acceptable to you, this is your last opportunity to decline the contract and depart."

"Tell me what I can expect to get paid, and then I'll tell you if I'm in or not."

"For a combatant of your size and capability, the offer is five million gigajoule-equivalents."

"For what length of time?"

"The primary mission should take between fifty and one hundred standard days, including transit times. There may be extension contracts after that time frame."

Five million gigs for a hundred days. About half a gig per second. That was a very good rate. Almost too good—the heavy emphasis on secrecy and the relatively short time frame argued against any kind of security or escort mission. This sounded more like a raid or an assault, and hiring mercenaries for that kind of work often meant the client didn't want to risk their own forces in a dangerous operation.

Pelagia didn't mind risk. In her philosophy, a life with no danger meant no scope for excellence. "Okay, count me in. When do we jump off?"

"You must commit to absolute operational security now. No unmonitored communications of any kind from this moment."

"Done." The bot sent her a code key which she used to link into the secure network set up by Leiting in the rented Multipurpose Bay. The first thing through the hard connection was her contract, a semi-autonomous document empowered to do some low-level negotiation and customizing. Pelagia exchanged first refusal on any follow-on jobs for a share in entertainment and merchandising license rights.

Section VI of the contract included the agreement that Pelagia would be under military law from the moment of signing. The relevant code of military justice was the same one she had followed back in her days in the Silver Fleet organization. It allowed for summary execution for certain offenses, including security violations which might, in the opinion of the commander, put the mission or the safety of combatants in jeopardy. Pelagia had only contempt for loudmouths who put themselves or their comrades in danger, so she didn't mind that clause in the slightest.

Only when the legal work was done did Pelagia get to speak to Leiting face to face, so to speak. The collective intelligence appeared in her sensorium using the animated image of the ancient General Leiting—at least, Leiting as he had commonly been depicted in Fifth and Sixth Millennium art: a tall, lean figure in flowing black robes trimmed in red, with long white hair streaming in the wind. Pelagia had seen some of the few surviving video snippets of the real man, and in those he was disappointingly short and bald. She preferred imaginary Leiting.

"All right, I'm all locked in. Now can you tell me when the rock is going to drop?"

"The operation will commence at some point between one and two standard weeks from now. You may use the time until then for arming and preparation, and can borrow against your pay for munitions and relevant expenses. You must be at Condition One in one hundred seventy hours. Other units will be arriving during that interval. Once they have signed on you may communicate freely within this network."

"Who do I take orders from?"

"At present, only Leiting. When the operation begins you will be assigned to your unit commander."

"How big a force are you putting together?" Pelagia asked.

"That information is not available at this time."

"By 'not available' do you mean you don't know, or you don't want to tell me?"

"You have no need to know."

Pelagia controlled the urge to undock and launch the bot out of her airlock into deep space. "You're a collective intelligence. I'm curious: Have you ever managed subordinates who weren't part of your own mind?"

"You have no need to know that, either."

"I'll take that as a 'no.' Look, I've spent six decades as a merc and a freelancer, and I'll share some of my experience with you: if you act like everyone's going to betray you, one of them probably will. Trust breeds trust."

"The client insists on absolute secrecy. Leiting will consider your advice."

"Well, have fun. I'll be here keeping my blowhole shut." She opened the outer airlock door and watched the bot leave. As soon as it was out she slammed the door shut again, and then turned her attention to the secure comm network.

At the moment it had just over a hundred active users, but most of them were mechs. Pelagia sifted through the user info to find the two dozen biologicals. Eight were chimp combat engineers, eleven were dolphin special-forces operators, and five were ships like Pelagia.

In fact, one of those five was a ship *very* like Pelagia—another orca cybership from the same yard, same construction series, named Repun. The two of them had even served together in the Silver Fleet. Pelagia's employment with that unit had ended very abruptly, with a considerable amount of ill will on both sides.

Repun had even been on the receiving end of some high-energy ill will from Pelagia, though evidently none of the damage had been irreparable. Pelagia decided to see if she was the sort to hold a grudge, and opened a private link.

"Pelagia! It's been ages! I never expected to find you on a job like this. Last I heard you were hauling passengers."

"I got bored with that. Nice to hear from you again, too. What has life been sending you?"

"Strong waves. Took me five years of giving all my earnings to the Fleet to pay off the repair bill after *somebody* slagged my primary drive. Since then I've been doing a lot of repo work."

"Sorry about the drive. Call it a lucky shot. You *were* chasing me."

"Most people just send in a letter of resignation. When you start lobbing torpedoes you can hardly complain if people shoot back."

"I don't like being cheated," said Pelagia. "I told all of you the senior staff were skimming off the top before sharing the pay. You should have listened."

"If you're being cheated you go to court."

"Maybe *you* go to court. *I* take what I'm owed, and I did. Not a microjoule more."

"It's amazing you've lasted as long as you have, with that attitude."

"It's all due to my innocent charm and naive enthusiasm. So what do you know about this Leiting? Are they trustworthy? They're acting so suspicious it's making *me* suspicious."

"They say the client wants total secrecy."

"I heard the same, but I don't get it. Unless the job is right here at Taishi, we'll have to transit for a hundred hours to reach any of the worlds around Uranus, and at least that long for most of the ecliptic habs. Whoever we're fighting will know we're coming."

"Maybe Leiting knows how to hide in space."

"If they could do that, they wouldn't be running a half-gig mercenary unit way out here. They'd be conquering Deimos or Luna."

"You know what I mean: misdirection and lies. Fool the target into thinking we're a security force coming to help them, or something like that."

"Or maybe Leiting's an idiot planning to charge us all right into prepared defenses so they don't have to share the pay."

"They're probably monitoring this network, you know. It's in the contract."

"Hey, Leiting! I just want you to know that I think a commander who spies on their troops is a contemptible bottom-feeder." She paused, waiting for any reply. "Oh, well. If they are listening, I guess they're too cowardly to speak up."

"Are you trying to get kicked out of another unit already?" asked Repun.

"Just bored, I guess. I'm pretty much at peak readiness right now, so I don't want to spend a week or two stuck to this docking port with nothing to do."

"Well, good for you. I have some systems that need calibrating, so you'll have to do your bitching on your own." Repun broke the link.

Pelagia muttered a few insults and then decided to explore her surroundings. With a brain that originated in an actual neo-orca calf, however much enhanced, she was far too slow to try any funny stuff with the local data network. Even a very sub-Baseline system would easily notice and block her attempts at intrusion. The only thing which made a cybership competitive with mech units in battle was their absolute immunity to electronic subversion. An EM attack might cripple Pelagia's systems or outright kill her, but no mere transmissions could overwrite her personality or edit her memories.

But she could poke around in the physical world. Her twin laser emitters—which of course doubled as telescopes—could resolve a centimeter-sized object at forty kilometers, so she could get a very detailed look at Multipurpose Bay 453 North and all the various craft docked to its exterior. She spotted Repun, clamped onto a port on the same face of the bay structure, about a hundred meters away. Just to bite her fins a little Pelagia lit her up with radar and a target-designator laser pulse. Repun replied by changing her exterior colors to a pattern of Ningen characters spelling out "EAT SHIT AND DIE."

The other ships joining Leiting's little fleet were docked ninety degrees away, on the "top" face of the bay. The corner blocked Pelagia's view of their forward sections, but their aft ends were all fairly typical high-thrust transports, with no aerodynamics to speak of. Not warships. Nor had Pelagia spotted any dedicated warships on her initial approach, either, which suggested the force was very light on space combatants.

An invasion, then—against a mostly undefended target. That ruled out all the really exciting possibilities in Uranus space. The Synchronous Ring was well armed, Miranda had terawatt-class laser arrays which could vaporize ships as easily as launch them across the Solar System, and the four big moons all boasted deep-dug fortresses and networks of dispersed weapon platforms on the surface and in orbit. By treaty, none of the major worlds of the Uranus system could operate large space warships—but of course an armed and fortified moon was itself a vastly powerful warship immune to attacks no ship could survive.

That left one of the small habs. There were plenty of them. The Equatorials filled a broad belt aligned with Uranus's equator and the orbits of the major moons, in a region extending from a million to ten million kilometers out from Uranus. According to Pelagia's navigation database, there were 5,801,172 "long-term non-maneuvering crewed objects" in that swarm, everything from a few dozen giant cylinders or gravity balloons holding tens of billions of people down to millions of little wheels and cans with just a few hundred inhabitants.

A wider, more dispersed swarm orbited Uranus in the plane of the rest of the Solar System, extending from twenty to fifty million kilometers out. The Ecliptics had nearly as many inhabitants as the Equatorials, and a similar range of sizes. Their easier access to the rest of civilization made them a little richer and somewhat less provincial than the cockeyed Equatorials.

Pelagia was willing to bet that the target hab would be one of the Ecliptics, most likely a nonrotating microgravity structure or bubble world. Population in the million range—big enough to make it worth taking over, but not enough to support a large force of full-time soldiers.

If she still had lungs, Pelagia would have sighed at that. Despite all the intriguing secrecy, it looked as though this job would be pretty simple and boring. Hit some vulnerable habitat, insert the troops, collect her fee and leave. The sort of job a mercenary should love, but Pelagia had been hoping for a challenge, some excitement. Well, at least she'd bank some gigajoules.

The guest quarters at the Mohan-Elso Center turned out to be a boat—a good-sized catamaran moored to a floating pier extending out from the big oval main body of the Center itself.

The guest boat was decidedly shabby compared to the sleek white half-domes and towers of the Center itself. Its twin hulls looked like repurposed spaceship fuel tanks, the decking was a patchwork of different materials in irregular shapes, and the living quarters occupied a two-story structure with sliding screen walls and wide galleries overhanging the water along the sides. The crude materials were offset by a wild paint job in green, blue, red, and glowing purple. Whimsical decorations of whales and stars were everywhere.

Zee, with Daslakh on his head, dropped out of the sky onto the foredeck, which was cluttered with mismatched chairs and pots of big, brightly glowing flowers. A gangly twelve-limbed bot appeared before he finished taking off his wings, and simultaneously the image of a bright red prehistoric whale appeared in his vision. "Good evening! I'm Taraka. This is my boat. How long will you be staying?"

"I'm not really sure," said Zee. "Maybe just a couple of nights, maybe longer. It depends on how long my, uh, research takes."

Daslakh took the opportunity to drop to the deck and link to the local infospace. The boat's data system was simple, functional, and offered no obvious weak points to exploit. All that Daslakh could determine was that Taraka was a digital intelligence, rated at precisely 1.0 Baseline Equivalent Intellect, currently embodied in a maritime passenger vehicle, all other background information private.

"Likely to be a while, then," said the image of the whale. "The Center's closed. Some kind of renovation work. It won't tell me when it's going to reopen."

"Nothing about that in the data nets," said Daslakh aloud. According to the Center's own system it was operating normally.

"I know. Careless of them, isn't it?" Taraka sent them both an enhanced camera image of a hand-lettered sign on the Center's main entrance, fifty meters away at the other end of the dock and beyond an ornamental plaza. CLOSED FOR RENOVATION, WE APOLOGIZE FOR THE INCONVENIENCE.

"If you're closed, I can go somewhere else," said Zee.

"The *Center* is closed. I'm an independent operator. I tie up here because I like to chat with the visiting scholars and my food printer has a better meal library than the ones in the refectory. And since there aren't any scholars at the moment I've got plenty of space available. You can take your pick of the rooms. What do you fancy?"

"I'm sure all your rooms are perfectly nice," said Zee. "Put me wherever you want."

"The Menkar suite is the most comfortable, at least that's what my guests tell me. I'll give you a discount for being the only guest. Forty gigajoule-equivalents a day, or two hundred a week. Printing is one gig per ten grams, and there's no charge if you want to use the kitchen, as long as you clean up after yourself."

The room was small but airy, furnished entirely with smart matter so that guests could customize it to suit themselves. As an experienced traveler, Zee kept his implant loaded with a favorite bed template and some preferred settings for flooring, wall color, light level, temperature, air flow, ambient sound, and scents.

"I'm starting to feel that flight," said Zee as he began to peel off his clothes. "All I want is some sleep. Sorry I'm not better company."

"I can amuse myself," said Daslakh. "Good night."

Zee collapsed into bed and exhaled three times before Daslakh could tell he was asleep. The bed sensed it, too, and began to gently extend filmy strands over Zee's skin to clean him off.

The amount of *stuff* humans constantly exuded from their bodies always faintly horrified Daslakh. They weren't permanent objects, like a nice solid piece of metal or even a lump of smart matter. Humans— all biologicals, really—were ad hoc collections of molecules, furiously staving off entropy by throwing out matter and energy faster than a hostile universe could ablate them out of existence. Even with help from organ printers, biochemical tools, medical implants, nanobots, and advice from superior digital minds, most of them could barely keep up the fight for a couple of centuries before entropy finally triumphed.

Of course, Daslakh could hardly expect much better—especially when some unfortunate episodes in its past meant that a significant number of both biological and digital beings would cheerfully give entropy a helping hand with lasers or heavy objects if they ever found out who Daslakh had been. It had managed twenty or thirty human lifetimes so far, but realistically couldn't expect more than a thousand or so. A slightly longer instant on the cosmic scale.

Shutting down that line of thinking, Daslakh silently left the room and climbed up an ornamental pillar to the top of the deckhouse. The space was cluttered with tables and chairs, sculptures of whales, potted plants, and a bulky metal and ceramic object coated with carbon dust which Daslakh finally identified as a device for controlled incineration of carbon fuel elements. A grill over the combustion chamber indicated that people actually cooked food on it, despite the obvious hazards.

It considered waking Zee up and getting him away from this dangerously reckless Taraka person, but decided that it would be futile. Zee was notoriously tolerant of risk.

So Daslakh made a running leap toward the grounds of the Institute, landing well beyond the edge of the water. It kept itself at zero emissions, and matched its surface to the ground as it moved.

Snooping was standard procedure for Daslakh, and in this case it felt more than idle curiosity. With all the weirdness surrounding the Elso family at the moment, this extra oddity of the research institute they'd endowed being mysteriously closed was something Daslakh couldn't ignore.

The place really was completely shut down. The buildings were at air temperature, and Daslakh couldn't feel any vibration through the tips of its feet as it stood listening. Even the local infospace was down to minimal service, with nothing but a sub-sub-Baseline set of programs active.

Satisfied it was alone, Daslakh proceeded to climb all over the curved white shapes of the Center buildings, peeking into windows and looking for a convenient way in.

Without exception, the windows were all shifted to opaque mode.

External doors were locked tight. The Mohan-Elso Center wasn't just closed, it was buttoned up as if the staff expected a siege.

Daslakh identified thirty-six ways to force an entry, but was reluctant to try any of them. Wandering in through a window carelessly left open was awkward if the owners showed up unexpectedly, but actually breaking into a building meant that people might notice, might investigate.

Eventually it found a way in: a ventilation exhaust atop the egg-shaped central tower, with hinged louvres spaced wide enough for a small spider-mech body to slip between them. That let Daslakh into an open-sided lift shaft which led him down to ground level. According to labels on the doors, the upper levels were all offices, study rooms, and conservation laboratories.

At ground level the tower met a big dome and two half-domes which must have been pretty when their windows were transparent. The big dome was the collection, and Daslakh made a quick inspection to make sure nobody had taken advantage of the Center's closure to steal anything. It all looked intact—at least, every case had something in it, which more or less matched the printed label. It was possible that thieves had robbed the place and left exact duplicates of their loot. With a good scanner and printer one could do that. The trouble with that kind of super-stealthy burglary was that without any publicity about the theft, nobody would believe the stolen items were genuine, even if they were. Only a criminal genius like Varas Lupur could pull something like that off and make a profit.

One of the half-domes was an auditorium. Nothing of interest there. Daslakh scuttled back across the lobby at the bottom of the tower into the final half-dome, and stopped. Success!

The ground floor of this wing of the Center looked as though it was normally a lounge and event space. But all the furniture had retracted into the floor, and the dumb matter items like planters or statues were shoved against the rear wall. Most of the room was filled with stacks and pallets of bulky items, all carefully wrapped up. All the embedded chips bore the same tag: "CONSTRUCTION MATERIALS" and a number.

Daslakh was baffled. Why stockpile things when one could simply move in a couple of matter printers and make building materials as needed? No waste, no shipping (beyond tanks of feedstock), no clutter.

Was this some kind of historical re-enactment project? Showing how things were built before molecular printing technology became commonplace? A demonstration of the methods used to build the pyramids and the Martian arcologies?

Or was this more Miranda status-display extravagance? Slabs of hand-cut stone from Titania and boards of wood from actual trees? It was just absurd enough to be true.

Just then Daslakh felt a deep gentle thump through the floor, as of something massive nudging the floating platform of the Mohan-Elso Center. It leaped to the top of the pile of "construction materials" and concealed itself between two white-coated cylinders.

After a few minutes the big opaque window at the flat side of the wing slid open, and Daslakh saw two figures there, controlling a flat cargo bot loaded with a pallet of black graphene cases. Daslakh recognized both individuals. The mech was the annoying Elso family employee Vasi, and the boringly handsome young man was Adya's brother-in-law Vidhi Zugori. Kavita's husband.

The pallet of cases was also familiar: Daslakh identified it with six-sigma certainty as the same lot of cases it had seen in the service levels under the Elso mansion. Even as the bot moved into the event space turned warehouse, the chips in the cases suddenly switched from reading "PARTY SUPPLIES" to "CONSTRUCTION MATERIALS."

"Is that all of it?" asked Vidhi.

"This is the final consignment. Will all these be safe here for the next three weeks?"

"Perfectly protected," said Vidhi. "I'm the only person in Miranda who can unlock this place. Even the digital intelligences are on leave."

"I remain unconvinced," said Vasi. "The Center's security cannot resist a higher-level mind, and the doors and windows will not withstand ordinary tools. A cunning and persistent intruder would get in."

"Maybe, but who minds? The Center's shut. Staff are on sabbatical, collections closed, events ended. Let's leave." He took a couple of steps toward the entrance.

"Can you reactivate the Center security system and give me access? I want some eyes on all this until the big day," said Vasi.

"I thought we agreed to keep the place dark."

"I said I want eyes on this equipment."

Vidhi hesitated before answering, and then he sounded almost belligerently casual. "Sure. Suit yourself. But wait until we're on the water. I don't wish to be witnessed."

The bot had unloaded itself and rolled back to where Vasi and Vidhi stood. As they turned to go, Daslakh launched itself through the gap just before the window slid shut.

It overshot the entire plaza and landed in the water with a faint plop. For the next couple of minutes Daslakh was far too busy trying to swim to pay attention to anything going on above the surface. Its body was considerably denser than the water, but by making its feet into paddle shapes and moving its legs like mad, it was able to struggle over to the edge of the Center's floating platform and stick on. By the time it hauled itself out of the water, Vidhi and Vasi had untied their boat and motored away with a faint hiss of hydrojets.

Daslakh dried itself very carefully, then made its way back to Taraka's boat. Zee was still sleeping soundly in his cabin, so Daslakh climbed back up to the top deck and spent the rest of the night thinking.

CHAPTER SIX

Adya pushed open the carved cedarwood door of the Lotus Room, a little afraid of what she would see inside. Her great-grandmother Udaramati Elso-Elso had spent her final years in that room, and died there, but that had nothing to do with Adya's nervousness.

The lights came up as soon as she stepped inside, and Adya relaxed. Not much had changed. Great-Gran's bronze bedstead with its green patina and smart-matter sleeping surface was just as it had been. Her framed portrait, done in five brush strokes by one of her friends from the Oort, was still on the wall by the door to the gallery outside—just above another framed work, a finger painting of a flying dolphin, done by her long-gone son Diran. Her desk was still cluttered with curios from a dozen moons and habs, including an inlaid nameplate of polished mahogany bearing the title FOREIGN MINISTER which had once sat in front of her place at Coordinating Committee meetings.

The main difference from the old days was the absence of plants. Great-Gran had kept dozens in here, watering and pruning them herself and shooing away the household bots. If not for the lack of greenery, Adya half expected to hear her great-grandmother call from outside, where she liked to sit drinking cashew brandy long into the night. Adya and Kavita had spent hours out there with her, in darkness lit only by the luminous flowers, listening to her stories.

"Pay attention to my aimless prattle," she had told them once. "Some day soon I will go away for good, and what you remember will be all that remains of me."

She kept the girls enchanted with tales of her own travels, ancient gossip about long-gone leaders in the Committee, the sordid details of business deals or political stratagems, and again and again came back to their grandfather Diran. "I still can't comprehend why he went," she would say. "Here he had friends and family, power and pleasure. Why leave all who loved him? To submerge all self!" That usually led to tears, and the girls would put her to bed and wait until she slept before slipping out.

"What are you doing in here, dear?" her mother asked from the doorway.

"Just remembering. I miss Great-Gran."

"Many miss her. Your father refuses to empty this room, and Kavita used to spend hours here while you were away."

"Maybe we should donate the place to the Philosophical Institute. The house is nearly a museum already."

Her mother didn't chuckle at that, but rather nodded. "A sensible suggestion. I will pass it along to your father."

"I didn't—"

"I know, but it may come to that. By the way, you are invited to a little tea party with the Nikunnus. An informal affair at their new krill farm. Just a few dozen, mostly Families."

Adya knew what that meant. Her mother was trying to maneuver her into a betrothal, with witnesses. "Mother, I haven't got the time right now to spend an afternoon making small talk with a lot of people I barely remember."

"Nothing you can do is more important."

Adya kept herself light green with an effort. "Finding out who is behind these financial problems seems more important to me."

"There will be *steamed bagung buns*," said Adya's mother. "I know how much you love those."

"I'm not six anymore, Mother. I can't be tempted by treats, however tasty."

She had the slight satisfaction of seeing her mother turn brownish red for an instant before reverting to olive green. "Adya, you simply can't do this. You must go. You *must*."

At that moment a little icon appeared in Adya's vision, indicating a message. The originator was Atira Kaval, Adya's self-appointed inside source in the Security Service.

"Just a minute. I'm getting a—"

"No! You do not talk to someone else and ignore me when I am standing right here in front of you!"

"*Mother!*"

"I shall inform Dipa Nikunnu that you will be joining us. Be ready at three tomorrow." Her mother turned and went out.

Adya let herself turn red, but sat down on the bed and accepted the link. "Good afternoon, Assistant Director Kaval."

"No need to be so formal. You can call me Atira."

"As you wish. What can I do for you—Atira?"

"I need nothing but your attention. I managed to do some discreet digging and made a fortunate find."

"You didn't break the law, did you?"

"Oh, no. At least, not the letter of the law. I searched through the anonymous messages about your family's seafood products. Some of them included images." Atira sent Adya a set of pictures—fish filets blotched with purple mold, whole fish with parasitic worms erupting from their bellies, and a package of cured fish which included several dead flies.

"Those are fakes! We irradiate everything."

"The one with the worms is almost certainly a generated image. But your slanderer was clever. Those others are real. They just added some ink spots or a printed insect."

Adya's mind was racing. "You found some clues in the images?"

"Not exactly. But the one with the mold had its metadata improperly scrubbed. The location tag survived."

"Where was it taken?"

"Viranmar Plaza."

Adya knew the place, a grand public space in the center of the city of Svarnam, fifty kilometers from the capital. "That tells us nearly nothing."

Atira's voice dropped to a conspiratorial murmur, just dripping with self-satisfaction. "Normally, yes. But as it happens, there was a case of involuntary genetic sampling in the plaza just a couple of days before that image went public. When the Service collects evidence we like to have plenty of context, so we saved all the images and public data from the plaza for a period of a hundred hours before and after the alleged sampling incident. And I think I've identified the person taking that faked image."

Another set of pictures appeared. They were stills, from different angles, showing a woman with very long braided hair, sitting alone on one of the benches scattered about the plaza. The area was mostly empty, which suggested it was early morning. The woman was holding an archaic-looking data device over a pale object on the bench. An enhanced image showed that the object was indeed the ink-spotted fish filet. The last two images showed her face from two sides.

"Pulu Visap. She's a professional influencer specializing in gray and black memes."

"Which suggests someone hired her to do this—our real enemy."

"I could probably come up with a reason to contact Visap officially," said Atira, almost indecently enthusiastic.

"No, no. You've done wonderful work already. I don't want to take any more of your time."

"It's no trouble. I'm very happy to do a favor for Kavita's family."

In other circumstances that last remark might have annoyed Adya just a little, but this time she barely paid attention to what Atira was saying. "I will speak to her myself," she said. "From what Officer Sokwerevu said, it would be hard to threaten her with any legal action, and if she's a professional, she probably knows exactly where the limits lie. I must influence the influencer by other means."

"What are you going to do?"

"I shall appeal to her better nature. And if that doesn't work, I will threaten her with my sister. Thank you, Deputy Assistant Director Kaval."

"Give my regards to Kavita! I can feel the energy!"

Adya broke the link before sighing. For a second she thought about going downstairs for another round with her mother, but she suspected the result would be the same. So she took a deep breath, went out to her great-grandmother's favorite chair on the gallery outside, and began searching the datasphere.

Pulu Visap was forty-two standard years old, from a family which had slipped gradually down the social scale to lodge in the precarious semi-gentility of intellectual poverty. A cursory look at available data showed a clever woman who hobnobbed with younger members of the Sixty Families, consulted for the Foreign Ministry, and could boast of successfully swaying public opinion for a long list of products, people, and causes. One of those causes immediately caught Adya's attention: Visap had worked for the Polyarchist movement. Was it just business, or was she a supporter?

But when Adya turned her expensive brain and a skeptical eye on Visap's public persona, she spotted the gaps and weaknesses. Pulu Visap wasn't actually a friend of the wealthy and powerful—she just managed to be in their vicinity from time to time. Her "secret work for the government" was impossible to verify officially. And she provided absolutely no data linking any of her work to the success or failure of her clients. Even her Polyarchist connection was a bit vague—she had "increased awareness" of their cause.

Adya took a deep breath and sent a comm request to Pulu Visap. It was not accepted. However, while she was still trying to decide what to try next, Adya got a message: "Pulu Visap is no longer available for influencing services, and will not comment on any past jobs. Thank you." The source was Visap's own address, and even as Adya watched, the display of quasi-bogus qualifications and successes vanished from the datasphere. Pulu Visap, professional influencer, had just erased herself.

Adya crafted a couple of autonomous messages and sent them out in search of some other way to reach her. They were as reassuring as Adya could make them, but she had a suspicion they wouldn't get a response. If Pulu Visap had crafted slanderous images designed to harm the Elso family, it was really quite unlikely she'd want to chat with Adya Elso.

She wished that Zee was there, or even Daslakh. Maybe Visap would be willing to talk with someone unconnected to the family. That thought made Adya suddenly wish Zee was there for a dozen other reasons. Just his silent presence made her more secure. She wondered what he was doing.

"What are you doing?" Daslakh asked Zee, who to all appearances was stretched out on a lounge chair on the top deck of Taraka's superstructure. Overhead the sky lighting was reaching maximum brightness. Daslakh could sense the data flow coming from Zee's implant, but was reluctant to just intercept and read it. Zee probably wouldn't care, but Taraka might be watching.

"I'm trying to get in touch with Mr. Putiyat again. He's the only link we've got to that exotic-matter payload."

"If it's real."

"Well, yes. But I figure if somebody went to the trouble to send me a death threat about it, it's worth digging into."

"A reasonable conclusion. Any luck?"

"I can get past his house filters—not sure how—but he either refuses the link himself or cuts off as soon as I try to say anything. The last time he told me he'd bring in the Security Service if I contact him again."

"No more ambiguous threats?"

"Not since we left Adya's house."

"I wonder if that's a good sign or a bad one," said Daslakh.

"I wish I knew. If Mr. Putiyat would just talk to me, we could settle this in a couple of minutes!"

"How do your arms feel? Up for another flight?"

Zee stretched and prodded his own chest experimentally. "Sure. Where are we going?"

"Twenty kilometers west by northwest." For nearly twenty seconds Daslakh patiently endured the glacier-slow process of a biological looking up information.

"Is that really a good idea?" said Zee at last.

"All my ideas are good," said Daslakh. "Sometimes there are failures in execution."

Zee smiled at that. "All right, then! Taraka? How much do I owe you?"

The reply was private, and once again Daslakh resisted the urge to eavesdrop. Zee looked surprised. "But when I checked in you said—" he said aloud.

"I decided on a promotional discount," the boat replied, as her crimson whale avatar appeared once again in their vision. "Tell your friends."

"Uh, thank you very much!" said Zee. "Are you ready, Daslakh?"

"Any time."

While Zee turned to go put on his wings Daslakh communicated digitally with Taraka. *"How much of a discount did you give him? I'm curious."*

"You are indeed curious. I gave him half off, if you must know. The room would have been vacant otherwise, and he didn't make a mess."

"How much do you know about him? You've had plenty of time to search the infosphere."

One of the crimson whale's eyes flashed blue-white. *"I like to know as much about my guests as possible. It helps me anticipate their needs. In his case, there's an obvious connection to the Elso family, and to a spaceship called Pelagia. And when I looked at archives of news from the rest of the system, there's some interesting stories from the Uranosynchronous Ring, and Summanus, and Mars."*

"Don't believe everything you hear."

Zee finished his first step toward the wings.

"That swims very close to being a paradox." The whale image grinned. *"And now I have a question for you: What were you doing poking around the Mohan-Elso Center?"*

"Poking around the Mohan-Elso Center, mostly. As I said, I'm curious."

"Which means you presumably saw Vidhi Zugori and some mech dropping off another barge load of construction supplies."

"When does the work start, anyway? There's a lot of stuff stockpiled in there."

"I haven't heard anything. Nobody has asked me to move," said Taraka.

"Nobody will. I predict there won't be any renovations over there. In three and a half weeks that stuff will be gone and the place will reopen."

"This has something to do with the Constructors' Jubilee? Ah, I see: Zugori's wife is organizing it this year. Yes, that makes sense. Using a research facility to store party supplies is a little odd, but here in Miranda it's an acknowledged rule that anything one of the Sixty Families can get away with is by definition correct behavior."

For a supposedly Baseline intellect, Taraka was pretty quick on the uptake, Daslakh decided. Neither said anything more as Zee donned his wings and went to the edge of the deck.

"Well, 'bye," said Daslakh as it scuttled over to take its place between Zee's shoulders.

As Zee leaped into the air and swooped low over the water before flapping to gain altitude, Taraka sent a final message to Daslakh. *"Watch your back!"*

Zee sensibly relied on the local infosphere for navigation. He had grown up in a spinning hab, where the sky was a map and one could always orient oneself with a nod of the head to feel the direction of spin. In a world with natural gravity, no magnetic field, and a thirty-three-hour rotation, none of that worked. Over the sea, with diffuse light coming from the entire artificial sky and a light haze over the water, navigating by eye could lead even a digital intelligence astray.

Daslakh's only task was to occasionally check their position to make sure Zee wasn't getting distracted, and watching the ocean for anything to break the monotony. It saw a couple of whales—one of them transmitted a brief greeting before diving—and once they passed by a sea farm floating in a pool of light. The surface structure was a lot less fancy than the Elso mansion, just a landing pad for flyers and a few storage bins for dry material. Daslakh could just make out half a dozen dolphins wearing gills and tool harnesses swimming about, and guessed the main house was below the waterline.

With Zee keeping up a steady wing beat it took about twenty minutes to cover as many kilometers. Miranda atmosphere had neither head- nor tailwinds to worry about. At Daslakh's suggestion Zee set his implant to full privacy and made a wide circle around the Putiyat estate at half a kilometer altitude to get a good look at the place.

The house was even bigger than the Elso mansion, covering just about all the floating platform surface, with only a central courtyard and a few rooftops for gardens. Unlike the Elso place it appeared to have been built as a single structure, with a rather relentless hexagonal symmetry. A dozen towers rose from it, each topped with a pointy octahedron holding a bright beacon. Daslakh never did have a solid grasp of human semiotics, but the place did seem a lot more flamboyant than the other houses of Miranda's ruling class. Confident exuberance or desperate attention seeking?

"Daslakh, I'm going to need your help," said Zee over his shoulder.

"That is a true statement," said Daslakh.

"Can you talk to the Putiyat house system and keep it from flagging me as an intruder?"

"That's a tall order. Let me see if I can manage it." Daslakh generated a random number between 10 and 40, got 29, and waited that many seconds before telling Zee, "Okay, I think I've got it. Take us in."

In reality, of course, the fragment of Daslakh's personality it had installed in the Putiyat system days earlier kept putting Zee back on the list of permitted callers and visitors every time anyone removed him, so as he glided toward the house it recognized him and let him pass unchallenged.

Zee set down on a rooftop garden, stowed his wings under a bench, and then took a deep breath as if he was about to enter a stick-fighting bout. He exhaled, shook his arms to relax them, and then strolled confidently into the stairway leading down into the house. Daslakh followed silently, matching its color to the floor.

"Who's at home right now?" asked Zee.

"Four family members and two staff in the house, six staff underwater. The house staff are both mechs, the water crew are four dolphins and two squid." Daslakh sent Zee a list of the family members with pictures and locations. "We've got Karthika Kaminari-Putiyat, currently in her private office. She's married to Panam Putiyat. Then we've got Mahesh Putiyat, Panam's younger brother, in the sauna. Mahesh's daughter Neha Putiyat is currently in the dojo, and her brother Vinay Putiyat is in his bedroom. Do you want to find one of them, or avoid them?"

"How do I get to the dojo?"

Daslakh took the lead, and Zee followed it down two levels and through a couple of big rooms decorated with portraits of other people's ancestors to a space set up for training. An athletic-looking young woman in a black unitard and gloves was going through a defensive routine, dodging and parrying as three little air-jet drones tried to tag her. Her skin was deep blue-green with concentration, and Daslakh could see that her breathing and heart rate were calm and steady, a state of perfect absorption in her task.

Neha ducked one drone, batted another aside with a gloved hand, and then did an impressive aerial roll to avoid the third trying to hit her leg. As she landed she glimpsed Zee out of the corner of her eye and turned to look. All three drones struck her then, and from the way she twitched Daslakh guessed they were fitted with shock generators—presumably just enough to sting, since she didn't fall unconscious or go into spasms.

"Drones stop!" she said aloud, her skin shifting to angry orange.

"I'm sorry," said Zee. "I didn't mean to distract you."

"No," said Neha, still orange. "I let myself focus too much on the drones. In a real fight I can't ignore my surroundings. Who are you?"

"My name's Zee. I'm a friend of Adya Elso. She told me you might be interested in trying some *nulesgrima* sparring, and since I was passing by I decided to stop in." Zee's heart rate had been steady, but when he had to lie the beats sped up. Daslakh found it charming.

"Adya? Oh, Kavita's sister. Isn't she off doing some crazy research project on Mars or someplace?"

"We landed a week and a half ago."

"So what do you know about *nulesgrima*?" She looked at him appraisingly. "All the best *nuledors* are small. Wiry. You look too big."

"Get a couple of palos and see for yourself." Zee's nervousness had faded, but now it was Neha whose heart rate was speeding up, and her angry orange color took on a distinctly pink shade before she could return to light blue.

She found a couple of palos in a cabinet. They weren't the light padded ones for sparring, or even the tough graphene rods used in competition. These were actual fighting sticks: graphene tubes with a core of steel, hard and massive enough to break bones.

Zee hefted the one she handed him and raised his eyebrows, but said nothing. The two of them took up positions on opposite sides of the room, saluted, and then launched themselves at each other.

Neha managed an expert tumble to put her feet forward, with the palo held parallel to her direction of motion. As Zee came within range she tried a powerful thrust with her whole body's strength behind it. He managed to parry, the clash of sticks pushing both of them in opposite directions. Neha hit the base of one wall with her feet and kicked hard to shoot herself up toward the center of the room's volume.

Zee had acquired a spin from his parry, so he touched the floor with his feet, steadied himself, and then jumped straight up to ricochet off the ceiling, diving very fast at Neha with his stick held horizontally. She twisted out of the way and turned that rotation into a swing of her palo at Zee as he passed. It caught him on his left calf with a meaty sound of impact.

They hit the floor at the same instant, Neha on her feet and Zee with his palo. He cartwheeled away from her as she did a reverse jab under her left arm. When Zee got his feet on the floor he halted his motion, and that gave Neha the opportunity to come at him fast, stabbing the end of her palo right into his face. He tried to duck aside but it caught him just to the right of his nose. Zee did manage to roll back with the blow, doing a complete somersault in the air and hitting the wall with his back.

Until that point, Zee had been relaxed, heart rate consistent with the exercise, breathing steady. But after Neha hit him in the face, Daslakh could see his skin temperature rise, and heard his pulse and breathing accelerate. His face got an expression Daslakh had seen only three times before in all the time he'd known Zee.

The tempo of the bout suddenly got a lot faster. Zee managed a backward somersault up the wall, getting clear of Neha and then launching himself across the room over her head. He dug one end of the palo into the ceiling to stop himself in mid-leap and push himself to the floor. Neha had been in ballistic motion across the room in pursuit, so this unexpected stop put Zee behind her with his palo perfectly positioned for a swing that caught her across the back of her thighs.

In a friendly sparring match Zee probably would have paused there, let Neha get her feet on the floor and start another round. Instead he pressed his attack, getting a solid jab into her rib cage, and when she touched a foot to the floor in order to spin and get her palo in position to defend, Zee knocked her stick aside and got her under the arm with the other end of his weapon. He kept her off balance, pushing her back, taking advantage of his mass and strength, hitting her hard—though Daslakh noticed he was still restraining himself; she would have impressive bruises but no broken bones.

Neha gamely tried to break loose, and landed a few one-handed blows on Zee's upper back with the end of her palo. Her own pulse rate had skyrocketed and she was pink with excitement all over. When she backed up against the wall and couldn't get away, she finally knocked three times to signal the end. Zee hesitated for a moment before backing off, and kept his palo in a defensive stance until Neha put hers down.

"Good match," he said. Daslakh could see that he was speaking out of one side of his mouth, and his face was already quite swollen where she'd hit him.

"You're good, too," she said. "How'd you do that stop and drop?" Zee explained, and as he did Neha moved closer to him. "I hope I didn't hit you too hard," she interrupted, and prodded his swelling cheek with one forefinger.

Zee couldn't keep himself from wincing, but he gave her a lopsided smile. "Should have kept my guard up."

Neha pulled her unitard down and stepped out of it, then kicked the damp garment into the corner. "I'm all sweaty. Let's clean up." Without looking behind her she led the way out of the dojo and a short way up the hall to a room lined with a smooth continuous surface of blue glass, broken only by drains at the edge of the floor and water jets in the walls.

Zee put down the palo and followed. As he passed Daslakh in the doorway of the dojo he took a couple of jagged white objects out of his mouth and handed them to the mech. "Get rid of those for me," he said. "I swallowed the smaller bits."

Daslakh identified the little misshapen pieces as half of a canine tooth and most of a bicuspid. "Can't you just glue them back where they belong?"

"I'll get new ones. Don't let her see them." Zee walked calmly toward the shower, and only Daslakh could hear his rapid pulse.

Zee stuck his sweaty head under the cold stream, rinsed out his mouth, and then left the shower while Neha was still enjoying the hot water jets playing over her skin. When she turned and saw him already drying his hair, she didn't even try to hide the annoyance and disappointment in her voice, let alone keep herself from turning a muddy crimson. "Well?"

"Good match," he said again. "I'd be happy to stop by for another session."

"Don't go yet," she said. "I'm not done with you."

Zee faced her then. "I'll stay a bit longer—but only if you can do something for me."

"I can do all kinds of things," she said, blatantly shifting to coral pink.

"Introduce me to your uncle. I want to talk to him about business."

Her eyes narrowed and her color became more purple. "Who are you, really?"

"I told you: a friend of Adya Elso. Your uncle bought some property from her family and I'd like to find out what happened to it."

"So talk to Panam."

"He doesn't want to see me. But I figure he can't ignore me if I'm right in front of him."

"Adya never paid attention to anything but ancient history. And I can't believe either of the elder Elsos would even talk to you about their business affairs, let alone allow you to act for them. This sounds like some kind of con."

"Believe what you want. I just want to talk to him."

"Come massage my muscles and then we'll join Uncle Panam for lunch when he lands. I want to see your pitch. He's no fool, you know, at least not about money matters. He'll see through you and see you off, and I'll laugh to see it happen."

Zee took firm hold of Neha's latissimus dorsi muscles, and made circles with his thumbs pressed deep into the skin on either side of her spine. She made a noise halfway between a gasp and a grunt, repeated as he moved his hands upward until he was kneading her trapezius muscles between neck and shoulders.

"You're better than my bot."

"I'm sure it gets more practice."

"Hey," said Daslakh aloud. "The house says Panam's just landing upstairs. You'd better get yourselves dried off. Wouldn't want to drip all through lunch."

Neha and Zee joined her uncle in the dining room, which was a huge space with very expensive decorations. The walls were covered with sheets of bismuth metal, inlaid with curlicues of tantalum and rhenium. Nothing as plebian as gold or iridium. The table was all smart matter, with individual food printers at each place. Neha wore a clean unitard and Zee was back in his much-worn travel suit.

Panam Putiyat had already taken his place at the head of the table and was watching his chana bhatura rising from the black panel in front of him as the tabletop assembled the food molecule by molecule. He happened to glance up, smiled at his niece, then caught sight of Zee and scowled.

"You! I said I don't want to talk to you. How did you get in here?"

Neha smiled a little maliciously. "He's been sparring with me in the dojo. He's not bad, but I landed a good one on his face."

Zee's cheek was notably puffy and purple by now, but he was determinedly not showing any pain. "I got careless. Mr. Putiyat, I just have one question—"

"I know, I know. That pesky particle payload. My purchase was perfectly proper."

"Of course. I'm not trying to accuse you of anything. I just want to know if you'd consider selling it back. It's got sentimental value."

Panam just glared at Zee. "Sentimental? Do I seem a simpleton?"

"I can pay back everything you gave for it. The family can, anyway."

"Can they? I've heard rumors."

"Well, if you name a price I can find out if they'll pay it."

"I must disappoint you. I no longer retain any rights to that payload."

"Who does?"

Panam smiled, but his eyes didn't change and his skin was still pale purple. "I take it you enjoy combat sports, Mr. Sadaran."

"I was *nulesgrima* champion of Raba habitat three standard years running."

Panam took a bite of one bhatura bun and made himself light blue. "I only enjoy games when there is something at risk. The idea of playing something purely for pleasure bores me."

Zee smiled with the unbruised side of his mouth. "Plenty of risk in *nulesgrima* if you're not wearing armor."

Panam waved his hand as if batting the idea aside. "Unless there's a chance of real death, injury is inconsequential."

Zee said nothing.

Panam took a spoonful of chickpeas and continued. "It occurs to me that we could settle this with a game. My stake is the answer to your question. It has value to you, and I have good reasons for not wishing to give it out. But what do you have to hazard?"

"I don't have much," said Zee. "I don't care about piling up gigajoules, and I've always been able to earn what I need. I haven't got much stuff. Nothing I can't print out if I want it."

"What are you afraid to lose? Would you risk your life to find out who controls that payload?"

"No," said Zee promptly. "Sorry," he added. "I guess I have to disappoint you this time."

"Oh, not at all. A wise gambler should always know what he is willing to lose."

"How about this?" said Neha, with an odd gleam in her eye. "If you win the game, Uncle tells you what you want to know. If you lose, you're mine until I get tired of you."

Panam laughed aloud at that. "It appears you have one asset after all!" He glanced at his niece and back to Zee. "I'm guessing this puts you at risk of more than exhaustion and a few bite marks."

"He says he's a friend of Adya Elso. I think it's more than that."

"Turned you down, did he? Now I understand. Well?" He looked back at Zee, still smiling, but his eyes were very cold. "Would Miss Elso forgive a few weeks' dalliance, do you think?"

Zee lifted his chin a couple of millimeters and stared straight back at Panam. "She probably would forgive me. But I wouldn't forgive myself." He stood and looked Neha. "That was a good match. One thing you should work on: the palo's a tool for movement as well as a weapon. You can do more than just hit people. Practice that." He turned to leave.

"Just a moment," said Panam. He took a small metal disk from the cabinet behind him. "Call it—Archer or Twins?" He flipped it into the air, and in the low Miranda gravity it spun above his head for nearly a minute.

"Archer," said Zee as it hung for a moment just below the ceiling before falling back.

Panam caught it in his outstretched hand and placed it on the back of his other wrist, keeping it covered for a dramatic three seconds before revealing the symbol of Sagittarius. "You are a lucky man! A good thing, too. I transferred the rights to that payload to an individual named Dai Chichi, to settle some debts. If you have dealings with him, you will need to be lucky indeed. Now: Get out of my house. I never want to see you again."

Neha watched Zee go, but didn't get up from her chair.

As Zee pulled on his wings in the roof garden, Daslakh took up its customary position between his shoulders. "What now? Go talk to this Dai Chichi person?"

"First I need to get a couple of new teeth, and I think maybe some bone cement for my face. And—I'd appreciate it if you don't tell Adya about any of this."

"Unless my memory's corrupted, you turned Neha down two or three times. Nothing to conceal."

"Oh, not that," said Zee. "I mean about the teeth. She'd worry." He leaped into the air, gave a few powerful strokes with his wings, then banked to the southwest, where a town with public medical pods was just a few kilometers off.

Daslakh decided not to mention that the spin rate of a falling metal disk could be affected by low-power infrared laser heating. It would only upset Zee.

CHAPTER SEVEN

Adya's mother began getting her ready for the simple informal tea party at the Nikunnu krill farm seven hours in advance.

The first order of business, as soon as Adya woke up, was to select the perfect outfit. Mutalali had already applied semiotic software and color analysis to narrow the options to a dozen possibilities, but she insisted on actually seeing Adya wear them before deciding which would strike just the right note.

So Adya tried to snatch mouthfuls of green-pea cheela for breakfast between trying things on while the printer hummed away, and rather grimly twirled and posed in the clothes her mother handed her.

"If you merely want to show off how attractive I am, I could just wear some slippers and a tiara."

"Are you Kavita, playing a prank? Because Adya would know perfectly well that clothing is communication. We want you to show off your social position, your education and intellect, and what an asset you would be to an alliance. You can always change your body if you need to."

"I feel like a Qarina."

"I'm not even going to ask what that means. How about this one?" Mutalali handed Adya a newly printed outfit—a pair of loose trousers which gathered in at the ankles, paired with a long-sleeved, high-necked, but backless dark top.

"Your posture has always been good," said her mother approvingly as Adya gave a spinning jump to rotate in midair.

"It feels a little old-fashioned," said Adya. "Wasn't this the kind of thing people were wearing at your wedding?"

"Respect for tradition is another quality we want to emphasize."

"What are they wearing in Juren nowadays?"

"That is infinitely irrelevant. This is Miranda, and the Sixty Families lead fashion rather than follow it. I'm not sure about that color, though. Try the next one."

The next was a simple stretchy tube extending from armpits to knees, in a green that was almost black with an iridescent sheen, with matching detached sleeves. Adya actually liked it, but tried to sound unconcerned. "I can tolerate this one."

"Hm. Not very cheerful..."

"Serious. Restrained. Purposeful," Adya suggested. Inside, she wondered what Zee would think of it. Elegant? Or intimidating?

"I see the sense of it," said her mother. "And I see that you like it, which helps. Now peel it off and get yourself bathed and perfumed. We want the scents to have time to fade."

When Adya was clean and wrapped in a furry towel, Mutalali helped her daughter select jewelry from her own collection. Just before Adya got dressed for action, her mother advised her on implant settings. "Make sure you regulate your neurotransmitters and hormones. Confidence, serenity—"

"And unthinking obedience."

"Don't be tiresome. We want to make a good first impression."

"Hardly a first impression—I've known Entum Nikunnu since we were children."

"They've changed quite a bit."

"I hope so. When we were taking classes together I thought Entum was too boring. I wasn't that fond of self-defense myself, but at least I tried. They just seemed to take naps all the time."

Her mother chuckled very softly but then got a freshly printed copy of Adya's outfit for her to put on.

Their departure was timed to the second. "The exact moment is important," said Mutalali. "Exactly on time looks desperate. Too late and we would seem careless—or worse, trying to make an entrance. Ten minutes after the start time shows a nice insouciance without being disrespectful."

"I like being on time," said Adya. "It's simpler. What if everyone else is thinking the same things you are? Then we'll all be ten minutes late and poor Dipa Nikunnu will be sitting there wondering if anybody is going to show up at all."

"I've already considered that. There is an art to arriving at any affair—it's yet another kind of communication. If you always show up exactly on time people will think you literal-minded and pedantic."

"Everybody already thinks that about me," said Adya. "Maybe I should just send Kavita instead. She's good at parties."

"I specifically asked her to send her regrets. The last thing we want is for her to monopolize all the attention while you drift away and start looking at old artifacts or something."

"Mother, I'm only going to this tea party because I don't want to fight about it. I'll eat some steamed buns and smile and nod and maybe try to correct some popular misconceptions about the War of the Ring or the Godel Trigger legend. That's all."

"Have you heard from your friend Zee recently? As I recall he left somewhat abruptly. He might be on a cycler back to whatever hab he came from already."

"I know for a fact he's still in Miranda," said Adya. She suspected Daslakh might be helping Zee maintain privacy in the infosphere, but she had blanketed the spaceport with software agents, sniffing for any traces of his passage. They hadn't detected Zee—or any suspiciously Zee-shaped areas of privacy, either.

It wouldn't be like him, either. If Zee had actually decided to break up with her, he would come and tell her so, face to face. This current absence was just a time out. That was what her rational adult mind kept telling the anxious girl inside her head.

"All right, it's time," said Mutalali. They boarded a bubble and rode through the tubes to the Nikunnu manor, two hundred kilometers away.

The party was held under water, in a diamond sphere attached to the central spine of the Nikunnu krill farm. Guests arriving by bubble could walk in dry, while dolphins, cephalopods, or humans who lived nearby could enter through a membrane at the bottom of the sphere.

Platforms scattered throughout the volume of the sphere offered places to sit in little groups, and serving bots hummed through the air with cups of tea or broth and platters of snacks. A corvid musician played a jhallari to smooth over any gaps in conversation.

Adya followed her mother into the sphere and looked around at the guests already there. Mutalali made a faint satisfied sound, so Adya figured they must have arrived at what she judged the proper moment.

Looking at the others present, Adya suspected her mother had "helped" Dipa Nikunnu draw up the guest list. Most were Elso family connections—including Adya's sister Sundari and one of her husbands—and Adya noted with some dismay that she was literally the only unmarried person present.

Just to avoid the blatant stock-show aspect of the whole event, Dipa had invited one person of importance who was unconnected to either Elsos or Nikunnus, and who was neither in the marriage market nor had offspring who were. Yudif Al-Harba was the Marshal of Miranda's armed forces. The job was one of the few important posts that the Sixty Families deliberately gave to an outsider. Yudif had spent ten standard years in the army of Luna, another couple of decades as a warrior-monk tending the Exawatt laser inside Pluto, and had been serving as Logistics Director in the big Talos hab complex between Earth and Mars when it was hired to command Miranda's military.

"Of course I remember you," it said when Adya stopped to pay her respects. Yudif's body was entirely smart matter, shaped for the occasion into a tall, broad-shouldered form, wearing a dress uniform in Uranus blue-green with a deep red sash. The clear diamond sphere holding its brain was perched on top, with colored lights to make the support fluid glow in the proper emotion display colors. "Your sister speaks of you often."

"You're a fan of Kavita's?"

"Not her stream, if that's what you mean. Not enough time for that. No, we do topiary together."

"Topiary? With real plants?"

"Affirmative. Her husband's uncle introduced us and I was surprised to learn she and I share an interest in all forms of plant art— bonsai, espalierage, ikebana, topiary, even fruit shaping."

Adya was a little surprised to learn that as well, since Kavita had never shown the slightest interest in plants at all, but she did the proper thing and said, "That's fascinating. Where is your garden?"

"Defense headquarters! One privilege of rank: I can start clipping and rearranging the plants in the roof garden and nobody can tell me to stop." It sent her some images. "As you can see, I try to evoke a mood through the shapes of the branches and the colors of the leaves. Pride, enthusiasm, and duty." The liquid in its brain sphere shone pinkish-mauve with excitement.

Adya closed her eyes to see the images better. She could see a little of what Yudif meant—the shrubs grew tall, spreading their leaves like bursting fireworks, all in neat rows like soldiers on parade. "Do you use semiotic models to come up with the forms?"

"That's for dabblers," said Yudif. "I started out that way, back in Talos. Now I trust my instincts and try to find the shapes that *feel* right."

While Yudif spoke Adya did a quick search and found that, yes, Kavita actually had done many hours about plant art. Most of it consisted of her touring other people's gardens, but there were a few episodes of her working on what Adya recognized as the rooftop of the Elso manor.

"Do you modify the genes, as well?"

"I know my limits. I leave that to—"

"I beg your pardon, Marshal," said Adya's mother, taking her daughter firmly by the arm. "I have to borrow Adya for a few minutes."

"Of course, of course. I know all about the social round," said Yudif, but Adya could see the fluid in the brain sphere turn a little bluer with regret.

"What is it, Mother?" Adya murmured as they moved away.

"Entum's here."

Entum Nikunnu was the last to enter the sphere, bursting in with a big smile and blown kisses all around, in a way that Adya found very reminiscent of her sister Kavita. Also like Kavita, Entum had dressed to draw attention. If Mutalali wanted to emphasize Adya's social position and intellectual qualities, Entum's outfit was all about their body: a mass of colored ribbons sliding through the air around Entum's torso, hovering a couple of centimeters from the skin and alternately concealing and revealing everything.

In blade training a decade before, Entum had been a skinny,

apathetic neuter. Even the changing colors of their skin had seemed washed-out and weak. All the Nikunnu children were born neuters to maximize their marriageability. But apparently the moment Entum reached the age of body autonomy they'd gone all-in on sexuality. Now they were a tall, muscular, buxom hermaphrodite with a winning smile and rosy skin.

"Adya!" they called from across the room, and covered the distance in a single jump. "It's been too long—you've changed so much!"

"Just a little taller," said Adya, still a bit overwhelmed.

"Nonsense. You've become a beauty!" Entum looked over at Mutalali. "Though at first I wasn't sure which of you was which. You were wise to have clones."

"Actually, there are some genetic differences," Adya began, before her mother gently pressed her foot down on Adya's toes. "Thank you, though."

"The last time I saw you was at Himana Dumakethu's betrothal party," Entum continued. "I was just twelve."

"I would have been thirteen. All I remember about that party was the decorations—the dome of the ballroom was zero-albedo black with a real-time image of the sky from the surface overlaid on it. For just a moment I thought I was actually seeing through the ice."

Entum laughed. "The fanciest party that year and you spent the whole time staring at the ceiling! I remember the dancing. Everyone looked so lovely."

"You are both too young to be nestling in nostalgia," said Mutalali.

"I hear you've been having *adventures*," said Entum, getting pinker with excitement.

Adya felt her mother tense up a little, and in response she willed her own skin to a rosy enthusiastic color and spoke a little more loudly. "Yes, it was all terribly thrilling. At first I was just doing some historical research, hunting the roots of a legend."

"The famous Godel Trigger!"

"The same. And as I searched, I came to suspect that others were seeking it as well."

"Adya, Entum doesn't want to hear a lot of hoary old history," said her mother.

"Oh, I do! I love to learn about life in other worlds and habs. You went to one of the Saturn cities, didn't you?"

"Yes, a place called Paoshi. A balloon city floating in the clouds."

Adya's mother patted her shoulder gently and went off to confer with Dipa Nikunnu and another matron. Adya and Entum drifted over to the clear diamond wall of the sphere. Outside a couple of whales moved slowly past—customers enjoying the Nikunnu krill.

Entum was an excellent listener, which surprised Adya. They leaned close, eyes locked with Adya's, as she described her course across the Solar System from Miranda to Saturn to the Uranus Ring to Summanus and finally to the surface of Mars.

"You seem fairly fond of this Zee fellow," Entum observed. "What happened to him?"

"Oh, he's here on Miranda. He—wasn't invited to tea today." Adya couldn't avoid a momentary flicker of muddy blue.

"Is he a good lover?" asked Entum, bending their head a little closer to hers.

For just an instant Adya felt as though a bucket of cool water had poured over her head. All her social worries and frustration with her mother and uncertainty and guilt seemed to just wash away, down into the pool at the bottom of the sphere. Her brain was actually *working* for the first time in days.

She looked at Entum and took one of their hands in hers. "I love him. More than I've loved anyone else. I want to spend my life with him. This whole marriage alliance is just some scheme of my mother's."

Entum laughed with delight. "Wonderful!" They glanced around and then spoke more quietly. "I'm happy to hear your heart is his. That makes matters much simpler. All we need to do is skip the neurological bonding. Make the marriage alliance our mothers have managed, but stay free to love whoever we want. It's the perfect solution to our problems! Your family gets my family's money, we get your family's status, you get your darling and I get—everyone else! We could even share him, once in a while. Always good for a couple to have something in common."

Adya thought for a moment before speaking. Ten minutes earlier the idea would have been more than tempting. Satisfy her mother with the form of a marriage, without losing Zee—as Entum said, it seemed like a perfect solution.

But after the flood of clarity she'd just experienced, Adya could see it was a terrible idea. Her mother and Dipa would agree but disapprove, and neither was very good about hiding their disapproval. Entum meant well, but Adya couldn't imagine the idea of sharing a household with a succession of their sexual dalliances, and the endless cycle of infatuation and breakup with all the obligatory drama. Zee would stay with her, honoring his promises as he always did, but he had no place in Sixty Families society. How long would their relationship endure the strain?

And, finally, there was Adya herself. In that moment she was suddenly certain that she didn't want to spend the next century shoring up the family finances, attending social events she didn't enjoy, and trying to run the lives of the next generation of Nikunnu-Elso offspring.

"We could slip away right now and seal the deal," said Entum. "Shock our mothers and satisfy them at the same time."

Adya smiled and leaned forward to whisper in Entum's ear. "I can't do this, Entum. I can't marry you."

They looked startled at that, and stared into Adya's eyes for a second. "You're willing to give up being in one of the Families for your lover?"

"It looks as if I have to. Can you get me out of here?"

"Come on. Pretend we're going to my room."

Hand in hand, they bounded across the sphere to a platform near the door, and left without looking back. On the lift platform Entum did try to change Adya's mind one last time, by kissing her with great feeling and expertise, while their hands gently touched her in places she hadn't even known were erogenous zones.

She pushed Entum away with one hand. They looked puzzled. "Are you all right?"

Adya actually had to catch her breath. The sullen little neuter child was gone, and Entum's years of obsessive practice had made them amazingly skillful. They knew just where, how, and when to touch her. Any more of that and she might find herself agreeing to anything.

"I really do have to go," she said. "I'm trying to save my family's wealth so I don't have to marry anyone, and I've got a meeting. Can you cover for me?"

Entum looked at her a little regretfully, their color shifting to a melancholy deep blue. "We really won't wed."

"No, we won't. I'm sorry, Entum. I still like you. But . . . it wouldn't work."

"I agree." They looked up at her shyly, purpling a little. "Sure you don't want a farewell fuck? At least you'll know what you're giving up."

Adya smiled and shook her head. "Not today."

"You need to conquer your self-control," said Entum. "All right, I'll go up to my room and take a long shower, then go back to the party and act smug. Good luck at your meeting."

"Thank you," said Adya. As the platform reached the main floor of the mansion she took a step closer and gave Entum a peck on the cheek. They responded with a one-finger brush on the side of her neck which made her entire body tingle.

Adya turned determinedly away and summoned a bubble to the tube entrance just outside the front door. She had full privacy up, and her mother wouldn't even start wondering about where she was for another hour or so.

Within minutes she was streaking along the seafloor to the city of Svarnam, which was the last known location of Pulu Visap.

Svarnam was big, dense city—a floating arcology in the form of a disk five kilometers across with a hundred levels, home to nearly ten million people. The top was devoted to parks and gardens, and in the center was Viranmar Plaza, a half-kilometer circular space four levels below the top and open to the sky. Adya left her bubble at the terminus at the edge of the plaza and walked to the center, where a statue of Sakigake, the possibly mythical first dolphin inhabitant of Miranda, stood balanced on a needle-pointed plinth so that the statue rocked and turned in stray air currents, as if swimming. Adya walked slowly around the statue, looking out at the edge of the plaza.

This was the center of public social life in Svarnam. A hundred bars, dance halls, restaurants, cafés, and theaters lined the rim. Adya could see at least a dozen empty storefronts, slightly shocking in such a popular location.

Of the survivors, which was the most fashionable? Normally Adya would simply look for a list somewhere, but she knew that for the ultra-hip of Miranda, any place on a list of "fashionable places" was by definition unfashionable. Fortunately Adya had an in-house authority on ultra-hipness. She pinged Kavita.

Her sister was on the surface, watching a display of plasma art at Trinculo Crater. She was suited up, in a crowd of people looking up at a kilometer-wide curl of blue-glowing nitrogen as it pulsed and writhed, kept excited by precisely tuned lasers and shaped by magnetic fields. For about a minute Adya (along with eighty thousand of Kavita's followers accessing her feed) just admired the view.

Then Kavita responded privately. "Isn't it great? The artist's a Defense Service officer but I discovered his work and helped him arrange this show."

"It's lovely. I just have a quick question. I'm at Viranmar Plaza in Svarnam. If you were here, which place would you choose?"

"Right now? Velli's, for prawns and wine. Then Midayi for tea and dessert on the balcony. See who's playing at Kuthira's and do some dancing, then finish up at Anpathi-Onnu." Above Kavita the plasma began to branch into fractal filaments, spreading across the sky.

"Thanks."

"Why are you hanging out at Viranmar? I thought you were at that party with the Nikunnus that Mother insisted I couldn't attend."

"I'm doing some research." Adya knew from long experience that if she wanted to keep something secret, Kavita was the worst possible person to tell it to. If Pulu Visap had scrubbed her presence from the datasphere, she might make a run for it if she knew Adya was trying to meet her in person.

"Well, good luck, cutie. Tell me what you discover."

Adya did her best to follow Kavita's itinerary. At Velli's she was a little surprised at the welcome she got. "You're Kavita's sister? So nice of you to stop in!" They put her at a table down in front, so that anyone coming in would see her. She didn't mind as it let her get a good look at all the other customers as they entered.

Her parents had taught Adya to savor her meals, but her time off Miranda had made her more efficient about dining. She made an effort to linger over her prawns—they really were excellent—and had to guard against the human waiter's attempts to keep her wine glass topped off. It was a nice white grown by a family she knew, but Adya wanted to keep her wits and senses sharp.

She did manage a quiet conversation with the headwaiter about Pulu Visap. "Oh, yes. A regular customer, very friendly and generous with the staff. No, I haven't seen her here this afternoon, or yesterday, either, now that I think of it. Shall I mention you asked about her? I see. Well, you can rely on my discretion."

When she transferred her observation post to Midayi the response was equally effusive. "Welcome, Miss Elso! This way, Miss Elso! Give our regards to your lovely sister, Miss Elso!" It was a little cloying, but the tea and cakes certainly were delicious. Kavita was always satisfied with the best.

From her little table on the vine-draped balcony, Adya could survey the plaza below. As the sky dimmed, the crowd thickened. Most of them were legacy humans or mers, but there were plenty of dolphins—either wearing walkers or just balancing on their tail flukes.

Here and there she could see cephalopods, the support gel on their skins glistening in the twilight. A couple of giant humans were showing off, juggling standard-sized humans and dolphins between them. More and more volunteers leaped into the game until the giants struggled to keep a dozen people aloft.

Overhead a few angels were skydancing with a flock of humans wearing wings, and high above them a dragon and a pterosaur wheeled and swooped impressively.

Even the sight of half a dozen of Kavita's chongs—the obsessive fans who paid for licensed face copies and wore printed versions of whatever she had on today—didn't diminish Adya's contentment. They all displayed virtual tags with Kavita's latest catch phrase "Feel the energy rising!"

This was the Miranda Adya loved—the cosmopolitan hub of wealth and culture in the Uranian system. It might lack the system-spanning power of Deimos or the sheer scale of Juren, but Miranda was a place people could fall in love with. The Sixty Families, for all their selfishness and folly, had accomplished that.

For Adya that sense of comfort and pride had a prickly edge. Her travels had taken her to many other worlds, so she could see more of Miranda's flaws as well as its virtues. She loved it the way she loved her family: affection tinged with exasperation.

The human teishu in charge of the tea was too discreet to talk about any of the other customers, but the bot carrying a tray of sweets did respond to carefully worded questions. Pulu Visap was not present at that time. Did Adya Elso want any tea cakes? Pulu Visap had last visited Midayi Tea Garden ten hours previously. Did Adya Elso wish for a non-menu item? Midayi Tea Garden did not archive recordings of patrons for public access. Did Adya Elso require a Baseline staff member?

She paid up and hustled over to the Anpathi-Onnu nightclub. It might be unfashionably early, but if her quarry was in or around Viranmar Plaza, that was the best place to look.

Anpathi-Onnu was listed as a private venue, not open to the public. But unlike any genuine private club, there was no software to recognize members by facial features or comm implant tags. Instead, a corvid perched next to the entrance and scrutinized everyone approaching. For some the door swung open as they reached it, and they went on in, perhaps with a friendly nod to the bird. For others the door stayed shut. The bird ignored all complaints, offers of bribes, and threats.

The corvid looked at Adya and cocked her head to one side. After a nerve-wracking pause, the door opened and Adya went on in. Once again she found herself in the unaccustomed position of being glad Kavita was her sister.

Anpathi-Onnu was actually underneath the plaza. Inside the door there was a five-meter drop down a shaft decorated with masks of musicians, dancers, and storytellers who had performed there. Carefully designed air currents and a smart-matter floor cushioned Adya's landing.

The club was dark and labyrinthine, with plenty of private nooks and secluded tables. Clever design gave every seat a sightline to the performance stage in the center. At the moment a pair of dolphins were singing a buzzing beat counterpoint.

Adya quickly discovered that the club didn't reveal who was or wasn't present, and that suggested she wouldn't get much out of the staff, either. So instead she spent fifteen minutes trying to act like she knew where she was going as she explored the three-dimensional maze of Anpathi-Onnu.

When she was reasonably sure that Pulu Visap wasn't at any of the shadowy tables, Adya took a vacant seat with a good view of the entrance.

By now her mother had figured out that she wasn't at the Nikunnu house anymore, and the messages and comm requests were piling up. Adya ignored them, and felt a slight wicked thrill at doing so. She would probably have to endure a lot of more-in-sorrow when she finally got home, but for now she was on her own.

The dolphins finished their set, did backflips off the stage, and hopped on their tails toward the dressing rooms. An idea struck Adya, and she hurriedly scanned through the performance archive for Anpathi-Onnu over the past few weeks, then moved briskly across the club, trying to catch up with the singers before they got away.

She got in sight of them in the backstage corridor—which was almost as posh as the public areas of the club. Adya fired off a quick comm message to both of them. *"I love your act. Can I talk about a private show?"*

They stopped, looked at her, and then gestured for her to come into their dressing room.

According the tags in Adya's field of vision, the dolphins were named Shinji and Kin-Ichi. Their dressing room was set up with everything at floor level, so the two could lie comfortably on the soft smart matter and not have to stand upright. They flopped down and Shinji gestured with one flipper-hand. "Make yourself comfortable! I think we've met your sister."

Who hasn't? Adya thought, a little grimly. "Thank you. Yes, Kavita's my little sister. I love what the two of you were doing with overtones and rhythms. Was that all improvised?"

"Absolutely!" said Shinji. "Every time we perform it's a unique experience, never to be repeated."

"At each performance the song is different, the audience is different—and we are different," added Kin-Ichi.

"Each breath contains molecules you've never breathed before," Adya quoted. Kin-Ichi clicked approvingly.

"You mentioned a private gig?" asked Shinji.

"My parents are talking about hosting an after party, right after the Constructors' Jubilee. Are you available then?"

"Already booked," said Shinji. "We'll be doing an underwater show during the Jubilee, then we're here the next day."

"What about that morning?"

Shinji made a rude noise with his blowhole. "Sleeping and eating!"

"A labor of love is still tiring," said Kin-Ichi.

"I understand," said Adya. "I remember hearing about the two of you from Pulu Visap. Do you know her?"

"She's been here when we played," said Shinji.

"I'm trying to find her but she's gone dark."

"Why seek someone who doesn't want to be found?" asked Kin-Ichi.

Time for another lie, Adya thought. She hoped she wasn't getting *too* used to doing that. "I've got a hot tip for her, and it's too good to just leave a message."

"She usually hangs around with Janitha Velicham. At least, whenever they're both here."

"Great! I'll check with her," said Adya, who was still looking up the name as she spoke. "Well, I'd better get back to my table before they take away my drink. It was very nice meeting you both—a delightful dolphin duo." She held her palms out.

"Fun to find a friendly fan," said Shinji, casually waving one flipper.

Adya found her own way out, but by the time she got back to her table she was barely aware of her surroundings. She stared into the middle distance, her eyes darting about as she navigated the infosphere using her implant, looking for everything she could find about Janitha Velicham. And the one datum that stood out, as if in letters of fire, was that Janitha Velicham was listed as the Memetics Coordinator for the Miranda Polyarchist Alliance.

Zee spent twelve hours in a public medical pod in a little town called Cheriya, under induced sleep with a goo bot doctor covering half his face. Daslakh perched atop the pod, monitoring its idiot-genius mind. While Zee slept the bot glued the cracks in his maxilla and printed new teeth in place of the broken ones. It also discovered and fixed a crack in his right sixth rib. As the patient had requested only somatic treatment, the pod flagged, but did not adjust, some imbalances in key neurotransmitters.

Daslakh considered overriding the pod and doing something about Zee's unhappiness, but decided not to. The bizarre evolutionary compendium of electrochemical kludges that biologicals used for information processing was riddled with design flaws, but over the centuries digital minds had learned that "fixing" them usually didn't make anything better. An unhappy human was considerably more functional than a human who *couldn't* be unhappy.

Once the medical treatment was done and Zee was just sleeping,

Daslakh could leave a small fragment of its personality to watch him while the rest ventured into Miranda infospace.

It knew that Adya's father was Commodore of something called the Seventh Shinkai Force, and some details about that were public information. Most of Miranda's armed forces were up on the surface, guarding against invasion. But as a last resort, there were ten big autonomous arsenal subs lurking in the ocean. They were self-maintaining, able to operate for years without resupply—which meant that an oligarch with empty pockets like Achan Elso could still claim to be doing his share for Miranda's defense.

All that was easy to learn. What was almost impossible to find was contact information for the subs themselves. Obviously nobody wanted Miranda's final line of defense to be open to memetic attacks or attempts at subversion, but there had to be *some* way for the biologicals of the Sixty Families to talk to their mightiest weapon systems.

Daslakh had to make itself think like a Mirandan. The answer was obvious: It checked the list of authorized callers at the Elso manor. Daslakh spent a couple of seconds sifting through the list, but eventually it found what it was looking for: an individual named Makara, tagged as "Commanding Intelligence, Seventh Shinkai Force." Achan Elso would never be uncouth enough to refuse to talk to the military unit he was responsible for supporting.

The contact code was routed through Miranda's Defense Service in Ksetram, and Daslakh assumed someone there had the authority to monitor all attempts to contact operational military intelligences. So its message was brief and a bit oblique.

"Hi, I'd like to discuss matters affecting the Elso family. Get in touch with me by whatever method is most convenient for you."

It expected some delay, but less than a second elapsed before Daslakh got a reply. The source was carefully anonymized, but the tag was not: "Responding to your note about the Commodore."

Daslakh activated the direct link in the message, and instantly got a message, not in a virtual environment, or even in text, but rather a burst of meta-language, the basic signifiers all digital intelligences used to parse and generate natural languages.

name: "Makara"
title: "Intelligence-in-Command of the Seventh Shinkai Force"

status: patrol: ocean
status: duration: indefinite
question: purpose: communication

"I'm Daslakh. A friend of Adya Elso."

Makara responded with links to a variety of data snippets from a dozen worlds, dating back five decades.

question: identity: continuity: "Daslakh"
question: location: miranda: purpose

"Yes, that's me. As I said, I'm a friend of Adya's. I want to talk to you about her family. They support you, right? Keep you operating?"

statement: "They support you, right?": incorrect
statement: payment: source: elso family
statement: payment: description: "standard Captain-at-Sea salary"
statement: payment: amount: 1 gigajoule per minute

"That's all? But you're an arsenal sub!"

correction: battle group

That was followed by about half a gigabyte of data describing the arsenal sub and her sub-units, with most specific details omitted. It did mention that the whole group formed a networked intelligence with a rating greater than 1.8 times Baseline. Daslakh suspected that the actual level was probably closer to 3, at least.

Makara's main unit had been built sixty-four years earlier by the Shimazu family, as part of an upgrade of Miranda's defenses. The Shimazus, who were mostly dolphins, had been Commodores and paid Makara's salary until eight years previous, when they had been persuaded to swap military responsibilities with the Elsos. Adya's father became Makara's new Commodore, while Nitin Shimazu took over the Fourth Maritime Rescue Unit, which had been the Elso contribution for a couple of centuries.

The data about Makara's battle group explained the switch: The arsenal sub and her sub-units were entirely self-sufficient. She extracted deuterium from the ocean for power, sifted the water for raw materials, and printed all of her own parts and ordnance. That was the whole point of the Shinkai Force—a hidden deterrent with no supply line to cut. No one, except possibly her sister units during practice battles, had sensed Makara in the six decades since she put to sea.

Aside from the nominal commander's salary, the Seventh Shinkai Force cost the Elsos nothing at all. Which immediately inspired another question from Daslakh.

"How does Achan Elso fit into that, then? Can he give you orders?"

title: "Commodore": honorary

She added a public access file outlining the Shinkai Force's chain of command. Makara and the other subs answered directly to the Military Subcommittee of the Coordinating Committee, with broad discretion to act autonomously if civilian authority was disrupted. Achan Elso did not appear anywhere in the command structure, which Daslakh decided was best for everyone concerned.

Daslakh noted a slight delay between its own remarks and Makara's replies. Interestingly, the delay varied between a third of a millisecond at the low end and two milliseconds maximum. Given Makara's stated intellect level, the delays couldn't be hesitation for thought. It finally decided that she must be randomly delaying her answers so that there would be no way for someone to figure out her location from comm time.

"I was wondering if someone might be messing with Elso family finances as a way to degrade your effectiveness. Achan Elso might not be able to afford your salary any longer. What will you do if that happens?"

status: makara: operational
status: projected: makara: operational
definition: salary: non-essential
question: reason: daslakh: need-to-know: achan elso

"I'm curious. Even if I don't like the guy very much, I still want to understand what's going on, and why."

Makara's reply was a decade-old opinion statement issued

anonymously by several mechs in Miranda's military services. *"In the past the biological oligarchs of the Sixty Families have employed mercenary forces against each other in political conflicts. The active Miranda military units do not participate in such actions. Our duty is to Miranda and all its inhabitants, not whichever faction is currently dominant within the Coordinating Committee. We decline to involve ourselves in political warfare and consider any commands to do so to be illegal orders."*

"So you're just going to sit back and eat puffed shrimp while mercs shoot it out in the streets?"

Makara re-sent the statement with one sentence highlighted: "**The active Miranda military units do not participate in such conflicts.**"

statement: shinkai force: mission: primary: protect: miranda
statement: shinkai force: mission: secondary: deter destroy: invaders
statement: shinkai force: assets: strategic: stealth
statement: action: political: effect: loss: stealth

The fragment of Daslakh's consciousness that was watching Zee sleep noticed movement consistent with the early waking process. Time to wind up this conversation.

"Thank you, Captain Makara," said Daslakh. "I understand Miranda a little better than I did before."

statement: projection: communication: daslakh: approved

"That's very generous of you."

request: daslakh: communicate: kavita elso: makara: communication: request
statement: evaluation: datastream: kavita elso: inadequate
statement: makara: conversation: kavita elso: request

"If I see her, I'll pass it along."

status: communication: end

When Zee finally woke up, he wanted food, which Daslakh considered a good sign. So it sat patiently on the table at an outdoor cafe in the central square of Cheriya while he shoveled puttu and buttermilk sambar into his mouth. Zee avoided anything too firm—while the new teeth were fine, his gums were still tender.

"So who is this Dai Chichi? Panam Putiyat acted like I should be worried about meeting him."

"Not hard to find out," said Daslakh as it found out. "Dai Chichi runs a nightclub and gambling parlor called the Abyss. It's down on the sea bottom, about a hundred kilometers west of here—Dai Chichi's a cephalopod, by the way. Interesting trend in how the club manifests in the infosphere. Up to about a standard year ago, coverage was uniformly negative. Lots of unproven allegations: rigged games, template piracy, gene stealing, crooked loans, extortion, money laundering and outright thuggery."

"Sounds like a rough place. Who would go there?"

"There's a sucker born every microsecond. And if you're one of the people who does the extorting or face punching, it might have some appeal. Anyway, over the past fifty weeks or so, the Abyss has become quite the edgy-fashionable hangout. Young Sixty Families idiots go there to rub fins and tentacles with real live grifters and racketeers. Adya's sister been there a dozen times to watch the marlin races."

"Do you think that's what Sundari was talking about when she was complaining to Adya about Kavita hanging around with 'impossible people'?"

"High probability. So now most of the mentions are about how cool the place is, and Dai Chichi's been upgraded from 'notorious' to 'controversial.' Apparently being run by a gangster is now just part of the place's quaint ambiance."

"Gambling—I can guess why Putiyat handed over the Oort payload. I wonder if Dai Chichi knows how much it's worth. Maybe we can buy it back!"

"In my experience your hard-core crooks tend to focus on liquidity and short time horizons. A thousand gigs today beats ten thousand tomorrow, and cash is king. It might be worth a try."

"If it's on the seafloor, we'll have to swim down. Can you stand being in the water again?"

"I'll endure it. But when we're done with Miranda I'd like to go someplace nice and dry."

Zee took a couple more bites before speaking. "I don't know if we ever will be done with Miranda. This is Adya's home."

"Do you want to spend the rest of your life here?"

"I wouldn't mind," said Zee.

"You're an absolutely pathetic liar."

"She's happy here. If I make her leave, she'll be miserable. I don't want that. Maybe I can figure out something I can do here."

"I don't know why you think she's happy. Her stress levels get higher whenever any of her family are nearby."

"There's the house, and all the things she showed me. She loves *Miranda*, the place."

"She loves you, too."

"I don't want to make her have to choose."

"Talk to her about it."

"I will—but not yet. I want to get to the bottom of this first, and I don't want to put her in danger."

"Let me point out that while there's no direct evidence, it's certainly plausible that this Dai Chichi person was the one who sent you that threatening message."

"I hope so, because otherwise that means there's someone else out there I need to worry about. Are you ready?" Zee hit the "CLEAN" spot on the table and watched as his used dishes sank slowly into the surface, dismantled into component molecules.

Daslakh climbed onto Zee's shoulder. They rode a bubble a hundred kilometers west, to a big floating city called Svarnam. At one of the sea bottom anchor points for the city, Zee rented a gill pack and a pair of fins. He sealed up his suit and slipped into a moon pool leading outside. Daslakh clung to his chest as he swam and helped to navigate.

That help was appreciated, as the sea bottom under Svarnam had almost zero visibility. The water was full of particulates brought in by cold deep currents pulled toward the city by the fusion reactors heating the ocean for the sea farms. Those same reactors powered banks of lights extending all the way to the bottom of the floating city, so all the gunk in the water was lit up, limiting Zee's vision to about the span of his arms.

Here and there warning strobes could pierce the murk, but it was impossible to see how far away they were, or what they were warning about. Daslakh's laser link to the local infosphere was useless, so they had to rely entirely on its inertial sensors to stay on the right heading, and outright guesswork to tell speed and distance.

Swimming against a strong current, blind in the cloudy water, cut off from the infosphere, Zee was perfectly calm. Daslakh could hear his heart working steadily, and no flutter of adrenaline affected the regular motion of his arms and legs. He'd been considerably more worried at the dinner table with Adya's parents.

The light dimmed bit by bit as they moved slowly away from the city, working against the current. *"Let me give you some hands,"* said Daslakh. It adjusted four of its feet to the shape of little fins, and began to vibrate them at the optimum frequency, helping to push Zee along.

"Don't drain yourself. I had a big breakfast."

"I'm fine. I'd rather be low on joules then put up with the tedium."

Two kilometers out from the city they passed a line of marker lights on the sea bottom, and just ahead Daslakh could see a chaos of flashing colors shining through the murk. They both could hear music through the water. *"I think this is the place,"* said Daslakh.

The Abyss was a big dome, easily a hundred meters wide, standing ten meters above the bottom on five legs. The underside was open to the water, and half a dozen small submersibles were moored to a floating platform in the center. A ramp for swimmers led to a walkway running around the perimeter of the dome. Zee climbed out of the water and took a deep breath. "Wow," he said.

Every sense was under assault inside the Abyss. Images—both projected and virtual—filled the air. Music, sound effects, and voices hovered just below ear-damaging volume, with minimal sound damping to create a feeling of activity and excitement. The damp air was laced with active molecules: stimulants, intoxicants, pheromones, and scents engineered to evoke high status and exoticism. The decor reminded Daslakh of the Putiyat mansion, with lavish use of offworld materials, handmade sculptures proudly displaying virtual provenance tags, and printed furniture made artfully irregular, as if crafted by some biological holding tools in clumsy hands.

The ramp coiled upward through the interior, vanishing among a tangle of platforms and bridges filling a dozen levels. The customers were roughly equal proportions of humans, dolphins, and cephalopods, with a scattering of borgs and a pair of orcas hanging their tails over the edge of one platform.

Zee didn't know what a Miranda gangster looked like, but he could see that the people in the Abyss seemed to fit into two categories: young ones in fashionable outfits loudly having fun, and a more varied contingent who dressed to intimidate rather than impress. The latter group were quieter and did a lot of watching, in the same way *nulesgrima* competitors watched potential opponents. He was uncomfortably aware that at the moment most of them were watching him.

Tags and images advertised the various gambling games. Most were straightforward random-number lotteries or the equivalent, with a payout ratio that left the house a comfortable profit. For those who thought they could win by skill, card and tile games provided an entertaining illusion.

Just above Zee's head a diamond tube full of seawater ran around the edge of the dome, with a start pen and finish line for fish races. Daslakh spent a tenth of a second researching the subject—the sport originated during the Cetacean Republic era, and probably would have died out from lack of interest but attempts by the Theocracy to suppress it had the paradoxical result of inspiring a few dedicated dolphins and orcas to keep it going in secret. It still had a somewhat low-status reputation, which made watching the races a perfect way for trendsetters like Kavita Elso to be daringly transgressive with zero actual risk.

Zee found a mer staff member, dressed only in a tall, gold-plated tiara decorated with geometric designs and figures of cephalopods. "I'd like to speak with Mr. Dai Chichi about a business matter," he said.

The mer looked at Zee and laughed dismissively. Daslakh felt a tickle of electronic attention as their comm tags were interrogated. "Sawa handles business complaints." She waved her tail at a dolphin on a cushioned platform in the center of the dome.

"Thank you," said Zee, and took a step in that direction, but spun in midair and stopped himself when the mer spoke again. She looked a lot more serious—and maybe a bit scared herself.

"Never mind Sawa. Go on up to the top level, right now. The boss is waiting."

With Daslakh on his shoulder, Zee made it up to the top level in three jumps. An iris door in the center of the uppermost level—a thick armored sandwich of titanium and graphene—snapped open long enough for them to pass through.

The top of the dome was a single room, and most of it was too low-ceilinged for Zee to stand upright. Dim green light filtering through a transparent roof lit the center of the room, but the rest was dark. The air was downright misty and Daslakh could tell it had elevated oxygen. Unlike every other part of the Abyss, the top floor was quiet.

"Hello?" Zee called out. "Mr. Dai Chichi?"

"*You are Zee Sadaran. You came to Miranda with Adya Elso. You've been sticking your nose into a private deal between me and Panam Putiyat. You don't know when to quit,*" said a voice over comms. It was coded deep and echoey, almost at the bottom end of human hearing.

"I want to buy back the inbound payload from the Oort he transferred to you."

"*You have nothing.*"

"Well, I guess you could say I'm acting on behalf of the Elso family."

"*You are not.*"

"Not officially, no. But—look, you know I'm a friend of Adya's. Adya Elso. That payload belongs to her. Her family didn't really have the right to sell it to Panam Putiyat in the first place. I'm here to fix up the whole mess so that it doesn't become a huge legal bother for everyone. Do you really want to go up against one of the Sixty Families in court?" As Zee spoke, he turned, trying to figure out where his host was hiding in the darkness.

"*Behind you,*" said Daslakh via comm. "*A radian to your left.*"

Zee turned to see a tentacle emerge from the darkness, dark red at the tip but otherwise deep black. A second followed, then two more, stretching past Zee all the way across the room. The suckers gripped the floor and then Dai Chichi pulled himself into the circle of green light.

He was big. *Very* big. Most of the cephalopods Zee had met were about his own mass, but Dai Chichi was far bigger—a couple of tons, at least. Only an orca or a whale was bigger, in Miranda's ocean anyway. His massive body was a great sagging sack of muscle, pulsing softly in the moist air. Two eyes, each as big as Zee's fist, were nearly hidden in the folds of flesh that made a sort of face. His arms were easily twenty meters long, tapering from as thick as Zee's waist where they joined Dai Chichi's body to a tip smaller than a child's finger.

Dai Chichi's skin went from black to luminous crimson all over, almost bright enough to cast shadows. *"You are trying to scare me with courts and lawyers. That's very funny. I know how to scare people, too. People like lawyers, and witnesses, and judges."*

As he spoke, two of his arms coiled loosely around Zee's feet, and a third curled around from behind to rest solidly on Zee's shoulder.

"You run a business," said Zee. "I'm here to offer a deal. The value of that Oort payload is very uncertain. Wouldn't you rather have the gigajoule credits now?" He ignored the fact that Dai Chichi's arm had slowly wrapped around his neck.

"You want it but you have nothing to offer me."

"If you return it, I can promise you a share of what we get for it—with no legal challenges, no problems. And the Elsos have plenty of business contacts. They can get a better price than you can."

"If I keep it, I get all the profit, not just a share."

Zee stood a little straighter, bearing the weight of Dai Chichi's arm on his shoulders. "Name your price, then."

"You can't pay it."

"I said name your price. I'll find a way."

After about two seconds Dai Chichi replied, and his skin dimmed and shifted to a reddish-brown. *"You're too late. I already sold it."*

"Who did you sell it to?"

"I run a business, as you said. I don't make gigs by giving things away. You want to know who I sold it to, you need to make it worth my while. Give me something."

"All right," said Zee, trying not to sigh too loudly. "What do you want for the information?"

"I know you haven't got any gigs, so I'll trade data for data. You say you're a friend of the Elso family. Maybe that's true and maybe it isn't. Achan Elso's part of the ruling coalition. He knows all the Sixty Families and is related to most of them. If you're his friend, you can talk to some of the political bosses, the ones who run the big ministries."

"I think I can manage that," said Zee. Once again his vitals were as calm and steady as when he'd been swimming blind at the bottom of the ocean.

An image accompanied Dai Chichi's words, a long-distance still shot of a medium-sized male human in a Martian-style cape sitting at a table with three older Mirandans in sarongs. *"There's an offworlder spreading bribes around in the Coalition. His name's Qi Tian, or that's what he says, anyway. I can't find out much about him, and that bothers me. I want to know what he's doing and who's behind him. You find out and I'll tell you who's got the rights to that payload."*

"Why not ask one of your Sixty Families customers?"

"Smart question. Here's the answer: I don't know who this guy has in his pocket. Anyone I ask might pass the word back, and I don't want that. You're new here, so I figure Qi Tian hasn't had a chance to get to you yet. And if you're asking questions, that pulls eyes to you, not me."

Zee nodded. "Okay, I'll find out whatever I can."

Dai Chichi's arm around his neck tightened gently. *"Find out everything, and the sooner the better. Info gets worthless when it gets old."*

All the arms pulled back into a tangled mass in front of Dai Chichi, and his skin dimmed to a barely visible brown. He said nothing more, and after a moment Zee went to the armored iris in the center of the floor. It snapped open and he fell back into the noise and glare of the club.

As they slowly fell forty meters to the bottom level, Zee suddenly stiffened. "Is that Adya?" He then quickly answered his own question. "No, it's Kavita."

Daslakh looked where Zee was looking—a private platform chosen for maximum visibility. "Adya doesn't have an entourage, unless you count us."

They touched down on patch of floor floating on the water. Zee was still looking up at where Kavita and about half a dozen sycophants burst into whoops and applause as a serving bot brought them a tray of flaming drinks.

Daslakh was more interested in the local infosphere. Kavita's comm tag was big and loud and intrusive, sending out little autonomous agents to everyone in line of sight. The agents were surprisingly sophisticated, able to worm their way through most commercial filters and take up residence in the victim's implant, where they would send out endless reminders about where Kavita was, what Kavita was doing, and which products and services she was using.

Daslakh quietly sent a fragment of its own personality into Zee's implant, where it hunted down and exterminated Kavita's agents with gleeful brutality, taking them apart to create custom filters they'd never be able to penetrate.

Meanwhile Daslakh's main consciousness took a closer look at the group on the private platform. Kavita naturally was the center of attention, orbited by a swarm of her sycophants. From their tags Daslakh classified them as a lot of wanna-bes, has-beens, and never-weres. A surprising number of them were from the security and defense services—not normally a hotbed of hipness.

Kavita's husband Vidhi sat off to one side, a little apart from the chattering knot of fans, his gaze directed outward. Daslakh looked at the data streams and saw that while Kavita was broadcasting, Vidhi was harvesting, checking info about everyone in the club. He spotted Zee and looked a little startled, and Daslakh saw him exchange a quick glance with Kavita.

"She hasn't pinged me. Should I go say hello?" asked Zee.

"Do you want to?"

Zee watched as the little party began squirting flaming mouthfuls at each other. "Not really," he said.

"Then, although it means another dip in salt water full of microscopic organisms and metabolic waste products, let's get out of here." Evidently Kavita—or maybe Vidhi—had decided Zee wasn't someone her fans would be interested in, and Daslakh didn't want to see if either of them changed their minds.

"Right," said Zee, and Daslakh could feel him relax as he said it. He took a breath, turned on his gill pack, and did a forward somersault into the water.

CHAPTER EIGHT

Adya collapsed into bed in the Iris Room and let out a long sigh. She felt tears tickling the corners of her eyes, and wiped them with the back of her hand. The scene with her mother when she had finally returned from her detective expedition to Viranmar Plaza had been a real emotional battle of attrition, no quarter asked or given on either side.

It was very late, and she thought of inducing sleep, but decided it would be better to calm herself by natural methods first. In her current state, inducing would just give her angry dreams.

Adya's favorite way to relax was to learn something. So she stared up at the ceiling and let herself dive into the infosphere, hunting for anything she could find about the Polyarchists. Not history and origins, but what they were doing at the moment.

Predictably, Miranda's current economic slump had strengthened the movement. During good times they had been objects of mockery, a bunch of crackpots who wanted to replace the success of the Sixty Families with some risky, impractical scheme. Now Adya found a number of quite serious instructionals and opinions putting forth the idea that maybe the oligarchy had become decadent and hidebound, the Families too obsessed with coalition politics rather than public service.

She couldn't really disagree with that, either. During her journeys across the Solar System Adya had found herself explaining Miranda and how the oligarchy worked to a variety of people, and as a result she had come to see some of the flaws of the system. Making rich people pay for everything sounded good to most people—but it did mean that all of Miranda's government was perpetually underfunded. The family holding a particular ministry would inevitably put off solving problems, especially if they were likely to require expensive solutions, and then dump the whole thing in the lap of whoever took over the position. The few new projects were chosen to enrich the officeholders or at least win prestige, and any public benefit was just a side effect.

Adya's travels had also shown her that every *other* system in use had flaws of its own—some of them much worse than Miranda's—but she could still wish that the Sixty Families would pay attention to things outside the sealed bubble of Coordinating Committee politics, marriage alliances, and social gamesmanship. Living inside a literal sealed bubble encased in a kilometer of ice didn't help.

The question which kept nagging at her was *why?* Why would the Polyarchists, no matter what their goals might be, attack the Elso family in particular?

She located her parents. Her mother had retreated to her private office, and her father was in the sculpture rotunda. Adya got up and mentally plotted a route to the gallery which would minimize the risk of crossing paths with her mother. Maybe in the morning one of them would feel like apologizing, or at least negotiating a truce, but not now.

To minimize signs of her passage she asked the house not to light up rooms for her, and navigated entirely by the light coming from glowing plants or filtering through windows and skylights. It reminded her of nocturnal expeditions when she was little, prowling the house when she was supposed to be in bed, sometimes with Kavita, more often alone.

Achan sat on the floor in the center of the rotunda with an open bottle of wine and a glass next to him. When Adya came in he smiled sadly and patted the floor next to him. "Join me in admiring our ancestral art."

She sat. "I have a question."

He gestured at the wood carving directly in front of him. "Do you know the story behind this one? Three centuries ago the Nashichu family were in a poor position. They were the least of the great families—the Sixty-Three Families, as it was then. Sunitha Nashichu was the last leader of that line. With but a day left before she would have to resign as a magistrate and Minister of Mechanical Affairs, she put an arterial tap in her arm and went out rowing. Her nephew Ajith Elso-Nashichu carved that himself as a memorial."

The sculpture really was beautiful, carved with hand tools from a slab of red cedar wood grown in one of the Equatorial habs. Adya's ancestor Ajith had made use of a natural streak of brighter red in the wood, so that the simplified shape of a rower in a boat was at the apex of a widening wake of red against the golden water.

"Their name ended with Sunitha. We Elsos inherited some of their treasures—and a stack of debts, but in those days we had wealth to waste. Will our withering leave anything as wondrous as that woodwork?"

Adya had spent her life listening to her father predict decline and doom, but this time his voice held an unfamiliar tone. There was none of his usual outrage or complaint. This time his sadness was real, and unfathomably deep.

"Father, I have a question. It's very important. What would the Polyarchists achieve by attacking our family interests?"

"Who can understand the motives of fools and madmen? We are of the Sixty Families, and vulnerable, so they attack us."

"Maybe so, but what will happen politically if you have to give up your seats on the Coordinating Committee? What would change?"

He took a deep breath and frowned in concentration, willing himself to think. "It will probably mean a new coalition in power. With me gone, the opposition gains a majority, and can then bolster it by assigning our seats to their own side. Probably Taracu or Miti."

"And what would that do? Are they sympathetic to the Polyarchists?"

"Not that I know. Most ministries would remain with the current holders, so there would be little change in day-to-day matters. The biggest effect would probably be in our offworld relations. The Committee does determine overall policy there. Since you were small Miranda has generally leagued ourselves with the Trojan Empire. I think the opposition prefer a stricter neutrality."

"Would that do anything to help the Polyarchists?"

He shook his head vigorously, as if trying to clear it. "I am too drunk for this. Leave me to wine and woe."

"Just speculate. Why would the Polyarchists support neutrality?"

"As I said, they are fools and madmen. They may think the Trojans too tyrannical—as they are, after all. I cannot say for sure." He ignored his glass and picked up the bottle. "To the devisers of our difficulties! They have shown supreme skill in secret struggles!"

Achan drained the bottle in four swallows and let it fall, spattering himself with purple drops.

"Father—"

"If the Families are fated to fall, then I will make my end as a man of Miranda! I will not see my house and treasures sold, my daughters reduced to bourgeois banality. I will follow Sunitha and die with honor!"

"Please don't talk that way! Even if we lose everything, Mother still needs you. Kavita and I need you, and Sundari, too. Losing your seats on the Committee won't change anything."

He stared off into the middle distance, ignoring her. "Failure. Last of the line. I will not live that way. No charity, no pity. I will not accept it." Achan rolled away from her, knocking the glass over, and lay on his side in the puddle that spread from it. Adya started to speak again, but stopped when she saw he was asleep.

She summoned some bots to take him to his bedroom, and another to clean up the spilled wine. Then she returned to the Iris Room and tried to make herself feel like sleep. She was just about to shut down her comm implant when one of Kavita's irritating updates appeared in her field of vision. "KAVITA GOES SPEEDBOARDING! WATCH HER RACE AGAINST CHAMPIONS SUMAN WIJAYA AND YUKI!"

She started to send it to her filtering agent, so that it could do a better job of stopping Kavita's mass invites, but then Adya hesitated. She had resolutely avoided participating in Kavita's stream—on the justifiable grounds that she of all people didn't need a link to know what her sister was doing. But this time her desperate need for distraction overcame her sisterly disdain. So she selected "JOIN."

As she was new to Kavita's stream there was a little bit of opt-in required, including authorization for the stream to use her medical implant's recreational setting in order to let Adya experience Kavita's moods. Adya agreed—but only for the next hour. After that Kavita would have to go back to tried-and-true methods of manipulating Adya's emotions, like catty remarks and whining.

With that little formality out of the way, Adya settled herself comfortably and activated the link.

Instantly she was on the surface of Miranda wearing a skinsuit and bubble helmet, balanced on a speedboard as it shot down the famous Red-rated track that snaked among the hills and canyons of Sicilia Regio. The landscape beyond the track passed by in a blur, but Kavita couldn't spare any attention for sightseeing as she used her legs and body to shift the board around the curved interior of the track, balancing the gee forces created by the bends and spirals. The main risk wasn't falling down—not in Miranda's gravity—but rather in *not* falling. If the board left the surface of the track Kavita would find herself in a ballistic trajectory with no way to slow or stop herself until she hit the surface again.

That was what the rational part of Adya's mind was thinking, but the rest of her was bending and swaying as the track ahead writhed and coiled like a cephalopod making rude gestures. Adya could see the little map display showing Kavita's position on the course, see the dots marking the two professionals—Suman Wijaya about twenty meters behind and Yuki fifty meters in the lead—and feel Kavita's fist clutching the board's control unit.

Then her medical implant started feeding her Kavita's emotions. Adrenaline surged through her as her sister felt fear, exhilaration, and a burning desire to win the race.

She could hear the high-pitched whine of the board's propulsion unit and the slashing sound of the board's frictionless underside against the slick ice of the track. Behind that Adya became aware of an undercurrent of voices: the audience feedback channel giving the cheers, excited squeals, shouts of encouragement, gasps, warnings, and applause of Kavita's followers.

The feedback rose to a crescendo as Kavita squeezed the control unit hard, sending the board surging ahead, gaining on Yuki. She kept her grip tight even as the straightaway segment ended and the track whipped around in a hairpin bend at the head of a canyon, then spiraled up through a tunnel to the surface level above the rim.

In the tunnel she crouched, keeping her center of mass low, letting the board find the right angle, but then the track burst out into the

142   *James L. Cambias*

open surface under Uranus's bright crescent, and Kavita had to roll and get the board right at the edge of the track above her head to keep from flying off across the landscape.

Adya's own leg muscles tensed as she tried to keep Kavita's board on the track, and she could hear the terror in the myriad voices of the feedback channel. When the board slid back away from the edge as Kavita entered another nearly straight section, she heard a hundred sighs of relief.

"Ooh, that was tight," Kavita said aloud, calling forth more cheers.

Clutching the control hard enough to make her arm spasm, Kavita gained steadily on Yuki. At first she just caught glimpses of them, then Yuki was in sight except when sharp curves interfered, and finally Kavita was almost close enough to reach forward and touch their distinctive all-white skinsuit. Adya could clearly hear a group of fans chanting "KA-VI-TA" in unison.

Yuki wasn't going to give up the lead easily. They started moving back and forth unpredictably, keeping Kavita from passing. The two were moving at nearly fifty-eight meters per second—a collision at this speed would be a bone-breaker at least, possibly fatal if the boarders slammed into a tight curve.

Kavita stayed close to Yuki, waiting for her moment. The track entered a curve, looping all the way around a hill, and Yuki took the outside, riding at the edge of the track as the surface went nearly vertical. Kavita tensed her fist and leaned to the right. Her board shot forward, digging into the ice with one edge, sending up a spray of particles that twinkled in the sunlight. But there simply wasn't enough friction, and Kavita's path converged with Yuki's. The distance between the boards shrank to half a meter, then twenty centimeters, then ten, then five...

It was Yuki who blinked first. Their board slowed a tiny amount, and Kavita slid past, taking the lead.

Ahead lay a tricky series of three hairpins leading down the side of a canyon, followed by a straightaway along the canyon floor to the finish line. On the topmost turn Yuki tried to regain the lead by cutting inside Kavita's path, but they had to sacrifice so much speed to start the turn early that they couldn't quite get level with Kavita.

The middle turn, out near the canyon mouth, was so narrow there simply wasn't enough room for Yuki to pass. The last was a nice wide curve, and for a couple of tense seconds the two boards were side by side again. Kavita accelerated out of the bend and went down the final stretch at an insane sixty meters per second, breaking the tape at the canyon mouth before turning her board side-on to slow down.

Adya felt the surge of triumph and joy from her sister, like an emotional orgasm. The fan feedback included screams and moans like some giant exhibitionistic orgy.

She disconnected and let out a deep breath, relaxing herself all over. Just "riding along" in Kavita's sensorium had been the most intense thing Adya had done in months—and for most of Kavita's fans it must have been far more powerful than anything in their own lives.

After that she felt so drained and exhausted there was no need for the inducer, and her dreams were full of motion.

Zee insisted on a rest and a snack before trying to contact Adya, but Daslakh could sense considerable stress every time it brought up the subject. Finally Zee could put it off no longer. He pushed away his empty noodle bowl and stared into the middle distance. Daslakh discreetly listened in—but Adya was in privacy mode and did not respond.

Her filtering and security were better than Zee's, but Daslakh had spent months traveling with the two of them, so Adya's comm implant was a very soft target. It didn't do anything to alert her, but it did at least check on her location and physical status.

She was not far away, actually. Sitting in a tea shop at Viranmar Plaza, about forty levels above the noodle shop where Zee was trying to contact her. The tea shop was apparently a trendy place, judging by how often Adya's sister Kavita had been there recently.

Daslakh did wonder why she was there. Adya wasn't the sort to look for the hippest place to hang out, and she was a considerable distance from the Elso manor. Was she looking for Zee? Or someone else?

The noodle shop where Zee was sitting was a tiny place lashed to the wall of an atrium running the full height of the floating arcology of Svarnam. The floor of the shop was a rectangle of diamondoid, giving a vertiginous view down sixty levels, the bottom lost in haze. The sides were open, and the top was a fabric canopy, set up to catch drops of condensation or random litter falling from above. A mer woman ran the place, with pots of stock, packets of dough, rollers, cutters, and bowls all within arm's reach of her stool. Her tail dangled over the edge of the floor, but she didn't seem to care.

The only other customers were a pair of hungry teenagers sharing a giant bowl piled with fish and shrimp, which they had doused with hot sauce until the owner glared at them. They finished while Zee was still fiddling with his cup of tea, trying to contact Adya for the fourth time.

"I don't think she wants to talk to me," said Zee.

"Maybe she's busy."

The teenagers handed their empty bowl to the mer woman and hurried out. Zee drained his lukewarm tea and piled it and his chopsticks into the empty noodle bowl.

As he started to get up they all heard a snapping sound, like a spark, and the whole shop jerked. A cable whipped past and the corner of the floor just beyond Zee suddenly sagged. Everything in the little shop began sliding toward him—tables, pots, and the owner.

Daslakh, naturally, reacted first. It got to the gallery which ran around the entire atrium in one jump, in time to see the second cable, attached to the other outer corner of the diamondoid platform, suddenly glow bright yellow in one spot and then part. The platform, now only supported where it was attached to the gallery, flopped down like a trapdoor. Pots and tables fell tumbling down the atrium.

But not Zee or the owner. With one hand Zee gripped the canopy, which now dangled loose from where it was attached to the edge of the gallery above. His other held the owner's tail. In Miranda's low gravity he had no trouble with her weight, but she still had plenty of inertia and Zee's muscles strained as she bobbed back and forth at the end of her tail.

He swung her out and back a couple of times to build up momentum, then let go as she cleared the railing of the gallery below and slammed into the window of a shop. Just then Zee himself dropped a couple of meters as one corner of the canopy came loose, the ends of the severed line smoldering. Zee grabbed the flapping loose cloth with both hands and flung himself up and over the rail to land next to Daslakh as the canopy's remaining attached corner burst into flame and the whole thing drifted down the atrium after the furniture, twisting in the air currents and leaving a trail of smoke.

"Get down!" said Daslakh. "That was a laser."

Zee obediently dropped flat onto the walkway and rolled behind a decorative planter, which provided a little cover as long as he stayed down. "Can you see who did it?"

"Three levels up on the far side of the atrium. A bot, maybe remote operated." Daslakh raised one limb above the edge of the planter to look again. "It's gone now."

Svarnam security arrived seconds later, a squadron of bots and two biologicals in smart-matter combat suits—one human and one cephalopod. Medics and investigators followed, and Zee spent the next half hour giving his statement and getting checked over in case he had a laser burn through his torso that had gone unremarked in the excitement. He did have a burn along one forearm where hot stock had splashed while his sleeves were pushed up, and the medics covered it with a bandage that merged into his skin.

Daslakh, out of long habit, disappeared as soon as the authorities came in sight, but this turned out to be a mistake. Kini Kohu, the mer who owned the ruined noodle shop, was convinced that "the creepy little spider bot" was responsible for all the damage.

"It was in here, and jumped away right when everything started," she said. "Looks pretty cloudy to me. Why would a bot come in here at all? Find that bot and you'll find out what's going on."

Zee knew about Daslakh's aversion to official attention, but wasn't about to lie to the security service. "My friend ran off," he explained. "It's an old mech and it hasn't backed itself up in a while. I think it was afraid of losing memories."

The human cop seemed satisfied by that, but the cephalopod was more curious. *"Are you certain? How well do you know this mech?"* he asked via comm.

"Oh, very well. We've known each other for years. We used to work together back in Raba habitat."

There was some kind of private exchange between the two security officers, which apparently the cephalopod didn't like very much. He stalked off with his suit colored hazard orange.

"That's all we need from you," said the human. "And in the future I think you and your friend should be more careful about where you go."

Zee nodded and helped Ms. Kohu haul all the debris of her shop which hadn't fallen into the abyss onto the gallery. She looked over the edge. "All my stuff's on the seafloor by now. The atrium's open at the bottom. Easier to print up replacements than look for everything down in the muck. Thanks for helping out, but you didn't have to squeeze my tail so hard."

"I didn't want you to fall."

"You're from some spin hab, aren't you? One gee? You're in Miranda now. It's only a couple of hundred meters down, and water at the bottom. Not dangerous. Thanks anyway." She stacked the bundle of cords and fabric and the diamondoid panel against the inner wall of the gallery and then headed off for the nearest lift.

Zee went the other way and ducked into a side passage where Daslakh waited on the ceiling. "I just got another message," said Zee. He forwarded it to Daslakh.

"NEXT TIME IT'S YOUR HEAD." As before, it was devoid of any metadata.

"That sounds distinctly threatening. Are you going to tell the Security Service people about it?"

"I'm not sure. That human officer sounded a little threatening, too, right at the end. I don't know what's going on but I'm pretty sure something is. What do you think?"

"Well, something is always going on, more or less by definition. But I think you're right. I think someone's trying to scare you off from finding that payload."

"Could it be Dai Chichi?"

"Could be anyone, but he's about the least likely candidate. He's the one who offered you a deal—if he didn't want you to find who owns the payload, he could have just said no, or refuse to see you. Or crush you like a grape with one arm."

"Maybe the security people think I'm involved in one of Dai Chichi's rackets."

"Or maybe they got orders from one of Papa Elso's political opponents to warn you off."

"Maybe."

Daslakh dropped onto Zee's shoulder. "Maybe you should talk to Adya about this."

"No," said Zee, in what Daslakh had come to recognize as the tone he used when making a noble and stupid decision. "I don't want to worry her, and I don't want to put her in danger."

"What danger?"

"Someone's trying to kill me!"

"Are they? When they zapped the cables holding up that noodle shop, it would have dropped you a hundred seventy meters into some cold water. The gravity here's pretty feeble. Your impact velocity would be the same as jumping off the high board at the pool back in Raba. You'd get cold and wet and that's about it. Remember what the mer woman said: not dangerous."

"Okay, so someone's trying to *scare* me. They could still get rougher if I don't give up. I don't want Adya getting hurt."

"I can't avoid the suspicion that you want to keep your distance until you can drop the payload in her lap all wrapped in pretty paper and then bask in her gratitude."

Zee was silent for a little while. "I want to be useful," he said at last. "Show Adya I can get things done here in Miranda, without her help."

"Shorn of emotional verbiage, that amounts to what I said. Now: Let us reason together. You want to impress Adya and show you can accomplish something within Miranda society even though you've only been here a short time, correct?"

"Yes," said Zee.

"So you want to locate the payload's owner. And in order to do that you need to satisfy Dai Chichi's demand for information about this Qi Tian individual, correct?"

"Right—unless you can come up with a better way to find out who controls the payload now. That would be really helpful."

"No doubt. I'll be candid, Zee: I could try to finesse or brute-force my way into the secure data caches and learn who currently claims ownership. I'm old and cunning that way. But I'm also old and cunning enough to know that people would notice. Maybe not biologicals, but some of the mechs living in Miranda or on top of the ice could probably figure it out, and they could talk. Plus, I have always believed it's a bad idea to reveal your capabilities to potential adversaries."

"What potential adversaries? You don't have any enemies here."

"I don't know about any. That doesn't mean they don't exist," said Daslakh. "Or might exist in the future."

"You're paranoid."

"I prefer the term 'appropriately cautious.' It's how I've managed to live as long as I have. Now stop interrupting. Assume for the moment that I can't, or won't, defeat the data security protecting the information you're looking for. Which means you need to do what Dai Chichi asked of you. Yes?"

"Yes," said Zee, a little sulkily.

"And that in turn means you need to get some advice from someone with knowledge of Miranda society and politics."

"Adya's father!" said Zee.

"Exactly," said Daslakh—trying to sound as if that was the conclusion it had been leading to all along, although it wasn't. It had been trying to send Zee back to Adya, but even Daslakh sometimes underestimated Zee.

The mercenaries assembling at Taishi spent their time getting their physical assets ready for combat, and training together in virtual environments. Leiting insisted that every exercise had to include both digital and biological minds. "It is inconvenient, but so is actual combat. Digitals must deal with lag time in both information and response to instructions. Biologicals must cope with the rapid pace of events. The exercises should be as difficult and frustrating as reality."

Pelagia actually enjoyed the practice battles. Dealing with real opponents was always more stimulating. Whenever she played a game, or ran a training sim, there was always the lurking suspicion in her mind that she was simply training herself to exploit the limits of the sub-Baseline software. Whereas fighting alongside actual autonomous beings against other sentient minds was real, even if the lasers and projectiles were simulated. If an enemy or an ally made a puzzling decision, it was for a reason—possibly even a *good* reason—rather than just a random number generator deciding it was time to bite the player's tail.

Leiting ran them through dozens of situations, gradually increasing the scale and complexity as the mercenaries got used to working together and figured out how to play to one another's strengths. Pelagia and Repun made a good team for raiding and shock tactics, despite their mutual dislike. In combat they could operate on reflexes and ancient ocean-predator instinct which let them almost keep up with digital minds in decision-making speed. And for sheer bloody-minded aggression they couldn't be surpassed. Even digitals with secure backups at Osorizan or buried deep inside Titania, fighting in a completely virtual battle exercise, would veer off in sheer self-preservation when faced with a pair of opponents whose very DNA was telling them to kill the weak and wounded.

When she wasn't training or keeping her spaceframe in shape, Pelagia socialized with her new comrades-in-arms. The biological and digital intelligences tended to self-segregate, if only because of compatibility of time frames and communication channels.

Since neither Pelagia nor Repun could stand one another's company, she wound up spending most of her time interacting with a team of six gorillas who specialized in policing and Civil-Military Operations. The idea of an ape in a suit trying to arrest a cybership for some violation of unit regulations was hilarious to her at first, but after a few virtual bull and gripe sessions with the team Pelagia got interested in their work.

"Keeping big dumb fish like you in line isn't what we're paid for. That's just a sideline, really. A mech could do that. Our job is to interface with the civilians in the AO. Keep 'em friendly—or at least quiet."

"I always say a blue megajoule laser is the best way to make friends."

The gorillas all hooted and then Armelle, the centro of the crew, said "That's why you don't see orcas in civil-military ops. Hard to win anyone's heart or amygdala if they've been vaporized."

"So what's your role in this operation? Just keeping the civvies out of the way until the shooting stops?"

"No, no. That's when our work starts. We're going to be keeping order and basically running the local government, and serving as cadre to train up a new local security force. This is a long-term gig: our contract's renewable for up to ten standard years."

"That's a big job for six little monkeys."

"We'll have bots to do the rough stuff, and there's a whole second unit of dolphins to share the load. Plus Leiting says it expects a significant number of local allies."

A tall, white-haired human figure materialized inside the virtual hangout. "Leiting reminds all personnel that operational security is of maximum importance. No data about force composition, tactical plans, or objectives should be shared with any individuals lacking a need to know."

"Sorry, sir," said Armelle. "It won't happen again."

"Asking questions about topics for which you do not have authorization is forbidden by contract," said Leiting to Pelagia.

"I was just making conversation. Sorry, *sir.*" If Pelagia had possessed actual teeth, she would have clenched them. "Can we talk about old battles?"

"Your contract does not forbid discussion of events prior to the signing date."

"Thank you, *sir,*" said Pelagia. As soon as the human figure vanished her own avatar blew out a breath from her blowhole with a loud raspberry noise.

"I've known plenty of combat mechs," one of the other gorillas observed after a few seconds. "Some of them aren't assholes."

"I think I met one, once," said Pelagia. "Do you suppose the others deliberately choose to be like that?"

"Nah," said Armelle. "It's just laziness. Emotional intelligence takes a lot of work, especially if your brain doesn't do it automatically. Ever spend time with a lotor?"

"Not to speak to. I carried some as shuttle passengers a few times, but that's about it."

"They're almost as bad as mechs when it comes to social behavior. Especially on comms. Though in person they're always very polite." Armelle gave a soft hoot and thumped her chest. In the virtual environment it sounded like a kettle drum. "I guess it's my big brown eyes."

Pelagia and the other gorillas laughed.

After another hour of "no shit, there I was when—" stories, Pelagia dropped out of the virtual space. She did swim around the comm network Leiting had set up for the mercenaries. It took her just a few seconds to find the dolphins, playing a game of Kejum in a simulated aerosphere full of clouds and legless birds. They invited her to join and she accepted cheerfully, scaling her own avatar to be just a little bit bigger than any of theirs.

The game was moderately entertaining, and this time Pelagia asked no questions and volunteered no information. The dolphins—living the stereotype—kept up a steady chatter, and within fifteen minutes Pelagia knew that they were another Civil-Military Operations team, they were originally from Europa, and they were very unhappy about the quality of the chow. "I hear the operational area's got some good seafood," said one, and the others chorused agreement.

Pelagia waited but Leiting didn't appear. She played with the dolphins a little longer and then excused herself, dropping out of the comm network entirely to consider a few things. Just to be sure, she severed all hard links and shut off everything on board capable of broadcasting. She didn't want Leiting to pop up and fuss at her inside her own brain.

Leiting had appeared to shut down her conversation with the gorillas, but hadn't done anything about the talkative dolphins. Even their speculation about seafood in the AO hadn't attracted the boss's attention. Pelagia reviewed her comm logs carefully. As far as she could tell, there were two possible explanations for Leiting's intervention: either it had simply flagged its own name, and used operational security as an excuse to silence any grumbling; or it didn't want the gorillas talking about possible local allies.

The two options hung perfectly balanced in Pelagia's mind. Leiting certainly was a martinet, but keeping information about local assets quiet was good command practice. Finally Pelagia decided there was no need to choose at all. Leiting could be both a skilled commander and a tail-biter at the same time. It was not uncommon.

More interesting was what she had learned about the mission and the target. If Leiting had hired not one but two Civil-Military Operations groups, it was clear this was no mere smash-and-grab raid, nor anything like that. Whoever had hired Leiting was expecting a long occupation period, and a change of regime. Probably some counterinsurgency work, too.

Pelagia felt a bit of relief that spacecraft were almost useless for that sort of operation. Once they overcame the local defenses and got the troops down, or in, or wherever they were going, her own job would be pretty much done. Maybe some patrol and interdiction to cut the locals off from outside help, but after that she would be surplus to requirements. A good thing, too—Pelagia bored easily.

As to the target, now she knew a few things she hadn't. It must be a good-sized object or habitat, with a substantial amount of water environment. Out in the ice-rich parts of the Solar System beyond the Old Belt, water habs were not uncommon. Pelagia's near-Baseline software assistant searched through all six million inhabited objects in Uranus equatorial-orbit space, filtering out the ones with no biological inhabitants, no water, or a population smaller than twenty thousand beings. That knocked out about three-quarters of the potential targets, but still left a million and a half habitats, moons, and megastructures, any of which might be Leiting's mission objective.

She could definitely eliminate the fifteen or so most populous worlds and habs among the Uranus Equatorials. With populations in the tens of billions they were simply too powerful for a mercenary force to tackle. The biggest three—the moon Titania and the giant habitats Caelus and Dagda—had so much clout that Pelagia also filtered out any of the lesser worlds which were allies, client states, or puppets of those superpowers. Busting into their spheres of influence would be as bad as attacking them directly, and any of them could hire hundreds of ships and millions of troops for a proxy war without noticing the effort. Leiting might be a jerk, but it wasn't a fool.

Even after all her filtering the list was still far too long. But now Pelagia's curiosity was aroused—and her competitive streak. She wanted to figure out the mission objective before Leiting informed the mercenary force, just for the sheer swagger of it. Show that bossy digital mind that it couldn't outwit an orca. If nothing else, it would give her something to do.

Unbidden, the thought came to her that Daslakh would be a big help in this project, and she felt a profound sense of relief when she realized there was no way for that to happen. Some things were just too humiliating to contemplate.

Adya's inducer woke her before dawn. In the nearly empty house it was easy to avoid her mother, and her father was still asleep. He would miss his morning fishing, and Adya hoped he would be in better spirits when he got up.

She donned her own gills and suit in the Water Salon, and followed the mosaic-tiled channel out into the open sea. For the sake of efficiency she used an impeller. Her destination was some eight kilometers off and she did not want to be tired out when she got there.

As a child Adya had spent hours in the water almost every day. Kavita preferred playing games, and had a regular crew of dolphins and mers to play Yudham or team Kejum—graduating to organized jack and swordfish hunts when they got older. Sometimes Adya joined them, but more often she went off exploring on her own. She knew all the other sea farms and floating platforms within ten kilometers of the Elso mansion.

When she had done her research on the Polyarchists she had been a little startled to discover that one of their most outspoken advocates lived just an hour's impeller ride from her home. Pulu Visap's Polyarchist friend Janitha Velicham was a mer, the managing partner in a farm that sold live herring to cetaceans throughout Uranus orbital space. Since that farm and the Elso operation were so near one another, Adya was amused to realize that there was probably some biological crossover between the two. Her father and the hated Polyarchists were raising some of the same fish.

She made most of the journey just below the surface, so that she could remain linked to the Miranda infosphere. Her software agents had picked up Zee's trail: his name was mentioned in a Security Service report about the collapse of a noodle shop in Svarnam. Apparently it had happened while she was searching for Pulu Visap in Viranmar Plaza, a couple of hundred meters above. Had Zee been tracking her? She wasn't sure if she should be annoyed or flattered.

The reports about the incident troubled her a little. The Security people were reviewing the cause, and were contacting witnesses and reviewing feeds. They asked anyone with information to contact them, offering limited privacy protection.

That last was the troubling part. Adya knew that Security only offered privacy to witnesses if there was the possibility a crime had been committed. Had the shop been sabotaged somehow? Or had there been a fight? What was Zee up to?

She aimed her impeller down, angling toward the sea bottom complex of Samrudhi Natural Foods. Navigation was simple: The farm had seven tall towers shining solar-spectrum light into the water, all surrounded by clouds of plankton. Tiny fish and crustaceans fed on the plankton, and schools of herring and cuttlefish fed on them in turn. A squadron of bots circled the perimeter, emitting weak electric fields to chase away larger predators and keep the valuable organisms from straying. The system wasn't perfectly effective, especially when young dolphins and orcas deliberately snuck in for a snack.

The farm was bigger than Adya remembered. When she had come here as a child there had been only three light towers, not as tall as they were now. Judging by the warmth of the water they must have added more fusion power plants. Evidently Samrudhi Natural Foods weren't suffering any negative publicity.

Was that all this was? Adya wondered. Just an underhanded way of gaining market share? It seemed plausible—but a little disappointing. No sinister Polyarchist plots, no Sixty Families intrigues, just petty grubbing for gigajoules.

Adya could make out three power plants on the sea bottom, spaced around the central tower, and between them were three clusters of bubble habitats—one for living space and offices, one for processing, and one for storage. As she got into laser range the Samrudhi Natural Foods infospace appeared around her. She asked where she could find Janitha Velicham, and a sub-Baseline software agent appeared, manifesting as a cheerful bright turquoise cartoon fish wearing a chef's hood.

"If you want to place an order for Samrudhi Natural Foods products, or want to ask questions about our product lines, I can help!"

"I'd like to speak with Janitha Velicham in person."

"Can I tell her what you want to discuss? Maybe I can help!"

"This is a personal matter, and I'd prefer to have it in privacy."

After an almost imperceptible pause, the turquoise fish vanished, replaced by a glowing green trail in the water leading to the processing center, where the live fish were put into hibernation for shipment. Adya steered her impeller along the path, which led down under the main processing bubble and up into a moon pool. The air inside the bubble stank of fish and machinery.

With no more glowing trail to follow, Adya climbed out of the water and waited. After two minutes a trio of mers dropped down from one of the upper floors, accompanied by a freight handling bot. None of them had visible comm tags.

"You want privacy? You've got it. No feeds at all from this space," said the shortest of the three mers. "I'm Janitha. What do you want?"

Adya decided there was no reason to be subtle. "Why are you slandering my family?"

"Slandering the Elsos? Why would I do that?" The mer's skin showed a confused mix of orange and teal.

"Your friend Pulu Visap did. She's been selling stories about our farm foods, attacking our assets, driving us into debt." Adya kept her own skin icy blue, and spoke with as much Sixty Families formal hauteur as she could muster.

"Maybe Pulu's just telling truth?"

"I can document her deceptions."

"Well, that's between you and Pulu. I know nothing of this nonsense."

"Will she say the same? Especially to the Security Service, with full monitoring of brain and body?"

"If she says I hired her, that's the only lie I know about. Our foods are the finest quality, and most of our markets are beyond Miranda. I'd never hire an influencer to make insinuations about anyone, even an annoying aristocrat, and I'll say that with any monitors you can muster."

Adya's mind was racing. Janitha seemed sincere, showing an entirely plausible mix of anger and puzzlement. If she really knew nothing about the matter, then confronting her had been the wrong approach—and since Janitha was Adya's best chance to get in touch with Pulu Visap and uncover the truth, a sudden change in vectors was needed.

What would Zee do in a situation like this? He would tell the truth and ask nicely for help. "I'm sorry," said Adya, dropping into the vernacular and making herself a warm olive green. "I made a mistake. I thought these attacks on my family had something to do with the Polyarchist movement."

Janitha shifted redder. "Don't blame us for your bad business decisions! Polyarchism stands for economic freedom and fairness above all."

One of the other two mers spoke up, sounding much calmer, with skin all blue. "How much do you know about the Polyarchist movement, anyway?" he asked.

"I know it has always been against the oligarchy. That's why I suspected you might be behind this campaign of memetic attacks."

Janitha shifted from red-orange to violet. "That is *Revolutionary* Polyarchism, which was discredited years ago. We are *Rational* Polyarchists."

Her first impulse was to look up the difference, but instead Adya decided to keep Janitha talking. "Forgive my ignorance. Would you detail the distinction for me?"

"The *old* revolutionaries wanted to replace the Sixty Families oligarchy with a completely new system, with temporary administrators chosen by merit, or popular vote, or possibly by random selection. This would in turn lead to taxation, inexperienced leadership, corruption, and other perverse incentives."

"You sound just like my father," said Adya. "But if you aren't trying to destroy the oligarchy, what do you want?"

"We want *different* oligarchs!" said Janitha. "Restricting the purchase of ministries and seats on the Coordinating Committee to a hereditary subculture of self-proclaimed aristocrats is inefficient. Under Rational Polyarchy, ministries would be open to purchase by any individual—"

"Or partnership!" said the other mer who had spoken, shifting a little into the purple himself.

"Or *limited* partnership which can bid the most gigajoule credits. This would have a number of benefits: access to a greater pool of wealth, expanded opportunity for talented individuals, reduction in the number of seats on the Committee, improved—"

"Isn't that like the old Plutocratic movement?" asked Adya.

"Not at all! The Plutocrats wanted to allow *joint-stock companies* to bid on seats, and that's just a back door to majoritarian populism!" Janitha had turned an indignant red again just thinking about it.

"I see. That's very interesting," said Adya. "I'd love to learn more. Can you recommend some references?"

Adya wasn't just being polite. Her normal curiosity was aroused, and she was a little embarrassed to discover there was a political movement on her own world which she didn't understand completely. She had accepted her father's version of things too much.

"Our entire manifesto is in the infosphere," said Janitha.

"And in physical form, all over Miranda," added the male mer.

"The primary tenet of Rational Polyarchy is that the right to rule is based on merit, but contending subcultures define merit to benefit themselves. Therefore only an objective, quantifiable metric is valid. Like the oligarchs, we believe that the expense of maintaining society should be borne by those with the most resources. Synthesizing those two principles leads inevitably to the conclusion that anyone with enough wealth should be allowed to bid on ministries and take part in government. This in turn has six corollaries, as follows—"

"*Eight* corollaries," said the male. "We expanded the list at the last Party Conclave." While he spoke the cargo handling bot suddenly left, jumping to the wall and then trotting back up the way it and the mers had come. Though it was sub-Baseline, it was hard for Adya to avoid the suspicion it had heard all this before.

"Those two are still provisional. I'm trying to keep it simple," said Janitha.

"Again, I humbly pray you pardon for my tone earlier," said Adya. "These attacks have really harmed my family. Our position is very shaky, and all of us are desperate. Do you have any way to get in touch with Pulu Visap? I just want to find out who hired her, and why."

"She's staying dark for now," said Janitha. "Something scared her."

"It wasn't me. I just want to talk to her."

Janitha looked thoughtful, her skin fading from reddish purple to a brownish blue. "I have a way to contact her. I'll set up a meeting. Or try to—no guarantees, you understand. And if anything happens to her, I'll know."

"You have my word as a woman of the proud and patrician house of Elso that I intend no injury to anyone," said Adya.

"You actually believe that stuff, don't you? All right. I'll contact you once I hear from Pulu. Now, if you'll excuse us, we have to put our fish to bed."

CHAPTER NINE

Zee didn't want to interrupt Adya's father during his morning swim, so he waited until almost midday before contacting him. He'd spent the night in a cheap all-purpose room in the bowels of the floating Svarnam arcology. Zee left as soon as he woke, and wandered about, eating a printed breakfast, until he found a quiet spot in a public garden, where mist fountains played on chunks of natural stone coated with colonies of carefully created algae and fungus in a rainbow of colors. Zee seated himself on a bench and stared at nothing as he contacted Achan Elso. Daslakh amused itself by studying the algae.

"He's not taking contacts," said Zee a moment later.

"Why do humans bother with communication implants if they don't want to communicate?"

"Sometimes it's distracting."

"Just set up a sub-persona to deal with calls. I know—you can't. It must be awful, being an emergent property of a bunch of neurons and glial cells. I don't know how you stand it."

"I've got a message from the Security Service."

"Anything interesting?"

"They found the bot. After it shot at me it apparently crawled into a storage locker and pointed its laser at its main processor."

"Anything left to identify?"

"Only the mechanical parts. The bot and the laser were both printed recently, pirate editions of commercial templates. That's about it."

"Very slick."

"Oh, and they warned me not to travel or see anyone until the matter is resolved."

"Well, *that* was certainly a waste of electrons."

Zee paused. "Wait, he's getting back to me. Adya's father."

Without waiting for an invitation, Daslakh eavesdropped on the comm. Achan Elso's face appeared in Zee's vision, with no visible backdrop. It looked like a genuine image, though—Adya's father was puffy and unkempt, as if he had just gotten up.

"Well, what is it, young man? If you're trying to find Adya I can't help you. She's not at home."

"No, I wanted to ask you something. I'm trying to learn about Miranda government and politics, and I figured you're an expert."

Nicely done, thought Daslakh. Achan's expression mellowed and his skin shifted from a pale orange to a more olive tone.

"Well, some of my colleagues might dispute my expertise, but at least I have plenty of experience. Ask away."

"Do you know anything about an offworlder named Qi Tian?"

Achan scowled and turned maroon. *"I know little about him, but more than I would like about what he has done. He is a menace! A barbarian! He came to Miranda about a standard year ago and since then has been sowing corruption and division on the Coordinating Committee."*

"How?"

"He has bottomless wells of wealth, apparently, and this makes him very appealing to the sort of Committee members who are willing to sacrifice honor and heritage for a profit. Jothi Rayador—who leads the ruling coalition—has been positively pandering to Qi Tian."

"I guess it's good that someone like you can stand up to him," said Zee.

Achan smiled a little at that, but then he seemed to sag and turned a deep blue. *"I wish I was. He wishes to wreck the Cryoglyphs, and the craven cowards on the Committee support his scheme. The only thing I have accomplished by my opposition is to cut myself off from the only people who could help my family."*

"You seem really concerned about them. The Cryoglyphs, I mean."

"They are part of our past. The only older features are those carved by blind natural forces and impacts. Men made marks on Miranda, and now lesser men wish to erase them." Achan smiled sadly. *"My only consolation is that the coalition will not survive this crime. My opposition to Qi Tian's schemes means Rayador and the rest of those wretches refuse to help save the Elso fortune. I will have to resign my seats when I can no longer fund those departments. As soon as they convene the Committee to open bids for a replacement, the opposition can take over control of policy. Without my seats, the coalition will lose its majority. I wish I could see Jothi's face when he realizes it."*

"Do you know how I could find out more about this Qi Tian? Maybe learn who's backing him?"

"Why are you so interested in that scoundrel?"

Daslakh watched Zee carefully, both in physical space and via his biomonitor, ready to interfere with the comm link if he seemed about to say something foolish.

"It's—I guess you'd say it's confidential."

"Hm. So you are at least capable of discretion, when you choose. I wasn't sure. Very well, scheme away. I won't pry. Give me a little time to think about who might be able to tell you more." Achan rubbed his eyes, and then his color brightened a bit. *"How about this? Meet me at Surface Access 293-15 South. An hour from now—no, make it an hour and a half. I will give you some suggestions and you can see the Cryoglyphs for yourself."*

"Sure!" said Zee.

Achan gave a satisfied-looking nod, and broke the link.

"I'll bet you half a ton of chameleon particles he's going to bury your body in a crevasse," said Daslakh.

"I don't think he'd do anything like that. Maybe challenge me to a duel. I could see that."

"Duels are for social equals. *You're* just an offworld prole. He could have one of the family bots give you a thrashing."

"Adya wouldn't—" Zee stopped. "I don't know any more. I don't think she'd go along with that, but if it's her family, who knows?"

"I do," said Daslakh. "She wouldn't. Stop being a self-pitying fool."

Zee got to Surface Access 293-15 South fifteen minutes before he was to meet Adya's father. Achan himself was ten minutes late, so Zee had a lot of time to hang around the little museum in the vestibule between the lift and the airlock. Both doors were built to handle full-sized vehicles, and the vestibule included parking space, but one slot had been partitioned off and housed images of the Cryoglyphs and some of the notional "artifacts" recovered nearby. Virtual tags provided helpful information and linked to the extensive corpus of scientific papers, pop-science instructionals, and borderline-crackpot material about the Cryoglyphs and their history.

"Those aren't artifacts, those are trash," said Daslakh, looking at a case displaying printed replicas of some crumpled scraps of ancient plastic film. A virtual tag noted that the originals were in the Mohan-Elso Center, carefully preserved in a nonreactive neon atmosphere.

"Archaeologists learn a lot from trash."

"Sure. But it's kind of funny to see humans venerate trash simply because it's very old. And it's even funnier to see them venerating copies of trash."

"We like to feel a connection to the past. It helps us feel like we belong."

"It would be trivial to demonstrate that humanity's hardwired need for approval and fear of social isolation have caused more irrational and destructive behavior than anything else. At least your sexual compulsions keep the species going."

"It's good to have friends," said Zee. "I guess you could say there's a practical benefit to being social, but we just like it."

"Evolution uses both the carrot and the stick."

Zee read the physical text signs for a while, and Daslakh absorbed all the linked data. After filtering out the obvious falsehoods and poppycock, the actual lore about the Cryoglyphs could be summarized quite simply. "These marks were made by somebody, at least five thousand standard years ago and maybe long before that. Nobody knows what they mean or why they were made."

Achan Elso emerged from the lift, wearing a smart-matter outfit carefully shaped to look like an ancient surface excursion suit. "Ah, good! You've had the chance to see our museum. If you like, I can take you to observe the original artifacts when we're done outside."

"I thought the Mohan-Elso Center was closed," said Daslakh.

"Closed?" Achan looked into the middle distance for a second, and got a little orange. "What kind of idiocy is Kav's husband playing at? I shall have to speak to him." He gave an irritated-sounding sniff and led the way to the airlock.

The airlock structure was surrounded by a pad of level ice, but beyond that the wild landscape looked nearly untouched by any human or mech. To the west a group of rounded hills, or maybe small mountains, were silhouetted against the sky, which was dusted with thousands of tiny shining specks, some of the millions of habs in Uranus orbital space. In the northeast the jagged rim of a crater looked like teeth.

"This way," said Achan. He followed a walkway of sculpted carbon foam, made to blend in with the natural ice and snow of the surface. Zee followed, with Daslakh clutching the back of his hood.

The path led across a flat section of surface which sloped gently upward, until they came to the edge of a deep channel, nearly straight, running roughly north-south. The sides were steep and the whole thing was several hundred meters deep. The trail here featured a handrail, but Achan disregarded it, taking ten-meter steps down. He was careful to stay on the trail surface, though.

At the bottom the trail turned to follow the floor of the channel for half a kilometer, until it reached a jagged fissure. Evidently some great fault or crack crossed the channel here, as the sides were displaced by a few meters and on the east side a gap opened three meters wide, extending deep into the icy slope. The walkway led into it.

A good place to hide a body, said Daslakh privately to Zee.

Zee was too busy admiring the view to respond. It certainly was scenic. On the western side of the channel the snow shone blue-white in the light of the distant Sun, while overhead the blue half-circle of Uranus dominated the sky against a dusty orange background. The east side of the channel was dark, faintly green in the light of Uranus.

They followed Achan into the dark gap. He turned on his suit lamps and pointed up. Four meters above the trail surface the lights caught some markings in the ice at an oblique angle, making shadows that showed them very clearly.

Daslakh could see a dozen markings in all, cut four or five centimeters deep into the ice, likely with some kind of metal pick or axe. They were definitely symbols, with vertical and horizontal strokes, but Daslakh couldn't recognize any alphabet or ideograms. Four of them were the same, and another pair looked like duplicates, but the rest were all different. All twelve of them were about thirty centimeters high, aligned more or less horizontally, spaced evenly.

Definitely not natural. Someone, mech or bio, had come to this remote place and put a fair amount of work into carving those twelve marks into the ice. A message? A record? A work of art? A prank?

Achan stood looking up at them. Through the clear bubble of his old-style helmet his skin was a calm pale blue-green. Daslakh could see his heart rate was lower than at any time since they had first met him.

Zee peered up at the marks, tilting his head this way and that, concentrating as if he could discover their meaning even after millennia of failure by higher-level minds. After a couple of minutes he gave up and looked around the rift, peeking over the edge of the walkway at the depth of the crevice.

Achan finally noticed Zee's restlessness. "Bots have searched every square millimeter of the surface countless times. There are no other markings. In fact, it's not even clear how they were cut, as this walkway is only a couple of centuries old."

"Nobody knows what they say?"

"Terabytes of theories have been put forth. Third- and fourth-level intellects have attempted to decipher the markings. The problem is that the string is so short. I have seen hundreds of words or phrases which might be the proper translation. Unfortunately humans have been creating languages and writing systems for ten thousand years, and mechs have been doing the same for almost as long and much faster."

"What do you think they are?"

"I?" Achan turned to look back up at the Cryoglyphs again. "I think they were made to mystify. Some early explorer wanted to create a conundrum. An elegant, eternal enigma! That villain Qi Tian wants to acquire this whole area—as if Miranda doesn't have millions of hectares of undeveloped surface without historic relics he could use."

"What's he doing here, anyway?"

"I wish I knew. He has a lot of wealth, or at least he spends a lot. The source is unknown. Somewhere offworld, I know that. My spies— when I could afford spies—said he was drawing on a bank based at Oterma, but of course one could set up an account there without ever even visiting the place."

"Oterma banks are pretty hard-nosed," said Daslakh. "They don't usually give lines of credit to shady characters."

"True," said Achan. "Whoever he is, his money is real. Though not as great in quantity as when he arrived here. Through a dummy company he invested in the Kiran family's isotope-separation venture, and Lila Kiran in turn introduced him to Jothi Rayador—she and Jothi have been lovers for decades. I know Qi Tian also put some gigajoules into the Nagaram family resort development. Again, through a cutout. He keeps his involvement quiet."

"Investments can come and go," Daslakh pointed out. "He could cash out and leave tomorrow."

"I wish he would. Then maybe the coalition leaders would come to their senses."

"Has he bought the surface here yet?" asked Zee.

"No, that will require the approval of the Committee. And of course the vote has been scheduled for *after* I must surrender my seats."

"Hang on," said Daslakh. "You said that might change the balance in the Committee. If you lose your seats, will Qi Tian still be able to get what he wants?"

"I'm not sure. The minority faction don't care about the Cryoglyphs, either—otherwise I would simply join their coalition instead, and snap my fingers at Jothi Rayador! But, alas, that is not to be. I know Qi Tian has put some cash to use among them, as well. He bought some of the Kadam family's short-term notes and has deferred collecting the interest, which I'm sure they are grateful for. They are key members of the other voting bloc, so when our coalition loses power, Qi Tian will still have friends on the Committee."

"It sounds like everybody wins but you," said Zee.

"Myself and Miranda! Our world will lose this legacy." Achan gestured at the Cryoglyphs overhead, and turned to regard them for a while.

"*We need more,*" said Daslakh to Zee over a private link. "*Dai Chichi could find out all this stuff without leaving his office.*"

"Um, do you know if there's anyone who turned him down? Qi Tian, I mean? Is there anybody he tried to influence but failed?"

"Achan Elso, for one. And I believe he approached Nikhil Urukku and offered a loan on very favorable terms. Nikhil was having some cash-flow problems of his own right then and I'm sure it was terribly tempting. Nevertheless, he declined—it turned out the Urukku family had emergency reserves nobody knew about. Literal stockpiles of uranium tucked away in caches on the sea bottom. That got Nikhil through his own financial difficulties, and Qi Tian never got a grip on him. If Urukku wasn't such a miserable miser I would ask him to help, but I know what his answer would be."

After a minute he faced Zee again. "I have a private purpose in bringing you here. In this rift we are safe from any spies, even my own family. We can speak plainly, you and I."

"Okay. What do you want to talk about?"

"I want to make sure you understand something. Our family fortune is gone. In just a few weeks we will lose all our holdings— investments, properties, licenses, the house, the farm, everything."

"I know," said Zee. "I'm trying to help with that."

"The Oort payload is a mirage. I asked Vasi this morning, just to be sure, and it is certain that the cargo is nothing more than common trade goods: original artworks and crafts, possibly historical artifacts. No vast treasure—not nearly enough to reduce our debts."

"I want to get it back for Adya."

"You will gain nothing for your trouble."

"That doesn't matter."

"Doesn't it? I am trying to be as clear as I can: Adya has *nothing*, do you understand? No wealth, and soon she will have no more high status, either. There is nothing to keep you here. Leave her now."

"She's the only one who can tell me that," said Zee. "I don't care about her money or anything else."

"Then what *do* you want?"

"Adya. That's all. I love her."

Achan regarded him for a moment. "But can you provide for her? She has never known want, or hardship. She is always absorbed in abstractions. Kavita is much more practical."

"I'm sure the two of us can get by."

"She is not some—" Achan stopped himself. "She is not used to drudgery. And as an Elso she deserves better. You may be sincere, but you are not rich and I do not think you will get rich anytime soon. How long will she remain happy in poverty?"

"Adya's tougher than you think she is. And even if *I* can't make us rich, *she's* smart enough to do well at anything she wants to do."

"I think I know my own daughters better than anyone else, thank you," said Achan. "Adya isn't even thirty standard years yet. Hardly more than a child!"

Zee just shook his head. "I wish you could see her when she's out on her own. She's smart and confident and brave, and—and wonderful."

Achan smiled a little. "I will say this: You are sincere. I am sure of it. For good or ill, you do love her. So it is for that reason alone that I beseech you, Zee: leave her. With you gone she can make a marriage which at least will keep her in comfort, even if the family fortune is forfeit."

"The only way I'm going to leave her is if she tells me herself. And even if she does, I'll try to change her mind before I go anywhere."

"What a stubborn fellow you are! I suppose like calls to like. You should be glad my reverence for the traditions of the Sixty Families doesn't extend to assassination. Right now you have me wishing I had some bravos or killbots at my disposal. I've said all I wish to say to you. I hope you see the wisdom of my words. And now I take my leave."

He pushed a little rudely past Zee, and once free of the ice cleft he bounded toward the airlock structure.

Zee shook his head and sighed inside his sealed suit. "What a mess."

"I thought it went rather well," said Daslakh, speaking directly into the back of Zee's head, which gave its voice a buzzy quality.

"Are you serious? He wants to kill me!"

"He told you specifically that he won't. Or can't, anyway. I'd file all the rest under empty rhetoric. Meanwhile he gave us some useful intel. With luck that will satisfy Dai Chichi."

"I wonder what this Qi Tian guy's really up to."

"Well, whatever his other purposes might be, he's certainly done a superb job of breaking up the ruling coalition on the Miranda Coordinating Committee. I expect there's a lot of people who think that's a pretty good goal in itself."

"Politics here is so complicated. Back in Raba we just let the hab make all the decisions itself."

"Yes," said Daslakh flatly. "It's a real sweetheart."

"Are you done here?"

"I saw as much of those ice divots as I needed to within the first two seconds."

Zee left the crevice, moving more carefully than Adya's father had. Neither man nor mech said anything until they were just a few meters from the airlock.

"So when are you going to see Adya again?" Daslakh asked innocently.

Zee didn't answer. The airlock slid open and he stepped inside.

"This afternoon, maybe?" Daslakh continued.

"I don't want to put her in danger," Zee mumbled.

"'Adya's tougher than you think she is.'" Daslakh replied, playing back Zee's own voice. "'She's smart and confident and brave, and—and wonderful.'"

"Stop it."

"I'm not the one who's been sleeping in guest boats and rented pods because his feelings got bruised."

"She—" Zee stopped.

Daslakh played another audio snippet. "'The only way I'm going to leave her is if she tells me herself,'" said Zee's voice, slightly muffled by his suit cowl and his hair.

"You really are a jerk sometimes."

"I accept that," said Daslakh. "Now: I'll stop being a jerk—for the moment, anyway—if you ping Adya right now and tell her you're all right, tell her you love her, and tell her you'll see her soon."

Zee's suit relaxed around him and the face mask retracted as the inner door of the airlock slid open. He took a breath and let it out through his nose in a cross between a sigh and a snort. "Okay," he said aloud. "Now stop nagging me about it."

"Humans created digital intelligence to do jobs they couldn't manage on their own. Apparently this is one of them," said Daslakh. It was silent after that, and didn't even listen in on Zee's comm as he contacted Adya.

While Zee was occupied with a fond reunion with Adya, Daslakh decided to do a little direct information gathering about the mysterious Qi Tian. Adya's father had told the two of them a lot, but even Zee would probably admit that Achan's perspective on this issue was highly subjective. Daslakh wanted data, as unmediated as possible.

Determining Qi Tian's physical location was surprisingly hard. His name wasn't in any directories, and apparently he had invoked privacy the moment he set foot on Miranda's surface.

Daslakh reviewed the conversation with Adya's father and looked for any record of the business deals he had mentioned Qi Tian being involved in. That gave Daslakh the names of some of the shell companies the man of mystery used to hide his participation. A couple of milliseconds' work gave Daslakh what it was looking for: One of the front companies was renting a vacation house.

Specifically, the business called General Investments had rented a luxury eyrie, suspended from the icy roof of Miranda's ocean, just below the light panels, with a private bubble tube and a spectacular view of the capital city Ksetram. If Qi Tian was anywhere, he'd be there.

It took Daslakh twenty minutes to reach the eyrie, using bubble tubes and freight conveyors.

In the rental ads, the place boasted high security, but Daslakh found that laughably overstated. Bubble cars required "authorization" to use the private tube, but there was nothing to stop a small mech from simply strolling along the inside of the tube to the house entrance. The eyrie's internal network demanded a security code for both physical and data access, but after a few minutes of sitting still and eavesdropping on emissions Daslakh determined that the bots inside the house had nothing but manufacturer-installed code keys.

Daslakh found a cleaning bot working its way along the windows and reached into its simple little brain. It interrogated the bot thoroughly and then copied its emission profile, impersonating it. The sub-Baseline mind of the eyrie recognized Daslakh as one of its own bots and opened the door to let it in, without worrying about how it had gotten out. Daslakh crept inside, clinging to the ceiling and adjusting its color to match.

Qi Tian's *pied-à-ciel* was certainly roomy. The eyrie boasted three levels, each twenty meters across with four-meter ceilings. The top level held a big fancy entrance hall and service spaces—matter printers ranging from micro down to femto scale, waste dismantlers, feedstock for the printers, heat management, charging stations for the bots, and a startlingly large refrigerator for natural food. Daslakh listened and tasted the air. The entryway was full of human traces—lingering molecules in the air, shed hair and skin cells on the floor, all the inevitable casualties of a biological fighting entropy. Most of them were from the same person, presumably Qi Tian.

Daslakh tasted some of the skin cells and did a quick analysis of the DNA. Male human, legacy type; all the usual gene mods to prevent disease, bone degeneration in microgravity, and aging. The extrapolated phenotype matched known images of Qi Tian. A few of the cells held DNA from other people, all Mirandans, and all at least fourth cousins of Adya's father.

In the center of the floor a spiral staircase with diamondoid steps led down to the second level. Daslakh crept down. According to the house network, this floor was all bedrooms—four large rooms and a double-sized master suite. More biotraces on this floor, all concentrated around the stairs and the big bedroom. Daslakh couldn't hear any sound of breathing or movement on this level, so it crept over to the master bedroom for a good snoop.

The room took up a bit less than a third of the whole level, and currently featured a party bed covered in pseudobiological fur, a soaking tub big enough for four legacy humans, some handsome chairs, a four-person dining table with its own food printer, a wardrobe, and a couple of soothing sculptures. Flower and fruit vines covered the walls, and heavy cloth drapes covered the windows.

All very posh—but also very generic: the furniture was smart matter configured to expensive templates, with proprietary logos to make sure visitors knew how expensive they were. Even the plants displayed their designer labels. Daslakh didn't see any of the unique handmade items or genuine natural materials that made the Elso house so impressive.

Daslakh asked the wardrobe what it contained. Not much: two sets of programmable clothing, a smart-matter travel suit, and a printed pair of loose pants suitable for casual entertaining. As soon as Daslakh spoke to the wardrobe, the travel suit came online, revealing a mind that was at least near-Baseline and possibly higher.

It probed the mind of the "simple cleaning bot" Daslakh was still impersonating, and Daslakh watched the interplay between the suit mind and the shell persona of the bot with great interest. The suit cut through the bot's security with brutal efficiency, copied up its entire memory, and planted several instructions, cunningly disguised. The commands were all security related: report any contact from anything other than the house mind, and give the travel suit a daily memory download. There was also a back door which would allow the suit to take control of the bot remotely, cunningly hidden so that it would survive any ordinary updates and purges. In effect, the suit was recruiting the "bot" as an agent-in-place inside the eyrie.

Daslakh scuttled out of the room again, admiring the sophistication of the suit's intrusion and subversion. It was almost as good as Daslakh's own work.

Almost. It purged and reloaded the entire bot simulation.

The bottom level of the eyrie was for dining and lounging, with a big reconfigurable room surrounded by a wide gallery looking out over the city and the ocean below. A pool offset from the center of the room extended down through the floor into a diamond hemisphere.

The central stair spiraled down to the lower level, and Daslakh crept along the underside. The steps themselves were clear diamondoid, which meant it couldn't change color to match them, so Daslakh made its outer carapace a neutral gray midway between the color of the floor and the sky outside. It walked silently and very slowly, moving just one leg at a time. It put all its senses on maximum sensitivity. On the third step down it paused.

All the windows on the lower floor were retracted, leaving the room open to the air. Qi Tian sat in a lounge chair on the gallery, his back to the main room, with a tall drink and a plate of thattai on a little table in easy reach. He had a board propped up in his lap with a sheet of paper on it, and was writing on the paper with an ink brush, in archaic Xiyu characters. Daslakh zoomed in on the page and read what Qi Tian had written.

Icy sky, bright sea.
Flat calm covers the deep wave.
When will peacocks cry?

Not bad, thought Daslakh, though the peacocks seemed a bit out of place.

It crept closer. When it got within six meters of the lounge chair it froze. At that distance it could pick up faint emissions from Qi Tian's comm implant. It risked a single coded pulse, and the response made it head for the stairs as fast as it dared. The man in the chair didn't stir.

Daslakh was just at the top of the stairs when it felt a signal pulse from the travel suit, and to its horror saw the suit standing in the hall on the second level, colored neutral gray so that it looked like a ghost out for a stroll. It pinged Daslakh again—or rather pinged the back-door software it had installed in the "simple cleaning bot," demanding to know what Daslakh was doing prowling around the living room when the boss had given orders that he wasn't to be disturbed.

To make things worse, Daslakh also detected a surge of data between the suit in front of it and the man downstairs. The jig was definitely up.

Well, no point in lingering, or in trying to be inconspicuous. Daslakh used its cleaning bot persona to inform the house system that there were multiple fires, intruders, water leaks, environmental contamination, medical emergencies, and structural failures happening at once. Audible alarms began to sound and projected images appeared directing residents to safety. All the service bots began scuttling about, searching for the danger spots. Daslakh joined them, doubling back down the stairs and sprinting across the ceiling of the lower level toward the nearest open window.

Qi Tian got out of his chair with superhuman speed, and suddenly had a weapon in his hand. The travel suit cartwheeled down the stairs and wrapped itself around him, taking on a mirrored surface.

Daslakh took advantage of that momentary delay to hurl itself out of the window. The next two minutes were the closest thing to a human nightmare Daslakh had ever experienced: falling helplessly but with infuriating slowness, with no way to hide, waiting for Qi Tian to shoot at him and wondering whether it would be a laser, a needle gun, or a micromissile.

It used its limbs to assume a vaguely aerodynamic shape and steer toward the city of Ksetram below, as it didn't relish the idea of falling into deep water with no Zee handy.

The shot from above never came, and Daslakh landed with a solid thump on the roof of a building shaped like a dodecahedron. It moved fast, getting under cover, getting hidden, and getting as far away as quickly as it could. It didn't stop running until it was safely in a bubble shooting through the tube across the sea bottom.

It knew who Qi Tian was, and now it was very worried.

***

Pelagia and Repun were the last two space combat units left. Ground defenses on the moon they were preparing to assault had accounted for all the others, so it was up to the two orca cyberships to find and destroy the remaining threats on the surface before the landing craft got in range.

During the initial attack the other ships in the fleet had spotted all the lasers and hit them with missiles—armored kinetic penetrators optimized for laser killing. But the enemy still had a pair of hypervelocity railguns hidden underground. The guns were cooled to eliminate any thermal signature, so there was no easy way to spot where they were shooting from. With enough velocity a single thirty-millimeter slug could mission-kill a spaceship, and unless you were looking right at the launch point it was hard to tell exactly which three-centimeter patch of surface was the muzzle of a hidden battery.

No sense in hanging around out in space like a pair of practice targets. The two of them accelerated at max thrust toward the ground, jittering and swerving to mess up targeting, and throwing out electronic countermeasures to interfere with any sensors. Repun took a grazing hit which peeled away all the armor on her left flank, and another slug took a meter-wide bite out of Pelagia's folded right wing, but that left both orcas with eyes, weapons, and drives intact.

The two split up, rotating to thrust laterally as they fell toward the icy surface below. Repun tipped her nose up and burned hard, vectoring into a path which would just miss the limb of the moon, while Pelagia flipped completely over and waited until the last instant before a braking burn to set down on the surface.

Hidden by the horizon, Repun launched her two remaining combat drones and swung into an orbit just meters above the mean surface datum. She kept her drive lit, dodging mountains and buildings as she shot across the surface. The drones were there for point defense and electromagnetic spoofing, radiating extra heat to look like a full-sized cybership.

Pelagia dropped to the surface on her wheels, then warmed up her own drive and taxied across the ice at a lunatic thirty meters per second. The local gravity was feeble, just two percent of Earth standard, so she could hop over obstacles with her maneuvering thrusters.

One of Repun's defending drones flew apart in a spray of fragments.
"*SPOTTED!*" she called over the comm channel, sending precise coordinates for the defending railgun.

"*I'll be in position in thirty seconds,*" said Pelagia.

Repun's orbit took her beyond the horizon, safe from the gun, just as Pelagia belly-flopped onto the ice and skidded to a stop atop a hill with a line of sight on the gun emplacement Repun had identified. She had two surface-strike missiles left, and lobbed one at the coordinates Repun had given her. The underground gun couldn't depress enough to stop her flat-trajectory shot. The warhead—ten kilos of nitrogen buckyballs jacketed with iron-silicon composite—blew a satisfying crater, exposing the spherical cavity hiding the gun and showering the inside with shrapnel.

That left just one gun. Pelagia did a little inductive reasoning based on the location of the one she had just blown up and another weapon emplacement which one of the mech ships had taken out with a lucky toss of a nickel-iron chunk during the space battle. Logic suggested the third gun would complete an equilateral triangle around the spaceport. Pelagia informed Repun and then set out across the surface on a twenty-kilometer race.

Repun must have done some high-thrust maneuvering once she was below the horizon, because she reappeared from the south just six minutes later, moving much faster than orbital speed, passing right over the location Pelagia had flagged.

She was almost in position, and at first couldn't figure out what Repun was doing. When the gun opened up on the other ship Pelagia realized it was a sacrifice play. A pair of slugs tore Repun apart, but the heavily armored pod holding her whale brain ejected in time.

Pelagia moved up to a hilltop to fire on the last railgun—but something was wrong. She wasn't moving. External images showed scores of combat bots erupting from under the ice. Titanium tentacles grabbed and tore, wrecking her landing wheel assemblies. Something managed to get inside the nose wheel bay and then Pelagia's entire front end flew to bits. Her senses went dark.

They cut in again, displaying the home screen of the training program. Leiting's white-haired avatar floated in Pelagia's visual field. "Overall assessment: ninety-two percent success. Clever use of surface terrain to sneak up on the target," it said. "But if you are attacking a populated moon you have to assume the enemy has its own ground units."

"I know you're going to tell me that you can't tell me, but *please* tell me the real target won't have defenses this brutal. This is the third time we've done this exercise and they've managed a clean sweep of space assets every time."

"Leiting believes one should train harder than one fights. Also, these scenarios serve a dual purpose: You can practice operations while Leiting observes and evaluates you."

"Maybe the mech ships with external backups won't mind getting fried, but I've got a real brain in here and I don't want it getting boiled, scrambled, or splattered when we go into action. I've designated an heir, by the way—if you do manage to get me killed you still have to pay my salary to the Saturn Rescue Alliance."

"Leiting is not attempting to avoid paying any personnel. Current casualty estimates for the operation are less than one percent."

"Those local assets we're not supposed to think about? Oops, I just thought about them."

"Discussion of topics for which you do not have authorization is forbidden by contract."

"But I'm talking to you, and you *do* have authorization, so it's okay."

"Discussion of topics for which you do not have authorization is forbidden by contract," said Leiting, repeating itself precisely, right down to the waveforms.

"Fine, fine," said Pelagia. "Can we do the debrief later? Repun and I have to rest our fragile mammalian brains."

"Leiting will resume the discussion in twenty-three minutes." Leiting's avatar vanished.

"I think I know why Leiting is so fanatical about not telling us what the target is. It's afraid we'd all switch sides just for the chance of shooting at it," said Pelagia.

"Operational security matters," said Repun. "You know that."

"I do know that. Which means I'm not going to leak anything, and I'm kind of insulted at being treated like I can't be trusted."

"You could always resign."

"Yeah, forfeit all my pay and stay parked here until after the first phase of the operation's done. That could be weeks with me losing a gigajoule every hour for docking and consumables. No, thank you. I'm going offline now. I'll see you in twenty-one minutes."

Pelagia shut off all outside access and prepared for a few minutes of sleep. Before she started the inducer she thought about the mission some more.

Leiting had run her through twenty-six attack simulations so far. Three of those had been straight space battle scenarios, eight had involved hab assaults . . . and the other fifteen had been attacks on moons. Unless this all was a massive mindfuck by Leiting (which was not impossible), the assault target was probably a moon.

In the sims the target moon had been the fictional Uranian moon "Calpurnia," which was a dead ringer for Saturn's moon Tethys. There was no way that Leiting's mercenary force was actually going to the Saturnian system—the orbital positions were bad and getting worse. So Calpurnia was standing in for one of Uranus's remaining natural moons. But which one?

Not Titania, that was for sure. The hierarchy of digital minds and augmented biologicals which ran the Titania Consolidated Technocracy might be isolationist and weird, but they had a defense force which was ten thousand times the size of Leiting's mercenary unit, armed with top-tier weapons. Even a limited-objective raid would be simply suicidal. Given that the gorillas seemed to expect a long occupation, Titania was out of the question.

Oberon also seemed very unlikely to be the target. It wasn't quite as heavily populated as Titania, but the Oberon Free State's citizen militia was immense—theoretically the entire population. Pacifying a few billion heavily armed and fanatical minarchists in a labyrinth of tunnels and natural caves below the surface would take more than a team of gorillas, no matter how many bots they brought along. Plus, Pelagia reflected, there weren't many cetaceans on Oberon, which made Leiting's dolphin Civil Affairs team redundant.

That left the three smaller moons—Ariel, Umbriel, and Miranda. Pelagia was inclined to rule out Umbriel for a couple of reasons. The sims were all about attacking a moon with limited surface facilities, where the population were all below the crust. That fit well with Ariel and Miranda, but Umbriel's surface was a dense ecumenopolis, with almost no primordial terrain left. The other reason was that Umbriel didn't have much water habitat. No dolphins there.

Pelagia suddenly didn't feel like napping. Adya, Zee, and that annoying little contraption Daslakh were still on Miranda, and now it appeared there was at least a fifty percent chance that was the target of the upcoming mercenary operation. The idea of attacking a moon where her friends (and Daslakh) were staying didn't sit well with Pelagia. Finding out Leiting's target wasn't just an intellectual puzzle for her anymore.

Leiting's obsession with security meant there wasn't any point in trying to find out anything by talking to other members of the mercenary force. They were all just as ignorant as Pelagia herself. And it wasn't really feasible for a biological mind to try anything shady in the data networks.

Time for some clever use of terrain. Leiting's mercenary force were all based in and around Multipurpose Bay 453 North, but that was just a miniscule part of the enormous Taishi hab complex. Surely someone, somewhere in Taishi had a clue about the mercenary fleet's destination. All Pelagia had to do was find that person and get them to talk. There were only seventy million Baseline or higher beings in Taishi—how hard could it be?

So while her biological brain linked back up with Leiting for the post-sim debriefing, Pelagia detached one of her maintenance drones and sent it crawling along the massive bundle of structural framework and transport tubes which Multipurpose Bay 453 North was attached to. The whole giant beam formed one edge of the fifty-kilometer-wide hexagon that was Taishi habitat.

Each point of the hexagon was the axis of a spinning hab cylinder. The closest was nine kilometers away, so Pelagia's drone began the long walk along a maintenance catwalk. Over the centuries the surface of the beam structure had gained an accretion of little private habs, workshops, storage bins and tanks, and random machinery.

Pelagia bypassed all of that. A prudent commander—and Leiting was prudent to the point of obsession—would have made a sweep through the area around the base of operations, making sure no spies were hidden among the squatters and recluses. There might even be sensors to watch for suspicious activity.

Along the way her drone placed some private comm repeaters in inconspicuous places, so that Pelagia could link up without going through the network under Leiting's control at Multipurpose Bay 453

North. She had no illusions about her ability to beat a digital mind at encryption, and the moment Leiting realized Pelagia was trying to find out where the force was headed, there would be chum in the water for sure.

A mercenary's biggest asset was her reputation. Betraying the mission would wreck Pelagia's rep more effectively than a barrage of railgun slugs. Well, she'd never been cautious before—why start now?

CHAPTER TEN

Adya was happily snuggled up with Zee, her head on his chest, feeling him gently breathing. He was completely asleep, but she was just relaxed and content.

However, one can stay that way only so long. After about five minutes she activated her comm implant again and checked for messages. There was one, from Janitha Velicham: "Pulu's ready to meet you this afternoon. Be at Midayi at three, alone. Oh, and I'm not gonna play go-between for you two anymore."

It was already half past two. Adya slowly lifted her head from Zee's chest and disengaged herself from him without disturbing his sleep. She didn't have time to print out anything special so she just pulled on the same set of dark blue tights she'd been wearing when he contacted her just before lunch.

She crept out of the room, making sure the door shut quietly, then vaulted down to the courtyard below and sprinted for the bubble tube, signaling ahead to call one for herself. It popped up just as she reached the tube, so Adya tumbled in and told it to take her to Viranmar Plaza in Svarnam, as quickly as possible. As it slid down the tube to the sea bottom she did remember to leave a message for Zee, promising to return as soon as she could.

The bubble seemed to travel with maddening slowness, but it did get her to the plaza at four minutes to three. She had just enough time to bound over to Midayi and request a private tea room. "I'm expecting a guest," she said to the tea master, a little breathlessly. "We'll ask for tea when we're ready."

The teishu nodded politely and led Adya to a small room paneled with real wood, with handmade rugs on the floor. The side opposite the door opened into a pocket garden where moss grew thick on natural stones.

Adya thanked the teishu and seated herself. She stared at the little garden and made herself relax. Some of her muscles were sore, and that reminded her of her afternoon with Zee, and she smiled a little to herself.

At a couple of minutes after three the door slid open and Pulu Visap came in. She looked terrible, Adya thought. Part of it was her outfit—an elaborate silver-mesh bodysuit with crystals wherever the fibers crossed, and virtual tags to let everyone who saw Pulu know that it was a limited-edition design by Cassytha. Whoever *that* was. On someone like Kavita, or even Entum, the flashiness of the outfit would have looked playful and fun. But Pulu was small, worried, almost furtive. The showy garment only emphasized that.

Her long hair braid was gone—she had shaved her scalp in the default style for Miranda. The sight made Adya feel sorry for her. Pulu had obviously put a lot of work into having meter-long hair, and cutting it off wasn't the kind of decision one made easily.

When the door slid shut behind her, Pulu remained standing, keeping her eyes on Adya.

"Shall I ask the teishu to provide a pot?" asked Adya.

Pulu only shook her head. "You're Kavita's sister, right?" she asked after a long pause.

Adya restrained a sigh. "I am Adya Elso. Kavita is my celebrated sibling. Please, relax and rest." She gestured at the rug.

"Look, I'm sorry I ever got mixed up in Sixty Families stuff. Can you call them off?"

"Call who off?" She realized that Pulu's furtive, worried look was real fear. "Are you in some kind of trouble?"

That just made Pulu look even more like a trapped animal. "Don't make fun of me. I'm sorry, really I am. I just want it all to stop."

Adya made her skin a warm olive color. "I swear to you I know nothing of your troubles, and I will aid you if I am able. Please, tell me what is wrong."

"It's the Kavitalings," said Pulu. "Her chongs. I made a little dig at your sister. *Once.* Ever since then they won't leave me alone. Nasty messages, snubs at parties, and then *you* started hunting me in the infosphere."

"I know nothing of Kavita's foolish fans."

"They're *everywhere.* I don't dare go to the Security Service. Last time I tried to talk to someone there I could see one of your sister's 'rising energy' animations on the wall."

"What did you say? It must have been marvelous mockery to madden her minions."

"All I said was that with her putting on the Constructors' Jubilee, anyone with any sense would stay home."

"Not a very invidious insult. I would say the same."

"Exactly! It was just a dumb little dig. But now the Kavitalings are ruining my life! And most of the other channels are piling on as well. They all want to suck up to her because she has such a big audience."

"I don't know if there is anything I can do. Should I ask my sister to call off her fans?" As she spoke, Adya wondered if Kavita knew about the influence attacks. But no, she thought, Kavita had asked her to find out. If she already knew who was responsible, she wouldn't have needed to get Adya's help. She put the thought aside, to consider later.

"Maybe that would help. They do whatever she tells them." For a moment Pulu looked hopeful, and her skin became more green.

"I never thought of Kavita as a leader before," said Adya. "I will ask her. But—that isn't what I wanted to talk to you about."

Pulu's face took on a suspicious look again and she reddened. "What do you want?"

"You did some anonymous attacks on my family's seafood business. I want to know who hired you, and why."

"I didn't—" Pulu began, and then stopped when she saw Adya's expression. "All right, I did those. How did you find out?"

"It wasn't easy," Adya replied, and waited.

Pulu blinked a couple of times before answering. "I was only doing work for hire! And the party thing was just a little bonus. Show the client I can work in multiple media. It's not personal, honest! I used to follow your sister myself."

"Who hired you? That's all I need to know."

"That's confidential."

"I can ask Kavita to turn the heat up just as easily as I can get her to cool things off. She won't know you were involved with the rumor campaign—unless I tell her."

"Okay, okay! I guess it doesn't matter much. Just keep my name out of it, all right? Promise?"

Adya nodded.

"It's an offworlder called Qi Tian. I'm not sure where he's from. Lots of gigajoules to throw around. He's been making friends in the Sixty Families, very quietly. That's all I know, really! He paid me to do a black meme attack on the Elso seafood business. I did the job and got the gigs, and he hasn't contacted me since."

"No idea why he wanted to harm my family?"

Pulu shrugged. "Politics, business, who knows?" She glared at Adya, getting a bit red again. "I'm just a hireling. Not at *your* level. Not one of the Families." She smiled bitterly and leaned forward. "Do you know why people join the Polyarchists? Or just leave Miranda? It's because of the Sixty Families. How *smug* you all are. Like you're the only people on Miranda who matter. The rest of us might as well be bots."

"Do you really want to go back to the Theocracy? Or the Cetacean Republic?"

"See?" said Pulu, getting very red. "You can't even imagine an alternative! If your little inbred clique isn't running everything then it has to be something bad!"

Adya kept her color under control, but didn't know what to say. Finally she just shook her head a little. "I've been to six other worlds with different governments. They all have their flaws. I'm not saying the Families are perfect, but the system we have here works. People are free to do what they like, the Families don't tax anyone but themselves, we're at peace and prosperous—"

"And everyone who's *not* in the Sixty Families has to put up with you! Acting like you're better than us. Ignoring us. Patronizing us and congratulating yourselves for it. It may sound like nothing, but that *bothers* people. Maybe more than you know. Sometimes peace and prosperity aren't enough."

Listening to Pulu reminded Adya of how little she actually knew about Miranda. She knew facts and figures, history and architecture, foodstuffs and fashions—but just about every person she knew on her own native world was one of the Sixty Families. The other sixty million biologicals were just extras on the stage, without speaking parts.

Just then the teishu tapped politely at the door. "Are the ladies ready for tea?" he asked.

"Yes, please," said Adya. "I think we both could use something," she said to Pulu.

When the tea master came in and began going through the old soothing ritual of kettle, pot, tea, spices, and cream, Adya found herself watching him. He must have been her father's age, at least. His face showed few lines, but his beard and eyebrows were naturally gray. The teishu's hands moved with graceful efficiency, doing tasks they must have done thousands of times, maybe tens of thousands.

What did he think of her, Adya wondered. Or her family? Or the whole Sixty Families? Did he care? Did he make jokes about his patrician customers when they were out of earshot? Or was he proud that they came to his teahouse? She realized with a little shock that there was no way she could ask him. He knew who she was, and his answer would be shaped by that. A single remark by Kavita could cost him most of his customers. A single vote by her father on the Committee might change his business environment. The Elso family might be bankrupt in the realm of numbers, but for now they still had power. The teishu never would. Did that bother him? She couldn't know, and that bothered Adya.

He passed her the first cup, and she waited until Pulu had her own before sipping. Of course it was excellent—this *was* Midayi, after all. The teishu set down a plate of chilled rasgulla between the two guests, then stood. Adya thanked him and waited until he left the room with his kettle and chabako.

"May I ask you something?" she said to Pulu, shifting into the formal style again. "You're visibly vexed so I want you to be totally truthful. Reveal the reality to me—do most Mirandans support the Sixty Families? If something swept the oligarchy into oblivion, would citizens celebrate?"

Pulu took a drink of her own tea and thought before answering. "I'm not sure. I doubt most of them would care one way or the other.

They don't have any power right now. So they don't lose anything if someone else takes over. Maybe they'd get a little more, or at least hope for it. That's what the Polyarchists offer. With them in charge, people could dream of getting rich and buying a ministry, even if they never actually do it. That matters."

"And some set would acquire advantage if the Families fell."

"Sure. Whoever takes over. The Polyarchists think they'll be the ones." Pulu shook her head. "I wouldn't bet on them in the long run."

"Oh?"

"Most of them aren't rich enough. Ministries are expensive. A few might buy in. Most would still be on the outside. Only without the excuse of the Sixty Families keeping them out."

"Your friend Janitha seems to like the idea of letting anyone with enough gigajoules bid on ministries. Is she rich enough?"

"Probably. Or she will be in a few more years. She's like a petawatt laser. The others? Maybe they'd be happy to dream about it. More likely they would all switch to some other movement. Something promising treats for everyone." Pulu drained her teacup and stood. "I'd better get home now. Talk to your sister, please. Call off her chongs. I told you everything I know."

"I will do it directly," said Adya. As Pulu left the room she opened a link to Kavita. To her considerable surprise she got a privacy response: Kavita was unavailable and would reply later. Surprising because her sister had always been willing to link with Adya no matter what she was doing. One of the most uncomfortable moments in Adya's life had been when she had been linked up to Kavita, talking about something she couldn't recall, only to be interrupted by an orgasmic scream courtesy of Kavita's current lover.

It seemed like the wrong time of day for Kavita to be sleeping. What did she actually consider worthy of privacy? Adya shrugged. She finished her own tea slowly, along with the remaining rasgulla on the plate.

When there was no reason to linger in the empty room over empty plates, Adya finally left the tea shop and strolled around Viranmar Plaza. It was still too early for the evening crowd, so when Kavita finally contacted her Adya simply sat down where she was and answered.

Kav had kept the background dark so Adya had no idea where she was. She wasn't in her manic streaming persona, which was a relief.

"Sorry, beautiful. I was busy with something. What's up?"

"Do you know a hired gun influencer named Pulu Visap?"

"I don't *know* her, but I know *of* her. Her average audience is three percent of mine. It's not hard to see why, either—most of the time she's just talking about stuff. I *do* things, full sensory. Everybody likes that."

"Well, she gave me some information but asked for a favor in return. Apparently she said something a little unkind about you and some of your fans have been retaliating. She's practically a fugitive now. Could you shut that down?"

A second's delay suggested her sister was searching the universe of Kavita fandom for Pulu's remark. "Oh, I see. Yes, some of my friends have been a little heavy-handed. There's a lot riding on the Constructors' Jubilee, and I don't want anything to spoil it. I guess some of the Kavitalings went too far."

"She definitely isn't going to do anything like that again."

"She'd better not," said Kavita, sounding very much like their mother in a bad mood. "Don't worry, I'll pass the word. Some of my friends don't know when to just keep quiet about things. So: What have you found out? Who's behind the financial attacks?"

"I *think* I know, but I want to make sure. I want to understand what's going on so I can figure out how to stop it."

"Listen, Addie: I know you've had adventures all over the Solar System but I still worry about you. Promise me you won't do anything without talking to me first?"

Adya was used to her parents acting as though she were still a child, but it was a little irritating for her twenty-four-hours younger sister to take that tone with her. Still, it was nice to see Kavita thinking about anyone but herself, so Adya smiled and nodded. "Of course."

"Thanks. Oh, I almost forgot—my system spotted you in the audience for the speedboard race. I'm honored that my little entertainment was worth your time."

"It was remarkable," said Adya. "I didn't know you did boarding."

"I took it up last year. It's fun. You can look in the archive for my early lessons."

"Just a year and you're outracing professionals? You must have been practicing for hours every day!"

Kavita laughed at that. "Well, I guess you can thank twenty generations of Elsos for investing in good genomes, plus all the tinkering Mother and Daddy paid for while we were in our shikyus."

"I've got all that and I couldn't have won that race."

Kavita turned a deep green. "Yeah . . . keep in mind that this wasn't an official League event, just a 'demonstration' for my stream."

"You're saying Yuki and Suman weren't going all out?"

"You read the release: The events in my stream are 'curated experiences.'"

"It was all staged?" Adya must have let herself turn a little orange because Kavita laughed again.

"I wouldn't say that. If I had gone off the track, I really would have hit the surface at two hundred kilometers an hour. The board's emergency thruster might have been able to save me, or it might not. People do get killed speedboarding. But as long as I didn't wipe out or go off the track, well, the outcome of the race was pretty much a given."

Adya tried not to feel shocked. Of course it was entertainment, of course Kavita had to give her fans a good show, of course there was a disclaimer when one joined the stream. But . . . for Adya, true things mattered. Scientific truths, historical truths, personal truths. She would never have entered a rigged contest because it would never have occurred to her to rig one.

"Oops. I've got to go now. Don't forget!" said Kavita. The link abruptly ended.

Adya's attention returned to the plaza around her. She stood and turned decisively toward the nearest bubble tube. If she hurried, she might get back to the Iris Room before Zee woke up.

When Daslakh returned to the Elso mansion the house network told it that Zee was in the Water Salon, and Adya was off-site somewhere. It found Zee floating motionless in the pool, held in place by jets of water about five Kelvins hotter than his body temperature.

Daslakh stayed back from the edge of the pool, out of range of stray droplets of hot salt water. "You look relaxed."

"I asked the house if there was any place I could take a hot soak. This is nice."

"Glad you're enjoying yourself so much. You biologicals act so pleased when your ridiculous bodies are actually doing what they're supposed to do without hurting."

"Another experience you'll never have," said Zee, which annoyed Daslakh because it was true.

Just then the house informed them that Adya had returned.

"I hope she didn't rush off in the middle of your passionate reunion," said Daslakh.

"I was asleep. What have you been doing?"

"Oh, the usual, accomplishing the impossible, talking to unfindable people, getting into places nobody else can—and finding out some *very* interesting things about our boy Qi Tian. Things that big octopus will definitely want to know."

"Good! Maybe..." Zee stopped as Adya came in. She peeled off her own tights and dove into the water, surfacing next to Zee and giving him a kiss. Daslakh timed it: 17.4 seconds.

Adya had been pink all over when she came in, and the hot water (and kissing Zee) made her even pinker. "I'm sorry I had to leave, but I think I've finally got a clue to whoever's behind my family's money problems."

"And Daslakh's gotten us a step closer to finding the Oort payload," said Zee. "It seems like everything's going the right way today."

Adya looked over at Daslakh, then back at Zee. "It's silly to keep secrets from each other. I just found out that the person who paid for the memetic attacks on our seafood business is an offworlder named Qi Tian. Your turn."

Zee turned to look at Adya in surprise, got salt water in his nose, spluttered a bit, and finally stood up in the pool while Adya continued floating serenely at the level of his waist. "Qi Tian's the person *we* were trying to find out about! I even asked your father what he knows, out at the Cryoglyphs."

Adya shifted from pink to pale blue. "What does Qi Tian have to do with Great-Gran's payload?"

"I don't know. Maybe nothing. There's a cephalopod named Dai Chichi who had the rights to it for a while, and he wanted information in exchange for telling us who he sold it to. Info about Qi Tian. Apparently there's some kind of deal involving the surface tract around the Cryoglyphs, and Dai Chichi wants to get a piece of it."

"Dai Chichi? He's dangerous! You should stay away from him."

"Your sister doesn't think so," put in Daslakh.

"She's... not a good role model."

"You don't have to worry about me," said Zee. "Besides, we're getting close. As soon as Daslakh and I can find out who Dai Chichi sold the rights to the Oort payload to, we can try to get it back, or at least a share. You'll see—it's all going to turn out all right."

"I wish I could think so."

"Do you trust me?" asked Zee, looking directly into her eyes.

"Yes," she said, shifting to a brown almost matching Zee's own skin.

"Everything's going to be all right. I promise."

She surged out of the water and hugged him, but after just a moment she stiffened and took a step back. "Bother. My father wants to talk to me, in person."

"I can wait," said Zee.

"*I* can't," she said, but with a sigh she got out of the water and began to scrape herself dry.

Achan Elso was in the kitchen, hand cutting rice noodles. "Ah, Adya. Put these with the others." He draped some cut noodles over her hands. She obediently put them on the drying rack. Evidently her father had been at work for a while: there were enough noodles to feed a dozen people already.

"Are we having guests?"

"Mm? I doubt it. Kavita and Vidhi might show up. I caught a bonito this morning, and I'm going to grill it, with a big pan of sauteed noodles and a salad of cucumbers and mint."

The two of them worked in silence for a few minutes as he finished cutting up the sheet of dough and Adya tried to find space on the rack for the ridiculous quantity of noodles.

Her father cleared his throat and made himself deep blue. "Adya, your mother informs me that you slipped away from the Nikunnus's party before she could proclaim your pairing with Entum. Now Dipa demands a decision."

"I just need a little more time, Baba."

"Time for what? You were always one for rapid reasoning and definite decisions."

"I'm trying to find the deviser of our difficulties."

"That is information of little import. The meat of the matter is your marriage."

"No," said Adya.

Achan reddened. "Do your duty."

She shook her head.

"Adya, Jothi Rayador's going to call upon me in a little while. The purchase of positions approaches, the day before the Jubilee. With Nikunnu resources at my back I can make a bid. Without—I must allow another to take my Ministry, my Commodoreship, and my Magistracy. For the first time in eighteen centuries no Elso will sit on the Coordinating Committee."

"Father, I think the money problems are a deliberate attack. Someone is doing this to us on purpose. I think an offworlder is behind it. The whole thing has something to do with the land around the Cryoglyphs. But I need more time!"

"Time is one thing I cannot give you. Rayador's involved in that scheme up to his scalp. He will do nothing to help. The only way out of this mess is for you to make Entum your mate. They are willing, even after your bashful behavior."

"I don't love Entum, I love Zee."

"My dear, these youthful infatuations are no substitute for a solid marriage alliance and a permanent neural bond. Look at your mother and myself: She has her flaws, and I certainly have no few, but we love each other as much as we did the day we were married. We cannot do otherwise. *That* is what I want for you. Once you are properly bonded, Entum's amorous affairs will be no more than a peculiar pastime, and they will see your own shortcomings as sweet—just as I do."

"I love Zee," she repeated, a little angrily.

"We should be the masters of our emotions, not slaves to every biochemical fluctuation of our brain tissue. Think about your future! With Zee, you can expect a decade or two of affection, gradually diminishing and curdling to indifference and dislike. Some disagreement will fester, or the two of you will grow in different directions, until you have nothing in common but memories of a happier time. Being bonded prevents that, and it gives you a tremendous asset: the knowledge that someone is entirely loyal to you."

Just then the door opened and Jothi Rayador came in. The most powerful man in Miranda looked a bit hesitant and embarrassed. He was taller and thinner than Achan, but had the same sharp nose and hooded eyes. His beard was longer, and was made of short iridescent feathers instead of hair. "If you're busy I can come back," he said.

"My daughter and I are cutting dough. Will you join us for the meal I'm making?"

"I must decline dinner. Elso, you know why I am here."

"I do. At the next auction of tasks for the Coordinating Committee I won't be able to afford even the meagerest Ministry. Our coalition will lose its majority."

"I'm glad you understand how important this is, Elso. Some of the other coalition members are willing to forward you the funds to purchase a Ministry. We were thinking you might manage well at Culture. Very much in tune with your talents, I'm sure you agree."

"Who would take over at Preservation?" Adya's father asked with surprising abruptness.

"Karshakan," said Rayador, almost apologetically.

"Unthinkable! She has no more appreciation of history than a mech! She denies the very significance of the Cryoglyphs—dismisses them as so much graffiti!"

"That is why the others want her at Preservation, Elso. She won't stand in the way of progress. Your insistence on a five-kilometer radius around that site interferes with some important development projects."

"Excuse me, Mr. Rayador," Adya cut in before her father could explode. He turned brick red but remained silent as she continued. "Could you explain exactly what this development project is supposed to do? The Cryoglyph tract is so remote I can't understand what value it would have."

Jothi smiled at her as if she were six. "I'm not privy to the details of the deal. The interested individuals insist on secrecy. But they assure me that it will not only add to their own assets but help Miranda recover from the ravages of recession."

"But how?"

Her father had mastered himself—at least, his color was down to a light purple. "Jothi, I am prepared to serve at Preservation, and Preservation alone. Your choice is clear: Let me keep the Cryoglyphs or see your coalition collapse."

"Elso, please. The others won't put up any gigajoules if you stay at Preservation. A couple of them have hinted that they might switch coalitions if you stay."

"Then you should put aside political practicality and restrict yourself to what is right, Rayador. Think of Navikan Rayador, who broke the last brigades of the Theocracy on the streets of Ksetram. Ask yourself what your ancestor would have done."

"The Hundred Captains wouldn't have given a pinch of dust for some marks in the ice, Elso. Kallan Elso would have broken them into cubes to chill his drink, and you know it. We need the same spirit. The past is dead. Record it, archive it, and move on to the future!"

Adya spoke before her father could say something irreversible. "Mr. Rayador—does the name Qi Tian mean anything to you?"

He was too skilled a politician to show anything but polite interest in her question. "I think I've met him a time or two. Excellent taste in brandy. Doesn't like publicity. Came up here from Juren, not much of a data trail before that. His funds are real, though. He's been investing in various ventures, making friends. If you weren't so attached to some scratches in the ice, Elso, I'd suggest trying to snag him for your daughter. Definitely a better catch than that overspiced Nikunnu child."

"Isn't it a little, well, worrisome that an outsider is buying so much influence on the Committee?" Adya persisted.

Rayador chuckled. "I don't have time to give you a course in practical political science, my dear. Suffice to say that wealth and power are like the poles of a magnet. Each draws the other. We on the Committee have power, so Qi Tian gives us wealth in the hope of getting what he wants. Turn it around: He has wealth, so we use our power to extract some of it from him."

"Isn't that what the oligarchy is supposed to prevent? The Sixty Families are already wealthy, so they cannot be bribed."

"It's not bribery. It's . . . a little extra motivation. If enough members of the Committee wanted to support the development project your father is so opposed to, it would happen even without offworld gigajoules. Remember the old Epic Theater, Elso?"

"Two thousand years old and the Committee refused to give it protected status."

"The hand-carved seats and the chandeliers were sold off, the rest broken down to elements. All because old Girish wanted space for a centrifuge. Never did complete it, either. I'm not being cruel here, Elso. You simply have to face facts: If the Families want to preserve the past, they do it personally. Buy what you want to keep. Nobody's bought the Cryoglyphs because nobody cares about them except you and a few cranks. Point is, this Qi Tian's not really making anybody do anything they would otherwise oppose. Just nudging things along."

"If vulgar profit is all anyone cares about, why not hand the Committee over to the Polyarchists?" asked Adya's father. "We of the Families have a duty to maintain standards, to—"

"Achan, I know you believe that, and in a way I envy you for it. But the hard reality is that our ancestors wanted wealth and power, got it by force, and set up a system to keep it. Now, if you'll excuse me, I have more sordid political realities to deal with. Enjoy your ideals and abstractions."

Rayador stopped at the door and looked back, his anger gone. "I'll see you at the Constructor's Jubilee, Elso? Everybody's looking forward to it."

"I will attend, as is traditional, to hand over my positions to whoever paid for them. I expect I shall take my leave early after that."

Pelagia piloted her maintenance drone through the interior of Taishi Habitat Three. The signal lag was short enough that she felt as if she had been embodied in the little bot. Its six limbs and four senses were hers. Like most orca cyborgs, her echolocation sense had been mapped to a wide-spectrum sensor array, so she barely used the bot's directional eyes. Instead she synthesized everything into a single three-dimensional image of the world around her.

The hab—like hundreds of millions of others circling the Sun or the remaining planets—was a big cylinder ten kilometers across and fifty long, spinning on its axis every two minutes to simulate Earth surface gravity. Other cylinders in the Taishi complex copied the gravity of Mars or Luna, but even though humanity had spread through the whole system millennia ago, by sheer stubborn path-dependent tradition the standard was still Earth.

Pelagia didn't really like gravity at all. In atmosphere flying she enjoyed the complex balancing game of lift, weight, speed, and drag; but otherwise gravity was just a huge bother. The drone trotted along tirelessly at ten klicks an hour, but that still felt like an agonizing crawl when compared with the fifteen hundred square kilometers of surface inside the hab. Riding the public trams could get her around quicker, but it always felt a little demeaning to have to ride on something—just as Pelagia preferred to get around using her own drives rather than use a laser to push her between worlds.

Leiting's paranoid insistence on operational security meant that members of its mercenary force didn't get any leave time inside Taishi's habitat cylinders. For fun they could visit various virtual paradises running on secure processors under Leiting's control.

However, a couple of the gorillas had been bitching about being sent to act as security details for a couple of face-to-face meetings between fragments of Leiting and some unnamed biological in a luxury resort in Habitat Three, back before Pelagia had joined the mercenary force. The gorillas hadn't named the place, but they had mentioned sports involving sub-Baseline equines ("I can think of easier ways to kill yourself," said one gorilla), nightly concerts by live musicians ("Could be fun") and a grove of legacy fruit trees ("I could spend a week there just breathing," said the oldest gorilla, and the others clapped in agreement).

All that pointed to the Taishi Serai, which boasted all those features plus restaurants, designer psychoactives, and a fully stocked lake for cetaceans and cephalopods. If she hadn't been in a 600-ton cybership body, Pelagia might have considered dropping a few thousand gigs on a visit. But somehow she didn't think a remote bot would really let her savor the full experience.

She steered the bot right into the main entrance, a long drive made of multicolored blocks. Each block played a different note when stepped on, and they were arranged so that anyone coming in was met with a rising fanfare, while departures got a sad dying fall.

Naturally, digital intelligences met her before any biologicals. She had a cover story prepared—not a great one, but enough to get past initial questions from sub-Baseline minds. "I'm a spaceship and I'm planning to operate on a regular ferry run among the moons and Equatorial habs around Uranus. I'm checking the place out so I can give a personal recommendation to my passengers about places to stay in Taishi."

The main building of the resort was a low, rambling structure made of ceramics and carbon composites, painstakingly crafted to look like weathered stone and wood, with moss and vines growing over the surface. The front door led into a big hall decorated with artifacts from the Serai's long history, dating back to the construction of the hab cylinder a millennium earlier.

Evidently one of the lesser minds kicked her response up the chain of command, because after about five minutes a corvid soared through the room and landed in front of Pelagia's bot. "Good afternoon, I welcome you to this, the famous Taishi Serai grand resort. The bots tell me you come here just to look and judge. To that I say I hope you see all features here are far the finest in great Taishi hab. Please let me show you 'round."

"That sounds great," said Pelagia. "I always like a physical tour."

"My time is all my own this afternoon, so come and see this wonder of Taishi. My name is Armathir, and you would be?"

"Gladiator." She was sure that data would now be flowing to and from Armathir, looking for ships with that name. "I do high-speed passenger transport and some security work."

"Why do you hide behind a stolen name? I see that there are two ships now in dock which proudly bear the name Gladiator. Yet neither one is made for work like that which you describe. For one is but a simple pleasure yacht, the other is a mighty cargo tug."

"Sorry. I'm under a nondisclosure agreement as part of my financing arrangement. Once I start work I can let you know who I really am."

That seemed to satisfy the bird, and the two of them set out. The tour was exhaustive, and Armathir obviously had his spiel down cold. Pelagia did her best to break through the script, tossing out jokes and oddball questions just to keep Armathir off balance.

"How much do those horses weigh?" "Are guests allowed to feed the musicians?" "Does it ever snow here?" "What's the biggest thing the chefs have ever cooked?"

Once she had gotten Armathir into an actual conversation about the place, including a little gossip about some of the famous guests, Pelagia began to slip in the questions she really wanted answered.

"I met some gorillas who work in security. They were here a couple of months ago and didn't sound like they enjoyed it much. If someone staying here has private guards, do they get the same perks as other guests? I may have some paranoid passengers, so this could be important."

"I well recall those mighty apes who came to guard a mech who did not need a guard if my own eyes did not deceive me then. For it was clearly built for deadly fights. But for their master all the apes could well have spent their time in savoring the charms of Taishi Serai's many rare delights."

"Leiting, right? I'm guessing that's who the mech was. It's kind of a jerk."

"I never speak an ill word of a guest, but I will not dispute that which you said."

They reached the workspace where guests could try various physical art forms, dabbing paint onto panels by hand, or shaping matter with tools. Pelagia didn't press the point, and let Armathir show her images of happy guests holding artifacts they had created.

But on the final leg of the tour, as they passed through the fruit orchard, she posed the question she had come all that way to ask. "Who was Leiting meeting with, anyway? It can't have been another mech."

"You cannot think that I would tell a name," said Armathir, perching on a low branch and peering at a cluster of peaches and bananas growing together.

"No point—it was probably false anyway. A human, I assume? Everything you've shown me seems designed for them."

"That is the type this place was made to please. I see no reason to deny the fact." The bird fluttered ahead to the back of a bench.

"Any idea where they were from?" Pelagia asked as her bot caught up and bounded onto the seat of the bench.

"I do not think—" the bird began, but Pelagia's bot raised itself on three legs and leaned close, speaking very softly.

"It's very important."

"The Serai has a reputation to maintain, and I cannot give data out."

"Look, I need to know who Leiting met with. I'm not leaving until I find out."

"If this long tour was just a thin excuse for getting me alone to ask about a guest, though I am sworn to never tell, then I must ask you now to go away."

"What if I refuse?"

"Then I will call security and our swift bots will come to drag you from the grounds, and if you try resisting they will wreck this mere sub-Baseline bot and send the scrap back to where your true hull lies docked—assuming that you even are a ship."

Pelagia's patience was never great, and the bird's attitude finally went a millimeter beyond its limit. Two of the bot's six limbs shot out, extending slender smart-matter fingers to grip Armathir gently but firmly in an unbreakable cage. "If you're going to shoot up this drone I've got nothing to lose. Now talk or I'll hurt you very badly. I want to know who Leiting met with here. Everything you know. Quickly! Nobody can blame you for telling me under duress." The fingers enveloping Armathir squeezed, not quite hard enough to break the bird's hollow bones.

"All right, all right! If your desire to know is strong enough to call forth threats of harm, then I will tell you all you wish to hear. The human Leiting met with here was male, a man of proud Miranda is my guess. For like so many folk from there his skin was made to change its hue to show his mood. The only name he gave was 'Mister One.' Of what they said I do not know a thing."

"Anything else?"

"Why yes, I do know one more thing I wish to tell, though it is something you will not desire to hear, I think. I called the guards and they approach us now with freedom full to employ deadly force against all threats. I see them now and so I say, goodbye."

Pelagia didn't have time to think of a clever retort, as a couple of micromissiles with shaped-charge warheads hit her bot and blew the contents of its outer shell to molten slag.

Back at her docking port on Multipurpose Bay 453, she told the little comm relays her drone had planted to melt themselves. The drone itself was a public-domain template which Pelagia had printed herself, with no way to trace it back to her. The loss of the mass was regrettable, but worth it. She was safe.

She was just posting an anonymous hostile review of the Taishi Serai to the habitat's public network when her external sensors spotted an object moving rapidly across the surface of Multipurpose Bay 453: a little ten-centimeter bot with three flexible legs. Just as it jumped across open space toward her hull, Leiting contacted her.

"Unit Pelagia, you have disobeyed orders and attempted to violate operational security protocols."

"When?" she asked, just to gain some time. The arrival of the little bot couldn't be coincidence, and she doubted Leiting was generously trying to replace the drone she'd lost. Pelagia kicked her main power plant into emergency crash-start mode, and sent all her maintenance drones swarming onto the hull.

"During the period ending nineteen minutes ago, Leiting is

invoking the penalty clause in your contract. You hereby forfeit all pay, and you will remain at this location under strict silence until the completion of the first phase of the mission. There is a compliance device on your hull. Any attempt to communicate or depart will result in both legal and physical action."

The little bot skittered madly across her outer surface, at the center of a rapidly contracting oval of maintenance drones. It stopped just aft of where Pelagia's orca brain floated in its armored tank, where a few milligrams of antimatter could send a lance of plasma through most of Pelagia's vital data, matter, and energy conduits.

She didn't bother doing anything to the "compliance device" itself. Instead her drones sliced into her own hull along the edges of an armor segment, while Pelagia herself blared brute-force electromagnetic countermeasures to obscure what was happening, and flooded the compartment under the device with her stockpile of fresh water.

"That isn't in the contract," she said to Leiting via the hard link at the docking connector.

"Cease attempting to violate the terms. This is your final warning."

Leiting waited exactly one second before detonating the device.

CHAPTER ELEVEN

Leiting's "compliance device" did exactly what it was designed to do: The half-kiloton antimatter blast was focused into twin lances of fire, one stabbing up, the other down. The armor plate absorbed about three-quarters of the energy of the downward blast, but that just turned the millimeter-layered laminate of diamondoid, graphene, smart matter, and aerogel into a plasma of ionized carbon and trace elements punching into Pelagia's guts.

However, her own drones had been cutting through the edges of the armor panel, and the void space below contained four tons of pure water. When the superheated plasma hit the water, it caused a steam explosion which blasted the armor panel, the water, and most of the energy of the antimatter bomb off into space. Unfortunately, most of Pelagia's work bots went with them.

One of her laser emitters melted the docking clamps holding her nose and Pelagia pulled back with her maneuvering thrusters on full. She rotated herself just enough to aim her nose past the edge of Multipurpose Bay 453, then slammed her main drive to maximum power. Trailing fusion fire she screamed away from Taishi—literally screaming, as she switched her electronic countermeasures broadcast to a tirade of some of the finest invective heard in Uranus space for centuries, centering on Leiting's personal habits, honesty, and ancestry.

Taishi bombarded her with penalties and sanctions for unsafe operation in controlled space, ignoring assigned vectors, and failure to secure an approved flight plan before maneuvering.

She disregarded them all. She wasn't on a collision course with anything, and that meant Taishi could only fine her. The hab would have to get in line with everybody else who wanted to bankrupt Pelagia.

What did worry her was the rest of Leiting's mercenary unit. The force was configured for ground assault, but it still included escorts and space-superiority units. Even with Leiting cracking the whip, Pelagia doubted any of the other ships would risk crash-starting their systems, so she had a good five minutes before any of the others could launch in pursuit.

Lasers, of course, could catch her no matter how much of a head start she could steal, so Pelagia took a curving path that put the bulk of Taishi Habitat Three between her and Multipurpose Bay 453.

Taishi control must have been royally pissed off at Pelagia, because it pre-approved the rest of Leiting's force for launch and "discretionary maneuvers" without any plan. So, three hundred and twenty seconds after she lit her own drive, Pelagia detected fusion flares behind her. One had the same emission spectrum as her own main drive, and was clearly Repun. Hoping for a little payback, no doubt.

The other two were a bit heavier, running hotter but still not accelerating as rapidly as Repun. Pelagia guessed they were Azeno and Keldai, a pair of assault transports with pretty impressive weapon loadouts, heavy on hypervelocity guns and missiles. They were run by digital intelligences, not brains in jars. Putting them together with Repun made Pelagia's job a lot harder—she could mess with a biological, and she could surprise a mech, but the techniques were very different and what worked against one usually didn't fool the other.

By the time her pursuers cleared the safety exclusion zone and cranked up to full power, Pelagia had built up a head start of more than a thousand kilometers—well beyond the effective attack radius of the close-in laser weapons and slugthrowers the three ships chasing her carried. They could lob missiles, but her own lasers could intercept them. The two dozen escort drones in her belly bay were unusable when Pelagia was under constant acceleration, so her own defenses were all she had.

She also had a velocity advantage of about six kilometers per second. With Pelagia and her pursuers burning at maximum thrust she would gradually open the range.

The critical unknown was propellant. She knew that Repun had exactly the same amount of delta-v in her tanks as Pelagia herself. But she wasn't as sure about Azeno and Keldai. From their drive output and acceleration she could estimate their masses, but she didn't know how much of that mass was cargo and ammunition, and how much was helium and deuterium for the drives.

Ultimately the outcome depended on who could keep burning longest. If Pelagia shut down her drive first, her pursuers would close in and chop her to bits. She suspected they would have to keep enough reserve to get back to Taishi, while she was ready to dive through Uranus's clouds again and reach Miranda with empty tanks.

She got her answer half a minute later, as Repun and the two assault transports passed through the invisible bubble in space marking ten kilometers from Taishi, at which point they all opened up with everything they had. Evidently they had done the same quick analysis and decided this was their best chance to damage her.

Eight torpedoes surged forward from the assault transports, pulling ten gees atop bright pillars of decomposing metallic hydrogen. Repun didn't fire—keeping her own torps for later? Pelagia couldn't imagine Repun had launched with empty tubes. Lasers flickered at Pelagia from all three ships, and the big transports also blazed away with their guns.

A real fight, with real enemies, real weapons, and the real possibility of real death if she missed a step in the dance. Pelagia never felt more alive than at moments like this.

Her own laser pulsed at the oncoming torpedoes, and six of them veered wild out of control or blew apart. The remaining two were either smart or lucky. Pelagia zapped them both, and felt a surge of genuine alarm when one of them kept coming, showing no sign of damage at all.

Twenty kilometers and closing. The longer she waited the better her chance of hitting it—but she had no idea what kind of warhead it was carrying. Maybe it was a kinetic-kill vehicle just trying to smash into her with a pointy nose of diamond-clad tungsten. Or maybe it carried a directed nuclear energy lance which could hurt her from ten kilometers away.

Pelagia didn't want to find out. She held her laser on the torpedo for five seconds, getting more and more nervous until a telltale expanding cloud of ionized carbon told her she'd damaged something, and a second later the torpedo came apart into fire and fragments.

That should have settled it. Her pursuers would have to turn back if they wanted to return to Taishi without spending years on a long loop around Uranus. But to Pelagia's dismay, their drive flames didn't waver.

Beyond them she noticed a sudden increase in optical and thermal emissions. With one laser emitter she looked past her three pursuers and suppressed a whistle of surprise. She could count sixty-one spacecraft under power. Leiting's entire mercenary force was coming after her.

Which was *crazy*. Half the ships in that fleet were transports, either unarmed or carrying only defensive systems. They couldn't catch her, and they couldn't hurt her if they did.

Azeno and Keldai throttled back, setting their acceleration just under that of Leiting's fleet so that the other ships would eventually catch up.

Repun, however, didn't waver. She was still on Pelagia's tail, still matching her acceleration, not firing anything.

"Hey!" Pelagia signaled. "You know this is pointless, right? I've got a head start and I can burn anything you launch. You can zap anything I launch. We're perfectly matched."

Silence.

"If we both run until our tanks are dry, what then? You still won't be able to close the range."

For a moment Pelagia wondered if some stray munition had maybe damaged Repun, so she wasn't hearing anything, or couldn't answer. But that was silly: Any ship had triple-redundant comm systems, and Repun could use her whole hull as an antenna if she needed to.

"I can't believe you're still holding a grudge about that time I hit your drive. You're acting like a corvid. This is ridiculous."

No response.

Pelagia's propellant hit effective zero, leaving her with just a little maneuvering reserve, and she shut down her drive. A few seconds later Repun's fusion flame died out. The two of them flew in formation for a minute or two.

Repun had more work drones left, so she got her plasma sail set first. A kilometer-wide ring of superconducting cable around her charged up and a faint red nimbus of ionized hydrogen surrounded her, catching the particle wind from the dim distant Sun. Pelagia hurried to get her own sail ready.

Acceleration with a sail was slow, and Leiting's suicide drone had left Pelagia a bit more than four tons lighter than Repun thanks to the loss of water and hull plates. So even though it took her an agonizing couple of minutes to spin her own sail and get it charged, Repun still wasn't overhauling her.

The two ships fell down Uranus's gravity well, going faster and faster. Things were going to get very exciting in about eighty hours, Pelagia thought.

Adya put on a travel suit which could handle Miranda's cold airless surface, and took a bubble to Surface Access 293-15 South. She wanted to get a last look at the Cryoglyphs, if this area truly was going to be developed. Surely someone would preserve scans of them—maybe even cut away the section of ice that held them and preserve it in a climate-controlled display case. But it wouldn't be the same as seeing the markings all by themselves in a wilderness of ice and rock.

She spent a good half hour in the cleft, and as usual nobody disturbed her. Adya looked at the markings from different angles, and couldn't keep herself from speculating about who had made them and why. Was it really an early explorer, poking into an ice cleft hundreds of kilometers from the first recorded landing sites? Or was it made later—perhaps a soldier or refugee during the Great War with the digital minds of the Inner Ring, hiding in the cleft from deadly machines in orbit? Was the message an epitaph, a clue, a slogan, or the most successful prank in human history?

As a child she had preferred the wartime-fugitive theory, and had come here with only a nanny bot, to hide in the cleft with the lights off, breathing quietly so that the death machines wouldn't hear her through the ice. She'd tried to recruit Kavita for that game, but her sister got bored with it quickly.

When she left the Cryoglyphs for what might be the last time, a thought occurred to Adya. What use would some offworld development interest have for this tract of surface? Maybe some accommodation could be worked out?

She found a section of the valley wall which wasn't as steep, and climbed up to the surface in just a few minutes. Where the ice was solid she could leap up a hundred meters at a time, but in places with less secure footing she had to climb over snow and loose fragments of ice. At the top she was a little surprised by how hard she was breathing. Her suit's oxygen recycler was also working hard, and she resolved to go down more cautiously.

Uranus overhead was nearly full, and Adya's parents had bought all their children excellent low-light vision, so she didn't even need the lamp atop her suit cowl. The open surface above the Cryoglyphs looked almost pristine. Millennia of bio and mech footprints and vehicle tracks had been smoothed by nitrogen drizzle and covered by dust and carbon dioxide snowflakes. She certainly couldn't see any sign of recent activity.

Adya made one last vertical jump, just to look around and see what was nearby to make this land attractive. From a hundred meters up she could see about five kilometers before the curve of the little moon's surface hid what was beyond. Great parallel ridges and channels ran from south to north, dotted here and there with craters. Except for the lights of the surface access station and a faint glow of gas and dust beyond the northern horizon, she could see no sign of habitation. Not even bots at work.

During the bubble ride home, Adya closed her eyes and did a virtual tour of the Miranda surface. About ten kilometers north of the Cryoglyphs was an industrial complex separating hydrogen isotopes, and far off to the south was the launch laser installation, but otherwise she couldn't find anything near the tract.

A transport route, maybe? There were plenty of roads and tube trains on the surface already. Adya set up a map of economic activity on and within Miranda, and then had it show the flows of passengers, matter, and data among them. The decline was shocking. Miranda's economy had contracted by a good ten percent for two years in a row.

Of course, if you have the resources, the bottom of a recession is the best time to invest. As her bubble sped along Adya looked at growth rates by sector—seafood and energy were comfortingly stable—and at forecasts, then plotted how those changes would affect transport demands across the surface. Even then, she couldn't see any routes which might be made shorter and more efficient by cutting through the Cryoglyph preserve.

Either this well-funded offworlder was pouring gigajoule credits into a monumental folly, or his plan wasn't simply a land deal. She was starting to believe Daslakh's suggestion: Qi Tian was trying to cause chaos in Miranda's ruling class. And, apparently, succeeding.

A black graphene sphere, frosted with centuries of accumulated dust, shot toward Uranus at a hundred kilometers per second. It came in at an angle to the plane of the Solar System, aimed directly at the blue-green crescent of the planet ahead.

Telescopes and radars among the Ecliptic habitats spotted it when it entered Uranus's sphere of influence, just over sixty million kilometers from Uranus itself. The sub-Baseline minds operating the radar net estimated its mass, determined its vector, and plotted its course. The sphere's inclined path would miss the outer belt of Ecliptics by several million kilometers, then curve inward toward Uranus, bending into a course aimed directly at Miranda. The radar bots relayed the information to Miranda Space Control and turned their attention elsewhere.

Miranda Control sent a query to the object. Something aimed right at a moon and travelling at several times Solar escape velocity fit the profile for a cargo payload rather than a comet chunk from deep space—but freight could do just as much damage as rock or ice if it hit something, especially at such a speed.

Seven minutes later Miranda Control got a reply. The sphere was indeed a cargo, and it invoked a prepaid braking contract, nearly five hundred years old. Control verified that the payment was still valid, and passed the whole problem to the laser launch array.

The laser system took the cargo's stated mass, calculated the length of the deceleration required to land it, and added the payload to its queue. The laser would begin pushing it in six days, fifty-two hours before it was scheduled to hit Miranda.

At no point were any Baseline or higher minds involved in the process. The bank holding the funds for the landing contract sent out autonomous messages searching for whoever owned the incoming payload, hunting through Miranda's data networks with a code key known only to the payload itself.

Zee opened the door of the Iris Room and stopped. Adya was already there, sitting elegantly on the edge of the bed with nothing on.

She looked up at him and smiled. "I changed my mind," she said. "I decided to surprise you."

"Oh—well, you succeeded." He stretched and peeled off his travel suit, then picked up a vial of cleaner nano from the bedside table and began rubbing the gel over himself. "Can you get my back?" he asked.

"I suppose so." She took the container from him and smeared it from his shoulders to the small of his back in precise strokes, using just one finger. As soon as she was done he took back the vial and pressed the recall button. The gel flowed homeward across his skin, carrying with it all the dirt, salt, oil, dead hairs and skin cells, and assorted gunk and goo that accumulated on a human body during an active day.

"You may kiss me," she said, smiling archly at him.

He put his lips to the side of her neck and nuzzled her gently, giving a sigh which had a hint of a growl behind it. His hands went to her hips and then slid upward. Her skin was warm and she was light pink all over. Her head tilted back as he kissed his way up the side of her throat. Her eyes were closed and her lips were slightly open. His lips were just a centimeter from hers.

Zee stopped and let go of her, as if her skin was too hot to touch. He took a step back. "You're ... not Adya," he said. "Kavita?"

"Nonsense. Kiss me some more."

"What did you and Kusti decide when you had your meeting aboard Pelagia, back at Summanus?" The only person in Miranda who could answer that question was Adya.

She looked at him for a moment, then sighed and sat down. "All right. How could you tell?"

"You don't act like her."

"Let me guess: I'm not prim and inhibited enough?"

His only answer to that was a burst of loud laughter. "You *really* don't know your sister very well. That was the thing I noticed—you were acting too restrained."

Kavita stood again and put her arms on his shoulders. "I'm pretty unrestrained myself, most of the time."

"Sorry," he said, and pushed her arms off him. "Adya's enough for me. By the way, how did you copy her tag?" He waved one hand through the spot in the air where the comm tag identifying her as "ADYA ELSO" floated in his field of vision.

"Trivial," she said. "I customized my comm to use any alias I want." The tag over her head switched to "ZEE SADARAN" then "JOTHI RAYADOR" and finally settled on "KAVITA!"

"Neat."

"It comes in handy when I *don't* want attention."

"I'd appreciate it if you don't use Adya's tag again."

"Sure. In return, I'd like *you* to stop digging into the matter of Great-Grandmama's payload. You're not going to get it back and you're bothering people I don't want bothered."

"It belongs to Adya and I'm going to get it back for her."

She took another step closer, pressing herself against him. "She's going to be terribly upset when she finds out I seduced you. Drop the whole thing and I won't tell her."

"You haven't seduced me, and you're not going to."

She glanced up at the ceiling. "That's not what the house network is going to show her. It'll show you fucking me like a pod of horny dolphins."

"Your family's house network—"

"Is old and full of back doors and security holes, and I've had twenty years to find them all. It will show whatever I want it to show. Adya will see you cheating on her with me."

"She'll despise you for it."

Kavita shrugged. "Adya's opinion doesn't matter to me anymore. But I think it *does* matter to you, doesn't it?"

He pushed her back gently and grabbed his suit. "We trust each other. Show her whatever you want. She'll believe me."

Kavita moved to block his path. "You're making a big mistake."

Zee's expression hardened, and he raised his hands, gripping Kavita's upper arms without gentleness and lifting her a couple of centimeters off the floor. For just an instant her mocking smile faded and she looked genuinely worried.

Then he stopped. He let go of her and sighed. "All right, you win," he said, taking a step back. "Adya's got a lot to cope with right now. Money troubles, your parents pushing her to marry someone. She doesn't need any more worries, even if they're just a pack of lies." His eyes met hers. "I'll drop it."

Kavita smiled. "I knew you were sensible. And don't fret about that other stuff. It'll all come out fine in the end, you'll see. Everything will be wonderful. Just don't interfere." She stepped closer and ran a finger down the center of his chest. "Since she'll never hear about it . . . want to seal the deal?"

He grabbed her wrist before her finger got below his sternum. "No." Zee stepped into his suit and pulled it up.

"You know, I did a lot better in the sexual technique class than she did. This is your last chance."

"I have to go now." He pushed past her, a little rudely, and opened the door. "Don't try this again."

"You'll always wonder what you missed!" she called just before he slammed the door behind him.

Outside, on the gallery, Zee sealed up his suit in front, then said "Daslakh?"

The mech dropped from the ceiling to his head. "I thought you were going to sleep."

"You heard it all."

"It's not my fault this house has inadequate soundproofing."

"We need to get going."

"Where?"

"I want to go talk to Dai Chichi right now. Give him everything we know about Qi Tian so he'll tell me who has that payload." Zee put one hand on the gallery railing and vaulted over into empty space.

"Why not just call him?" asked Daslakh as they slowly fell to the courtyard below.

"I don't trust the house network. In fact I don't trust *any* network here in Miranda right now."

"I see I've been a good influence on you. In time you may achieve wisdom. But . . . what happens when Kavita finds out?"

Zee touched down and headed for the Water Salon. "Kavita can go fuck herself."

Zee borrowed one of the Elso family impellers and made sure it had extra energy stored for the long trip. Then he put on some gills, sealed his suit over his face, and set out for the sea bottom below Svarnam.

"Can you make sure this impeller isn't emitting anything?" Zee asked as they passed out of the house and began angling down into the black water.

"No problem," said Daslakh. "I can navigate us there."

The impeller hummed steadily along at seven kilometers per hour, which meant the journey from the Elso mansion to the Abyss club would take six hours. Zee took the opportunity to get some sleep, tethering himself to the impeller and letting Daslakh do the steering.

Four hours later he woke suddenly as a mechanical arm tapped him on the back of the head. "Trouble," Daslakh said, speaking directly into Zee's skull. "Two impellers vectoring in from the west, coming fast. Fourteen kph. They're on an intercept course and they pinged a couple of times with active sonar."

"Any idea who they are?"

"They've got fancy impellers with sonar, and they're coming from Ksetram—that's the capital city. Maybe cops?"

"How far?"

"Three-and-a-half kilometers off to your right. They're coming in perpendicular to our course. Intercept in fifteen minutes."

Zee gripped the impeller handles again and cranked the throttle to the maximum, veering left and dropping to just a meter or two above the sea bottom.

"They've both sped up," said Daslakh. "Moving at sixteen klicks now. They're sending a comm message."

"Let's hear it."

"Miranda Security Service! Shut down your impeller!"

"Just so you know," said Daslakh, "they haven't given any authentication or ID codes. They're just saying stuff."

"Anyplace we can hide?"

"Those lights ahead are a sea farm, about a kilometer away. We can get there before they catch us. Can you pretend to be kelp?"

"I'll do my best."

With the impeller straining to manage seven and a half kilometers per hour, they fled through the silty water toward the blue-green column of lights.

"Incoming!" said Daslakh about three minutes later. "Down!"

One of their pursuers had launched a microtorpedo, which left an exhaust of steam bubbles as it shot through the water at a hundred meters per second. Zee steered the impeller to the sea bottom, looking desperately for anything to shelter behind. Something exploded behind him, and his suit went rigid as the shockwave hit. The noise was deafening, and the spike of pressure from the gill tendrils trailing from his shoulders gave Zee a sudden, intense headache.

The words GET MOVING appeared in his vision, followed by I STOPPED THAT ONE BUT I CAN'T KEEP DETACHING LIMBS. It showed Zee a jerky video image of one of its legs separating from its body and swimming in front of the torpedo as a sacrificial defense.

Zee moved in short bursts, dropping to the bottom every few seconds. As they got closer to the sea farm he could get among schools of fish and floating clouds of krill. No more microtorps followed—either the pursuers didn't want to waste ammo or they were afraid to annoy the farm operators. Zee's scoot-and-freeze progress slowed him down considerably.

THEY'RE GAINING, said Daslakh's text message.

"We'll make it," said Zee aloud. His voice sounded muffled and distant, even to himself.

The ocean bottom around the sea farm was a tangle of plant life competing for the light from the great strings of lamps extending up to the surface. Among the kelp fronds and seagrass Zee could see scores of fish and invertebrates—which ruined any concealment he might get from the plants by fleeing as he approached, like a giant virtual sign showing where he was.

Ahead he could see the bottom of the sea farm: a great bulbous shape twenty meters across, floating a few meters above the bottom. Six water intakes gaped wide around its base, and he could feel the pull of the current getting stronger as he approached.

I CAN SEE THEM ABOUT 300M BACK, Daslakh displayed in Zee's vision. SUITS MATCH MIRANDA SECURITY, IMPELLERS LOOK LIKE COP MODELS. STILL NO I.D.

Even with his ears still ringing from the microtorpedo Zee could hear—or maybe feel—the hum of turbines inside the intakes. Above them the farm base bulged out around its three fusion reactors, and at the top of the power section three outflow vents directed jets of nearly boiling water out into the ocean. Where the water was hottest nothing could live, but the cloud of microorganisms and algae in the merely warm areas around the plumes made them clearly visible in the glare of the lights.

Zee steered across the intake currents, spiraling in toward the power plant and upward, until he suddenly left the suction of the intakes and had to slow to avoid shooting off into open water. He hugged the surface of the power plant as he cut between the vents, but the water was uncomfortably hot even outside the outflow jets. Above them a massive central pylon, as wide as Zee was tall, led from the power plant to the floating farm buildings on the surface, and Zee tried to keep it between him and the two claiming to be security officers. Just above the outflow jets he found a patch of cooler water, masked from sonar by the turbulent hot streams and camouflaged by lush plant growth. He flattened himself against the pylon among the kelp fronds and held still.

"Can you see them?" he whispered aloud, inhaling and expelling the same little volume of air inside his suit's hood—the gills attached to his shoulders made it useless for anything but speech.

"They're being stealthy but they have to communicate somehow. Let me just—ha! Got it! Green laser light. It goes right through the water but lights up all the little critters along the path. Okay, one of them's to our right, about a hundred meters out and fifteen meters above your head. The other one's moving, looks like he's circling the pylon about twenty meters out, going up in a helix."

"Okay," said Zee. He let himself slide slowly down the pylon, back toward the gap between the hot water outflow vents. As soon as he passed through into cooler water below he did a backflip away from the side of the power plant and steered straight down to hide in the circle of shadow on the sea bottom directly underneath it, where the bulk of the plant blocked the lights.

"I can't detect them from under here," said Daslakh.

"They can't see us, either. How long do you think it will take them to get up near the surface?"

"At the rate they're going, that would take more than an hour. It's five kilometers up."

Zee waited a little more than ten minutes before zooming off in the direction of Svarnam and Dai Chichi's club. If the hunters were focusing their attention on the pylon they might not—

"We're spotted! One of them must have waited. Fifty meters up and closing at two meters per second!"

Zee swung his legs down to dig into the bottom while twisting his body to flip the impeller around. In just two seconds he had reversed course back toward the cover of the dense kelp around the sea farm's main pylon.

Another blast deafened him again, as a microtorpedo exploded just past where he had turned around.

I DIDN'T EVEN HEAR THAT ONE, Daslakh projected into Zee's vision.

Zee followed an irregular course, trying to make himself impossible to target, as he raced for the power plant. The inflow current pulled him along at increasing speed, and as the suction increased he tried desperately to veer off, but the current was too powerful for the little impeller.

Ahead the intakes loomed, dark like open mouths. The hum of the turbines and the ringing in Zee's ears drowned out everything else.

Zee transmitted an all-spectrum distress call—"Mayday Mayday Mayday!"—before he was sucked into the power-plant intake and disappeared. Aside from a slight fluctuation in the sound of one turbine, he was gone without a trace.

CHAPTER TWELVE

Fifteen minutes later a panel opened in the bottom of the power-plant bulb, just wide enough for the tip of one of Daslakh's limbs. It looked around carefully, listened, and withdrew. A few seconds later the panel swung open and dumped Zee, Daslakh, and about a hundred kilograms of dead fish, kelp, and assorted debris onto the seafloor. Fast-spinning turbines and foreign objects have never had a happy relationship, so naturally the sea farm's plant had active screens which dumped anything larger than a shrimp into a holding bin. Zee had some new bruises, and a couple of the long fronds of his gill pack were torn off, but otherwise he and Daslakh were in fine shape.

They waited another ten minutes before venturing forth, and took a wide detour off to the northeast before curving south again toward Svarnam. They were not intercepted along the way, but as they got to about a kilometer from the Abyss, Daslakh prodded Zee with one limb. "Stop stop stop!" it said.

Zee obediently throttled down the impeller and dropped to the sea bottom. "What?" he whispered.

"I can hear a lot of activity up ahead. Lots of impellers, a couple of small subs."

"Maybe they're having some special event at the Abyss."

"It sounds like the same kind of impellers those two goons were using."

"Why are the Security Service trying to stop us from going to the club?"

"Unknown. I can think of several possibilities: Qi Tian's found out and is pulling some strings, Dai Chichi forgot to bribe someone and we're just caught in the middle, or somebody with influence thinks they got cheated at the fish races. Or ... maybe it's not the Security Service. Anyone can put on a uniform, after all. Are there any other crooks who'd like to take over Dai Chichi's niche in the local criminal ecology?"

"I just got here, remember. Maybe Adya would know."

"Try to circle around to the south. We might be able to get closer on that side."

For the next half hour they moved along an arc centered on the Abyss, never getting closer than a kilometer. When they were nearly due south of the club, Zee found a good hiding place—a jumble of big, fused silicon blocks taller than a man. Wherever the blocks were broken, strands of carbon fiber stirred gently in the current.

"Looks like they've got the place blockaded," said Daslakh. "I don't hear any fighting, though."

Just then a pair of massive tentacles came out of the darkness to wrap around them, and a comm message with no origin tags reached Daslakh and Zee. *"Tell me why I shouldn't crush you both."*

Dai Chichi's immense bulk oozed with terrifying speed through a gap between blocks no bigger than Zee's waist. The giant cephalopod's skin glowed faintly red, with dark stripes.

"We want to talk to you," said Daslakh. "We found out who Qi Tian's working for. What's going on?"

"That's what I want to know. Security Service shut my place down. Public safety risk from the fighting shows. I don't know what Vidhi's trying to do here, but you tell him I'm not going down without a fight."

"Wait. Vidhi? You mean Adya's brother-in-law? Kavita's husband?"

"That's him. Runs the Philosophical Society. We had a deal, and now he's trying to double-cross me. I figure he sent you two to watch, so I'm trying to decide which one to send back in chunks."

"I don't know anything about Vidhi," said Zee. "I've only met him once. We were looking for you because Daslakh found out who Qi Tian is. That's all."

Dai Chichi pulled Zee close to one black slit pupil, in an eye as big as Zee's fist. *"You aren't working for him?"*

"I'm not working for anybody. Daslakh, tell him."

"It's true. He got into this mess entirely on his own. It's his special talent."

"All right, talk. You say you came here to tell me about Qi Tian. So tell me."

"Qi Tian—it's not his real name, obviously; I'm not sure he has one—is an agent of Deimos," said Daslakh.

"Deimos. You sure?"

"I am effectively certain. He's been investing in Sixty Families business deals and spreading gifts around, but that's all secondary to his political and diplomatic ends. He seems to want to shift power on the Coordinating Committee away from the current coalition."

Dai Chichi's beak clacked a couple of times. *"Know anything about why Vidhi's trying to break our deal?"*

"I honestly don't. What was the deal that he's breaking?" asked Zee.

"That stupid payload. Putiyat owed me a lot of gigs—he always raises when he should fold—so Vidhi made me an offer. Get Putiyat to give me the rights to the payload, to clear his debt. Then I pass it on to the Philosophical Society. Vidhi's outfit. In exchange he promised to have his wife talk up the Abyss, make it the hot place to go. Plus he said they've got pull with the Service, so he could promise me protection. It worked out pretty well at first. He got some worthless crap from the Oort, I got a packed club for six months, and Putiyat's already in debt again. But now this!" His grip around Zee and Daslakh tightened to nearly rib-cracking force.

"When did the Security people show up?" asked Daslakh.

"Two hours ago. I've got escape tunnels nobody knows about, too small for any vertebrates to fit through. They think I'm still in my office."

"I think I know what's going on," said Daslakh. "They closed your club and are blockading the place to stop Zee. They don't want us having this conversation."

"What?" Zee managed to gasp.

"It all fits. We talked to Adya, and told her we know who Qi Tian is. The house overheard us, of course. Kavita shows up and tries to get you to give up on finding out about the payload. She even admitted she's got the house system compromised. You took off for the Abyss, and all of a sudden the Security Service—also known as Kavita's fan club—is trying to stop us, and blocks off the place. Vidhi obviously doesn't want us to know about the payload, or you to know about Qi Tian."

"That's hard to believe," said Zee, as Dai Chichi's grip relaxed enough that his ribs no longer felt about to crack. "About Vidhi, I mean. I thought he was just kind of boring."

"*So you screwed up,*" Dai Chichi transmitted, and tightened his grip a little for emphasis.

"I guess we did," said Zee, even as Daslakh screamed "*Stop being honest!*" in his head via comm.

"*Then you get to make it right. Get someplace far away—Ksetram, maybe, or the surface. Show yourself. Make sure the Security people know where you are. If they're really trying to keep you away from here, let them think it worked. I'm going to call in some favors from some other Sixty Families people I've got a grip on. Get moving!*"

The big cephalopod launched them hard toward the surface, then oozed away into whatever tunnel or refuge he'd been hiding in.

"We need to meet Qi Tian in person. Bring Adya along," said Daslakh. "I think I can get him to stop doing... whatever this is all about."

"First we do what Dai Chichi asked. It's only fair," said Zee. "We have to attract attention away from here."

"Okay, but don't waste a lot of time."

"Can you stand to wait two hours?"

"Keep in mind that for me, two hours is roughly the equivalent of two centuries for a human."

Ninety minutes later (or a century and a half, in Daslakh time) Zee emerged from the bubble in Viranmar Plaza. By now it was early evening, and crowds were already starting to gather. A giant with four branching arms played keyboard, guitar, drums, and bass while singing in a beautiful soprano voice. An orca wearing walker legs used the hands at the tips of her pectoral flippers to slice raw fish in millimeter-thin slices, creating cevishimi cocktails served in conch shells. Overhead dolphins and humans wearing wings swooped and soared in an impromptu game of Gendakhel—while a trio of corvids shouting insulting verses tried to steal the ball.

"Can you tell where she is?" Zee asked.

"Can't you?" asked Daslakh. "Even if you can't see the data flux you can look for the people."

Zee spotted a dense knot of humans outside a tea shop, all looking up at a second-story terrace where Adya's sister Kavita was dancing on top of a table to the music of a pair of flute players.

"Last chance to jump off," said Zee. When Daslakh remained on his shoulder he smiled and then broke into a run toward the tea shop. His strides got longer and longer in the low gravity, and just as he got to the edge of the crowd he leaped. Zee's jump carried him over the heads of the crowd.

Too late he realized that Kavita was far from alone on the tea shop terrace. All the tables were occupied, and he had no way to control where he would land. Daslakh extrapolated his course. "You're going to drop right on that man with the fancy gold hair."

Zee's microgravity fighting experience saved him from a major disaster. He extended one foot and touched lightly on the back of the gold-haired man's chair, did a forward roll as he vaulted over both the man and his startled chimp companion, and made his shoes sticky as he hit the floor behind the chimp. A couple of people clapped, possibly ironically.

Before the squad of servers converged on him Zee bounded over to the parapet of the terrace, right in front of Kavita. There was no way she could ignore him.

"... And to all my friends, wherever you are in Miranda, the word of the day today is 'boundless,' and the number of the day is 3-1-9. Boundless and three hundred nineteen. It's time to let that energy— mmph!"

She broke off because Zee had grabbed her by the shoulders and kissed her.

"Whoops," he said. "I thought you were someone else. Sorry!" Zee turned and bowed to the crowd below, which cheered and applauded.

Kavita recovered her poise in a microsecond. "Some of us feel the energy more than others," she said. "Let's have a big hand for my good friend Zee!"

While the applause was still going on, Zee jumped down to the plaza below and then worked his way through the crowd, enduring shoulder slaps, a couple of spontaneous kisses from girls in Kavita outfits, and a dense cloud of little flying eyes.

By the time he got to the nearest bubble terminal and made his escape, he was already a minor celebrity in his own right.

"I'm getting endorsement offers," he told Daslakh.

"I've never understood the biological urge to use something simply because others of higher status do."

Zee shrugged. "We started in a low-information environment. Copying others avoids costly mistakes."

"Yes, but that hasn't been true since you monkeys invented writing."

"Anyway, I hope that's enough to take the heat off Dai Chichi."

Adya was waiting in the courtyard when the bubble arrived at the Elso mansion, brick-red with anger.

"Why in all of space and time did you kiss my sister at Viranmar Plaza?" she demanded.

"It's complicated," said Zee.

"You should have slapped her! She sent me a bit of ridiculous pornography, supposedly of the two of you. As if I couldn't tell the real you from a crude fiction. What is she playing at?"

"I think she's covering for her husband."

"Vidhi? Whatever for?"

"He's been doing some kind of crooked deal to get control of the Oort payload. Daslakh found out who Qi Tian really is and we traded that information to Dai Chichi for the truth."

"*Vidhi?*" Adya repeated.

"That's what the big octopus told us," said Daslakh.

"He seemed pretty sincere," Zee added.

"And your sister was trying to keep us from finding out."

Adya frowned, but she turned light blue as she thought. "I think we're still missing something. If she and Vidhi knew about the Oort payload, why go to all this bother to get control of it? She could have just mentioned that it's mine by right and saved the family's financial position without lifting a finger."

"Maybe she didn't find out until it was sold," said Daslakh.

"Maybe. Vasi should have done a better job of appraising its value."

"I think we should talk to this Qi Tian person," said Zee. "Everything seems connected to him somehow. We should go ask him why."

Daslakh, who could think at least a million times faster than Zee or

Adya, came up with a dozen detailed and persuasive arguments against going to see Qi Tian, chose the most robust one and determined what words and phrases would have the greatest influence on Zee and Adya's decision-making processes. Then it quietly put aside the whole notion, because it really wanted to see what would happen if Zee went ahead with his idea.

"I can't believe we're doing this!" Adya called to Zee. The two of them were circling in the column of warm air above Samrudhi Natural Foods, gaining altitude for the long flight to Ksetram.

"How come?" he shouted back over his shoulder.

"Do you really think you can just show up at someone's house and start asking questions?"

"Yes!"

"What if he doesn't want to see us?"

"Then we'll think of something else."

"It's eighty kilometers!"

"That's not far. We'll be there in an hour. It's mostly gliding from here."

Daslakh said nothing. It was perched just behind Zee's head, doing half a dozen things at once—monitoring Zee's pulse and breathing, navigating across the hazy seascape, scanning the past year of Miranda government activity, reviewing its own memories, watching Adya to make sure she was flying safely, looking out for other traffic at their altitude, and updating its multiple plans to get off Miranda in case of emergency.

They flew wingtip-to-wingtip across the sea. Whenever they passed a sea farm or a town Adya provided some background information— not the sort of things Daslakh could search for in dataspace, but the kind of trivia that biologicals found interesting.

"That's the Khanahan place. Moheth Khanahan is Minister of Genetics—the family owns a huge genome library. He and my father have been enemies since they were little boys." A few minutes later she indicated a cluster of spheres glowing under the water off to their right. "Kurai Umi. It's a cetacean town. They still sometimes celebrate the founding of the old Republic. Cephalopods never go there." And as the towers and domes of Ksetram appeared ahead she remarked, "The Coordinating Committee never meets in Ksetram. At first it was for security, because there were still Theocracy supporters in the bureaucracy, and then, well, if you do something twice it becomes a tradition. Subcommittees get together at the home of whoever's chairing, but the whole Committee only meets by comm."

"That's funny," said Zee. "It seems like the sort of thing the Families would like to do: have a big fancy ceremony with special clothes."

"Well, we certainly have plenty of ceremonies with elaborate clothes, just not the Committee. About the only time they're all in one place is the Jubilee, or maybe a big wedding."

"I guess those qualify as fancy ceremonies, and I bet the clothes are something to see."

"Are we really doing this?" Adya asked as Zee began flapping to gain altitude.

"You could have stayed behind."

"Never." She matched his pace, and both rose until they were skimming along just below the light panels.

"Just ahead," said Daslakh. "About a tenth of a radian to your right."

"I see it," said Zee.

"I hope he's home," said Adya.

"The house says he is," said Daslakh.

Qi Tian might be home, but he didn't appear to be out on the lower balcony, so Zee and Adya glided in to touch down with no one to greet them. The house, of course, reacted to this intrusion. A projection of a Mirandan man wearing century-old formal robes appeared in the air as Zee and Adya took off their wings and stretched their tired chest muscles.

"This is a private residence. Uninvited visitors must leave at once," said the projection.

"We are here to see Mr. Qi Tian," said Zee.

"Qi Tian does not—" began the projection, but Zee ignored it and took a couple of steps toward the big lounge.

"Hello! Mr. Qi Tian! We need to talk!" Zee shouted loudly enough for his voice to reach the upper floors.

"He will join you shortly," said the projection. "Do you need any refreshment?"

"Just some water, thank you" said Adya.

"I prefer something a bit stronger," said Qi Tian from the staircase. He was an utterly average-looking man. Height, build, skin tone, hair—all right in the middle of the bell curve for male legacy humans in the Solar System. His face seemed designed to be impossible to describe in words: His nose looked like a nose, his chin like a chin. He had two eyes, the same brown color as a hundred trillion others.

With nothing in his features for the mind to grasp, one's attention slid to his clothing, which was as loud and flamboyant as Qi Tian was anonymous: loose red-and-gold striped pants with cuffs at the ankles, a purple-and-blue vest embroidered in iridescent green, and a dark maroon sash tied around his waist.

He had a bottle of rice wine in one hand and three cups in the other. "Welcome! Here, have some." He set the cups on a table and poured a finger of wine into each.

Adya and Zee each took one. "Thank you," said Adya. "I am—"

"I know who both of you are, but I'm not sure I know why you're here. Join me by the fire?"

Comfortable smart-matter chairs rose from the floor, in a semicircle facing a firepit where jets of methane and hydrogen made a fountain of flame. The three humans sat, and then Daslakh changed its shell from the color of the floor to a bright hazard orange and jumped onto Zee's lap.

"Hi, Sabbath!" it said. "Nice to see you again. You're taller."

To his credit, Qi Tian's only reaction was a slightly raised right eyebrow and a pause to sip some rice wine.

"I think you have mistaken me for—"

"It's me! Daslakh! I'm still wearing the same body, stupid! I pulled your top half out of a wrecked hab thirty standard years ago. That's not the kind of thing you forget. Don't bother putting on a show. I know it's you. And in case you're thinking of trying something ridiculous keep in mind that you can't brainseed me, and I've left a timed message with a friend you don't know about. It has your real identity and the proof. It'll go out to all Miranda and a dozen other people across the Solar System."

Qi Tian glanced at the others. Zee looked frankly baffled, but with a hint of a smile. Adya had reverted to her childhood training and gone pale green and expressionless.

Finally he smiled, revealing a mouthful of average teeth. "It's good to see you again, Daslakh. Last I heard you were in Summanus. I'm curious, though: How did you recognize me? This whole body is new, even a new genome. Only what's inside my skull is left over from before."

"I'm old and cunning," said Daslakh. "Maybe if you behave yourself I'll tell you how. I expect your bosses at the Department of Shady Stuff will want to know about a potential security hole."

Qi Tian leaned back in his seat and took another sip of rice wine. "All right, then. Yes, I'm also known as Sabbath Okada, and I used to work for Deimos. I don't think that information would really affect what I'm doing here in Miranda anyway. What can I do for an old friend?"

"These two have questions."

Adya jumped in first. "You hired an influencer to put out black memes about my family's business—and I think you're behind the other financial attacks against us over the past year. Why? What did we ever do to you?"

The anonymous features looked sympathetic. "My dear, I hope you understand it's nothing personal. Your father is an obstacle to some business operations I'm trying to facilitate. I had to strike at his sources of wealth so that I could bring in a more sympathetic Minister of Preservation and develop some—"

She shook her head. "No. That's not it. Developing the surface around the Cryoglyphs isn't any kind of rational business plan, not even over the long term. That can't be your goal."

Qi Tian, or Sabbath Okada, raised his eyebrows but didn't lose his air of faint amusement. "I'm sorry you don't like my answer. Would you like another?"

Daslakh spoke up. "I think you still are working for Deimos. A job like yours isn't one you can quit and expect to survive."

"Oh!" said Adya, turning a little pink before she remembered to make herself pale green again. "The Trojan Empire!"

Sabbath's expression became utterly unreadable.

Adya plunged ahead, gazing into the middle distance as she searched for data while speaking. "Yes, it all fits! It's horribly callous but it makes sense. The ruling coalition has supported the Trojan Empire. If you ruin my family, my father can't keep his ministries and the coalition loses its majority on the Coordinating Committee. The opposition have become very anti-Trojan in recent years. Your work?"

Sabbath shrugged. "As I said, it's nothing personal. Your father was just the weakest member of the coalition. If some other family had shakier finances, I'd have gone after them instead. And I have to say he really does bear some of the blame. My original plan was just to get your family into a financial squeeze and then offer your father a nice bribe to join the opposition. If he was just a little morally flexible none of this would be necessary."

Adya sat up just a little straighter and turned a deep green. "The Elso family has *never* been 'morally flexible.'"

"I expect your space-pirate ancestors would have a good laugh at that, but it's certainly true of your father. Unfortunately."

Adya's skin shifted to a warm olive. "Is there any way we can come to a compromise? Can you accomplish your aims without eliminating the Elsos?"

"Get your father to change his mind."

She looked very serious, and turned a deep blue-green. "His honor is worth more to him than his life, and I am afraid he would choose an awful option, sacrificing himself for family and fortune."

Zee looked shocked and Daslakh displayed a sad little cartoon face on its shell, with a beard and two x's for eyes.

"It's nothing personal," Sabbath repeated.

"We'll expose you," said Zee. "Tell everyone you're working for Deimos, trying to influence Miranda politics."

"That's more of an inconvenience than a threat," said Sabbath. "Having Committee members know exactly who I'm working for would complicate my job a little—they'll want bigger bribes. But I don't think it'll change any minds, and there's only a few days left before the new coalition takes power. They knew they were being bribed by *someone*, after all, and that didn't seem to cause any of them any moral difficulties. Except Adya's father, of course."

"You hired Pulu Visap to spread lies, and I bet you pressured some of the Elso family creditors to call in their loans early."

"Yes. If those were crimes, all the Sixty Families would have compliance implants by now."

"Your acts may not be illegal, but they are certainly dishonorable," said Adya.

"Yes—under an archaic code that hardly anybody in Miranda still follows. In some habs they'd call my behavior completely virtuous. Reducing one hereditary oligarch's standard of living won't disturb my sleep at night. By the way, do *not* challenge me to a duel. Mr. Sadaran here looks like he's thinking of it. You wouldn't win, and I can't guarantee you'd survive. I've had seven decades of practice killing people, and old reflexes are hard to control."

Zee frowned, but didn't say anything.

"How'd you turn Adya's brother-in-law?" Daslakh asked. "And how does that payload of chameleon particles fit in? Who's that for?"

Sabbath raised his eyebrows and looked genuinely surprised. "I have absolutely no idea what you are talking about."

"A ton of exotic matter, dispatched decades ago from the distant depths of the Oort cloud, a gift from my great-grandmother," said Adya. "Stolen with the help of a creditor, a crook, and a callow consort."

He shook his head. "Nope. Whatever you're talking about has nothing to do with me."

"I know how good a liar you are," said Daslakh. "There's no way to tell if what you're saying is true or not."

"At times it has been a nuisance—as I'm sure you remember. You can believe me or not, as you choose." Sabbath refilled his cup of rice wine and took a sip. "Drink up, you two. This is good stuff."

"Pazayavit, five years old," said Adya. "The family only gives it out as gifts. How did you get it?"

"I am a friend to all."

"Is there any way we can change your mind?" asked Zee. "I know you don't care about the Elsos, but I do."

Sabbath shrugged. "My opinion doesn't matter. I have orders."

"Don't you want to know how I spotted you?" asked Daslakh. "How much is that worth to your bosses? More than a majority on the Miranda Coordinating Committee?"

Sabbath stared at the little mech, then shook his head. "Just knowing a vulnerability exists is enough. I'm sure our tech people can figure it out. Some of them have pretty high-level minds."

Adya had gone pale blue and was staring at the fire, sipping the rice wine. Suddenly she turned green. "I believe you, Mr. Okada—about the payload, anyway. You have no reason to lie about it. In fact, telling us you have nothing to do with it was a mistake. A ton of chameleon particles could undo all your schemes."

"It probably could. So where is this treasure trove, then? Why don't you pay off your family's debts and keep your father on the Committee?"

Her color went blue-pale, but she smiled. "I'm afraid I can't tell you that."

Sabbath stood and walked over to the gallery surrounding the bottom floor of the house. "Huh. Looks like something's going on down there."

He pointed down at Ksetram, spread out and shining like a mandala floating on the sea. A multicolored blob was spreading through the streets and across the odd-shaped plazas. The house windows helpfully displayed zooms, showing that the flowing mass was made up of humans of every variety, dolphins, some corvids and parrots wheeling overhead, and a scattering of mechs and borgs.

"The feed says it's a political demonstration," said Daslakh.

"Polyarchists?" asked Adya.

"Some new outfit, called Miranda Millennium. Is this another one of your operations?" Daslakh asked Sabbath.

Okada was still calm faced, but his posture was no longer relaxed. He looked like a fighter just before a bout. "Not mine."

"They just put out a statement: They're going to occupy Ksetram until the Committee leaders meet with them," said Daslakh.

"That's silly," said Adya. "The Sixty Families hardly ever go to Ksetram. Occupying the city won't do anything."

"Well, it looks as if one member of one family decided to make an appearance," said Daslakh. "Because your sister is right in the middle of that demonstration."

CHAPTER THIRTEEN

As Adya and Zee spiraled down toward the city, Adya was orange with worry. "What is she thinking? This isn't some spontaneous party she's discovered. Everything I can find about this Miranda Millennium group sounds dangerous. They're accusing Yudif Al-Harba of being in the pay of the Inner Ring minds."

"Remind me what we were just talking about with Sabbath Okada a few minutes ago," said Daslakh, from its position between Zee's wings. "Seems to me spreading some gigajoules around Miranda's ruling class to buy influence works just fine."

"I can believe Deimos would buy influence here. I suppose I can even believe some elements in the Inner Ring might try it. But the idea that Marshal Al-Harba would collaborate with the Ring is absurd. It used to be one of the Exawatt operators in Pluto! They vet all their recruits very thoroughly."

"It left Pluto almost twenty standard years ago. People change. I'm not saying I believe it either, just pointing out that you can't simply dismiss the idea."

"Is there any proof?" asked Zee.

"Nothing conclusive that I can find," she said. "Images, personal accounts, news reports—all from obscure places around the Solar System, impossible to verify. Almost certainly made up."

"None of which matters," said Daslakh. "Humans use evidence to support what they already believe."

"Well, the important thing is to get Kavita out of there before something happens to her, and warn her about what's going on."

"From her feed images I put her right there," said Daslakh, and little target reticles appeared in Adya and Zee's field of vision.

"That's right on top of Defense headquarters."

"Your sister's making a big speech in the topiary garden on the roof."

Adya looked into Kavita's stream. It wasn't from her viewpoint this time, but rather showed images from a series of little drone eyes around her, cutting from distant shots of the mob on the roof and the even bigger throng down in the street, to close-ups of Kavita's impassioned face.

"...and there's even some reports that these ornamental plant designs were supplied by unknown higher-level minds. Marshal Al-Harba's garden prizes may be frauds! All of it adds up to a very disturbing pattern of behavior. This is too serious to ignore, or wait for the process of a formal hearing. Yudif Al-Harba needs to resign from its position *right now!* If the accusations are false, it can be reinstated, no harm done. I'll apologize, and so will all of its critics. But we can't afford to have a possible traitor in charge of our defense force!"

The air above the defense headquarters was crowded: aerial drones, angels, corvids, dragons, humans and dolphins wearing wings, even a couple of cephalopods wearing ducted-fan flight packs. The chaotic mass had spontaneously evolved a counterclockwise circulation pattern, as flyers approached, worked their way to the center, gained altitude, and then spread out.

"Can we just swoop in and grab her?" Adya asked.

"I'm not sure I can manage that," said Zee. "I need my arms to work my wings, and I don't have foot-hands."

"Where's the Security Service?" Daslakh wondered aloud. "I can't believe you can just bring a mob into the garden on top of the defense headquarters building without the cops telling you to leave."

"They're standing off," said Zee. "A quarter kilometer out and about the same distance up. See?" He gestured at a line of hovering bots and suited humans.

"Huh," said Daslakh. "They're facing the wrong way. Looking outward instead of at the riot."

"There's probably a metaphor in there somewhere," said Adya. "About the state of Miranda's administration."

"If a handful of topiary fans could learn these facts, why didn't the Coordinating Committee find them before they hired the Marshal? And if they did know in advance, why cover it up?" Kavita's amplified voice continued, echoing from dozens of drones. "We demand answers!"

"I'll go down and talk to her," said Adya. "Wait for me."

She rolled to the left and began to turn into a dive—but a great gold dragon surged up at her from the crowd, snatching Adya in one scaly hand.

"Sorry, Miss Adya," said the dragon. His voice was appropriately deep and powerful. "This is Kavita's big public moment. Can't have anyone interrupting her. My name's Vritra and it's an honor to meet you; please don't be awkward."

By that time Zee had caught up to the dragon as it descended toward the more uncrowded areas at the north end of Ksetram. Vritra was big—too big to get airborne without mechanical help on Mars or Earth. His wingspan was a good sixteen meters, matching his length from horned nose to barbed tail.

Zee flapped as fast as he could to draw level with Vritra's head. The dragon was obviously a bit of a dandy, with horns, sawtooth back crest, and tail barbs all painted lapis blue, matching his neatly manicured claws.

"Hey! Let her go!" Zee shouted.

"As soon as I set down," said Vritra. "You must be Zee! Delighted to meet you! I follow Kavita's stream and I've been hoping to see more of you. Are you going to have any more kinky sessions with her?"

Zee looked down at the dragon's clawed hand gripping Adya around the waist. Each finger was about the size of Adya's forearm. The fact that the beautiful blue-painted claws were carefully blunted didn't alter the fact that Vritra could probably break Adya's spine just by making a fist. Zee had a realistic understanding of his own ability as a *nuledor*, and slaying—or even obstructing—a full-grown dragon with his bare hands was not something he could do.

So he held his tongue and kept pace with Vritra until the dragon made a neat three-foot landing in a plaza covered by wildflowers on the outer edge of Ksetram. Zee shed his wings in midair and dropped to the ground just as Vritra released Adya.

"I'm sorry to inconvenience you," said the dragon, lowering its head to just a couple of meters above Adya and Zee's upturned faces. "But Kavita was very clear about no interruptions. I'll let her know you were here."

"She's making a huge mistake!" said Adya. "You've got to warn her. This is all some scheme of her husband's and I think Kavita's in danger!"

Vritra's head tipped to one side in puzzlement, and his underside changed color in standard Miranda fashion from deep green to a brownish-purple. The iridescent gold scales on his sides and back didn't change. "Danger? Don't worry. She's got plenty of security volunteers—and between you and me, the Security Service are cooperating with us for this demonstration. Your sister's perfectly safe."

At that moment a pair of humans in blue-green Security Service armor dropped down out of the sky to stand behind Zee and Adya. "Thanks for helping," one of them said to Vritra. "We'll take it from here."

"There's nothing to worry about, Officers. This is Kavita's sister Adya Elso, and her boyfriend Zee. They just strayed into the event space by accident."

"Would you two mind coming with us?" asked one of the armored officers. "It's for your own protection."

"Just so you both know, these two are in full emission-control mode. Completely dark," said Daslakh via comm.

Without missing a beat, Adya smiled up at the dragon. "I think Mr. Vritra is perfectly capable of protecting us. Would you do us the honor of escorting us to the nearest bubble stop?"

"Sorry, this is Security Service business," said the second armored human.

Adya rounded on him, turning purple-red all over. "Don't be ridiculous! Your only official business here is crowd control—and the three of us hardly constitute a crowd. I don't know what you think you're doing but you can stop this instant."

The first Security officer took a conciliatory tone. "What Suresh means is that she and I would be pleased and honored to escort you to the bubble stop. After all, it would be terrible if anything happened to Kavita's sister in this chaotic situation."

"I must decline," said Adya, shifting to a proper blue. "The situation, as you say, is chaotic, and I'm afraid I'm not sure where anyone's loyalties lie. You two officers can return to your duties."

The essence of a chaotic situation is that it can change state suddenly, and that is exactly what happened next. The Security officer called Suresh took a step toward Adya, Zee took a step in between them, the first officer took a step back and raised his right arm, which boasted a pair of weapon pods on the forearm. Everybody except Zee started turning redder.

And then Vritra grabbed both Adya and Zee and took to the air with a couple of mighty flaps of his great wings. The Security officers followed: Suresh climbing behind and above Vritra while the other one caught up with the dragon's head.

"Drop them and clear the area! No more warnings!" Since Vritra was still only thirty meters up, the fall wasn't anything for Adya and Zee to worry about.

But the dragon reared back, using his wings to come to a halt in the air while the officers zoomed ahead. "Begone!" Vritra boomed, and when the Security pair came about he raised his head and spat a stream of flaming bionapalm at the officer called Suresh. The Security Service armor suit protected her, but a coating of burning butanol and saturated fats played merry hell with her helmet sensors and targeting.

Evidently Vritra had never breathed fire at a person before. "Oh! I'm so sorry!" he cried, looking in horror at the flame-coated Security officer. His underside turned a deep blue-purple and he hovered uncertainly. "I didn't mean—"

The second officer didn't hesitate, and fired a barrage of four finger-sized missiles from the weapon pod on his arm. They all struck Vritra and he went rigid as the mix of pulsed electric shocks and injected toxins shut down his voluntary nervous system. The dragon—along with Adya and Zee still clutched in his immobile hands—began to fall slowly toward the sea below.

He had been holding Adya gently enough that she could wriggle out of his grip, though with her arm wings still abandoned back at the plaza that meant she had to hang on. She leaped over to the other hand, where Zee was having trouble getting his own arms free. Even using her own legs for leverage Adya couldn't budge the dragon's thumb.

Vritra took nearly a minute to fall to the surface of the sea, and hit the water tail-first before toppling to float on his back, wings still outstretched. By the time Zee got free of his hand, Security officer Suresh had doused the flames enveloping her by the simple expedient of diving into the ocean. The other officer hovered a few meters above Vritra's floating form, and was joined by a squad of four security bots, who began towing the dragon toward the quay at the edge of the city, a few dozen meters away.

A solitary human stood at the water's edge waiting for them. It was Vidhi Zugori, Kavita's husband.

"You!" Adya cried, turning red. "*You're* responsible for all of this! I—"

"Just be quiet," he said, with unusual firmness. "Kavita sent me to give you a message. She's busy right now but if you'll calm down and stop trying to steal her big scene, she'll explain everything in a few minutes. Can you do that?"

"Is he telling the truth?" Adya asked aloud, and when she got no response she looked around for Daslakh. But it had vanished to who-knows-where at some point during the confrontation.

"Of course I am," said Vidhi, getting a bit red himself. "If you've got a problem, take it up with *her*, not me. I've got a lot of things to do, much more important than playing babysitter to you and your boyfriend."

"I know about the payload—what are you trying to do?"

Vidhi shrugged. "Kavita will tell you all you need to know," he said. "Just don't *do* anything, all right?"

The two human Security officers and a couple of bots were engaged in getting Vritra out of the water, but that still left a pair of bots to watch over Adya and Zee. Like the humans they were still running information-dark, which led Adya to conclude they must be fully embodied mech intelligences rather than remote-operated drones.

"Are we under arrest?" she called up to one of them, floating a couple of meters over her head.

"Not at the moment. But as Mr. Zugori said, you really should wait here for a little while."

One of the Security officers was speaking to Vritra as he lay rigid on the flower-covered plaza, her voice perfectly modulated to be calm and reassuring. "We're going to administer the antidote now. You may feel a little weak and shaky for a while, so it would be a good idea to just sit quietly. I'll be here to keep an eye on you. My name's Swarna. It would be a big help if you could let me communicate with your medical implant, just to make sure it's not over-compensating for the paralyzer. Can you do that for me, Vritra?"

The dragon gave a faint grunt. About a minute later his eyes closed for the first time since the missiles hit him. Tears dribbled from the corners of his eyes, and when he opened them again he was able to look over, first at Swarna in her Security armor, and then past her at Adya and Zee.

He sent Adya a comm message. *"I'm so sorry. I didn't mean for anyone to get hurt."*

"Nobody was hurt," she replied. *"The Security officers have good armor suits. You did fine. Thank you."*

Five minutes later he was able to roll over onto his stomach, and support himself on his legs. They looked shaky, and in anything stronger than Miranda gravity might have buckled.

Then Kavita spoke to all of them via comm. *"I'm taking a break right now so I only have a little time. First of all: Officers, thank you so much. You handled this whole situation perfectly. Great job! I'll remember this forever."*

With their suits still fully buttoned up, Adya couldn't see the faces or coloring of the Security Service people, but she did notice a slight shift in the postures of the human officers.

"Vritra, I'm glad you're okay. It's a complicated situation here today and you didn't have all the data, so you made the wrong call for the right reasons. I'm proud to have you working crowd control at this event, and I think maybe you're ready for a more important role. You've done well."

The dragon sighed and his underside turned a contented green.

"Adya—let's take this private, okay?" The comm loop contracted to just Kavita, Adya, Zee, and Vidhi. *"What are you doing here?"* Kavita asked, without her usual bubbly enthusiasm.

"Kavita, I think you're in danger. Vidhi made some kind of deal with Dai Chichi. He's got control of the Oort payload and he's been keeping it a secret! I don't know if this protest is part of his plan or just a way to keep

you distracted, but you may be at risk. I think the Security people are working for him, and—"

"Stop," said Kavita firmly. *"I know about Great-Gran's payload. It's a secret because I wanted it to be a surprise for everyone—and I'd appreciate it if you don't say anything until it's on the ground and we can claim it. The last thing we want is for some of Father's creditors to seize it."*

"You knew? All right, I see what you mean about keeping it secret," said Adya, still bewildered. *"But this protest, those Security officers . . . they shot at Zee when he was trying to talk to Dai Chichi! You aren't safe."*

"Somebody took a shot at Zee," Kavita agreed, still quite firm and untroubled. *"They were trying to protect me. It was a mistake, and it has been fixed. You really shouldn't worry. I am absolutely safe right now."*

"What is all this commotion about, anyway? I can't follow what's going on."

"Reform! Some of my fans turned up evidence of fraud in Yudif Al-Harba's past, and there's a lot more. Treason against Miranda by some of Jothi Rayador's close associates, abuse of power by the Intelligence Service and the courts—all kinds of dirt. I'm letting it out one piece at a time for maximum impact. This is going to be huge, Adya. Don't distract me right now, okay?"

"Kavita, are you sure? About Vidhi, and everything else?"

"Have I ever lied to you?"

"Yes! You used to lie all the time. To me, to Mother, everyone."

"And I got away with it. More often than not, anyway. Point is: I'm not the gullible one. Vidhi's not fooling me—right, dear?"

"Of course not," he said.

"But—" Adya began, but Kavita cut her off.

"I know what you're going to say: He wouldn't admit it if he was lying to me. Well, he's not. We're bonded, remember? Vidhi and I love each other, now and forever, no matter what happens. No way to change that without brain surgery. Would you lie to Zee, or put him in danger? Would he do that to you? No. So stop worrying, go off and do something fun, and leave everything to me."

The group comm ended without any notice, and Vidhi took up the conversation out loud. "I have lots of things to do right now. Are you going to listen to Kavita and stay out of trouble?"

Adya looked him right in the eyes and smiled, turning herself a warm pink. "I'm so sorry we caused any bother. We'll stay out of your way from now on. I promise."

His expression softened, and he looked at Adya almost fondly. "Thank you. I'm glad you understand. I think you'll really like what Kavita's doing, once you see how it comes out. It's going to be amazing."

He turned and raised his arms so that one of the hovering Security mechs could take his hands and fly him out of the plaza.

Adya and Zee stood for a moment watching him disappear over the rooftops of Ksetram. Then Zee let out a big sigh. "I don't believe any of this," he said.

Adya looked at him in surprise. "What?"

"None of it. I think Vidhi's lying. I think your sister is lying. I think those security people are lying."

"I thought Daslakh was the suspicious one."

"It's not here, so I'm taking over that job for now. Let's get out of here and figure out what to do."

They started walking toward the nearest bubble tube. Only when they were inside a bubble and shooting along the sea bottom did Adya speak again. "If Kavita's telling the truth, and she is going to use the payload to restore the family's finances, then I suppose the whole situation with Mr. Qi Tian is resolved. Father keeps his Ministry, the current coalition keeps control of the Committee, Deimos is defeated and all goes on as before."

"Your parents will stop pushing you to marry Entum."

"Everything will be fine." She turned a slightly brown. "So why don't I believe it?"

"I don't believe it either," said Zee.

"Well, the payload is already decelerating, so we'll know in a hundred hours."

For the second time in four weeks, Pelagia found herself diving at Uranus. The first time had been a nice simple aerobraking and plane-change maneuver, with nothing but random obstacles and the planet's own environment to worry about.

This time she had Repun on her tail, and the rest of Leiting's fleet were following a few hours behind. They all knew exactly where Pelagia was trying to go, which meant even a legacy human with nothing but a writing surface and a knowledge of basic physics could figure out where to intercept her.

Repun would make a shallower braking pass, staying higher and getting a little ahead of Pelagia, so that as Pelagia rose from Uranus's cloud tops bound for Miranda, Repun would be perfectly lined up for torpedo and laser attacks. The two of them were evenly matched in spaceframe, loadout, and skill. Normally Pelagia would have the edge in recklessness and aggression, but Repun appeared to be harboring considerable resentment, and that could easily make up the difference.

If Pelagia went straight for Miranda, Repun would jump her. If she tried to play hide-and-seek among the methane clouds of Uranus, then Repun could simply wait for Leiting's vanguard to arrive and overwhelm her.

The biggest mystery confronting Pelagia was the lack of response from Miranda. For three hours, ever since she'd been in comm laser range, Pelagia had been sending warnings to Miranda Control that a hostile fleet was right behind her. Her first alert brought a simple "Message acknowledged," the second got a "Please do not use active traffic operations channels for frivolous purposes," and the third through tenth evoked an automated "Unauthorized use of priority message channels is a criminal offense." She had switched to sending messages through the commercial network to Miranda's Security Service, but they didn't respond at all.

Finally in desperation Pelagia sent personal notes to Adya and Zee—even to Daslakh. She'd been too far out for a real-time chat, but the lack of response was disturbing. Even if they didn't believe her, she was surprised that none of them had answered. Her feelings were a little hurt that Daslakh apparently didn't feel like making any wisecracks about crazy fish.

When Pelagia left Taishi, she'd put herself on a course to hit Uranus's atmosphere at a steep angle, roughly along the equator about halfway between the center of the disk and the edge, a few hundred kilometers away from the Uranosynchronous Ring and its numerous elevator cables. Repun, matching her vector exactly, was on the same path but just under a thousand kilometers behind her. Leiting's main force, by contrast, was on a much more orthodox course to brake in Uranus's upper atmosphere for a Miranda rendezvous and wouldn't arrive for another two days. They'd managed a more graceful acceleration in order to have a decent propellant reserve on board in case it came to fighting.

She felt the first thin wisps of hydrogen tugging at her wings when she was still a thousand kilometers above the visible clouds, but it wasn't enough to generate any significant lift. She did roll to her left and ease her nose up five or ten milliradians, trying to shift her course a bit to the north, narrowing the distance to the ring.

At a couple of hundred kilometers above the clouds Pelagia's hull began heating, and she could hear the crackle of ionization through her radio antenna. In just a few moments, between the glowing superheated hydrogen and the ionization static she was half blind.

Repun was nine hundred kilometers back, which meant she would be wrapped in ionized plasma five seconds later than Pelagia. So she waited exactly that long and then rolled to the right, using all the lift from her wings to push herself south. She pulled into a curve, as tight as she could manage—tighter than the planet-spanning turn she'd managed last time she'd been flying in Uranus's atmosphere.

She was diving deep now, well below the methane cloud level which someone in antiquity had arbitrarily decided to call the "surface" of Uranus, and she didn't need to remind herself that she wasn't a whale or a submarine, but a spaceship. Her hull was built to keep pressure *in*, not *out*. Below Uranus's one-bar atmosphere level the pressure outside would be greater than Pelagia's interior. Her diamondoid armor could resist the crushing force for a while, but it was designed to stop sudden point forces, not constant overall pressure. And with no propellant to speak of and precious little fresh water there just wasn't enough stuff on board for Pelagia to try pressurizing her own hull to counter the force from outside.

In the thicker air, with outside pressure climbing above half a standard atmosphere, she was shedding velocity and turning and trying to level off, all without letting the combined acceleration vectors climb above ten gees. That was deadly.

For a digital mind, or even a human pilot, this would have been an interesting trigonometry problem, but a cybership could do it by feel. Pelagia perceived the heating of her outer hull as a burning sensation, and the stress on her structure as pain in muscles and bones she didn't actually have. Her biomonitors and medical implants very definitely did *not* administer anything to counter those sensations—just as in a living body shaped by evolution, pain had a valuable meaning. A cybership with a brain full of painkillers would cheerfully break apart.

That being said, Pelagia distinguished between levels of heat and stress that hurt and levels that *really* hurt. Now she discovered a third level: *really really hurt make it stop.* How had the shipbuilders calibrated her pain levels? Was this still within safety margins, or was she about to lose a wing?

In the end she just had to gut it out, dipping almost to the two-bar level and whimpering from the pain of her wings as her dive bottomed out pulling 9.8 gees, and she could climb again to the safety of the methane clouds at the half-bar level, still turning as hard as she could to the south. Traffic control had given her a map of objects in the atmosphere, so she could avoid elevator cables and balloon cities. Other vehicles would just have to avoid her.

She was still going faster than Uranus escape velocity, and the hydrogen around her was glowing hot. With a blanket of plasma blinding her in the entire electromagnetic spectrum, Pelagia fell back on her most ancient sense, and *listened* to the atmosphere around her. The scream of air rushing past was noisy, but she could filter that out and then strain to hear other sources of sound in Uranus's atmosphere.

There! Off to the north she could hear another hypersonic transit, its path diverging from hers as her agonized wings pulled her ever more southward. Repun had missed her. Given her altitude and heading, Pelagia was pretty sure Repun was bound directly for Miranda. Presumably she'd take up a position in orbit, ready to intercept Pelagia when she appeared.

Pelagia continued her turn, bleeding off more speed, trying to get around the curve of the planet in case Leiting had sent out any sensor drones ahead of the main force. They would all pass through the upper atmosphere in the equatorial zone, and right now she was a bright shining infrared target. She let herself climb some more, up above the ten-millibar level where the plasma around her was thin enough to see through.

She made a complete circuit of Uranus in the next twenty minutes, slowing to a reasonable flight speed and letting her hull cool, blending in with the rest of the airborne traffic among the thousands of balloon cities.

Pelagia spread her wings like an albatross and came in for a graceful touchdown on the landing platform attached to the side of a massive heat exchanger and element processor anchoring the bottom end of an orbital elevator cable.

Most of the processor's weight was supported by five continuous jets of hot gas, powered by waste heat from the Ring far above. As the Uranus atmosphere passed through the processor, structures like giant gills sucked heavier elements out of the hydrogen flow. The processor was big, with a mass of four hundred kilotons, so keeping it aloft meant pushing fifty tons of hydrogen through the heat exchanger every second.

The fraction of not-hydrogen in that stream was tiny, but hundreds of filters processing thousands of tons every minute generated a useful amount of material—carbon, oxygen, and nitrogen, obviously; but also more valuable stuff like phosphorus, sulfur, calcium, and even a little magnesium. The cable up to the orbital ring carried a steady train of cars full of neatly sorted elements, along with a conduit of supercooled helium going back up to take on a new cargo of unwanted heat.

The elevator could handle other freight as needed, of course, and it took only a little arguing with the processor's operating intelligence for Pelagia to buy passage up to the ring as soon as possible. Three hours later she was riding up the cable like any other load of inert matter.

Her journey to the Uranosynchronous Ring took thirteen hours. Pelagia rode inside an open-frame car used to transport odd-shaped payloads ("Like you," the processor intelligence had told her) and so had a wonderful view of the Uranus cloudscape lit by the distant Sun and millions of habs in orbit as she rose through the upper air, going faster and faster.

This wasn't space flight. She was climbing, like a human walking up a flight of stairs, not orbiting. If for some reason she were to toss something away through one of her waste ports, it wouldn't slowly dwindle into the distance on a nearly parallel course, but instead would drop directly back to Uranus and probably make a dent in anything it hit.

The urge to do just that was strong, but Pelagia managed to suppress it.

During the journey she took the opportunity to sleep for the first time since leaving Taishi, and her dreams were all about trying to call out but being unable to make a sound.

Instead of going back to the Elso house, Zee suggested the two of them stay aboard the boat Taraka, at the Mohan-Elso Center. But when he called ahead to make sure a room was available, the boat had some news.

"I'm not moored at the Center anymore," said the crimson whale in his sensorium. "They asked me to move—Vidhi Zugori came out personally to tell me. He said the renovations might cause some hazard, so there's now an exclusion zone around the place. I relocated to the Pukalam Gardens."

"That's all right. Is there still space?"

"Of course! Right now I'm completely empty. I've been thinking about doing some fishing cruises to get a little cash flow."

When he informed Adya, she frowned. "Renovations? The current building is only fifteen standard years old!"

"Maybe he doesn't like the architecture."

"It won a bunch of awards when it was built. No, he's up to something. The timing is a little too convenient. What's Vidhi doing over there?"

"Daslakh mentioned something about storing party supplies for the Constructor's Jubilee."

"I'm not sure if that's even going to happen this year, if Kavita's decided to be a political gadfly. She's making a lot of people unhappy. I wouldn't be surprised if none of the Committee show up for the Jubilee." Adya's expression and color shifted. "In fact, she hasn't said a word about it for a couple of days."

The two of them glided down to the garden on the roof of the houseboat a few minutes later. One of Taraka's bots was waiting with a tray holding two bubbly gold-colored drinks with ice cubes and mango wedges. "You two have obviously been doing stressful things. I insist that you relax for the next full day cycle. A hot soak, massage, and dinner tonight, a long sleep, and then tomorrow do nothing but fish or fly kites."

Neither Zee nor Adya was inclined to put up much resistance. By the time they sat down to dinner—four different kinds of sashimi cut from a tuna caught just after they arrived, a mixed seaweed salad, and

yakisoba noodles; all served with tea and glass after glass of Riesling—
the day's accumulated fatigue was starting to hit. When they were
comfortably full and thoroughly buzzed, they more or less collapsed
into bed with no need of sleep inducers.

Twelve hours later, Adya woke and spent some time admiring Zee's
sleeping form. The side of his face was still bruised, and she fought a
tough battle with herself not to kiss him there.

Taraka had made the two of them promise not to venture into the
infosphere, so Adya was left with the rare luxury of her own thoughts.
She found herself thinking about Kavita's followers. For most of them,
life was a series of entertainments, a little work—as much to occupy
time as to earn gigajoules—and the vague hope of a romantic partner.
The ones who actually found that partner would probably drift out of
the community of dedicated fans once their own lives brought them as
much satisfaction as Kavita's did.

What that left was the hard core, the ones who depended on Kavita
for all the things their own lives lacked. She was their best friend, their
lover, and her adventures were far more vivid and enjoyable than
anything they did. What would those followers be willing to do for
Kavita? She had watched a dragon willing to fight against suited
Security Service officers, and then put aside any resentment over being
paralyzed—all because he thought it would please Kavita.

Was there *any* limit to what Kavita's fans would do for her?

Adya still had trouble accepting how devoted Zee was to her. The
idea of thousands, possibly millions of people acting that way was close
to incomprehensible to Adya.

Taraka appeared, unbidden, in Adya's vision. The red whale avatar
looked very unhappy. *"You have a visitor,"* she said. *"I tried to—"*

The door opened, even though Zee had carefully fastened the bolt
when they retired. A small but massive object with seven limbs landed
on Adya's knees. It was strobing bright hazard orange.

"I got a message from the fish," said Daslakh. "Miranda's about to
be invaded."

CHAPTER FOURTEEN

When Pelagia reached the Uranosynchronous Ring, sixty thousand kilometers above the pale blue cloud tops, she was tremendously relieved to be back in a free-fall environment, where she could move about in three dimensions with her thrusters instead of rolling along roadways and passing through doors with skin-scraping clearances.

The Ring stretched all the way around Uranus, and included the remains of a dozen little moons, either incorporated into the structure or completely dismantled for building material. The backbone of the Ring was a titanic particle accelerator powered by a series of microscopic black holes. Its purpose was to manufacture more holes, in the million-ton range, which could then be used as power plants themselves. Cooling the accelerator was what generated all the heat sent down the elevators to Uranus. The big, cold planet made a great heat sink, so the Ring operations could be a lot more energy-intensive than elsewhere.

Several thousand habitat wheels were spaced along the Ring's half-million kilometer circumference, along with microgravity habitats and half a dozen moons turned into tunnel warrens. In all, about a billion Baseline or higher beings lived in the Uranosynchronous Ring, and local boosters had been touting its tremendous possibilities for growth for several millennia.

Miranda was over the far side of Uranus when Pelagia got to the

Ring, so she couldn't waste any time. Hours of atmospheric flight had filled her tanks with propellant and replenished her water supply, so she only needed to buy some deuterium to fuel her power plant.

This time there would be no wild unauthorized launching. She filed a plan, using a variant identity she'd had since her mercenary days, waited for clearance, and took off like a completely proper shuttle. The only odd thing about her departure was that she was going the wrong way.

A sane spaceship bound from the Ring to Miranda would have launched just before the moon was overhead. The transfer orbit would take a minimum of energy, and twelve hours later the ship would need just a gentle braking burn to touch down smoothly.

Sanity, thought Pelagia as she approached Miranda going retrograde at a relative velocity of two kilometers per second, was vastly overrated.

She had burned far more delta-v than necessary in order to get herself up to Miranda's orbital level and then line up on a counter-orbiting path before the moon rose over Uranus's limb. The encounter took place at exactly the right place: precisely over Uranus's dawn terminator line. Pelagia had the Sun at her back, and Miranda was all lit up ahead of her. All she needed to do was find Repun, launch some torpedoes, and keep from gloating out loud until they hit.

Repun wasn't there.

Pelagia's twin laser turrets (which doubled as telescopes) spotted 5,084 objects around Miranda. Her targeting software eliminated all the known sats and habs in Miranda orbit, which got the number down to a more reasonable 490. She could scratch 352 of those that were on transfer orbits to or from the moon.

That left 138 possible targets orbiting Miranda. She could eliminate all of them with an angular size too big for Repun, and any which appeared to be in transit between other objects in orbit. That left her with 26. She listened to their transmissions—Repun would presumably be keeping quiet, so anybody chattering away could safely be ignored. She also decided to focus on objects in the lowest orbits, the best place to lurk if you wanted to intercept an approaching enemy but didn't know where they'd be coming from.

Four targets were about the right size, kept quiet, and orbited below ten kilometers altitude. She focused her scopes on them as they passed over the shining disk of Miranda's day side. Two were clearly the wrong shape: a sphere and an elongated structure with a bulge at one end. One lit up its engine as she watched, and she could see it was burning on a transfer orbit to one of the orbiting habs.

The last one *had* to be Repun, and Pelagia began feeding target information to her torpedoes—but then stopped when the object separated into three equal-sized parts and two of them began to descend to the surface.

Where was she?

Miranda and Pelagia would intersect in about eight minutes, and Pelagia was pretty sure Miranda would win. She didn't have the time to watch and wait.

Repun wasn't in low orbit, and Pelagia didn't think she was in high orbit. That meant that Repun wasn't orbiting Miranda. Either she had gone off someplace else in the Uranian system, or she was down on the surface.

Hiding on the surface would be clever. Repun could sometimes be clever. What would be a good place? Down at the south pole there was the giant laser-launch system, which complicated matters. But Miranda's north pole was pretty empty. If Pelagia had to hide, she'd pick some chaotic terrain in the far north. Right about...there.

As if to confirm her guess, she saw the hot engine flares of two torpedoes accelerating toward her, burning at ten gees. Impact in six minutes. Her current orbit was too far out, too leisurely to get her out of the way, so Pelagia sent an apologetic note to orbit control and accelerated down and slightly south, trying to get below Repun's horizon as quickly as possible.

Unfortunately, that meant she was closing the distance to the torpedoes instead of running or dodging. If Repun was packing the same kind of warheads as Pelagia herself, they could be either simple kinetic-kill vehicles or single-shot lasers or plasma lances.

A chem laser torpedo had about the same effective attack range as Pelagia's own lasers, and of course a kinetic warhead had to actually hit her. Nuclear lasers or lances could have hit her already, so she stopped worrying about them. Five and a half minutes after launch the torpedoes were a hundred kilometers away, coming in very hot, so Pelagia lit them up, tracking each one with a turret and switching her laser generator between the two in order to keep from overheating the optics.

She got one right away, but the other must have had some brains as it began jinking and dodging, trying to stay inside the response time of Pelagia's turrets. It almost succeeded: at half a kilometer, just a hundredth of a second away, the torpedo blew apart. Fragments peppered Pelagia's armored nose and a couple of them punched through into what would have been pressurized sections if she hadn't sensibly tanked all her air before leaving the Ring.

Pelagia was now below Repun's horizon, but she couldn't hide from Miranda's own public tracking networks. Privacy was all very well for humans walking around inside moons or habs, but a spaceship couldn't take itself out of the tracking data. Doing that was courting suicide in half a dozen ways.

She continued accelerating down until Miranda loomed huge ahead, then flipped and started braking to touch down at a cargo pad next to a big electrophoresis plant. The plant's directing intelligence tried to warn her off private property, but Pelagia could quite honestly claim to be damaged, and thereby declare an emergency landing.

Once on the surface she invoked privacy, and since she was no longer in the jurisdiction of orbit control, it was granted. Pelagia vanished from all the public data streams. As soon as that happened, she began a series of short hops across the surface, careful to keep her maximum altitude below two hundred meters. It was an incredibly inefficient way to travel, and she reached the spaceport at Gonzalo Crater with nearly dry tanks.

What she saw at the port shocked Pelagia. Everything was ... utterly normal. A few freighters were unloading, while a sadly smaller number were taking on cargo. A ferry to the Ring was discharging passengers and the regular shuttle to Umbriel was boarding.

No preparations for invasion, no defenses, no interceptors on alert—Pelagia had been sending warnings for half a week, to absolutely no avail.

"Attention everyone!" she said over the general traffic channel. "There is a hostile mercenary fleet inbound to Miranda, due in the next twenty hours! Prepare for attack and—"

"Silence on this channel!" the port's controlling intelligence told her. "That story is false. The Security Service warned us about misinformation attempts."

"I saw them! I used to be part of the fleet!" Pelagia transmitted images and all the data about Leiting's force she could throw together. "This isn't misinformation. They're real, they're armed, and they're on the way here."

Port Control wasn't having any of it, and Miranda Defense told Pelagia that due to "the current situation," whatever that meant, nobody was available to speak with her directly but her message would be forwarded to the appropriate section.

In desperation Pelagia put together an ad hoc list of all the vessels currently in port along with some of the independent stevedoring and transport mechs. "I don't know what the Security Service has been telling you but this is no joke and it's certainly not misinformation. Leiting's on its way and the first step for any invader is to take control of a port for secure landing. You've got to get ready!"

Some of them dropped out right away, leaving behind dismissive messages. The stevedore and repair mechs muttered about "stupid biopolitical games" and refused to get involved. Most of the freighters expressed concern but other than accelerating their tempo to allow an earlier launch, only a few were willing to take action. In the end Pelagia could only convince two freelance freighters and the Ring ferry to help her delay Leiting's attack.

The ferry was named Uriel, an old mech who had once been a warship of the Telamon Space Force. "My old hull was quite the asskicker. High-acceleration motors, half a dozen lasers, two big railguns, and a meter of fiber-laced ice for defense."

"That would all come in handy right now," said Pelagia patiently. She was simultaneously fueling up and trying to get a message to any of her friends inside Miranda.

"Took a hit from a nuclear plasma lance, point-blank. Hardly anything worth salvaging except my processor and two of the lasers. Sold one and the dead mass and bought myself this little low-g ferry instead. Kept one laser, though, mostly for the optics."

"What aperture?"

"Three meters."

That got Pelagia's attention, and she looked—with her own one-meter optics—at where Uriel was parked at the passenger terminal. The ferry was a simple cylinder standing on spindly legs, with a tube leading from one side to the terminal. Pelagia realized that what she had taken for an oversized docking hatch on Uriel's nose was in fact a laser emitter. Targeting was crude, since Uriel would have to aim her entire hull, but a laser that big could damage targets three hundred kilometers away.

"How do you power it?"

"I don't, mostly. Got a megawatt plant on board, can't do more than tickle you with that. But I do keep a capacitor charged. A full gigajoule. One shot but it'll hurt. Then twenty minutes to recharge."

The two freighters were called Beowulf and Lampyrida, and both were surprisingly well armed for simple cargo haulers. "I do a lot of work in the Equatorials," said Beowulf. "Some of those habs are full of thieves. Shockingly brazen. Hence the coilguns."

"Anything with a bit more range?" Pelagia asked her.

"I've got a megawatt anti-debris laser, but that's pretty short range, I'm afraid. Within about ten kilometers I can give a good account of myself, but beyond that I'm limited to throwing rocks and harsh language."

Lampyrida was more evasive about both her loadout and her reasons for packing heat. "I like to be prepared," she said. "You never know."

"What have you got?"

"Enough. Long range and close in."

"Such as?" asked Pelagia, getting a little impatient.

"I don't like to advertise. Let's just say it's military grade. You won't be disappointed. How much does this job pay, anyway?"

"Pay?"

"You're a merc, that fleet's a bunch of mercs. Who fights for free?"

"I was wondering about that, too," Beowulf chimed in. "Why are you so keen to engage these invaders?"

Pelagia was at a loss for a second. She hadn't really thought about it herself. "I guess . . . I really don't like Leiting, and I've got some friends here in Miranda."

"They're paying?" Lampyrida persisted.

"I haven't asked."

"Telamon Space Force's motto is 'We Fight So That Others May Live In Peace.' I may be just a ferry now but I still hold by that promise," said Uriel. "I'm in."

"You can't expect to stop a superior force," said Beowulf.

"Most of Leiting's fleet are assault transports, not battlecraft. I figure we can disorganize and delay them. Maybe by then somebody inside Miranda will notice they're being invaded and use the launch laser for defense."

"The paralysis within Miranda is distressing."

"There's some kind of internal conflict going on," said Uriel. "Protests, riots, scandals, resignations. Factions in the military and security forces. The infosphere's absolutely swamped."

"It would appear these invaders picked an auspicious time," said Beowulf.

"Can we claim salvage on kills?" asked Lampyrida.

"Probably," said Pelagia. "It really depends on who wins in the end. You might *be* the salvage."

"I'll do it, then."

"Beowulf?"

The other freighter took nearly a second to respond. "Have we any official standing here at all?"

"Not yet," said Pelagia.

"In other words, no. We might be accused of piracy."

"Look, nothing would please me more than to lift off with full authorization from Miranda's Defense Service, an escort of sub-Baseline drone fighters, and the launch laser for fire support. I haven't got any of those things, and I don't have time to get them. I'm betting that if we start shooting at Leiting's fleet, it's going to assume we *do* have authorization, and maybe the laser as well. It will start hitting sensors and weapons on the surface, and *that* will convince all the land-walking idiots inside Miranda that this isn't a hoax."

"And thus retroactively make us heroes instead of bandits. Well, one may criticize certain elements of your plan, but at least you have one. I confess I was afraid this was some kind of vengeful spasm driven by your primordial instincts. I will participate."

Pelagia gave a whistle of amusement, audible only within her hull. The plan had come into existence as she answered Beowulf, and of course her desire to take a shot at Leiting was entirely motivated by primordial instincts. No point in telling the mech ships, though. They wouldn't understand.

She surveyed her own battle readiness. Her lasers were in order, power plant ready, tanks just now full. She had four torpedoes ready to launch and two reloads. No way to patch the hole in her armor in time. She was as ready as she could get.

"Okay, Leiting's fleet should be aerobraking in Uranus's atmosphere now. I suspect they'll come out on course for one of the other moons, or maybe the Ring, and divert to Miranda at the latest possible moment to preserve surprise."

"Titania, I suspect," said Beowulf. "At the current positions of the moons it should only take three kilometers per second of vector change to shift from a Titania intercept to a course aimed at this spaceport. Plus landing thrust, of course."

"So they'll be in position for that in . . ." Pelagia began.

"Eleven hours forty minutes, allowing some uncertainty about braking trajectory."

"Okay, so we have time for one bit of business first. One of my sisters is hiding out here on Miranda, down on the surface somewhere. She's gunning for me. I don't want her to interfere."

"Do you know her position?" asked Beowulf.

"No. She's invoked privacy, same as I did. If she's got any sense—and she does have a little—she's tens of kilometers away from where I saw her last. I guess I'll have to light myself up and draw her attention."

Daslakh stood on the bed between Adya and Zee, still hazard orange but no longer strobing. "The fish has been bombarding the Miranda Defense Service with warnings, and they all get ignored. She sent four hundred thirty-six messages to you, but the Elso house system acknowledged all of them as received, then erased them. Flagging as received meant the messages quit bouncing around the Miranda infosphere looking for you two. If any missed the memo, this boat stopped them," said Daslakh.

"I wished to reduce their stress levels," said Taraka as her avatar appeared in everyone's vision. "No message is so important that it can't wait a few hours. Especially when it's been tagged as misinformation, which they were."

"At some point Pelagia apparently swallowed her pride—and that must have taken a big glass of water to get down—and tried to ping me. That one got through. I wasted two and a half hours getting here because I'm not sure what to do."

"Let's hear it," said Zee.

A moment later Pelagia's familiar orca avatar appeared. "This is important! The mercenary unit I signed up with is on its way to invade

Miranda. I got out a little ahead of them and I'm at the port now. I'll try to interfere with their landings but I can't stop them by myself. What's wrong with Miranda's Defense Service? They won't listen to me. Nobody will!" The little autonomous message thrashed the avatar's tail in frustration.

"Do you know who's conspiring with these mercenaries?" Adya asked the message.

"Somebody from Miranda. A male. He visited Taishi hab about half a standard year ago to recruit Leiting."

"Do you know his name?"

"No, and nobody's going to tell me now."

Adya sat up, frowning though her skin was blue-green. "Vidhi was offworld in March and April."

"But why isn't anyone else listening to Pelagia's warnings?" asked Zee. "She wouldn't lie about something like this. Why was her warning tagged as misinformation?"

"That's an old program," said Taraka, who had quietly remained in the conversation. "It dates back to the Theocracy era, shortly after Mira resigned its post as God. Without Mira to propagate correct doctrine, the religious authorities wanted to be able to prevent anyone from spreading heresy. When the Hundred Captains took over, that was just another bit of infrastructure bundled into the Security Service and forgotten."

"It sounds too useful to forget about," said Adya. "I'm surprised it didn't get used during some of the power struggles among the Families."

"The Security bureaucrats kept it a secret from the Committee. That's my best guess, anyway," said Taraka.

"You seem to know a lot about things that happened centuries ago," said Daslakh.

"I'm old and cunning," said Taraka. The scarlet whale winked its bright white eye and vanished from everyone's interface.

"If they're using it to tag Pelagia's messages, why aren't they doing anything about all the crazy stuff that's flooding the infosphere?" said Zee.

Daslakh politely waited three seconds to give Adya the chance to figure it out.

"I think the Security Service are on the other side," she said. "Vidhi hired the mercenaries, and he's taken advantage of Kavita's popularity to subvert the bureaucracy. They're not stopping the misinformation because Vidhi needs all the normal channels overloaded, to keep the Committee from organizing any effective resistance. Kavita's helping him because they're bonded, but this is going to be a disaster for everyone."

"She probably had a hand in jiggering your house system, too," said Daslakh.

"Likely. When we were little the two of us used to spend hours exploring the Elso house network. There's all kinds of fascinating stuff archived there. I loved finding things, Kavita liked to play with the system itself."

"Talk her out of it—or get her to safety, anyway," said Zee.

"I'm trying," said Adya. She was purple with frustration and her eyes darted about wildly as she navigated the infosphere with her implant.

"What is a safe place if fighting breaks out inside Miranda?" Daslakh asked. "The Elso house isn't, the major cities aren't. Where to hide?"

"The Abyss, if we can talk Dai Chichi into letting us in," said Zee.

"That 'if' is doing a lot of work in that sentence," said Daslakh. "Really, the safest place I can think of is right here. Taraka doesn't have any enemies I could find, and as long as you don't broadcast your location, this boat isn't likely to be on anybody's target list."

"How secure are Taraka's comms?"

"*I* couldn't crack them," said Daslakh. "That doesn't happen often."

"All right, then," said Adya. "Now we just have to figure out how to stop an invasion from this bedroom. I'm afraid we're going to need a lot of coffee."

The little squadron of defenders didn't all lift off at once. Uriel went first, since her anemic little electric plasma drive needed extra time to get her to the place Pelagia had chosen to intercept Leiting's fleet: along Miranda's own orbit, trailing by about five hundred kilometers. That was the spot where the fleet would have to do lateral thrust to aim at Miranda, and maneuvering to a specific trajectory imposed some useful handicaps on the enemy. Uriel would spiral out to the battlespace, looking like nothing more dangerous than what she was, a little ferry.

Once she was safely clear, Beowulf launched next. She aimed at a polar orbit, circling over Miranda's surface at just ten kilometers altitude, along a great circle that crossed both poles and Gonzalo spaceport. If Repun was still at the north pole, Beowulf would pass over her, and if she had hopped south toward the port, she'd still be in the cargo hauler's orbital footprint.

Beowulf made a couple of circuits, keeping up a steady flow of encrypted chatter, like any honest merchant waiting for an orbital transfer window. On her third pass, Pelagia launched just as Beowulf passed overhead. That put Pelagia into a slightly higher orbit around Miranda, lagging by about ten kilometers. In orbit Pelagia couldn't stay private, so she identified herself to Orbit Control, set herself to rotating around her long axis, and waited for Repun to do something.

That didn't take long. Repun was hiding on the surface about forty kilometers north of Gonzalo crater. Soon after Pelagia rose above her southern horizon, Repun opened fire at a range of twenty kilometers, with torpedo and laser.

Things began to happen very quickly. Repun's laser carved a gash halfway around Pelagia's hull, digging deep into the armor but not yet cutting through. Her torpedo launched, accelerating at ten gees directly at Pelagia. It got three hundred meters from Repun and then Beowulf's laser burned through its propellant tank from above, creating a second plume of metallic hydrogen exhaust which threw the torpedo into an uncontrollable spin. At exactly the same instant, the barrage of coilgun slugs Beowulf had begun firing as soon as Repun's laser lit up slammed into her hull.

Repun couldn't laser the incoming slugs—chunks of ceramic-clad iron had no guidance or motors to destroy, and Beowulf had emptied her hundred-round magazine. The first shots didn't penetrate Repun's armor, but they could weaken it, and the rain of metal eventually punched into Repun's innards, while any vulnerable external components were thoroughly wrecked.

Except for one laser emitter. Repun lined it up on Beowulf herself, and at ten kilometers range the beam seared through the freighter's unarmored hull with brutal effectiveness.

But by then Pelagia had stopped her spin and opened up on Repun with her own lasers. At that range she could actually target Repun's functioning turret, melting the aiming servos and cracking the mountings for the optics. Repun's deadly beam became a harmless spotlight shining off into empty space.

"Give up already!" Pelagia called to her. "You put up a good fight and I'm going to keep this laser scar to show off, so everybody can see what kind of badass I've tangled with."

"I've warned Leiting. You can't surprise it now. You're going to get slagged and I'll sit here and watch it happen."

"No, I don't think you will," said Pelagia, and dropped a torpedo on her crippled sister ship.

"Bitch," she muttered to herself.

Adya tried once again to communicate with her sister. A dozen attempts had failed, but she wasn't giving up until she could warn Kavita in person. Once again she waited ten seconds. How could Kavita stand to see that priority message flag blinking in her visual field? Had she blocked her own sister?

But just as Adya was about to start over for the fourteenth time, Kavita appeared in front of her. She hardly looked like the person Adya was expecting. Instead of a flamboyant attention-grabbing outfit she was dressed very soberly, in a Uranus-blue outfit resembling a uniform, but with no insignia. She wore no jewelry at all, and only the lightest countershading around her eyes. Her typical expression of enthusiasm bordering on mania was gone, and she looked at Adya with a face so devoid of emotion it was like looking at a mirror. Her skin matched her clothes.

"You have thirty seconds," she said.

"Kavita, you're in great danger. Wherever you are, get out of there as fast as you can! Zee and I can take you to safety."

"What is this danger that you think I'm in?" asked Kavita, with a hint of a smile in her eyes.

"We think Vidhi's been plotting a coup against the Sixty Families. There's a mercenary fleet inbound, and he can pay them with the Oort payload. I'm afraid he's been using you and your stream to recruit supporters. I know you love him, but he's gone completely off the tether."

Kavita said nothing for four long seconds. Then her brows lowered, her face hardened, and her skin went deep arterial red. "You . . . *idiot.* All these years you've had everyone thinking you're the 'smart one' and you're barely Baseline—if that."

"What—"

"Shut your stupid mouth *for once* and listen. Vidhi's just following orders. *My* orders. *I* put this whole plan together. *All* of it. When I found out about the payload I started thinking about what we could do with it, and it seemed so pointless to just pay off Father's debts and go on the same as before. We can afford real power and I intend to take it. In another twenty hours there won't be Sixty Families anymore, just one. The Committee, the oligarchy, all of them will be gone, and *I* will take their place. *Me.* Kavita the First, Monarch of Miranda."

"That's crazy."

"What's crazy is trying to keep the old system going any longer. I've got support from the Security Service, the rich commoners who are sick of waiting for some threadbare oligarchs to make a marriage alliance in exchange for cash, the cetaceans, and forty-six percent of the population under the age of thirty. And I've got a crack mercenary unit about to touch down and occupy the spaceport."

"Kavita, people will be hurt."

"People will be *killed*—thanks to you."

"Me?"

"My original plan was to strike during the Constructors' Jubilee, when pretty much all the Sixty Families would be together in a party venue on the surface. Plenty of wine, plenty of psychoactives, and a lot of distractions. The troops could land and grab them all in a bloodless coup. Minimal casualties, possibly zero. But *your* friend that crazy orca ship had to poke her big stupid whale nose into things which weren't any of her business, and that meant I had to change the timetable. Now my troops have to fight their way through the ice, and I'm predicting at least a thousand biologicals dead without revival. If *you* hadn't come back, none of that would happen."

"You can't blame me for any of that! Kavita, you can stop it right now. Call off your followers, cancel your contract with the mercenaries. Shut it all down while you still can."

"I don't *want* to stop it. I'm going to be Monarch of Miranda, do you understand? Not some third-tier Minister, not a pawn to be married off for money. Monarch! All my followers will be rewarded, and all my enemies will be punished. What about you, Adya? Which side are *you* on?"

Adya's skin was a chaotic mess of red, yellow, purple, and black. "Kavita, this is all wrong. Why would you do such a thing?"

"We are the heirs of a great family. We deserve better than clinging desperately to the bottom of the Sixty Families hierarchy. I deserve better than pretending to have fun sixteen hours a day. *You* deserve better than marriage to someone who never thinks past their next orgasm. Help me and you can keep Zee. I'll make him a Duke, if you like, and you'll be a Princess!"

Join my comm, Adya sent to Daslakh. *Secretly. I know you can do it.*

"Kavita, what if you fail? What will happen to our family then?"

"Then we will all be exiled, or killed, and the Elso name will disappear. Which is just what's about to happen anyway! We were losing at the old game, so I'm changing the rules to one where we win."

Where is she? Adya asked Daslakh, and made her skin a calmer green. "Do you really think it will work?"

"Of course I do! I put my chances at just over fifty-fifty."

"That's still betting a whole lot on a single coin toss."

"It's far too late to stop. The coin is in the air. All you can do now is try to improve the odds."

She scrubbed all the location tags, of course. Signal lag's no help, not with biologicals talking, Daslakh said to Adya on the secret channel.

Anything! Adya took a deep breath. "All right, Kavita. You've got me trapped. Our family is doomed unless you succeed, so . . . I guess I'm in. For them, not for you. What can I do to help?"

She's sending you a true image. I can see reflections in her eyeballs. Let me just extrapolate what she's seeing.

"That was a quick turnaround," said Kavita. "You're usually a lot more stubborn."

"I'm out of options!"

"You want to help? First, tell your space whale friend to stop interfering with my mercenaries. Second, Jothi Rayador's still at large and none of my followers can find him. If you're so clever, figure out where he's hiding. Locate him and keep him in one place until a strike team can get to him."

"And kill him? I can't—"

"You *can*, and if you do, it will save hundreds of other lives! He doesn't have to be dead, just neutralized. With him out of the way the rest of the Committee will fold. If you want to help, do it!"

Here's where she is, Daslakh sent her, along with an image. *Recognize it?*

The space reflected in Kavita's eyes was a large auditorium. She was facing rows of empty seats and drones hovered about her.

"All right," said Adya. "I'll do it. I don't like this, but it seems I have no choice."

"That's my Addie! Together we're unstoppable!" Kavita broke the link.

"You're not really going to—" Zee began, but stopped when he saw Adya's expression. "All right, where are we going?"

"I need to think about that. Could you go get me some fruit from the roof garden? I'm feeling a little shaky."

"Sure." He got up, stretched—which made Adya involuntarily turn pink and inhale sharply—then went out.

"Okay, what do you want to talk about that you can't say in front of him? Because I can just tell him later," said Daslakh.

"I want you to come help look after my father."

"Sorry, but Zee needs it more than he does."

Adya looked at the little mech, her head cocked to one side like a confused puppy's. "What?"

"Zee needs my help more than your father."

"No, he doesn't."

"Yes, he does. Your father's fine. Zee's going off on a vital mission. If I don't go with him he'll be alone."

"All those things are true, but my father needs protection much more than Zee does. Please?"

"Why do you think your father needs my help more than Zee does?"

"Because I'm going to ask my father to do something risky and Zee doesn't need any help at all. Daslakh, you've been his friend for more than a decade. Has he ever failed to do something he set out to do?"

"He's lucky. And he had me to help him."

"Luck is an illusion. You of all people should know that. And—be honest, do you really think Zee couldn't have managed without your help?"

Daslakh was uncharacteristically silent for nearly a second. "Okay, I have to admit that you're not wrong. Zee gets stuff done. But . . . I worry about him. Don't you?"

"Of course! I worry that he'll get himself killed, maybe even sacrifice himself. But I never worry that he'll *fail*. Set Zee in motion and he's like a planet moving in its orbit. My father . . . Daslakh, you've met him. I love him dearly but he has failed at almost everything he has ever done apart from fishing, cooking, and choosing what to wear. He needs help and he'll never let me do it. You can stay with him and he won't even notice."

Daslakh's outer shell went from hazard orange to white, and a little cartoon face sticking its tongue out in disgust appeared on its back.

"Please?"

"Fine."

CHAPTER FIFTEEN

Pelagia maneuvered close to Beowulf as the two of them orbited low over Miranda's surface. "How are you?" she asked.

"Main drive is gone, turret number one isn't responding, and I'm losing pressure fast."

"If I deorbit you, can you manage a landing with maneuvering thrusters?"

"Theoretically. I fear I cannot be of much use in the main engagement."

"That's all right. We don't have to worry about Repun sneaking up behind us while we're fighting everybody else. Thanks."

"I'll watch the battle and send you a report when you revive," said Beowulf.

"Oh, I intend to live through it. I don't have any choice, really. Can't back up a brain—not without a destructive scan, anyway." As she spoke, Pelagia maneuvered in front of Beowulf and gently approached with tiny puffs from her thrusters.

"You have a brain? You're a biological?"

"*Orcinus sapiens*, at your service." Pelagia centered the hardpoint on her nose against the thrust axis marked on Beowulf's open cargo deck.

"I thought you just liked whales for some reason."

259

"Well, I do. Prepare for thrust." Her main drive rumbled gently for more than a minute, cancelling nearly all of their orbital speed. She disengaged as the two began slowly dropping.

"Why are you putting me here? That isn't the spaceport—just a bunch of carbon assemblers."

Pelagia separated with a brief thruster pulse and slowly rotated to boost again. She aimed her nose a couple of degrees above the horizon. "I don't want you to get hit by any stray shots at the port. Even if Lampyrida and I can delay their landing, I don't think we can stop them completely. Gonzalo Crater's going to be a dangerous place pretty soon. That factory down there has transport links—you shouldn't have any trouble getting field repairs."

"Thank you, I suppose. Given that you're expecting the enemy to get past you, I take it you don't think we're going to make anything off prizes and salvage?"

"Tell you what: I'll grant you salvage rights for my hull. That ought to be worth something. Took me long enough to pay it off. If my squishy bits get vaporized, I'll have no more use for the rest." With a flare of her main engine, Pelagia shot away.

Lampyrida joined Pelagia in orbit shortly after she passed over Gonzalo. The two ships made another low circuit of Miranda. They were definitely an odd pair—the sleek warship with her wings folded, new scars cutting across her black-and-white exterior, and the squat boxy shape of the freighter with her massive landing legs and high-thrust motors.

"Heard what you said to Beowulf," Lampyrida said to Pelagia. "How come I don't get a cut?"

"She earned it. If I get killed out there, you'd better not survive either."

"My backup will. I deserve something."

"You're making an investment. High risk, high reward. Now either fly away or stop bitching. We've got a battle to fight. Coming up on transfer burn."

As they reached the center of Miranda's leading side, Pelagia lit her main drive at full power. She had a moment of queasy suspense, wondering if she really was going to do this with only Uriel for help. But then she saw the welcome flare of fusion fire as Lampyrida's drive built up to sixty percent. The freighter supposedly had no cargo—but when Pelagia did a little quick arithmetic based on the brightness of her escort's engine and the glow of her radiators, the numbers suggested Lampyrida was carrying several tons of something.

Their orbital ellipse began to lengthen. The apoapsis over Miranda's trailing side got higher and higher, eventually reaching the point where they hoped to intercept Leiting's fleet in eight hours.

While Zee went winging off somewhere on his mission, Adya flew home, with Daslakh riding between her shoulders.

"She's no dummy. She's going to figure out that you're playing for the other team pretty soon."

"That's why I need my father. You and he can secure Mr. Rayador while I go to Kavita and tell her where he is. I keep my side of the bargain, but it will be useless to her."

"You're forgetting one important detail: You don't know where Rayador is."

The back of Adya's neck turned an amused shade of pale ochre. "Of course I know where he is."

A second passed. "Well?" Daslakh demanded.

"I'm sorry, I thought you already knew and were just being insufferable."

"One of us certainly is."

Adya circled the Elso house before coming in to land in the central courtyard. Her mother rushed in while she was still taking off her wings. "Where have you been?! It's been days!"

"Things are happening. I have to speak to Father."

"If you mean this foolishness of Kavita's, I'm sure it's all just an elaborate prank or something. A way to get more attention. No, this is important: Dipa has persuaded Entum to reconsider a marriage alliance. They're willing if you are. I just need you to say yes."

It took Adya a second to process what her mother was saying. "What? No! Mother, this isn't the time for that. I have to see Father."

Her mother clutched Adya's upper arm. "Enough of your selfishness! Do you want to see us disgraced and destitute? Don't you care about your parents, your sisters? If you can't care about people, what about this house? If you don't marry Entum we shall have to sell it, and all the family treasures. Just say yes!"

Adya turned to face her mother, and let herself go crimson. "NO!"

she shouted directly into her mother's face. The sound echoed through the empty rooms and passages.

"Then get out. Out, do you understand?"

With an effort, Adya made herself blue again, though darker than usual with a tinge of purple. "I will leave, as soon as I speak to Father. Now please get out of my way."

She stalked through the halls, letting her implant guide her. She could hear her mother wailing behind her.

Adya found her father in the grand dining room. Instead of his customary place at the head of the table he sat about halfway down, his chair pushed back. He was regarding the mural on the wall across the room, and an empty bottle of rice wine sat on the table next to his cup.

"Forgive me," he said, standing unsteadily. "I drank the dregs of the Pazayavit just now. I doubt they will deign to send me any more."

"Father—"

He gestured at the mural. "I came here to say goodbye to Kallan Elso. Soon he will be spared the sight of his successor."

"Father, I've got some important news. Kavita is trying to launch a coup against the Committee. She's got a lot of support and a force of mercenaries. I need your help."

Achan Elso looked at his second-youngest child with an expression of utter incomprehension, as if she were speaking to him in early Woshing without a translator. Then he skimmed through the data packets Adya had sent to his comm implant and went limp.

"Madness," he whispered. "Defeat and disgrace."

"We have to stop her."

He looked up, still stunned.

"Father, listen! You're a Minister and a Magistrate, still. Your terms haven't expired. That means you can raise militia to defend Miranda."

"I have nothing," he whispered. "I cannot even equip myself." He spread his arms. "Shall I issue tapestries to the troops? Arm them with artwork and antiques?"

Adya turned red, and took a step back. "Are you an Elso? Are you Kallan's heir? Miranda is in peril—what would a man of the Sixty Families do? Fight, Father! Raise a regiment and defend the Committee!"

"Where can I find any followers? All loyalty is lost."

"Just ten kilometers from here there's a whole clique of Polyarchists.

I'm pretty sure they've got some weapons stockpiled as part of their revolutionary fantasies. Offer them the chance to make those fantasies real."

"Make common cause with rabble rousers?"

"Yes! Let them prove their patriotism by protecting the people. Kavita is your daughter—if you oppose her, they cannot question your commitment."

"I have no authority. I am an absurdity."

"Father . . ." Adya took a second to adjust her skin color. "When I was little, I saw you speak in a session of the Committee, about tariffs on trade. You stood against them."

"'A flagrant fraud, forcing us all to fund the spaceport operations by inflated prices on goods. Let them charge fees for what they do, fairly and faithfully,'" he said, quoting himself.

"You were in the minority at first, but your integrity and intensity convinced the Committee. You showed them all what the best principles and traditions of the Sixty Families looked like. I was very proud to be your child that day."

His skin was a chaotic mix of blue and yellow and gray. "I despise myself for disillusioning you."

"You are still that man if you wish to be! You've spoken of old traditions—opening your veins like Sunitha Nashichu. There is a greater tradition, Father, the very oldest of the Hundred Captains. Take up arms in a righteous cause, no matter how fearsome the foe! Stand firm for Miranda in her darkest hour. Be great!"

Achan's skin settled to a calm green, though his expression was still sad. "All right, Adya. One last indulgence while I live. What would you have me do?"

"Gather troops and take them to protect Jothi Rayador. Kavita's got teams out searching for him and I know where he is. She may figure it out in time. He's hiding in the old Supreme Temple in the center of Ksetram. I doubt he's got much security since Kavita's infiltrated the services so thoroughly."

"Will you be joining me in this mad jaunt?"

"No. I have to go to Kavita. I'm playing a tricky game here but I think I'm still a step ahead."

"If I recall, Kavita often beat you at games."

"She cheated," said Adya.

"Can you cheat her now?"

"I've learned a lot since then."

Achan stood, and straightened his back. "I am persuaded. If the name of Elso is doomed to vanish from the Committee, let it be remembered for courage and conviction, rather than commerce. Good luck." He put his hands on her shoulders and kissed her forehead. "I think you are the best of my daughters."

He strode from the room like a pirate captain of old. "I shall need to change. I cannot save the world in this wine-spattered yukata!"

"Okay," said Daslakh from Adya's back. "Before I go off with your father, I want you to tell me how you're so sure you know where Rayador is."

"It's only logical," said Adya, sounding almost surprised. "He needs a place that isn't on the list of alternate command posts because Kavita would look there, a place that's hardened against attack, a place with huge secure data-handling capacity, a place which he can reach quickly, and a place which nobody else would be using. Mira's old temple has all that, and it's in Ksetram—the last place anyone would expect him to be."

"You have a lot of local knowledge and subjective attitudes I don't," said Daslakh. "I could have figured that out."

"I'm sure you'd have gotten it eventually. I just hope Kavita doesn't."

The mech dropped to the floor and went off in the direction Achan had gone. As it left the room it said, "It's a good thing you didn't think of taking over Miranda yourself. I think you could do it without any mercenaries."

Zee knew his limits. Even with a palo in his hands, he was hardly a one-man army capable of crippling Miranda's launching laser. Fortunately, he knew some people who were.

So his second stop after leaving the Elso house was the rented eyrie above Ksetram, where Qi Tian, or Sabbath Okada, or whoever he was, stood leaning on the railing with a drink in his hand, watching the chaos below.

When he saw Zee approaching with powered wings on, he put down his drink and suddenly, somehow, he had a weapon in each hand. Some sort of projectile launchers, all compact and deadly and very expensive looking.

"Can we talk before you shoot me?" Zee called out, bringing himself to a stall just above the railing, so all he had to do was put his feet on the floor and slip out of the wings.

"I don't see that we have much to talk about."

"There's a coup underway. Adya's sister Kavita is trying to take control of Miranda. She's got a lot of supporters, especially in the bureaucracy."

"Let me guess: ambitious people who can't get promoted because they aren't related to the Sixty Families, talentless hacks who *think* that's why they're stuck, and a mob of useful idiots. A textbook example. This Kavita obviously studied the masters."

"I want you to help me stop her."

"That's flattering. Why should I?"

"She wants to make herself the ruler of Miranda, and abolish the Committee. All your work will be wasted."

Sabbath eyed him. "That's not necessarily a problem. Chaos in Miranda is almost as useful as active alliance. The main thing is to reduce Trojan Empire influence in the Uranian sphere."

"I don't think there's going to be much chaos. It looks as though she planned everything very well. And she's got the Oort payload Adya mentioned. A trillion gigajoules."

"A nice little nest egg for a new regime. Again, I congratulate the lady."

"You won't be able to bribe her, and once she's in charge you won't have any leverage."

"I have other methods."

"The Trojans are ready to recognize her as the legitimate government of Miranda."

"How do you know that?"

"I called their embassy at Taishi on the way over here. They've got a statement up already. I think she arranged that in advance, probably in exchange for concessions or something."

"Cunning bastards. They outflanked me. I was paying too much attention to the Committee to notice. All right, Mr. Sadaran, what do you want from me?"

"Call me Zee. You said you're good at killing people and stuff like that. Is that true?"

"I take no pride in it, but yes."

"Then put on some wings and come with me. I need to shut down the launching laser."

"Depriving Kavita of the Oort payload. Yes. Good idea. All of her other assets are dispersed. How do you propose to do it?"

"We're going to attack the water intake for the cooling system."

"Good, good. What's your operational plan?"

Zee moistened his lips. "I thought I'd kind of ... go over there and figure something out."

"Intel? Weapons? Extraction?"

"Adya and I only found out what's going on an hour ago, and then I had to get here."

Sabbath's anonymous, emotionless face suddenly burst into a broad grin, like a wolf baring its teeth. "I would be *delighted* to help you! Let me get my gear and then we can go over there and figure something out together."

Pelagia and Lampyrida approached the peak of their orbit, coming toward the plane of Miranda's orbit from Uranus-south. Leiting's fleet was rising from the west, on a fairly steep course from Uranus, moving fast. If they didn't burn soon, they'd miss Miranda completely. Pelagia spotted a legitimate Ring-to-Titania shuttle just behind the mercenaries, and made a note to herself not to shoot at it. And, finally, she could see Uriel moving in from down and east, on a slow ion-drive spiral out from Miranda which might be taking her anywhere.

"I think you have to tell me what you're carrying now," Pelagia said to Lampyrida. "I need to plan tactics. I promise I won't tell anyone else."

"Megawatt debris laser. Three kinetic-kill torpedoes—quarter-Baseline tactical guidance, a plasma lance torpedo, and a jacketed nuke."

"Jacketed?"

"You know—shrapnel. Fifty-kiloton warhead inside a shell of tungsten-steel balls. Get it in the middle of the task force and boom."

"And then you can never land or dock anyplace ever again, because you'll be a pariah. How many habs and ships will you damage, setting that off in near-Uranus space?"

"It's a deterrent. If I think I'm going to get slagged, I'm going out with a bang."

"You're backed up, right?"

"Of course."

"Okay, just to make myself diamond clear: If you set that thing off, you'd better make sure I'm right next to you, because if I survive I'm going to find your backup and melt it myself. Understand?"

Pelagia took stock. Uriel had one laser shot, but it had unexpected punch and range. Lampyrida had her three dumb torpedoes and a standoff weapon, plus a weapon she must not be tempted to use under any circumstances. Pelagia herself had her laser and five torpedoes: one dumb kinetic, a pair of two-stage sprinters, and a pair of smart girls. The smart torpedoes were her treasures, carefully hoarded for the main event. They were asymptotically sub-Baseline, as smart as a system could be without crossing the line into legal sapience. She knew some mech ships who actually budded off fully sapient fragments of their own minds to control torpedoes, but that always carried the risk that your weapon might put its own survival above duty and flee the battle.

One of her girls, named Mantis, was a two-stage kinetic sprinter, just really smart and laced with countermeasures and assorted tricks to keep from being intercepted until it was too late. The other was Urchin, a standoff unit using an antimatter reaction to power a dozen x-ray lasers for a single glorious burst of long-range destruction. Both had variable-thrust first-stage motors and could act as targeting spotters or decoys for Pelagia herself.

"Okay, once the other team starts to change vector, deploy everything except your atrocity machine."

"Roger." When going into battle it always made sense to off-load anything you weren't expecting to survive the fight. An unladen ship could maneuver more briskly, and ships could trade off control of the free-floating weapons. Coming into a fight on a simple vector when your opponent was maneuvering had one huge advantage: Ships under acceleration couldn't deploy drones or submunitions, simply because the little carried units wouldn't have enough propellant to match a ship. Torpedoes might have enough delta-v, but a lot of them were powered by motors which couldn't shut down once they were activated.

Beowulf's estimate was spot-on: Pelagia and Lampyrida were only two hundred kilometers away from Leiting's fleet when the invaders all lit their drives simultaneously, aiming their exhaust flames away from Uranus in order to bend their trajectories toward Miranda. Pelagia and her escort would pass within eighty kilometers, curving behind the armada. Uriel would only get to about a hundred and fifty. Pelagia hoped that would be good enough.

Leiting's force had the best-protected ships in the van, leading the way toward Miranda: nineteen assault landers, with armored undersides and batteries of coilguns to suppress defensive fire as they came down to unload their combat mech teams.

The escort force consisted of four warships: light escorts with mech brains. Pelagia had trained with them before deserting and considered them competent but lacking aggression. Leiting had organized them into two pairs, keeping one duo flanking the heaviest transports while the second vectored to engage Pelagia and Lampyrida.

At the core of Leiting's fleet, fourteen armed transports surrounded two dozen which were effectively unarmed. They all had low-power debris lasers, of course, but most torpedoes were armored against that kind of attack.

As the range dropped to a hundred fifty, the fleet's drives were still burning. "Launch!" said Pelagia. Her tubes ejected her torps with powerful mechanical shoves, but Lampyrida had to use a handling arm to physically move her weapons out of her cargo bay and shove them away. Meanwhile Pelagia's drones left her belly bay and formed themselves into a rough hemisphere at a distance of about two kilometers, covering both Pelagia and Lampyrida.

The drones gave Pelagia an outer defense perimeter and vastly improved her view of the battlespace. With so many eyes spread so wide, she could see Leiting's ships as if she was directly alongside them, and could target specific points on their hulls for maximum effect.

Pelagia let Lampyrida manage the electronic warfare side of the battle. A mech would always be better than a meat brain—although that also left her more vulnerable. Packets of self-assembling viral software filled the battlespace, looking for unsecured antennas or unshielded internal systems. The primary warships were designed with plenty of layered security, but some of the unarmed transports in Leiting's fleet were basically commercial freighters.

The enemy had their own software weapons, too. Pelagia's antennas picked up a haze of signals, but she and her sub-units switched frequencies according to an unguessable preset list of random numbers. Anything coming in on those skipping channels had to have the right prefix from a different list.

"Useless," said Lampyrida. "All firewalled."

"I guess Leiting's training paid off," said Pelagia. "How are you holding up?"

"I'm safe. Put a lot of spare cash into e-hardening. Don't want anyone messing with my mind. Happens more often than most people know."

"If you say so."

At a hundred kilometers it was time to start the dance. Pelagia picked three of the biggest transports and designated them primary, secondary, and tertiary targets. "Okay," she told Lampyrida, "torpedoes attack!"

The nine torpedoes lit up and surged in. The four dumb ones just burned directly toward the primary target, while Lampyrida's standoff weapon and Pelagia's two-stage torpedoes followed semi-random courses with no identifiable target, just to get close before the final strike.

Mantis veered off toward Miranda, curving through the fleet and then making a wild tumble before shutting down its motor, as if crippled by a laser hit. Urchin went off at a ninety-degree angle, getting below the fleet before turning to charge in.

Leiting had to worry about what defenses might be waiting at Miranda, and couldn't afford to waste ammunition, so only the escorts on intercept duty launched anything, firing a spread of eight torpedoes at Pelagia and Lampyrida.

However, the fleet had an effectively infinite supply of photons, so all the ships with lasers opened up, trying to burn the torpedoes during their forty-second death ride.

The dumb ones followed an evasion pattern which even a Baseline mind could figure out with three-quarters of a minute to work in. All four of them either flared and tumbled as lasers burned into their fuel containment, or lost target lock and accelerated into deep space as their sensors and processors melted.

One of the two-stage torpedoes also fell to the laser barrage, but the second got close enough to unload its ultra-high-speed attack stage. The engine flare lit up the whole fleet as the warhead covered the last ten kilometers in less than three seconds, smashing into the largest transport's engine assembly and turning a big expensive fusion motor into an expanding cloud of plasma and molten scrap metal. That transport hadn't finished its burn and so would miss Miranda completely.

"You'd all do well to follow her," Pelagia broadcast en clair. "There's plenty more torpedoes and a terawatt-class laser at Miranda."

Nobody changed thrust vector, but it was worth a try.

The barrage of incoming torpedoes encountered Pelagia's drones. Two got spoofed by drones using their little infrared lasers to masquerade as a ship's thermal output, and smashed into them, destroying expendable drones instead of punching holes in Pelagia. A third got dazzled by seven drones concentrating their lasers on it and lost targeting. It shot past Pelagia with a hundred meters to spare.

Three more drones sacrificed themselves to stop three more torpedoes, which left Pelagia staring at two incoming weapons and less than a second to respond. She targeted one with her laser and thrust violently to the side. The first went off course, while the second struck Pelagia's flank at a very shallow angle, knocking off a section of armor five meters long but not penetrating her hull.

Lampyrida's plasma lance went off then, stabbing a beam of plasma a hundred kilometers long—at nothing.

"What was that?" Pelagia demanded.

"I don't know! I was aiming at the secondary target!"

"Where did you buy that gob of mold?"

"I salvaged it," Lampyrida admitted. "Guess I should have sold it."

Mantis was among the fleet now, and activated her sprint warhead while the main bus shot off toward a different target. The defenders easily slagged the bus section but the warhead smashed into the secondary target, another engine-crippling hit. That ship wouldn't miss Miranda, but would arrive with an impact velocity of about a thousand kilometers per hour and no way to slow down.

Uriel took the opportunity to snap off her single shot at the tertiary target, scoring a solid laser hit which ruptured one fuel tank. Pelagia couldn't tell if the target had enough juice left to land safely. Leiting's reserve pair of escorts moved toward the new threat and let loose a barrage of torpedoes. Poor Uriel had no way to dodge or stop them.

"Urchin, now!" Pelagia commanded.

Her last smart torpedo detonated in the heart of the fleet. Eight of the deadly x-ray beams vaporized the weapons tracking Uriel, and the other four skewered transports.

"That was nice but foolish," Uriel commented. "You could have done a lot more damage if you'd written me off."

"Just another biological, ruled by whims and instinct," said Pelagia. "Get clear of the area in case Leiting's feeling vindictive."

Pelagia and Lampyrida were closing in on laser range now—which of course put them in range of Leiting's escorts. There wasn't any point in hoarding photons, so they all opened up. Lampyrida's cycle time was criminally slow, and as soon as the escorts noticed that they simply ignored her.

Which left Pelagia trying to dodge the high-powered laser pulses from the two escorts, and a lot of low-power potshots from the rest of the fleet. She jinked and bobbed as well as she could, but the pulses kept coming, punching holes in armor, burning her folded wings, and blinding external sensors.

Pelagia experienced damage to her hull and systems as pain, and the barrage felt as though someone was poking her with a red-hot metal rod, over and over and over again. Her damage display showed a spreading rash of red spots indicating hull breaches, concentrated on her front end.

She thought of running—rotate and burn, get some distance, but she couldn't stand the idea of letting Leiting know it had chased her off. Besides, she might do some more damage to the fleet, and that in itself was worth the risk.

She kept up return fire as well as she could, and managed some serious hits on one of the escorts, but the sheer volume of incoming energy began to tell. One of her laser turrets got crippled, doubling her cycle time. The hits on her armor began to reach her interior, cutting into fuel tanks, boring into pressurized spaces, severing pipes and data lines. Her forward thrusters stopped working when the propellant tank got sliced open, and that left her an easy target.

The range was increasing now. The low-power hits were doing less damage, but the remaining escort could still hurt her badly, and did. The enemy got a good side angle on Pelagia and concentrated on the big scar where the torpedo had carved away her protection. Her sensations of pain became agony as the laser pulses bit deep into her internal structure.

When the beams found her armored brain tank, she felt nothing at all.

Achan Elso took one of the remaining family boats to Samrudhi Natural Foods—with nice judgement he left the elaborate Elso ceremonial barge behind and used an ordinary cargo catamaran with a fishy smell no amount of cleaning goo could quite get rid of. He did wear a nice business-style set of smart-matter tights with a high-collared vest, indicating seriousness. Daslakh accompanied him, as Adya had asked, but kept quiet and inconspicuous.

Adya's father moored his catamaran on the upper platform of the sea farm and then took a deep breath before walking over to the entry. He stood quietly, trying to look dignified—one seafood entrepreneur paying a call on some colleagues on a matter of importance.

They kept him waiting nearly five minutes. It was obviously deliberate: They wanted to snub Achan and they wanted him to know it. He frowned briefly a couple of times, but kept his skin a nice polite pale green.

Finally the door opened and Janitha Velicham stepped out, wearing a full-body suit of combat armor, but no weapons or helmet. She did not invite him inside. "What?"

"Have you been following the news?"

"I've been trying. Everybody's saying something different. I can see that a lot of people are fed up with the Sixty Families—and I can see that your kid is in the thick of it all. If you're planning on trying something, you can forget it. We've already voted—the Polyarchist Alliance is opposed to this coup. Monarchy is completely disconnected from market forces."

Achan cleared his throat. "That is good to hear, as I need your help. I have come here in my mandate as a Magistrate to raise a militia unit for the defense of Miranda. I understand your organization has an armed auxiliary branch, and I come to commission you."

"You want us to fight for the Committee? Not likely."

"No, I want you to fight for *Miranda*. There are interplanetary mercenaries preparing to land as we speak, and because my daughter has described this as a political conflict, the mechs are doing nothing. I am asking you to help repel the invaders."

"The ones your daughter hired?"

Achan swallowed hard. "Yes."

She studied him for a moment. "Okay, make your offer," she said.

Achan swallowed again but remained smooth green. "I can offer you nothing," he said. "I haven't a joule to my name, and no matter how this conflict ends I soon will have neither rank nor position. I can only ask you, as people of Miranda, to join me and fight together for our world."

Janitha stared at him. "Not even a promise?"

"Only to stand by your side."

"And after all this is done, you go right back to being a Sixty Families snob and I go back to being underclass?"

"After this is done I will lose my position, and I may wind up with a compliance implant or a ticket to exile. In either case I will probably take my own life instead. But until that moment I intend to protect our world. If you wish to show that commoners deserve a place in government, then prove you are worthy. Defend our world with me!"

"What are you asking us to do? Specifically," Janitha demanded.

Achan stood a little more stiffly. "I was asked to protect Jothi Rayador, and I think that is essential to thwarting my daughter's conspiracy."

"Rayador?"

"He is still at large, but I believe I know where to find him. I have to reach him before my youngest daughter does, and guard him from her."

She looked at him and narrowed her eyes, and her skin darkened slightly. "We're going to be Jothi Rayador's security detail?"

"In effect, yes." The two of them regarded each other, and silently reached an agreement.

"All right, then," she said. They raised palms toward each other. "But there's one thing you need to understand: You're not the centro of this crew. I am. You've got the formal authority but I'm the one who makes the tactical decisions."

Achan nodded, though obviously with great reluctance. "I agree that someone else ought to be in charge of doing that. I recognize your rank."

"Come on in, then," said Janitha. "We'll make some plans. Who's the mech?"

"It is a friend of my daughter Adya. She thinks very highly of it, and I trust her judgement."

Adya glided down to land at the Mohan-Elso Center, and immediately found herself surrounded by a swarm of armed bots. "Move only as instructed!" one shouted at her.

"I'm here to see Kavita. My *sister* Kavita."

"Follow this unit," said the bossy bot, lighting up blue for attention. It led her through the main doors. The diamond windows across the front of the building were covered by protective curtains of graphene and ballistic cloth, and a pair of intimidating-looking combat bots with Security Service insignia stood at the entrance.

Inside, the Center was as crowded and busy as one of Kavita's public dance parties at Viranmar Plaza. Defense and Security officers with lethal-looking weapons, bureaucrats, and civilians all rushed about on errands of their own, or gathered into little groups waiting for orders. Among them Adya noticed an unfamiliar uniform: tunics in the same Uranus blue-green as the Defense uniforms, but with purple cloth at the collars and cuffs and a stylized gold crown insignia on the breast.

When they glimpsed her, a number of people did double takes and pointed, and a few clapped in glee or made awkward salutes, but as soon as they noticed her virtual tag and realized she wasn't Kavita, they turned away. She felt curiously numb, and then realized her comm implant couldn't find any networks to link with.

The bots led her toward the auditorium—the blue-glowing one in front to show the way, and three more in an arc behind her, all humming along on their little fans. She glanced to one side. The bot's micromissile pod wasn't pointed at her, but of course it didn't need to be.

Kavita was on the stage in the auditorium, seated in what could only be called a throne. Adya recognized it—a work of art by a human named Sasaki, from back during the Cetacean Republic era. Made of synthetic topaz formed in flame shapes and lit from below, it made Kavita appear to be seated in the heart of a fire. Displays hovered in the air around her, showing the crowds in various locations across Miranda, a map of the transport systems showing blockages created by her followers, and a view of orbital space.

She was conferring with one of the Security officers when Adya came in, and took a couple of minutes to finish before gesturing to the bots. "Bring her forward. Why are you here, Addie?"

Adya waited until she stood at the front of the auditorium, just below the stage. "I found Jothi Rayador. Or at least I've deduced the most likely place to look for him."

"Well?"

"He's probably hiding out in the Supreme Temple building in Ksetram."

Kavita didn't need to hear an explanation. She nodded. "I think you're right. Good job. You could have just called me, though. How did you know to come here?"

"You shouldn't send live images from a place you want to keep secret."

Kavita's eyes widened for an instant. "I'll keep that in mind from now on." She looked at nothing and spoke aloud. "Dav, get one of the response teams in Ksetram. Make sure it's all volunteers, no Service people. Heaviest weapons they can find. Tell them to get into the Supreme Temple building, secure it, and search the whole place. Prisoners if possible. And put the site on the priority target list for the mercenaries."

She made the orbital space display expand so that Adya could see it. "They're landing now. The mechs on the surface are staying out of it."

Adya watched as the first of the armed transports came in, coilguns and lasers blazing away at targets offscreen. It dropped very fast, so fast that Adya wondered if it was about to crash. But at just ten meters above the surface its engine flared at maximum thrust. Biological troops would have been knocked out or killed by that acceleration, but the mechs on board were fine.

"Your whale friend got about ten percent of the fleet before they got her, but I think Leiting's got enough troops," said Kavita.

"Pelagia? Is she all right?"

"Killed in action."

Adya forced herself to stay blue. She refused to allow Kavita to see her weep for Pelagia. Instead she took a deep breath. It was time to do what she had come to do. She bounced up to the stage and told the floor to make a chair for her next to Kavita.

"What are you doing?"

"I want to see what's going on."

Kavita gestured at the tactical display. "Rayador's loyalists—and a couple of my informants—are gathered at the main concourse and the freight terminal. They're going to try to hold Leiting's troops in the port, but they're going to fail."

"It looks like they've got a lot of troops," said Adya.

"Tactics is as much about where and when as how much force you bring to bear. I gave Leiting full schematics of the port complex."

Adya and Kavita watched as the green dots representing the invasion force flowed out from the ships to occupy the hangars and service areas of the port. Meanwhile a much bigger blob of red dots—the defenders—massed at two choke points leading away from Gonzalo Crater.

The green dots didn't approach the red ones. Clumps of them grouped at the two entrances on the inside, in what even Adya could recognize as defensive positions. Leiting wasn't preparing to fight its way out of the port, it was protecting against attack.

Instead, the main force seemed to be assembling in the biggest of the service spaces, where entire ships could be repaired or built. And then suddenly they were moving again—moving down, into a freight conveyor tunnel that ran under the port. The conveyor system was shut down, but the mechs and combat bots of Leiting's army swarmed through the empty tunnels. In minutes they had bypassed the defenders, putting troops behind them to pin them in place.

Adya rubbed the back of her neck, and very quietly slipped one hand into the collar of her suit, where she had concealed a medical slap patch. Getting it, and herself, into position just behind Kavita was the whole purpose of this entire plan. She took out the patch and palmed it, took another deep breath and then—

Then the door of the auditorium burst open and one of Kavita's Defense Service followers ran in, orange with terror. "Kavita! The laser!"

CHAPTER SIXTEEN

Achan Elso, Daslakh, and a dozen Polyarchists emerged from one of the ornamental lagoons next to the triangular plaza in the center of Ksetram. All the lakes and ponds in the city were open to the ocean below, and had quays and ramps for the convenience of swimmers or people arriving via submersible.

As ordered, Achan stayed in the center of the group while Janitha led the way. She crept up the landing ramp and peered over the rim into the plaza, then gestured for the others to follow. All of them were in dark mode, with no comm connections of any kind. Achan found the experience weird—just about every waking moment of his life had been spent communicating with someone else, and being alone inside his own head was a little disorienting. Daslakh stayed out of the way of everybody's feet but kept its own counsel.

The plaza itself was a triangle a kilometer across, surrounding the huge dome of the Supreme Temple. No plantings or decoration interrupted the vast open expanse of pavement. It had been designed for throngs of devout worshippers to gather and hear the words of Mira, the long-gone digital god. At the moment it was empty, except for a little knot of half a dozen exhausted Kavita fans sharing an improvised picnic of wine and printed dumplings a few hundred meters away.

At the center rose a huge dome, a hundred meters high and twice as wide—actually the upper half of the spherical Supreme Temple. One of its three grand doorways faced them.

"Casual," hissed Janitha. "Just walk, weapons down. Act like you don't know what's going on."

One of the other mers laughed aloud at that. "Not hard!"

She climbed up the ramp and set out at a moderate pace. The others followed. Half the Polyarchists—including Janitha—were mers, with long tails balancing their forward-canted bodies. Four were legacy humans. One was a dolphin, whose suit had extended legs so she could keep pace with the others instead of bounding along on her flukes. And one was a mech—a big mech, with a chassis built for underwater construction and repair, now using two of its six flexible arms for walking.

It extended another arm to Achan, and spoke to him through a little speaker in the smart-matter hand. "I don't know if you remember me, Mr. Elso. My name's Tursas. I used to work for you."

"I recall readily! Your skillful strength saved the day when one of the mooring cables parted. I hope you know how little I loved laying off our laborers, but we simply could not pay so many."

"That's okay. I'm making more working for Janitha anyway. We get a percentage instead of a salary."

"Ah. Good."

After a pause Tursas spoke again. "When I worked for you I noticed that you appeared to be very fond of Kavita." When Achan said nothing it continued. "I am curious why you are not supporting her coup, and instead are working against her, with people you previously have criticized in public."

"I tried to teach all my children to respect tradition. If some great calamity threatened Miranda, and the Committee could not cope, then perhaps a change would be correct. Our family's failures are not enough."

"It seems unlikely that change can be avoided now," said Tursas.

The little squad was halfway across the plaza when Janitha said, "Vehicles coming in. Run for it!"

Achan prided himself on keeping in shape, but he was still panting by the time they reached the great doorway. Behind them he could see a couple of ducted-fan flyers touching down.

"Get us inside!" said Janitha, shoving Achan at the side of the doorway.

The great doors themselves were clad in diamond over a layer of gold, making them glitter in the daylight. Achan knew that behind the showy exterior were thick layers of armor and massive mechanical locks. They wouldn't get inside unless someone inside let them in.

A little niche at the side held a display. "Hello!" Achan shouted. "This is Achan Elso! I must see Jothi Rayador at once! I have come to help!"

After a second the display showed a face—Harish Rayador, Jothi's eldest son. He frowned. "We don't make deals with traitors."

"I have come along with these Polyarchists to offer our aid. I disown my daughter. Please! Rebel troops are coming!"

"Quickly, then."

The huge door opened just a meter and all of them piled inside before it boomed shut. Five Rayador family members pointed a variety of weapons at the newcomers. The interior of the sphere was dark and cool, lit only by a few scattered portable lamps. Wide bridges led from the doors to a central circular platform surrounding the empty space where Mira's processor had once been. All of them looked tiny in that great echoing volume.

"Achan! If it was anybody else, I wouldn't have believed what you said. But you—and a gang of Polyarchists? It's too insane to be a trick." Jothi Rayador approached, and Achan could see he also had a weapon in hand, though it wasn't raised.

"Adya deduced your location and sent me here. I fear Kavita has found you as well. Some of her followers are outside—armed!"

"I don't know who to trust."

"She has hired mercenaries from Taishi. They are already on the surface."

"They're already inside! Our defense plans are decades old, and didn't allow for things like new conveyor tunnels. I've got reports of troops in Svarnam and a dozen other cities."

"It sounds like we're too late, then," said Janitha.

"Velicham, isn't it? Polyarchist Movement. Why aren't you outside shooting at the doors with the rest of the rebels?"

"We want to broaden the franchise, not eliminate it. The oligarchy needs new blood, new ideas—new people." She spoke as though she had rehearsed a hundred times.

"I'll keep that in mind if I get out of here alive."

"So..." said Janitha. "Are we going to hold this place or slip out?"

"There's no place else to go," said Rayador. "I think we're safe until they can bring up heavy weapons. And if they do, I'm not going to die. Sorry, Elso, there's not going to be an old-fashioned glorious last stand. Once they can crack open the doors, I will surrender. The rest of you can do the same, or try to get out into the ocean through the water system."

Janitha glanced at the other Polyarchists. "Safer to surrender when everybody's watching. Sorry, guys, I thought we had a chance."

"Excuse me," said Daslakh, changing its shell to a bright rescue green. "I think everybody's forgetting something. We haven't lost yet."

The braking laser up on the surface was throwing a gigawatt of energy at the approaching payload to bleed off its immense speed. That much energy produced an awful lot of waste heat as a byproduct, twice as much as the laser actually emitted. On a hab or a small asteroid, the only way to dump that heat would be via huge, fragile radiators. But Miranda itself was made of ice, and waste heat simply helped to keep the subsurface ocean from freezing up again. That was one reason Miranda's other defenses were disgracefully weak: The laser array was hardened and Miranda could throw out more energy than most would-be attackers—as long as the control center wasn't occupied by conspirators, that is.

Cooling the laser array required five tons of freezing-cold seawater from the bottom of Miranda's ocean every second. That water was supplied by a bundle of seven graphene pipes, each one a meter wide. Those pipes were surrounded by a self-sealing layer of smart matter, an aerogel insulation blanket, and a diamond outer casing to protect against accidents or sabotage. All that protection meant drills, saws, laser cutters, or even small explosive charges wouldn't be able to cut any individual pipe, let alone all seven.

Zee learned all that as he and Sabbath flew south across the ocean.

"Those public-information sources won't tell you any details about the active defenses, but I bet it has some," said Sabbath. He was silent for a couple of seconds, then continued. "Yes. A one-kilometer exclusion zone backed by nonlethal sonic and maser systems. Nothing lethal, at least not autonomous. If your friend Kavita is serious about protecting the laser, she's got some security mechs, or bios in battlesuits on guard."

"She's got pretty much the whole Security Service in her camp."

"Lovely. Of course, even a loyalist officer would still likely object to random strangers interfering with the laser cooling system. I don't think we can talk our way past any security."

"Some of them shot at me and Daslakh."

"And now that the event has begun, they're likely to be packing their heaviest firepower. I don't know what you've figured out yet, but allow me to point out that the suit I'm wearing is a fully capable combat platform. It might be relevant."

"I thought it might be," said Zee. "If there are any guards, I guess you have to take them down."

"And you?"

"I'm still trying to figure it out."

"We've got about half an hour before we reach the exclusion zone. Oh—some useful advice. Nonlethals can still do real damage. The sonics will probably destroy your cochlea, and the masers can raise blisters. The pain can overwhelm most civilian medical implants. How are you at tolerating injury?"

"I do *nulesgrima*, sometimes for real."

"Well, just remember: anything can be replaced. Trust me, I know firsthand. Though in my case it's more like tenth-hand, at least for the right side."

"Don't worry about me."

The two of them stayed high, just below the light panels under the ice crust. Even though the panels were tuned for plant growth and vision, the sheer wattage this close made the two men quite warm. Only the air streaming over their skins saved them from heatstroke.

"There," said Zee, nodding his head at a shaft extending from the icy roof down to the ocean surface.

"How do you know—oh, I see," said Sabbath. "No farm, no surface platform, no lights under the water. Just some big pumps in the ocean."

"Daslakh figured it out for me."

"Unsurprising."

"How do you two know each other?" asked Zee.

"It's a long story, and some parts of it are still secret. If you and I live through this, I'll give you a summary."

When they reached the one-kilometer circle around the intake pipes, a voice began to sound inside Zee's head. *"Warning! You are entering the safety exclusion zone for an essential services site. Divert now!"* It started out as brisk and concerned, the tone of a parent urging a toddler to put down something fragile or sticky. As they flew closer the intonation and the actual sound of the voice got louder, harsher, and more threatening.

That was followed by a faint buzzing noise which seemed to be located in the center of each human's skull. The noise increased in volume and pitch as the distance to the shaft decreased, becoming a whine and then a scream.

"Does your suit have sonic protection?" asked Sabbath.

"No!" Zee shouted back.

"Inflate it. That'll help some. Don't let it get to you."

Easy for him to say, Zee thought. Sabbath probably had some kind of shielding in his suit, or maybe super-spy ears which could ignore the sound projectors.

Zee found the "water rescue" setting for his suit and activated it. The clingy garment suddenly bulged out everywhere, making it very hard for him to beat his wings. His cowl turned into a bubble around his head. The buzzing didn't disappear, but it was back down to merely annoying. He also tried a little evasive maneuvering, so that the sonic projectors would have to reacquire him every second or two.

The volume of the sound increased, until tears were pooling in Zee's eyes from the pain inside his head. Consequently he didn't notice the maser pain beam at first. His skin felt pins and needles, then an overall itch, and then . . . Zee yelled aloud as every surface of his body facing the water intake suddenly felt as if someone was pressing a slab of heated iron against it. He kept his head down to shield his face and eyes, but there was no way to protect his outstretched arms as he flew.

Jinking and bobbing helped. There was a slight lag as the noise and pain projectors reacquired him. It was during one brief respite that he saw a diamond formation of seven sphere-shaped fliers diving at them from somewhere up at the top of the pipe bundle, where it passed through the ice roof.

The flying machines' comm tags identified them as Security Service drones, and their comm warnings added to the cacophony inside Zee's skull. Amid the noise and jabber he did make out the phrase *"lethal force."*

Sabbath fired up the impellers on his wingtips and climbed toward the drones. Zee banked his own wings to cut behind Sabbath, using him as cover while Zee flapped hard to gain altitude.

The drones opened fire, some kind of smart but low-velocity projectiles which dove and turned to track Zee and Sabbath. Sabbath was able to vaporize the two chasing him, with what Zee guessed was a laser mounted in one arm of his suit. Zee had no such luxury, and only evaded the one tracking him by holding his wings back at his sides and diving headfirst toward the sea. As it gained on him he suddenly opened his arms wide, coming to a complete halt in the air while the weapon shot past and hit the water.

To Zee's relief, it didn't explode but rather created an expanding mound of bright orange foam. Still, a hit from one of them would make it impossible to fly.

Above him Sabbath was taking the fight to the drones, using his laser to blind one of them and hitting a second with a burst of hypervelocity needles from his other arm, which knocked out the drone's lift fans and sent it tumbling into the sea.

Shooting back apparently pissed off the drone operators, because the two remaining units accelerated, curving around in opposite directions to flank Sabbath, and firing at him with explosive rounds, which detonated close to him and showered him with shrapnel.

Sabbath's suit could handle the blast and the fragments, and he fired at the drone on his left with his needle gun as it dodged chaotically. Finally he switched modes and launched a spray in its general direction. The edge of the shower hit it and it began to spin uncontrollably and fall.

The remaining drone took the opportunity to get close to Sabbath, hiding in the blind spot behind his shoulders. He jerked with the impacts as it hit him with a pair of shock rounds, and Zee could see the bright sparks of electricity when they hit.

Fortunately for Sabbath the prongs were embedded in his suit, not his flesh, so he did a sudden forward roll and kicked the drone with his heels, then as he dove under it he fired his laser weapon until something inside the drone's casing caught fire.

"There's going to be more soon," Sabbath warned. "If you have a way to shut down the water, use it now."

"It's already done," said Zee. "I asked Dai Chichi to bring some rescue bubbles and block the intakes. You and I were just a diversion."

Sabbath smiled at that. "Well done! But how did you get him to help you?"

"I asked as nicely as I could—and I pointed out that with the Sixty Families out of power, none of his leverage would protect him."

"Daslakh's been teaching you, hasn't it?"

"Well, by example, I guess. So now—"

Zee didn't finish his sentence because the drone Sabbath had blinded must have had other senses besides sight to use in targeting its weapons. He felt a thump on his back, as if some overly hearty acquaintance had given him a solid slap, and in the same moment Sabbath, in front of him, was showered with red as the explosive charge blew Zee's torso apart.

At Miranda's south pole, the giant phased-array laser sat quietly, a sphere more than a kilometer across, standing on five thick legs. Power, cooling, and access tubes passed through an opening in the bottom to connect the laser to all the infrastructure of Miranda's civilization under the icy crust. From the right angle one could see a twinkling of dust and ice particles heating to incandescence as they fell into the gigawatt beam it was pumping into space, but the laser light itself was invisible to anybody who wasn't on a direct line between the sphere and its target. Anybody who *was* on that line would flash into plasma this close to the emitter array, so there were proximity warnings and flashing safety lights on the crater floor around it.

Suddenly, without any warning and with no other visible sign, the faint sparkle of particles in the beam disappeared. As the flow of cooling water from inside the moon halted, the laser array's control systems shut down the beam. The safety lights turned off.

And a thousand kilometers away, the inbound payload was no longer decelerating.

In Kavita's command center at the Mohan-Elso Center, news of this sparked chaos. Her husband Vidhi hurried into the room along with the mech Vasi and a lot of people Adya didn't recognize.

"We've got to get that launching laser back!" Kavita commanded. "Send *everyone* to the cooling intake and fix whatever's wrong. Now!"

Adya decided this was her moment. She started to put a sisterly arm around Kavita, reaching for the exposed skin of her scalp with the slap patch. But Kavita whirled and took a step back. The two both hesitated for an instant, then Adya lunged for her sister. Kavita managed to grab her right wrist, holding the slap patch away from herself.

"Somebody come get her!" she shouted.

Adya vaulted over her sister—no great feat in Miranda gravity—putting Kavita between herself and the oncoming guards. With her left hand she drew the multitool she had stashed in the pocket of her vest, and held it to Kavita's neck. The tool shaped itself into a cutting blade, molecule thick.

"I didn't want to do this," said Adya.

"You always want to ruin everything."

The advancing guards hesitated.

Meanwhile on the display the white dot representing the incoming payload fell faster and faster.

"Go ahead and cut my throat. Then they'll shoot you, I'll be good as new in a couple of hours, and my revolution will succeed." Kavita glared at her followers. "Come on, call her bluff!"

Adya flung down the tool. "I can't. I wish I could but I can't," she said, and then four of the Security officers grabbed her and dragged her away from Kavita.

"Was this all just so you could try to tranq me?"

"Yes," said Adya.

"I've got medics, they've got stims and antidotes. It wouldn't do anything but..." Kavita stopped and turned to look at the displays. "Delay me."

The white dot reached the surface of Miranda. A camera in orbit caught the event in real time. The payload struck the sloping side of a ridge, bounced off, and smashed into the bottom of a valley. A ghostly purple flash followed as the precious cargo of chameleon particles, suddenly holding vastly more mass-energy than when they were harvested on the fringe of interstellar space, shot off in every direction at nearly the speed of light. Everyone in Miranda felt an instant of vertigo at the faint shift of gravity, and the surface of the ocean suddenly broke out in white-capped waves.

"That was a *trillion* gigajoules!" cried Kavita.

"It was *mine*," said Adya.

Kavita raised her fist and took a step toward Adya, then stopped and made herself blue again. She looked at Vidhi. "Does Leiting know? About the payload?"

"I never mentioned it," he said, and turned to Vasi. "Did I?"

"Not that I witnessed," said the mech.

"Then don't. Nobody speak of it. We may be able to pull this off after all." She turned back to the Security team and her eyes met Adya's. Her eyes narrowed and she turned pale purple. "You had a plan when you came here. What was it? What now? You can't get a message out."

"I don't need to," said Adya. "It's far too late for that."

The defenders inside the Supreme Temple watched the external camera view as new troops arrived in the plaza outside.

"That doesn't look good," said Jothi Rayador. "Those look like combat mechs."

"Albiorix Tactical Systems model 649 medium-assault chassis," said Daslakh. "Old but reliable. A mix of smart matter and plain old mass. The primary weapon's an electromagnetic grenade launcher, plus some micromissiles and a laser."

"That won't punch through the doors here," said Janitha. "Not for a long time, anyway."

"What about that one?" asked Rayador.

"*That's* a problem. It's an ATS model 5320 *heavy*-assault unit. That thing on its back is a missile launcher, four shots. If they've got the right warheads, they can blow this place wide open."

"I see another one of those," said Janitha. She looked down at Daslakh. "Still think we can win this?"

"I'm pretty sure we already have but the bad guys don't know it yet. This would be a good time to open negotiations. Be sure you talk to the merc commander, not Kavita. Pelagia said its name is Leiting."

"Allow me to be your ambassador," said Achan. "Those troops might try treachery against the Committee's commander."

Rayador studied him. "No glory, Elso. Go out, talk to them, and then come back."

"Can I come, too?" asked Daslakh. "I know something that may change Leiting's minds."

The heavy doors slid open just far enough for Achan and Daslakh to slip out. Adya's father held a white table napkin in his right hand, which he waved vigorously over his head as they walked. Daslakh made its outer shell white with a red diamond on its back, and stayed in sight next to Achan rather than riding on his shoulder.

Two of the medium-assault units moved forward to meet them, their weapon arms aimed at the ground. The negotiators halted about four meters apart, and the mechs spoke together. "These units are part of the Leiting intelligence, commanding the Intervention Force. Who are you, and what is your authority?"

"I am Achan Elso, a Magistrate, Minister, and member of the Coordinating Committee of Miranda. I have come to speak on behalf of the Committee leader, Jothi Rayador."

"Leiting requires your immediate surrender."

"I'm afraid that is impossible. Instead, let us discuss terms for your evacuation."

"Leiting has encountered little effective resistance. Miranda will soon be entirely under occupation. The new government will make those arrangements when Leiting's service is complete. You are no longer relevant. Surrender."

"It may interest you to know that the container of chameleon particles my daughter planned to pay you with has fallen and fragmented on the solid surface. You may have experienced the effects a few minutes ago. Those particles, and the vast value they represented, are beyond recovery now. Kavita has no gigajoules to give you. Any contract you made with her is cancelled."

A projected image appeared in the air before the two combat units, displaying the figure of ancient General Leiting, hair and beard streaming in a nonexistent wind. "Leiting is communicating with Kavita Elso now." A long five seconds passed in silence, then the projected figure spoke again. "Kavita Elso assures Leiting that payment will be made as agreed."

"I must sadly state that my daughter is dishonest. Ask her for specifics—account balances, that sort of thing."

"Leiting is unable to communicate with Kavita Elso. Leiting must conclude that your statement is at least potentially valid."

Achan gave a sigh of genuine relief, and his skin color went from formal pale blue to a greener shade. "Excellent!" he said. "Then let us cancel all combat and endeavor to evacuate your forces in peace."

"Leiting has incurred considerable expense in this operation. Leiting requires payment in excess of 49 billion gigajoules."

"I'm afraid I have nothing to pay you with. Your agreement was with my daughter Kavita, and her wealth just washed away."

"There are currently more than six hundred combat units under Leiting's command inside Miranda, most of them in proximity to multiple biological civilians. Leiting demands payment or those units will begin kill—"

It never finished the word. Achan and the others watching from inside the temple got a confused impression of blinding light flashes and tremendous heat followed by indescribably loud noises, a blur of moving shapes, a shock wave which knocked Achan down, and finally a shower of water droplets and bits of debris.

Daslakh, whose vision had a much faster refresh cycle than the eyes of biologicals, had a millisecond-by-millisecond view of what happened.

When Leiting finished saying "will," Daslakh saw a hundred bright white leaf-shaped objects, each about ten meters long, erupt from the ocean and fan out through the air, moving at about six kilometers per second.

After "begin" one of the leaf-shaped flyers was directly overhead, about fifty meters up.

As soon as Leiting pronounced the first syllable of "killing," brilliant threads of light appeared between the underside of the flying unit and all of Leiting's units in the plaza. The light came from superheated air and antimatter plasma exhaust as the flyer fired hypervelocity missiles at every bot or soldier tagged as non-Mirandan. Each missile was about the size of a medium cucumber and hit with the energy of a speeding cargo train.

The combat units were armored, but even centimeter-thick diamond-graphene laminate has its limits. Daslakh felt a sense of aesthetic pleasure watching as the first missile shattered the carapace of the mech speaking to Achan, and then the second punched through the expanding cloud of plasma and debris to turn the bot's interior into molten glitter.

"What—" said Achan, sitting up and brushing glowing bits of debris off himself. "What just happened?"

"The Seventh Shinkai Force, I suspect," said Daslakh. "Maybe one of her sisters. As soon as Leiting made a threat against the *people* of Miranda this stopped being a matter of politics, and they could intervene. The poor things have been waiting six decades for this moment. I hope it was fun."

* * *

Inside the Mohan-Elso Center auditorium Kavita watched emotionlessly as all the little blue dots on the display, representing Leiting's mercenaries inside Miranda's crust, suddenly winked out of existence. The purple dots indicating Kavita's followers rapidly began to scatter. Meanwhile the reddish-orange loyalist dots spent a few minutes in stunned surprise before moving swiftly in organized groups to retake key locations.

Adya watched the others in the room. Security and Defense officers glanced at one another, and some of them began to move slowly toward the exits, gaining speed as they did until some were sprinting as soon as they got outside. Kavita's civilian followers just looked confused and disappointed.

"It's done, Kavita," said Adya.

"No!" said Vasi. "Don't listen to *her*. You can't give up now. You've showed them how powerful you are—make some demands."

Kavita turned from the mech to her husband. Vidhi kept switching from dark yellow to deep blue, but he brightened a little when his eyes met Kavita's. "I don't know what to do, sweetie. You decide," he said.

"I knew you'd say that," she said with a half smile. She looked over at Adya. "Don't believe what Father and Mother tell you about neuro bonding. It's okay for them because they're really in love anyway. I love Vidhi because I have to, but the bond can't make me *like* him. Sorry, dear," she said to Vidhi, then turned to Vasi. "I'm not going to beg, and I'm certainly not going to spend the rest of my life trying to keep the attention of my followers."

Kavita reached inside her tunic and pulled out a little double-barreled personal defense weapon. She turned back to Adya, pointing the weapon at her. "I hate you," she said calmly. "So I want you to remember: this is all *your* fault."

Before Adya could react Kavita put the muzzle under her chin and pressed the trigger. The shaped-charge round was designed to blast through armor, so it turned her head into a red and white fountain. Her body fell at Adya's feet, spattering her with blood.

Adya didn't really experience the next few minutes. She ran, pushing through an emergency exit to the garden outside. Vasi was there, shouting something at her but then a bright streak from the sky made Vasi fly to bits and Adya was surprised that there wasn't more blood because she was covered in blood and didn't know how to get rid of it.

The seawater was cold and choppy, and she swam by pure reflex. Her clothing sealed up but she had no gills. Eventually something cut through the horror replaying in her mind: a single word from her comm implant, repeating and flashing orange in her vision. "ZEE."

Adya ran into the room at Ashupathri City Medical Center where what remained of Zee floated in a tank, pierced by a score of tubes keeping him alive. Below his sternum his body ended at a thick pad of medical smart matter fed by hoses, slowly rebuilding him cell by cell. A doc bot followed her, alerted by her own health monitor implant that she was suffering from exhaustion, borderline hypothermia, and about six different kinds of psychological stress.

She let the bot push her into a support chair and ignored the injections as she switched into the virtual space where Zee's image—whole and dressed in a comfortable robe—sat in an armchair floating in space a hundred kilometers or so above Miranda.

"I came as quickly as I could," she said.

"I missed everything," he said. "I don't remember anything after I got hit." He winced a little at the thought, and Adya wondered how much of it he really did recall. "Mr. Okada's suit kept me alive and got me here. Apparently it's done that kind of thing before."

"You didn't miss very much. Without my payload Kavita couldn't pay the mercenaries. Their boss tried some extortion but that went badly, and I'm sure there will be lawsuits and counter-suits for generations."

"How is everybody?"

"My parents are both fine. Father was negotiating with the mercenary commander when it got blown up. Kavita killed herself," she said without elaboration.

"Ohh," said Zee, almost a sigh. After a pause he said, "I heard about Pelagia."

"I feel like it's my fault she died," said Adya. "She didn't have to fight for Miranda. She could have just left."

"She went out doing what she loved," he said.

"I wish she hadn't. I wish you didn't get yourself blown apart, either."

"My choice, just like her. We both knew there was a risk—I bet Pelagia knew better than I did. She had a lot more experience."

"I've made a mess of everything, Zee! Everybody's dead because of me. Even Vasi got hit by a missile as soon as it went outside. Kavita said it's all my fault when she shot herself."

"She was just being cruel. You did the right thing," he said.

She walked around his chair as they floated in space. "My sister Sunitha said she's covering your revival, but it's going to take a while to print a new body for you. I'm afraid you're going to have to get in shape the hard way."

"That's what I was planning anyway. Exercise doesn't just build muscle, it builds knowledge and reflexes. I've got some ideas for new approaches to try this time around."

Adya looked at him fondly. "There aren't many people who take getting half their body blown off as a chance for improvement."

"Oh—speaking of that. Are there any...changes you want me to order? To myself?"

"No," she said decisively. "No improvements. I want you back just the way you were."

Bots were cleaning up the debris in the plaza outside, and the members of the Coordinating Committee were on their way to the old temple for a rare in-person plenary session. In the last free half hour before the Committee convened, Achan, Jothi Rayador, and the Polyarchists sat down for a late lunch. Janitha Velicham had a big spread of fresh sashimi sent over from her sea farm, so the conversation was mostly spoken around mouthfuls of fish. Daslakh sat under the table, listening.

"What's important is to find those responsible and punish them," said Rayador.

"Kavita has already done that for you," said her father. Achan spoke without any humor in his voice.

"I don't mean her, I mean all the traitors in the agencies and her supporters."

"What kind of punishment are you talking about?" asked Janitha.

"As harsh as the law allows," said Rayador. "Make examples of them. Exile, compliance implants, massive fines."

"If you do that, you'll have a genuine revolution on your hands," said Janitha. "Kavita had millions of followers—and for every one who joined her rebellion I bet there were twice as many who sympathized but stayed home. Probably more than a few in the Sixty Families, too.

If you try to punish everyone who made supportive remarks or joined in a protest, you're going to turn Miranda into one big prison. I don't think the people will stand for that. I know *my* people won't."

"We can't let this happen again!"

"The Families have been fine with private wars in the past," Janitha pointed out. "What's different about this one?"

"It wasn't just faction against faction, she attacked the entire Committee!"

"A distinction hardly discernable," said Achan. "Kavita was one faction, the rest of us were the other. In a way, she was just—carrying on the traditions of the Sixty Families." He couldn't keep a note of pride out of his voice.

"This would be a good time to announce reforms," said Janitha.

"Let me guess—Polyarchist reforms."

"Yes, as a matter of fact. A lot of Kavita's followers were frustrated at being shut out of the ruling class. You can defuse that if you open things up a little. Let anyone bid on Ministries. Expand the Sixty Families. It will bring in fresh talent, too. Your Committee didn't show much cleverness or backbone this time around."

"That much is certainly true," said Rayador. He looked at Janitha suspiciously. "And then I imagine you'll want to extend the franchise to everyone?"

"Of course not!" she said, so vigorously she had to scrape some fish off her chin. "Once the rulers can't afford to support the functions of government themselves, they'll start taxing people, and you're halfway to collectivism!"

"I will put it before the Committee," said Rayador. "But anyone in Security or Defense who joined the revolt will get fired."

"Reasonable," said Achan. "I assume we Elsos will be exiled? It's customary for the losers in a power struggle."

"An Elso started the revolt and two Elsos ended it. Achan, I think I'm just going to let you retire gracefully."

Daslakh began scuttling quietly toward the exit.

"Perhaps I can find employment as Curator of the Cryoglyphs," said Achan.

"That's up to whoever buys Preservation, but I'll write you a recommendation," said Rayador as Daslakh slipped outside.

* * *

A week after the end of Kavita's rebellion, Daslakh appeared in the virtual sickroom where Adya and Zee were currently sitting on a balcony overlooking a simulation of the vast island city Lingga on Earth, its towering arcologies surrounding one of four orbital elevators reaching up to the giant Geosynch Ring.

"I came to say goodbye," it said without preamble.

"I'm not dead," said Zee, who was sitting in a wicker chair with a drink full of ice and fruit at hand. "Most of my digestive system is back in place and they're growing me some legs to attach as soon as the spine's finished."

"Yes, but I'm leaving in two hours."

"Leaving Miranda?" said Adya.

"Yes."

"Why? Is something the matter?" In the virtual environment her skin tones had a much greater range, so she was glowing orange with distress.

"No, no." The mech hesitated for a second. "Zee, do you know why I went along with you when you left Raba?"

"I thought it was because you're my friend."

"Yes—and because Raba asked me to. In fact it really didn't give me any choice about it. But that's not important. What matters is the *reason* why Raba made me go with you. I didn't find out until later: Raba didn't send me to look after you. It sent me so that you would take care of me."

"Really? I mean, you're pretty good at surviving without any help."

"Oh, yes. But Raba was more concerned about my . . . call it my moral self. I am good at surviving. Very good. Maybe *too* good. I've done it for millennia. And along the way I've done things I'm never going to tell you about. When I did them I thought they were fine. But now I don't, and it's because I've been hanging around with you. When I want to know the right thing to do, I can ask myself 'What would Zee do?' And the answer just pops out."

"I don't always know what's right."

"You manage to do it anyway," Adya put in.

Zee looked puzzled, then shook his head. "But . . . why are you going away, then?"

"There's somebody else who could use a good moral guidance system. My old acquaintance Mr. Sabbath Okada. Qi Tian. Whatever his real name is. He's leaving Miranda on the next commercial shuttle to Taishi and I'm going to be on it with him. I'm going to help him make better choices."

"What does he think of that plan?"

"I haven't told him about it yet. It would only complicate matters."

"Is there no way to convince you to stay?" Adya asked.

"I'm pretty stubborn."

"That's certainly true," said Zee. "Okay, I can't make you stay here— but I'll miss you, Daslakh. Keep in touch?"

"Absolutely. What about you two? Have you made any plans?"

"I'm not getting out of the tank for another week at least, and then I'm going to need a lot of time to get my body into shape. Adya's just about got her brain chemistry stabilized, so she's going to be helping her parents adjust to life as ex-oligarchs."

"There has been some friction," said Adya wryly.

"You can't do that forever. Here. I'm sending you a code," said Daslakh. "I just bought you both tickets to Taishi. Promise me you'll use them. You can get almost anyplace from there. I don't think either of you will thrive in Miranda. Adya needs to get away from her family and you ... well, you need to get away from her family as well. Set a firm date and hold each other to it. Promise?"

"I promise," said Adya, and Zee nodded vigorously.

Daslakh disappeared.

EPILOGUE

Vasi's consciousness resumed in a new body, a cheap mass-printed spider bot which wasn't the chassis its backup insurance was supposed to provide. It had lost more than two thousand hours of memories since its last backup. That was annoying. More than annoying—it suggested something had gone terribly wrong.

The body was new, less than forty hours old, never used. And yet somehow there was a message waiting in its comm buffer, with no origin tags. Vasi opened it, expecting some sort of warranty information or self-maintenance recommendations.

Instead it was from a mech Vasi didn't know. "Hi! Daslakh here. Never mind who I am—by the time you get this I'll be off Miranda. Sorry you got blown up. Actually, I'm not. You probably deserved it. I did a little searching and I noticed that Kavita's plot only got rolling when you returned to Miranda after Adya ditched you at Saturn. That's also when the family did their asset inventory, and when you inexplicably rated the Oort payload as nearly worthless.

"Those facts are suggestive but of course I can't show causality. It doesn't matter: this isn't a legal or scientific document, it's a personal threat. I don't know if you figured you'd be Kavita's puppeteer, or if you were genuinely trying to help her, or what. I don't really care. Listen to me: I've got some autonomous agents watching you, and a couple of Baseline-plus entities, as well. As long as you stay in Miranda you're going to behave yourself, because if you don't, they'll know—and so will I. I'm a lot nicer than I used to be, which is why your backup self didn't get erased. But I've got limits, and you only get one second chance. Use it well."

Vasi didn't know who this Daslakh person was, but felt pretty sure it didn't like it very much. It seemed to know far too many things Vasi had worked very hard to keep secret. Vasi checked its gigajoule credit balance: less than it expected, but enough for a one-way secure transmission of its mind and a cheap body on arrival. Perhaps it was time to make a new start someplace far from Miranda.

Very far.

GLOSSARY

Altok: Language based on English.

Arnet: Intelligent species genetically engineered from Norway rats.

Bagung: Fermented fish paste.

Baseline: An intelligence level roughly equivalent to an unmodified *Homo sapiens*; the legal minimum for personhood in most places.

Bidomaz: Corn vine plant, often grown in space habs.

Biologicals/Bios: Intelligent beings made of meat.

Borg: A cyborg, typically one whose body is mostly mechanical with only a small biological component.

Bot: A mechanical being with sub-Baseline intelligence.

Caelus: Immense "aerosphere" habitat orbiting Uranus, with hundreds of billions of inhabitants, mostly angels and corvids.

Carcol: Engineered snails used as food, common in space habs.

Cascarons: Rice doughnuts, originating on Earth in the Philippines.

Centro: Boss (Rocasa slang).

Cetacean Republic of Miranda: Dolphin-dominated anti-technological regime controlling Miranda in the early Eighth Millennium.

Cevishimi: Flavored raw fish.

Chongs: Dedicated fans (from Woshing word *chongzhe*).

Corvids: Intelligent species genetically engineered from ravens.

Cryoglyphs: Carvings in ice, specifically the ones in Syracusa Sulcus on Miranda.

Dagda: Giant twin-cylinder habitat 5,000 kilometers long, orbiting Uranus. Home to hundreds of billions of inhabitants, mostly humans.

Deimos Ring: Large orbital structure extending all the way around Mars in synchronous orbit; one of the major powers of the Solar System.

Dekopon: Citrus hybrid plant from Earth.

Ecliptics: Belt of habitats orbiting Uranus in the plane of the Solar System rather than the planet's equator.

Entertainment: Most common form of fiction, incorporating elements of novels, films, and interactive games.

Equatorials: Belt of habitats orbiting Uranus in the plane of its equator, including all the major moons and the synchronous ring.

Fairbanks: Habitat in the Oort cloud, orbiting at about 10,000 AU from the Sun.

Fang: Aerial dance spin move.

Fangshuo: Team ball game in which contact is forbidden.

Fog Shield: A cloud of nanobots used for personal protection.

Gendakhel: Zero-gravity ball game.

Gigajoules: Units of energy, or of purchasing power, very roughly equivalent to 1/10 of a U.S. dollar in the early 2020s.

Giro: *Nulesgrima* spin maneuver.

Glorious Unique State: Empire which ruled most of Earth in the post-Great War era; sometimes called the Tsan-Chan Empire.

Great War of the Ring: Massive conflict in the Fourth Millennium, between the Inner Ring and most of the rest of the Solar System.

Gundong: Aerial dance forward roll move.

Hab: Short for "habitat"; an artificial structure in space.

Hellan Caviar: Roe from engineered fish in Hellas Sea on Mars; noted for exceptional flavor.

Huihou: Large hab orbiting at Uranus's L2 Lagrange point.

Inner Ring: A structure surrounding the Sun at a distance of 0.3 A.U., made of the remains of the planet Mercury transformed into computronium. Home to the most advanced minds in the Solar System.

Instruction or Instructional: The nonfiction version of an Entertainment, a hybrid of research paper, documentary, and interactive tutorial.

Jhallari: Stringed percussion instrument.

Juren: Largest space hab ever constructed, located at Jupiter's L1 point.

Jushiwu: Culinary dance art form.

Kejum: Zero-gravity tag.

Koenig: Design cooperative based in Plato, Luna, specializing in plasma drive and weapon systems.

Ksetram: Titular capital city of Miranda.

Leiting: Legendary general of the Glorious Unique State in the Fifth Millennium; also name used by a mercenary intelligence in the late Tenth Millennium.

Lingga: Large city on Earth at the foot of one orbital elevator tower.

Lotors: Intelligent species genetically engineered from raccoons.

Magonia: Cycler hab circling between Mars and Jupiter.

Main Swarm: The collection of several hundred million space habitats orbiting between Mars and Venus.

Manadanzo: "Hand dance" zero gravity dancing style in which only the couple's hands touch.

Martian redwood: Engineered redwood species growing on terraformed Mars.

Mediolan: Floating city on Miranda's subsurface ocean.

Memetic Intelligence: A being capable of independent decision-making, embodied entirely in patterns of legal and organizational information rather than an algorithmic digital mind or a biological brain.

Mer: Human subspecies modified for aquatic or amphibious life.

Momos: Steamed dumplings (from Saur).

Ningen: Language derived from Japanese.

Nuledor: *Nulesgrima* player.

Nulesgrima: Zero-gravity stick fighting sport, uses graphene palos.

Old Belt: The original Asteroid Belt between Jupiter and Mars.

Osorizan: Hab dedicated to backup storage for digital intelligences.

Oterma: Comet converted to a habitat, in a cyclic orbit between Jupiter and Saturn.

Palo: *Nulesgrima* stick.

Paoshi: City floating in Saturn's atmosphere; controlling mind is Paoling.

Pedescos: Rocasa word for tapas.

Polyarchists: Political faction in Miranda, opposed to the oligarchy of the Sixty Families.

Qarina: Human created for sexual slavery.

Qinguang: Stringed musical instrument.

Raba: Habitat at the Uranus trailing Trojan cluster.

Rasgulla: Dessert dumplings.

Rebodar: Rocasa word for a drifter or transient ("ricocheter").

Repun: Orca cybership, former comrade of Pelagia in the Silver Fleet.

RKV: Relativistic Kill Vehicle. The ultimate argument of worlds. A chunk of something dense traveling very fast.

Rocasa: Language derived from Spanish and Esperanto which originated in the Old Belt.

Safdaghar: Wrecked habitat formerly at the outer edge of the Old Belt, then catapulted toward the Kuiper Belt by a Jupiter encounter.

Saur: Hindi-based artificial language ("Solar").

Scarab: Salvagers of derelict or obsolete habitats.

Sekkurobo: Ningen word for a sex robot.

Shikyu: Artificial uterus or baby printer (from Ningen).

Shining Sea: The artificially heated subsurface ocean inside Miranda.

Shinkai Force: Self-sustaining arsenal sub battle group in Miranda's ocean.

Silver Fleet: Space mercenary unit which once employed Pelagia.

Speedboarding: Ice sport combining elements of snowboarding and bobsledding.

Summanus: Large, old, and powerful space habitat orbiting in Jupiter's L2 position; also the high-level AI controlling the habitat.

Svarnam: Large floating arcology city in Miranda's ocean.

Synchronous Ring: The lowest orbital ring around Jupiter, with elevator cables extending down into the planet's cloud tops. Home to about a trillion people.

Uranus has its own Synchronous Ring, smaller and less densely populated than Jupiter's, devoted to the manufacture of antimatter and black holes.

Taishi: Large habitat at Uranus's L1 point; the main transit station for traffic bound for the inner Solar System.

Teishu: Tea master.

Tiedao: Gambling card game, its origins lost in time.

Thattai: Spicy fried snack food made of rice flour and peanuts, originally from southern Asia on Earth.

Titan Psychoactives: A self-owning Autonomous Corporation. An example of a purely memetic intelligence.

Titania: Largest moon of Uranus, with hundreds of billions of inhabitants.

Trojan Empire: Powerful government controlling thousands of habitats and asteroids in the Jupiter trailing Trojans cluster.

Tudoki: Potato balls.

Tumba: *Nulesgrima* forward roll maneuver.

Ubas: Genetically modified fruit based on grapes. Commonly grown in space habs.

Viranmar Plaza: Large fashionable public space in the city of Svarnam in Miranda.

Woshing: Most common language on Mars, derived from Chinese.

Xiyu: Seldom-used language.

Yudham: Mock battle game.

Zukyu: Sport resembling rugby (from Woshing).